Kristian's Rise

FOUR STARS OVER ARDATZ: JOURNEYS

Kandi J Wyatt

Copyright, 2025

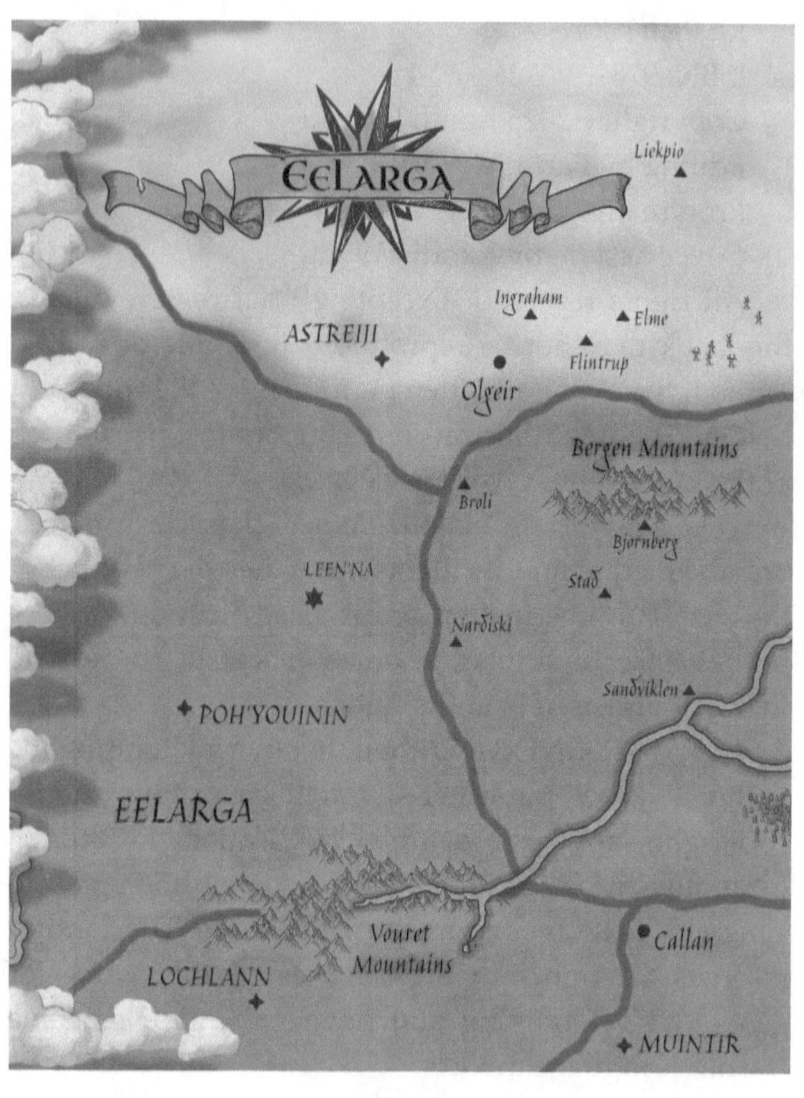
EELARGA
Liekpio
Ingraham
ASTREIJI
Elme
Flintrup
Olgeir
Bergen Mountains
Broli
Bjornberg
LEEN'NA
Stað
Narðiski
Sandviklen
POH'YOUININ
EELARGA
Vouret
Mountains
Callan
LOCHLANN
MUINTIR

Vilta
Storeheltur
Isholt
Aye'air Tundra
Kinuli Sea
Gamar
Toshesh
Edsbyn
Sletter Plains
Elv River
Soda Plains
SKYMNA
Kullar Hills
Sultiyelma
KHALKI
Youksengi
HUVUSTADEN
Boden Forest
ATSEGENA
Slieve Mish Mountains
DERBAC
THARRA
Legend
CAPITOL
COUNTRY
CITY
VILLAGE

*To all the Christinas and Davids out there
who've fought the battle and lost,
and to all the Benjamins and Juliannas
who fight the battle every day*

Acknowledgements

This story wouldn't have come into existence if not for Camp Fircroft and a chapel service. But along the way there were many who helped.

Mom and Bonnie kept me in their prayers as I drafted, while Kristina and Ralene prayed while I edited. The #Writestorm team helped me stay on task, and Allison Chaney was there for my annual writing retreat, cheering me on.

On the professional end, Tosca Lee encouraged me to pick up Donald Maass' *Writing the Breakout Novel Workbook*, and Christina Kuhn and I self-edited our stories concurrently, providing mutual feedback and encouragement.

As with the past fifteen books, Ally Morcom has been able to hear my voice and heart and bring my works an added breath of life by refining and editing them. I wouldn't be where I am today if it wasn't for her loving help. Sheri Williams is always willing to jump into my worlds and proofread them.

In the middle of the pandemic of 2020, Francesco Nigi photographed his brother from their home in Italy. That image sparked the physical portrayal of Kristjan, and Kat Heckenbach painted the moon and tree that I snatched up at Realm Makers 2019 that became the inspiration for Kristjan's thinking spot on Toppur. Both of these artists, allowed me to use their works for the cover.

Character List

Kristjan Jorvarsson—18-year-old son of the chief

Geirfinnur Jorvarsson—chief and father of Kristjan

Sæbjort Jorvarsson—wife of Geirfinnur and mother of Kristjan

Jorvar—original founder of Storeheltur

Iunn—Jorvar's wife

Froða Iunnsdotter—Geirfinnur's sister, midwife

Mikkael—Froða's husband

Bastian—Froða and Mikkael's son, Kristjan's cousin

Margeir Bergmundsson—Marko's dad

Telma Bergmundsdotter—Marko's mom

Marko Bergmundsson—Kristjan's best friend

Glyta Bergmundsson—Marko's baby sister

Myr Bergmundsson—Marko's oldest sister

Andri Bergmundsson—Marko's oldest brother

Hervin Bergmundsson—Marko's brother

Metta Arnorsdotter—Friðfinn's sister

Friðfinn Arnorsson—elder, Tinna's dad

Ebonney Arnorsdotter—Friðfinn's wife, Tinna's mom

Tinna Arnorsdotter—Friðfinn and Ebonney's daughter

Iðna—craftsman and elder

Karva—oldest of the elders

Orlaugur—elder and mining expert

Reinar—elder in charge of food

Arny—Reinar's wife

Hafnar—youngest of the elders

Sigmar—Hafnar's brother, expert on Toppur

Sungvari—Hafnar's wife and singer for funerals

Josebina—Sæbjort's best friend

Juli—childhood friend of Kristjan, Marko, and Bastian

Elias—Juli's son

Mani, Erika, Aldar, Ingvi and Mari—miners

Androw—merchant

Nikanor—chief of Isholt

Nyvarð, Tyr, Rikarður, Roskava, Eliros, Kubbur, Aðalsteinn, and Darri—Isholt explorers

Time Words

Span—hour

Moonstep (step)—day

Cycle—month

Rotation—year

Contents

Prologue

12 Ellefta, 382 AI

The sounds coming from the inner room were driving me crazy. I paced our living quarters without seeing the obstacles. One moment Sæbjort would be humming a soft tune, and the next she'd be shrieking at pitches I hadn't known she could produce. This had been going on for too long. Something had to be wrong. I wanted to barge into our bedroom and see for myself that she was all right, but the midwife—my sister, as it happened—had made it abundantly clear that birthing was a woman's job, and men were not wanted.

I wiped a hand across my face. All *had* to be well. I couldn't imagine life without Sæbjort's gentle guidance in my life. I might have been chief of our clans, but it was her voice as much as mine that led Storeheltur.

Another cry jerked me back toward the closed curtain that constituted the door. This time, though, there was a word in the inarticulate cries.

"Geirfinnur!" My name echoed off the stone ceiling.

Without waiting or even thinking about what I was doing, I thrust the tapestry aside and within three steps was beside my wife, her best friend giving way to me.

"Sæbjort, I'm here."

Her face was pale, her knuckles white where they clenched the back of a chair. She swayed back and forth, the moaning hum building again. I rested a hand on her back.

Froða huffed—a sound I'd known since childhood, and one I'd learned to ignore. "This is no place for a man, Sæbjort."

In answer, my wife clutched my hand. The strength in her grip surprised me. I blew air out through my nose, not about to complain about the loss of circulation to my littlest finger—not with Froða glaring at me.

"Fine." My sister shook her head. "Stay out of the way. Josebina, take this side." She relinquished her spot to my wife's closest friend to kneel in front of Sæbjort. Then she started humming, the same low and controlled sound I'd heard from the other room.

Sæbjort joined in, her voice creating the tune while the others backed it up. The repeating themes were simple enough that even I could pick up on them. And when my *kæra* broke off, her voice stollen by a contraction, Froða or Josebina would pick up the melody, keeping the music flowing—this song of my wife's own making, forged in the midst of bringing our child into the world.

"I…" Sæbjort panted, her face pinched. "I can't."

"Yes, you can," Froða encouraged her. "Every woman who's ever born a child has done this. You can too."

Josebina rubbed Sæbjort's back while my wife all but crushed my hand.

"It… It's too… too much!" Sæbjort ended with a yelp.

"There has to be *something* you can do," I beseeched Froða.

"Ferish Pools," Froða offered. "Being in the water may help. She'll not make the journey, though—the contractions are too close together; she won't be able to cover so much distance in time for it to make a difference."

"I'll carry her if I must." At last, there was something I could *do*! "Come, Sæbjort, let's go."

She took a couple of steps, but a contraction seized her, and she was rooted in place, groaning and crying out. "I… I… can't."

"Will you let me carry you?"

Sæbjort nodded. "Put me down if it's too much."

"I will." Defying my sister to stop me, I gathered my wife into my arms.

When she wrapped her arms around my neck, leaning into my shoulder, she fit perfectly. Well, not like she had nine lunar cycles earlier, but this was where she belonged, even if she was currently dripping some kind of fluid onto my trousers.

It took us twice as long as it would normally have taken to traverse the stone ways and reach the cavern with the pools, but finally, we arrived. I gently drew Sæbjort's robe off and placed it off to the side. Not eager to display my undershorts to my sister or Josebina, I glanced about. Froða had her back to me, and Josebina had gone to retrieve a poultice my sister had ordered. I shucked off my stained trousers, refusing to acknowledge that there was blood on them—too much blood—and led Sæbjort into the hot springs. The moment the water touched her legs, her balance failed; I quickly pulled her against me, thinking to cushion her fall with my body, if need be, but she landed seated in my lap, pushing me deep into the pool. My head barely stayed above the surface, and my hair floated out behind me.

Sæbjort's humming turned into a moan.

"It'll be fine, *kæra*." I brushed her dark hair out of her face.

She smiled at me, but it was weak. "Promise me, you'll be strong, Geirfinnur. You'll be there for our son."

"Hush, *kæra*, hush."

"No, you must promise me."

Before I could reply, she arched her back and cried out. Froða was beside us in an instant. Her steadying presence kept the terror at bay, but not for long. One look at my sister's face, and I knew something had gone terribly wrong. If it had been anyone else, I might have been fooled, but to her brother her eyes were as clear to read as the stars in the sky.

"Keep her steady, Geirfinnur. Don't let her slide in any deeper."

With a short nod, I held my wife to me. Tears worked their way down her cheeks; her breath came in short gasps.

The door opened, and Josebina's face turned pale as she set a basket down near Sæbjort's robe and hurried over. "How can I help?"

Froða shook her head ever so slightly. "Sæbjort, I'm going to see what I can do." Her hands faded from sight under the water—water that was murky with red.

I blinked, but Sæbjort cried out, then bit her lip, distracting me from all else but her.

"Hush, *kæra*, hush." I kissed her cheek, and she sagged into my chest.

"I can feel the baby's head." Froða's voice was calm, but still her eyes betrayed her. "We're almost ready, Sæbjort. All you have to do is push this little one out. Geirfinnur will hold you steady. You just push with the next contraction."

Sæbjort nodded, then put her hand up to my face, blindly feeling for my cheek even as her shoulders pressed back into my chest—already falling into the rigor of the next surge. "Geirfinnur, you didn't promise me."

Her fingers felt so frail. Why couldn't she have forgotten about whatever promise she wanted me to make?

"You'll be strong for our child, won't you?" She was panting; I could feel her body tightening. "You'll be there teaching and guiding him. You won't let leadership of the clan steal you from him, like it stole your father from you."

At least that was something I could readily promise. "Yes, I'll be there for our little one, but so will you, *kæra*. We'll teach him together."

Her fingers tightened on my cheeks, and she gritted her teeth. Her guttural groan was almost a growl like the snow cats that roamed Toppur.

"Good," Froða encouraged. "Keep that up, and you'll be holding this little one in your arms in no time."

Sæbjort's grip slackened, and she smiled—that lovely lifting of her lips that had drawn me to her six rotations ago even before my father had approached hers with a request for a betrothal.

Five more of those gut-wrenching growls, five more times squeezing the life out of my fingers, and Sæbjort fell limp in my arms with a weak cry.

"Keep her head above the water," Froða ordered as she stood, a small red form barely discernible in her hands, still obscured by the thickening cloud of red.

"Is…" I licked my lips. "Is that…"

"Your son." Froða's expression softened the gruffness in her tone. "I need to bring him up and get the cord cut, but Sæbjort's in no condition to help us. You need to lift her up onto the ledge."

Blinking back tears as I watched my son squirm, I nodded. Soon, I had Sæbjort resting on the upper step where the water lapped gently at her ribs. Froða placed my son against Sæbjort's chest and swiftly wound a thread tightly around the cord; she was probably glaring as she cut it, but I wasn't looking at her. I was too caught up in the small life before me.

Sæbjort smiled, her hands enveloping the tiny body—a mother's tender hands, holding her child, warming him, shielding him. "He's beautiful."

"Just like his mother," I said, through a heart that was ready to burst.

"Kristjan." Sæbjort caressed his dark head, her fingers too limp. "After my brother."

"Yes. He was a good man." At the moment I would have let her name him anything.

"Kristjan, you're going to be a strong man one step. Listen to your father. I…" Her eyes drifted closed, then lifted back open. "I love you, my son."

For one strained moment her gaze was trained on him, but she could only hold out so long. Her eyes slid shut and her hand fell from his back, and Kristjan squalled. The boy squirmed and without his mother's steadying hand, slid from her chest. I snatched him up before he could fall into the water.

His cry was pitiful, pure, demanding, as only an infant's could be. Such a large sound for such a small person. Every single detail was perfect—little fingers, toes, and eyes. He stared up at me, but it only broke me into pieces. He should have been looking up at his mother, learning the face that belonged to the loving voice of the one who'd carried him this far.

But no farther.

A sob escaped my lips.

Froða rested a hand on my shoulder. "Do you want me to take him so you can say your farewell?"

Numb, I handed Kristjan over to his aunt and knelt down beside Sæbjort. Her beautiful face was at peace. I caressed it, noticing a tear that clung to her cheek.

Gone. With the ancients now. If the stories were true, no more to cry. I regarded that single tear, wondering if I should wipe it away, but if I did, then I'd accept what had befallen us.

Why? Why had she left me? The dam broke, and my own tears flowed, splashing into her hair and then running into the hot springs, flooding over her face until there were too many to distinguish between what had been hers and which were mine.

I didn't know how long I remained there, but when I'd cried more tears than I knew I possessed, I passed into a state of quiet unreality, like I'd entered into the halls of the ancients myself, and it was only my spirit that stood and dried myself off. My trousers were blood-stained; I didn't want to put them on. They would bring me back into the mortal world, where everything was shattered obsidian. But I couldn't be wandering Storeheltur's halls in only my undershorts, so I slipped them back on, and none too soon. Froða returned with Kristjan.

"Here." She held Kristjan out to me; he was bundled in a blanket but still squalling. "Josebina went to talk to Telma. She may be able to help us keep this little one alive."

I hadn't even considered that it would be possible to lose my son as well. Without thinking, I pulled Kristjan close to me, while Froða went to see to her sister-in-law's body, and I stood there with a crying baby—and a hole in my heart.

Chapter 1

3 Fjorda, 400 AI

There might as well have been a chasm separating Kristjan and his best friend.

"Oh, come on! You can do it," Marko called down from the ledge.

Beside Kristjan, Bastian grinned. "Don't want to have rumors spread that the chief's son is a coward, do you, cousin?"

With a sigh, Kristjan forced the cold knot in his stomach aside and placed his hands where Marko had. The luminescent *yoma* on the rock walls gave off enough light to see each divot and crack in the cliff face.

"That's it," Marko encouraged him. "It'll be worth it. The dioptase up here is beautiful."

"Maybe even good enough to set in a ring for Tinna," Bastian added, scaling the cliff in moments.

"It'll take something spectacular for Tinna to think of marrying you, Bastian." Marko laughed.

Bastian slapped Marko on the arm. "Don't see you trying to impress any girl."

"I have time."

Kristjan's hand slipped, and he froze. He couldn't do this. If he fell, he'd break a leg—or worse!

"Easy, Kristjan." Marko's voice soothed Kristjan's fraying nerves. "You can do this. Bring your hand back up. There's a better hold right there." He pointed out the protruding rock.

"Come on, Kristjan. The sooner you're up here, the sooner I can get that stone."

"Would you shut up, Bastian?" Marko shook his head. "You'd think you'd be more considerate of your cousin."

Kristjan tuned their conversation out and concentrated on where to place his hand, then his foot, and then a hand, trying not to think about the burning strain in his arms. If he thought too much about the fatigue, his muscles might give out. At last, he hauled himself over the ledge, laying his ribs on the rock so he could finally step his feet up with the rest of him. He flopped back, not daring to look over to the ground below, or to think of how he was going to get back down, but exhilarated all the same.

"Ready?" Marko held out a hand. "You did it."

"Yeah, I did!" Kristjan allowed his friend to help him up.

"*Now* can I show you this deposit?" Bastian stood with his hand on his hip. At a nod from Kristjan, he sprinted off down the path, hunched over taking care to watch his head in the low-ceilinged cavern.

Shaking his head, Kristjan followed his cousin, although at a much slower pace. The green glow from the *yoma* minerals here gave off enough light to see by, but not much more than that.

"So, is this really worth it, or were you just humoring Bastian?" Kristjan bobbed around a low-hanging stalactite.

"I'll let the vein speak for itself." Marko caught up with Kristjan and as the path widened, came to walk beside his friend. "Bastian has a reason to want some of the dioptase."

"I know," Kristjan sighed. "I just wish he didn't have to constantly try to build himself up over me."

Marko shrugged. "I think it comes from being nephew to the chief. Mikkael has always lived in his brother-in-law's shadow, and that rubbed off on his son."

"Are you two coming?" Bastian called from ahead.

The *yoma* ahead were glowing more brightly—not only green, but a bright pink as well, casting a halo around Bastian who stood in the center of the way.

"Wish he was as much an angel as he looks there." Kristjan muttered with a friendly smirk.

Marko laughed. "You both are angelic if you ask me, just in different ways." He clapped Kristjan on the shoulder. "Let's go. He won't wait for long."

When Kristjan stepped into the cavern, he whistled. The sight was beautiful. The *yoma* here lent a yellow hue to the walls where among the copper, the deep blue-green of the dioptase sat.

"Told you it was worth it." Bastian bounced on the balls of his feet as he spread his hands wide, turning in an encompassing circle. "And it's all ours. We found it, so we can mine it first."

Technically, yes, but Kristjan knew that the mineral veins were growing sparse. The people of Storeheltur needed all the ore they could find to keep going. If they didn't have the minerals to trade, then they'd have to rely more on hunting and the limited resources around them, rather than the merchants who brought supplies in exchange for the ore mined from the caverns.

Bastian trailed his finger along a particularly strong strip of the cobalt rock. "Here's where I want to start. See this one?" He paused and tapped the stone. "This is the one that I'll ask Iðna to add to a ring for Tinna. I can see it now, so beautiful—just like her."

Marko and Kristjan exchanged glances, which did not at all help them tamp down their imminent laughter.

"What? It's true." Bastian turned to them.

"Sure, it is, but the way you say it…" Marko chuckled.

"Just wait until you find a girl. See if I spare you any teasing." Bastian pulled a pick from his belt and tapped along the rock.

Kristjan shook his head but followed suit. Soon the cave filled with the *tap, tap, tap* of three picks. Bastian had been right about one thing—this vein was deep and ran on for what seemed like forever. Before he knew it, he had several rough nuggets in a pile at his feet. He glanced around and saw Marko and Bastian also had excellent rocks.

"How long have we been at this?" Kristjan stretched his fingers and slid his pick back into his belt.

"Not long enough." Bastian grinned, letting Kristjan know his cousin was only half joking.

"Father wanted me back before the final meal of the step."

Bastian grimaced. "Uncle's still keeping you on a tight leash?"

"You know Father." Kristjan shrugged. "Always concerned with appearances and how I'm to be chief one step."

"Yeah." Bastian looked like he'd bitten into a sour cranleaf.

"We can always come back next step." Marko replaced his pick and pulled out a pouch for the gems at his feet.

"True." Bastian agreed, but the set of his shoulders said different. "At least I got this one mostly out—shouldn't take too long to finish excavating."

Kristjan joined his cousin and examined the crystal in question. "It *is* beautiful, Bastian. Tinna will love it."

"You really think so?"

"I do. Now let's head back."

As Kristjan had anticipated, he froze at the cliff. There was no way he was going to be able to make the descent, despite all the logic Marko tried. Kristjan's legs trembled and wouldn't listen to his brain, which was busy trying to tell them that they could work just fine if they would just *move*.

What type of chief are you going to make, if you can't even handle scaling a cliff? He could hear the condemnation from the elders. *Father wouldn't let a little height discourage him.* Yet it did no good.

Finally, Marko changed his tactic. "Bastian, go down ahead of him. That way if he slips, you'll be there to help him land on his feet. I'll come down beside you, Kristjan. You can grip ahold of my shoulder. I won't let you fall."

Like a snow fox pup led by its mother through the caverns, Kristjan allowed his friend to help him down. When his feet hit solid ground again, he collapsed into a heap, his face in his hands.

Bastian rested a hand on his shoulder. "It's okay, cuz. Even the best chief has to have some weakness. Yours just happens to be heights."

"Thanks." Kristjan scrubbed a shaky hand over his cheeks, ashamed of the damp that came away.

He hoped that what Bastian said was true. If it was, what was his father's weakness? He'd never witnessed it.

"Think you can stand now?" Marko offered a hand.

KRISTJAN'S RISE

With a nod, Kristjan accepted his friend's help. Together they followed the *yoma* until torches lit the smooth stone paths.

* * *

"Kristjan? Is that you?" Father called from his study.

"Yes." Kristjan steadied himself to face his father.

"Why are you so late?" Father entered the main living area, straightening his hair as if he was facing the elders. "The final meal has grown cold. I told you I wanted you back before then."

"I'm sorry, Father." Kristjan tried to hide his irritation at his father's tone, but from the way his father's eyebrow quirked up and he rested his hand on his hip, Kristjan hadn't done a good enough job. It was never good enough.

"It wouldn't have been too terrible if it was just our meal, but Friðfinn showed up. He wanted to discuss a betrothal."

"Betrothal?" Kristjan rolled his eyes.

"Kristjan, one step, you're going to have to take these seriously. Friðfinn's daughter, Tinna, would be a good wife—beautiful, able to cook, and keeps up with the best of the women in the mines."

And Bastian's had his eye set on her for who knows how many rotations. Kristjan didn't voice his thought.

Instead, he put on the face he used when the elders discussed all he needed to learn to be a good chief.

"I'll consider it in time, Father, but I have no intention of taking a wife at the moment. I'm perfectly fine as I am."

"Kristjan, son." Father rubbed the back of his neck. "I was two rotations younger than you when I married your mother."

And look where that got you. Kristjan had only voiced *that* sentiment once. The clenched jaw and fists had been warning enough.

"Maybe, but I'm not you, Father."

"But you're my son and will be chief after me."

"Which isn't for many rotations yet," Kristjan countered.

"Maybe not, but we can't let the Jorvarsson line die out."

Here it came: the story of Jorvar the Great. The man who had saved a whole village of people during the Impact with his quick thinking.

"If Jorvar would have thought only of himself, the *holdt* wouldn't be here, but he didn't. He took his people into Verndandi and waited out the storm."

"Yes, Father, I've heard it before. Then when he realized the storm wouldn't abate, he didn't think of himself, but took Iunn as a wife. Together they carved Storeheltur out of the mountain and provided a place for us all." Kristjan blew a breath out through his nose, calming his tone. "I'm not Jorvar any more than I'm you. Give me time, and I'll take a wife and be the chief you want me to be, but for now, just let me be me." Kristjan let the words hang, apprehensive. Would his father understand or turn away in frustration as he always did?

"Son, I know it's hard for you, but—"

The "but" always came.

Kristjan shook his head. "Father, I'm tired. I just want to eat and got to bed. I'll see you after the resting period."

"Where are you going, Kristjan? You can't push life away forever."

Stars forbid Geirfinnur's son would do as his father had for the past eighteen rotations.

"Father, I'm going to get some food and eat it while viewing the stars and then head to bed." Kristjan kept his tone civil. "I'll see you after Handi rises."

Not allowing his father any further say, Kristjan left the room. He filled a bowl and grabbed a roll. Balancing the two in one hand, he snatched his cloak from the hook and strode through the narrow, stone tunnel, wending his way until he came to a gradual slope. He rejoiced in it for that meant he was nearing Toppur—his place of peace.

According to Father, it was where Jorvar—everyone—had lived before the Impact. Kristjan couldn't understand how they would have endured the harsh climate, but Father said it hadn't always been this way.

When the air took on a crisp scent, and before the chill could get too uncomfortable, Kristjan set his bowl down on a ledge and wrapped his cloak about his shoulders. Then satisfied that he was as protected as he could be, he walked the rest of the way to his thinking spot.

* * *

I'd done it again. How many times had I pushed my son away? It had started that first moonstep when he was born and Froða had handed him over to Telma to nurse. From that moonstep on, no matter my intentions, it seemed that I'd been constantly watching my son leave me.

If only… How often had I thought that since Sæbjort had passed into the halls of the ancients? And it'd never done me any good—this step or any other. Instead, I stood there like an idiot while my son walked out the door to Toppur. I hadn't even asked where he'd gone with Marko and Bastian.

With a sigh that reminded me of my own father, I turned and walked back to my study. There Friðfinn's proposal sat on my desk. What was wrong with Tinna? She was as beautiful a girl as girls went—nothing like Sæbjort, but no one would ever match her beauty.

I thought I might as well try to figure out a way to phrase the rejection without injuring Friðfinn's pride. I'd already written four of these, but Friðfinn was an elder—and my friend.

Kristjan's Rise

But instead of putting quill to paper, I stared into the flickering flame and prayed — unburdening my heart to Jeeah.

The candle was burning low, the letter to Friðfinn unwritten, and only the *yoma* lit the room when I heard Kristjan's soft steps returning. He'd always been a quiet boy, even from the first. He'd hardly ever fussed, even when he was hungry. He'd even started losing weight because Telma couldn't always tell that he needed to eat. It'd been like he was waiting for his mother to appear — like she was the only one he'd tell if he needed something. In some sense, he'd been that way ever since.

Should I go to him? Sæbjort would say "yes," but any time I did, it seemed to make things worse.

Wiping a hand across my face, I stood and went to my room. There'd be time later to talk with Kristjan. Time when he'd listen.

Chapter 2

6 Fjorda, 400 AI

"**H**ey, Bastian, how's it going?" Kristjan called to his cousin as he headed to the water reservoir three moonsteps later, but Bastian ignored him.

What have I done now? With Bastian, it was always something. Shrugging it off, Kristjan resumed his trek. If he didn't bring the water, Father would be upset.

"Hi, Kristjan." Friðfinn fell into step beside him. "Your father is so fortunate to have you as a son."

"Thank you." Kristjan had a guess as to where this conversation was going, but he knew he needed to be polite.

"No, really. Most men wouldn't be caught dead gathering water or preparing a meal, but you're always willing to help no matter the task. It's what'll make you a wonderful chief when your time comes." Friðfinn stroked his beard. "It's also why I thought of you for Tinna. She has her heart set on you."

Kristjan bit his tongue. "Really? I thought she was interested in Bastian. He's a wonderful man."

"Your cousin's nothing like you, Kristjan, and Tinna sees that. He's impulsive and reckless. You, on the other hand, are steady, dependable, and kind. Everything a girl needs in a husband."

"When the time comes, I'm sure I'll take a wife, Friðfinn, but—"

"Listen to me, Kristjan. You're eighteen. When your father and I were your age, we'd been married for at least two rotations. You've had the time to grow up. Now you need to consider the next step to manhood." Friðfinn rested a heavy hand on Kristjan's shoulder. "As future chief, you need to consider wisely who you will marry."

Kristjan had to fight not to sigh. Would Friðfinn contrive to mention this every time they met now?

"Jorvar and Arnor worked together to bring Storeheltur into existence," Friðfinn pressed. "Why not join the two families as one officially? Consider my offer. Talk with Tinna if you must. I'll arrange for you to see her during the third watch this step. Come by after your final meal."

Realizing that, one way or another, Friðfinn would grind an answer out of him eventually, Kristjan forced out an, "All right, then." His refusal would go over better if he at least pretended to give it some consideration first.

Someone brushed against them. Kristjan glanced up to see Bastian's back. He knew that he'd better make things right with his cousin before it was too late, but first he needed to fill the water reservoir in their kitchen.

After five trips with the jug, Father stopped Kristjan.

"There's an elder meeting this watch. I want you to join me."

It wasn't a request.

"Very well."

"Be ready in a span. Oh, and Kristjan? Thank you for filling the water."

"You're welcome."

Father sighed. "I don't say it enough, but I appreciate all you do around here. I know you don't want to think of marriage, but it would ease your duties in the house."

Kristjan smiled. "Maybe, but who'd take care of you then?"

"Don't let that stop you from considering a proposal, son." Father's brown eyes were sincere, even tender. "No father should hold his son back. Our job is to give flight to your dreams."

"Thank you."

But would Father even want to know what my dreams are?

"Now, I have a few notes to gather before the meeting."

Back to business. Father always dealt with clan business better than he did with Kristjan. With a shake of his head, Kristjan returned to his room; he might as well get started on the schematic for an idea that he'd had to make things easier for the *holdt*. He picked up his journal, thumbing through the pages before wrapping a leather cord around it and placing it in its niche. He pulled the paper out of another stone cubby where various projects were kept in alphabetical order by name. Another alcove held his tools: straightedge along the side, eraser and adhesive in the middle, and old stubs of pencils that were good for shading tied together on the other side. Spreading out the curling sheet, he rested the straightedge on top to hold it down until he could place four unique rocks—tokens he'd claimed while traveling Toppur with Sigmar, learning the ways of the iced land—on the corners. Satisfied with the arrangement, he picked up his pencil from the bin of his favorites, and traced the distance between the well and their house. Next, he'd add the other homes along the route. Step by step, with meticulous, mind-settling precision, he worked until the clean lines had detailed every aspect of the proposed project area.

When Father came for him, he'd added a line to show where he'd put the pipe to draw the water from the well to the individual homes. If he could implement it, it'd save many spans for the whole clan.

The two walked side by side through the halls. People greeted them with nods and even a few bows as they passed by. Father acknowledged them all by name. Kristjan didn't know how he kept the names and faces straight. Those who interacted directly with them, made sense, but to know every single name of each community member was overwhelming for Kristjan.

You could do it if you put your mind to it. The voice was quiet but firm.

It's what's expected of the chief, another voice added.

Kristjan pushed them both aside. He had a meeting to attend.

The elders met in a chamber where the *yoma,* set into the high arched ceiling, illuminated a stone table inlaid with half a hand's breadth of deep green dioptase. Cushioned chairs sat around the table. Father took the one at the head and motioned to his right. Kristjan accepted his place. He could handle sitting at Father's right; it was the thought of sitting in Father's own seat that sent chills down his spine.

You'll be fine when it's your turn, the softer voice reminded him.

Or will you bumble it like you do everything else?

Always it was the two—one encouraging and one discouraging—much like Marko and Bastian.

It didn't take long for the six elders to join them and repeat the pledge that reminded them of their duty to the *holdt* and to Jeeah.

Father clasped his hands together, resting his elbows on the table. "Men, I've requested Kristjan's presence so that you can explain to him what you've seen, as well as your suggestion."

Kristjan schooled his face. When Father had told him of the meeting, he'd assumed that the elders had requested his presence, not that he was being foisted into their counsel.

Karva nodded. As the oldest, he'd be the one the others would look to lead. Yet, Karva didn't speak or meet Kristjan's gaze. This didn't bode well. None of the elders looked at him. Hafnar, the newest member, stared at his hands.

What have you done now?

Kristjan mentally sorted through his recent activities, but he couldn't think of any that would have disturbed the elders.

You're fine.

Father waited without saying a word.

At last, a man with greying hair sat forward, picking a piece of lint from his sleeve before folding his hands in front of him on the table. Kristjan knew Orlaugur well. He was in charge of the mines and had mentored Kristjan for a few cycles until Father had put an end to that, claiming it was too dangerous.

The elder spared Kristjan a grim smile before turning away to the chief. "Geirfinnur, as you know, mining has dwindled over the past cycles. The veins aren't as rich, and we're having to dig deeper into the ground to extract what we're finding. We don't have the equipment that our fathers had, or it's falling into disrepair, despite all the upkeep."

This was exactly what Kristjan had thought of when Bastian wanted to keep the new strain of dioptase to themselves.

Karva shook his head. "In all my rotations as an elder and even before I took my father's place, I've not seen a step when a merchant left Storeheltur dissatisfied."

Kristjan swallowed—hard. This was worse than he thought. Father adjusted his position in his seat, but that was the only indication that the news perturbed him.

Karva continued, "Androw left without a full load, and let it be known he'd inform any merchants he met that it wasn't worth coming this far north."

A sickly silence fell over the table.

No merchants meant no food, no supplies from the south.

"Wha..." Kristjan's voice wobbled, and he licked his lips. "What's more important—finding ore, or making sure we can all eat?"

Orlaugur's smile was hid in his thick beard, but his eyes sparkled. "Knew Geirfinnur was raising his son right. For now, we need to have food. That means hunting parties will have to brave Toppur. Every able-bodied person will be called in to help expand the mines and locate fresh ore."

"We'll need someone to be in charge of organizing all the efforts." Reinar ran a hand through his greying hair. "I can offer, but in reality, Arny's better suited for that than me."

Father smiled. It seemed an odd reaction to Kristjan, but the expression softened Father's face. "Then please ask her to help us."

Of the two options—hunting or expanding the mines—hunting was the one Kristjan felt he'd be best at. He loved going to Toppur despite the cold.

Before Father could interject with a denial, Kristjan leaned forward. "I'm willing to go on a hunting expedition. I know the ways of Toppur—how the moons glide through the sky, and how to read the stars. Bastian's the best hunter we have, and Marko can scout a trail better than anyone else his age. If I talk with them, they'll agree to form a party."

"Kristjan." Father's jaw dropped, but he shut it quickly. "Kristjan, Toppur has so much to comprehend—more than you've just listed. When was the last you were there for any extended length of time?"

Friðfinn cocked his head as if evaluating Kristjan's offer.

"I go up at least once a step."

Father wasn't to be deterred. "That's different, son. You go to your thinking spot. That's not the same as hunting. There are all kinds of dangers in Toppur. It's why Jorvar came down into the ground where the heated vents are. Without the warmth they provide, you'll not last long."

"Let the boy speak, Geirfinnur." Friðfinn was polite, but only barely. "I understand he's your only son, but if he's to be chief, he'll need to show himself capable—just as you did."

Pursing his lips, Father nodded.

Support from Friðfinn was unlooked-for, but Kristjan ran with it. "As I was saying, I believe my friends and I can make a safe hunting expedition and return in a phase, maybe two at the most, with food to last a phase. We won't have to worry about what we kill going bad like hunting parties in the caverns do. The climate is cold, but not beyond what we can handle." Kristjan wanted to rub his hands on his knees, but all of the elders were staring at him.

Karva pursed his lips. "I'm not sure risking the few strong young people that know Toppur, especially our chief's son, is a good idea."

"But if the situation is as dire as you say—" Kristjan cut off, realizing how condescending that might sound. "I mean, we need to start hunting and gathering in resources now. If we're so cautious about risking people, then we'll wait too long and put everyone at greater risk as we get more desperate. And at this moment, I believe I'm best suited to go. I've studied under Sigmar." He looked to Hafnar for confirmation.

"My brother's the best there is when it comes to knowing the ways of Toppur," Hafnar said.

At last, Karva nodded. "Very well, Kristjan. You and your friends have two phases to bring back as much meat as you can."

* * *

I sat staring at my son; he betrayed no fear, only determination. He was resolved that such a fate should not come to pass, and by stating the stakes so clearly, he was calling the elders to act to the best of their ability. There'd be no one slacking in the next phases, I felt sure.

Did I want him to go to Toppur for two phases? No more than I'd wanted Sæbjort to walk the halls of the ancients, but I couldn't deny him.

"Very well, then. Kristjan and his friends will make our first expedition into Toppur. Arny will organize the other parties, including the explorers." I glanced about to see if there was any other discussion. Seeing none, I rose. "I'll adjourn this elders' meeting."

Chairs scraped against the stone floor as first one and then another joined me and expressed their gratitude to Kristjan. At least he didn't beam with pride at their words.

Friðfinn settled a hand on Kristjan's shoulder. "When you return, please reconsider my daughter."

Kristjan nodded, but it was the type of inclination of the head that I'd used many times to say I'd think on the option without committing to anything. How much he reminded me of myself at that age. If only Sæbjort was here to see him. She'd have been as proud of him as I.

"Father, if you'll excuse me, I need to go find Bastian and Marko."

I studied his green eyes, so like his mother's that it'd sent me into despair at times when he was younger. Now, I saw it as a blessing—a reminder of better times.

"Son, I'm proud of you." My voice faltered, and I glanced down at my hands—anything to keep from looking up at him and losing all self-control and crying. "Take care. I…" I couldn't finish the thought or my greatest fear would come to life. "Come back safely."

"I will, Father." Was there a waver in his voice as well?

He turned before I could look at his face again; Reinar had commanded his attention. I watched them interact, again wondering at the young man Kristjan had grown into. Where had the rotations gone? Where once there'd been a small, insecure boy, there now stood a fledgling adult.

He strode out of the meeting hall with the confidence I'd taught him to have.

"You did well with him, Geirfinnur." Friðfinn nodded to Kristjan's departing form. "I noticed he didn't give me an answer. Will he marry my daughter?"

"I can't force him, Friðfinn, and neither can you."

"But we can encourage the arrangement. Will you press my case?"

I wanted to sigh but held it in check. Tinna *was* an excellent choice. Why didn't Kristjan want her? Was it true that he didn't have his eye on any particular girl? If so, then he should be happy with an arranged marriage. It was the way of our people. If a couple didn't have an opinion, their parents would settle on an agreement.

"Can't guarantee my word will hold any sway, but I'll try."

"Thank you, Geirfinnur. You're a true friend."

The words meant more coming from Friðfinn. The elder was quiet and kept to himself most of the time, yet his wealth of wisdom was great. Kristjan would do well to have Friðfinn as a father-in-law. If only the boy would see that.

* * *

Kristjan didn't have far to go to find his friend. Marko was bouncing his baby sister on his knee. It didn't make sense that Marko could be so happy with that many younger siblings running around his home. He was the oldest of nine, and the responsibilities that came with that seemed endless as far as Kristjan could see. The youngest smiled up at Kristjan with slobber dribbling down her chin.

"You'll want to wipe her mouth." Kristjan pointed, but his warning came too late. The drool landed on Marko's leg.

Marko laughed. "That's nothing, Kristjan. Wait until the cloth doesn't hold, and it leaks out the sides."

"Ew!" Kristjan couldn't keep the disgust from showing.

Marko laughed at his reaction and set his sister on the floor. "Myr, I'm going out with Kristjan. Can you keep an eye on Glyta until Mother returns from the market?"

Myr practically threw down her embroidery. "Oh, and abandon this knotted mess, which I'd much prefer to shred then sew? How unfortunate. O well." She grinned. "I suppose I can make some sacrifice. Have fun."

Marko waited until they were well out of earshot of the household before he spoke. "So, what has you so downtrodden?"

It always amazed Kristjan how his friend could see past the outer expressions to what Kristjan truly felt.

"Let's wait until we're not out in the open."

"All right." Marko drew the words out but didn't push for anything more.

Kristjan led the way to where he knew his cousin would be working. Bastian had been assigned to clean the heating ducts that ran throughout Storeheltur. The tunnels carried the thermal air and waters that warmed the cavern system, but they also built up gunk that needed to be scraped out occasionally. No one liked the chore, but it was a necessary evil that every male over twelve rotations endured.

The scratch of the metal spatula echoed off the walls as they drew near.

Instead of crawling into the tunnel, Kristjan called down into the hatch. "Bastian, come here. I have something you'll like more than scraping."

The clank of the handle hitting the rock was his only reply. Then his cousin's face, grimy and green in the light of the *yoma*, popped into view.

"Anything to get out of here. Don't you want to join me, cuz?" Bastian smiled, but his eyes were still hard.

Kristjan wished he could figure out what had changed his cousin's attitude.

"I'd rather not." Kristjan glanced about, and realizing they were alone, he let a sigh escape his lips. "Father called me to an elder meeting."

"What? Another wedding proposal?" Bastian waved his hand. "I'll go back to scraping if that's the case."

Suddenly, the pieces clicked into place. "Bastian, I'm not trying to woo Tinna. Her father's pushing the arrangement. I'm not sure if she really even wants it or if she just can't tell her father no."

Bastian glared at him. "You're trying to tell me; you want nothing to do with the girl of my dreams?"

"Why would I? Sure, she's nice and all that, but you've had your heart set on her for cycles now, Bastian. What type of cousin, or even friend, would I be if I tried to take her away from you?"

A smile twitched at Bastian's lips, and then he grinned. "Thank you, Kristjan. I'll take my ring to her as soon as Iðna has it ready."

"Well, hopefully, he can finish it by next step. Otherwise, you'll have to wait two phases."

Marko shook his head. "All right, enough mysterious little hints. Out with it."

Kristjan leaned against the stone wall and explained what he'd volunteered them for.

When he finished, Bastian pulled himself out of the tunnel hatch. "Count me in. I'll see if Iðna can complete the ring so I can give it to Tinna before we leave at first watch. Marko, we'll need you to get the sleigh and the rest of the equipment. I can help, but I'll want a bath first."

Marko gripped Kristjan's hand and then took Bastian's grubby one. "Let's go. The sooner our people's food supply is secure, the better."

Chapter 3

7 Fjorda, 400 AI

"Any idea where we need to go first?" Bastian glanced about the icy waste. "What creatures in their right mind would live here?"

"Like us, they find the thermal crevices and nest there." Kristjan pulled his cloak closer around his shoulders. The fur was a welcome warmth from the wind that blew snow against his boots.

"Then that's where we'll look first." Marko knelt to the ground. "The wind will erase any footprints, but there'll be other signs I should be able to find."

Bastian looked up at the large moon, Handi, and grinned. "You find me the critter, and I'll kill it."

That left Kristjan to watch their backs and make sure they all returned to Storeheltur in two phases. He could do this.

Of course, you can.

Unless…

Father was right. You've never led an expedition before. When was *the last time you were on Toppur for more than stargazing?*

Kristjan ignored the doubt and thought of what Sigmar had taught him. From the position of the moons, he'd say they had twelve spans to stalk and bring down their prey before they'd need to go to ground. Kristjan knew from time in his thinking place that once the moons settled past the ice ridge the winds would kick up and the temperature would drop even further, scouring the land and biting into any flesh still unsheltered.

Marko was good to his word. Within the span, he'd found their first hunt. Bastian shot it with his bow and skinned it. A snow fox was the first pelt to line the sleigh. By the end of the twelve spans, six more joined the first, along with a healthy brace of rabbits.

The young men settled down in a hollow out of the wind to rest and wait until the moons returned. With the fur tarp spread over them as a ceiling, they were toasty and warm.

"I could get used to this." Bastian blew on a piece of meat he'd roasted over the small coal stove designed for such expeditions. "Way better than cleaning the heating ducts."

"Don't you miss Tinna?" Marko hid his grin by grabbing his own piece of meat.

"If that came from anyone but you, Marko Bergmundsson…"

Kristjan wondered what Bastian would do, but his cousin just shook his head as Marko laughed.

"See, it's good to take a teasing now and again." Marko licked his fingers. "But I'll not tease you too much as long as you provide us with meals like this. Almost better than what my mother prepares."

"Why, thank you!" Bastian bowed. "I'll consider becoming chef of Storeheltur in the future."

"I think the cold air and exercise changes our taste." Kristjan snatched a second bite. "Telma still has you beat on a step in and step out basis. I've eaten her meals when there's not much food in their home. She has a way of stretching it to feed all the hungry mouths."

Bastian shook his head. "Still, I'll take the compliment. Now, eat before the meat grows cold."

His cousin's glare was such a perfect imitation of Aunt Froða that Kristjan laughed as he filled his belly.

As Tsiki, the smaller of the two moons, descended, a breeze picked up, but the tarp held. With their meal over, the friends crawled into their bedrolls and slid their heads out of the fur to watch the stars.

Marko extended his hand toward the sky. "They seem like they're so close. I should be able to reach out and grab them, but when I try, they're far away."

"Now you see why I enjoy sitting under the ice tree and thinking." Kristjan took a deep breath, the air invigorating. "I'm the only one out there, except the stars. It's easy to set aside the worries."

"What concerns do *you* have?" Bastian huffed. "You don't have any siblings to live up to."

Kristjan grimaced. "Oh, only the weight of Jorvar. Father's brought that name up so many times. Jorvar would do it this way. Jorvar would know what to do. Jorvar this. Jorvar that. I'll never measure up; despite how much I try."

Marko wriggled his hands in under his head. "No one's perfect, Kristjan, and no one's asking you to be perfect, except yourself."

"Be thankful you have the father you do. You have it easy, cuz."

Kristjan couldn't agree with Bastian. Despite his three older brothers, Bastian was the one who had it easy. No one expected him to be anything more than he was. They let him be Bastian, Mikkael's son, while everyone had high hopes and dreams for Kristjan Jorvarsson. He had two whole phases to be himself with his best friends; he'd enjoy it to its fullest.

When the stinging in their noses turned to numbness, they closed the fur back around them and soon drifted to sleep.

* * *

I caught myself staring into space at the most inopportune moments—my thoughts were drawn to my son like iron to a lodestone. How was he fairing? Had they found game? Would he be injured on the way? All the terrible possibilities flooded my mind, just as they always had from the time Kristjan had been little. I'd sit and watch him while he slept, making sure he was breathing. What father did that? Certainly not mine, but I couldn't help it. I'd already lost his mother. I couldn't lose him as well.

And yet, in some ways, it was as if I *had* lost him already. He wouldn't speak to me, not in any meaningful way; he'd rather be with Marko or even Bastian. Did he share his heart with them, the way he once had with me? There'd been a time when I'd known him best of anyone. When had that changed? *Why* did it change?

My heart stuttered, and I knew I needed to shift my thoughts.

"*Goðan*, Geirfinnur," Mikkael called at my door. "Can I come in?"

I reached for the wall as I stood, a momentarily dizziness delaying my answer.

"Come in, welcome." I hugged my brother-in-law. "What brings you here at this time of the step?"

"Probably the same thing that has you awake long after you should be in bed: my son." Mikkael held me at arm's length looking for something; what, I didn't know. He slumped into a chair—the same one Kristjan used to sit in, and Sæbjort before him. My heart still ached at the loss, if only she was here now.

"Froða says I'm..." He attempted a shrug, but it looked forced.

Shoving that pain back into the recesses of my being, I nodded, hearing instead my sister's voice as I finished the phrase. "…borrowing trouble." How many times had she told me the same thing growing up?

"Well?" Mikkael looked up at me with… Was that dread? There was an earnestness to it as if he was hoping my response would assuage his fear. Before I could form the question, he answered it. "It's been five steps since they left. They have another nine before we can even start thinking about going up there after them."

He echoed my own anxious thoughts, which rallied with the reinforcement. If something had happened in those first moonsteps, then they were already lost to us. But instead of dwelling on the worst possible outcome, I repeated the words Friðfinn and Kristjan had said at the elder meeting.

Mikkael smiled small, even though his hands were clasped in his lap, his thumbs circling each other. "And so we leave it at that, with nothing to *do* while we wait?"

"We're not out there on Toppur with them."

He shuddered. "I suppose you're right. Sometimes, I wonder at how life can strike us in the back when we're already down."

I nodded sympathetically, thinking of how Froða had miscarried their second child, and not even a cycle later his father had passed into the halls of the ancients. Grief upon a grief—both enough on their own to leave a man staggering, but combined they could bring him to his knees.

"Maybe it's not so much life as an evil force," I suggested.

"Like the old scrolls tell of an enemy of our souls?"

"Enemy of our souls," I mused aloud. "Sounds ominous that way, but it fits how I felt after Kristjan's birth. Something, or someone, was after me to steal my joy, but as long as I had my son, I had something worth living for."

"That about sums it up, and now our sons are out in Toppur with no way to contact us if something should go wrong."

"There is one thing."

Mikkael leaned forward as if my words were the textured lichen on a slick ledge and they could keep him from losing his hold.

"It's what I've learned to do over the rotations—pray. Jeeah will see our boys through this."

* * *

The storm came up on the ninth step. Kristjan had watched it build, but the ferocity of it, combined with its abrupt onslaught, caught them off-guard. They hurriedly dug out a hollow and piled their belongings along the edges before taking cover under the fur tarp they spread over it. The wind threatened to pull the tarp loose, but Bastian pounded spikes through it into the ice, and at last they could breathe for a moment despite the gusts that rattled through their little shelter.

"We need a fire." Kristjan shivered.

The wind had brought the temperature down further. He couldn't feel his nose, and their precious supply of coal was dwindled to almost nothing.

Bastian pulled a lump of coal from the sleigh. "This will have to do, but I don't know if we can get it started with this wind. Let's get the tarp weighted down as best we can, and then we might have a chance."

Together, the three arranged their packs to seal the windward edge of their makeshift tent. With that done, the biting cold lost a little of its edge, and they were able to take off their gloves for short turns with the flint and steel. Each of them lent their breath to the fragile sparks, and at last Marko had a small flame started in the bundle of tinder. He cupped that in his palms and set it to the coal, which began to burn brightly almost at once. The scant heat couldn't warm them, but it would keep them from freezing. They didn't speak much; they each knew that they needed to be heading home soon, but if the storm kept up, they wouldn't make it. Between the flapping of the tarp and the howling of the gale, Kristjan didn't sleep well.

Sometime in the late watch the fire died out. Bastian counted out their remaining coal and shook his head.

"We can't keep using it if we're to eat and still get home."

They looked at each other, their countenances grim, Marko was the first to speak above the roar of the wind.

"Maybe we should look for a better shelter. We're going to freeze in here if we can't get away from the wind."

Kristjan shook his head. "We'd get lost out there, if the snow lets up, then maybe."

Resigned, they snuggled into their bedrolls. Kristjan just hoped the storm would calm by first watch.

First watch came and went without abatement. The wind continued to blow, leeching the heat from their bodies bit by bit.

The moonstep dragged by with nothing to help with the passage of time. Marko entertained them with stories for a few spans, but eventually even his ever-cheerful attitude flagged. They were blowing their warm breath into their gloves to stave off the needling pain in their fingers when Bastian said what was thinking. "We can't stay here much longer."

Marko looked grim. "That means we need a better place to wait out whatever's left of this storm, and *that* means somebody needs to go scouting." He gritted his teeth and relinquished the warmth of his bedroll, giving a violent shiver as soon as he crawled free of its protection. "So I'll go look."

Kristjan shook his head. "We're blind out there, remember? No *yoma* means no light."

Marko slapped his forehead and dug in his trouser pocket. "Why didn't I think of this before?" He pulled out a piece of malachite along with something else that glowed, lighting up the shelter.

"You have *yoma*?" Bastian sat up, brushing snow onto his bedroll. "This could give us enough light to see."

"Yes, but in this blizzard, we might not be able to find our way back." Kristjan cautioned.

"Let me try, Kristjan. If I can't see to keep going, I'll turn right back around, but if it's safe, you and Bastian can come along." Marko settled his hood onto his head and wrapped a scarf around his face, tying it in place. "There's no harm in trying; we'll freeze if something doesn't change, and then all this meat will never reach Storeheltur. No one benefits if that happens. Time to take a risk."

His friend was right, but Kristjan didn't like it. Some internal instinct said to stay put, but he couldn't formulate an answer to Marko's logic.

"Fine, but be careful." Kristjan knew he sounded like his father, but he couldn't help it.

Bastian smirked. "Listen to your future chief, Marko."

"Shut up," Kristjan growled, but Marko joined Bastian in his laughter.

"You do sound like your father." Marko grinned. "I'll be careful."

With a final wave, he crawled out of the tent. Kristjan waited to hear a scream or to see Marko's head pop back in. There was neither. Bastian bundled up and followed after him; Kristjan sighed apprehensively and followed his cousin.

The wind tore at his face, legs, hands—anything it could get a grasp on, and everything else. Ahead, Marko's *yoma* glowed green and welcoming against the grey sky and white snow fighting for space around Kristjan. Bastian battled his way toward Marko, and Kristjan trudged along, his head down.

What are we doing? We'll get lost or hurt out here.

Or they'd freeze sitting down. Did it really make a difference which?

Where's your confidence now when it's needed?

Taking a deep breath, he plodded ahead.

You can do this. Just like Sigmar taught you.

Then, without warning, there was a yell in the howl of the wind and the light of Marko's *yoma* vanished. Not thinking of the consequences, Kristjan broke into a run, but Bastian beat him to the place where Marko had disappeared. His cousin's face was as pale as the snow swirling around them.

Afraid to look, and afraid not to, Kristjan knelt beside Bastian. The blistering wind faded to an annoyance, and the ice crunched as he rested his wrapped hands on the edge of the crusted snow, stray flakes falling away into the depths.

Below them, the *yoma* cast a greenish-blue hue around the pit, illuminating a scene that Kristjan couldn't immediately process. Marko's fur hood had come undone and his unruly brown hair was a stark contrast to the snowflakes that settled on it only to immediately melt away. His sprawled form lay at odd angles, his leg unnaturally bent, and a dark stain was spreading, soaking into the snow beneath him.

Too much blood. How had Marko lost that much in so little time?

"Kris…" Marko's strained plea unlocked Kristjan's feet.

He sprang up, but Bastian grabbed his arm before he could get anywhere.

"Don't," his cousin hissed. "There's no way out again, and what if you get hurt?"

"We can't leave him there!" Kristjan pulled his arm loose. "I'll be careful."

One side was shallower than the other. Kristjan lowered himself down into the hole, but by the time he made it to Marko, his friend's eyes had slid shut.

"No! Marko!" Kristjan collapsed beside his friend, his hands groping, trying to see what had happened.

They came away smeared in blood. *So much!* Then he saw the culprit. Marko lay on top of his pick. The tool had slid from its notch in Marko's belt, or Marko had been pulling it loose when he stumbled. Either way, the pick had pierced Marko's thigh.

"Marko!" Kristjan pressed one hand to the wound in an attempt to staunch the flow of blood, but he could already feel that the pressure had ebbed. Desperate, denying, he slapped his friend's chest, then shook him, trying to elicit some response. Some sign. Some hope.

None came. The wind gusting overhead was a distant rumble and shriek, and in the pit, there was black quiet and the scent of too much iron.

"Marko, please," Kristjan whispered low, gripping his friend's shoulders and trying to pull him upright, as if that would revive him. "Please, I *need* you."

"Kristjan?" Bastian peered over the lip, his eyes wild.

Kristjan swallowed back bile and took a shallow breath, letting Marko's weight pull them both back to the ground.

What now? They couldn't leave Marko here, and yet, what were they supposed to do? Sleep here beside him? Leave him to be embalmed in ice or worse? Kristjan shuddered at the thought of a scavenging animal happening upon his friend.

"Get the sleigh," he said. "We're going home."

"But—"

"We'll find one of the *lofti* and head down that way."

"Are you *crazy*?" Bastian shook his head. "It's blowing so hard that we can't even see the moons. There's no way we'll find a little hole like a *lofti*. Besides, we have a *sleigh*, Kristjan. It's not made for traveling through the caverns. It's designed for Toppur—for snow."

He was right, and Kristjan hated it. He measured his words before he answered, reminding himself that it wasn't his cousin's fault that they couldn't return so easily.

"Fine, but I'm staying here. You can either join me or go back to the shelter."

His vision blurred. He rubbed at his eyes, only to discover that his tears had frozen on his lashes.

"Kristjan. It… it's a good place to wait out the storm. He— he did…"

Kristjan nodded, angry and guilt-stricken. He'd let Marko go out, searching out a better place for them all, and now here they sat, sheltered, but at such a cost. He couldn't speak, not yet. Bastian couldn't see him like this—undone. He took a shuddering breath and blinked back the tears. He was too fragile to withstand Bastian's mocking, and he couldn't break down. Not now, not in front of anyone else.

Thankfully, he had time to regain his composure when Bastian vanished for a little while, though Kristjan began to worry that he'd gotten lost in the blizzard. But before much longer he heard the crunch of the sleigh's runners approaching the rim. His cousin lowered down some of their gear and fastened a line to help them get out again, then tacked their fur tarp over the mouth of the hole, leaving only the leeward side open where the pit's edge dipped down. Then he crawled in through the opening and climbed in, careful to avoid Marko.

In unspoken agreement, Bastian handed Kristjan a single lump of coal, and the two worked until they had a small blaze going. The cheerful flames were a stark contrast to the gloom between them. Always before when Bastian and Kristjan had disagreed, Marko had been the buffer that helped them laugh at their

differences and see past them. Now, he'd taken his contagious spirit to the halls of the ancients. Kristjan hoped with all his might, that the ancestors appreciated what they'd received, for he couldn't imagine his life without one more word, one more joke, one more of those happy smiles that he'd known since childhood. Storeheltur was poorer for his loss, but Kristjan, ever burdened by his doubts and once buoyed by Marko's presence, was utterly destitute.

Chapter 4

20 Fjorda, 400 AI

Friðfinn had alerted me that the boys were back, but the ice-encrusted cloaked figure couldn't have been mine. The blotchy red skin was nothing like the fair complexion he'd inherited from Sæbjort, more than that, when I saw his mouth moving, speaking to Telma and Margeir, his eyes caught my gaze like a tar pit, beautiful green eyes flat and devoid of life. He moved as if in a trance, operating from memory and not on conscious thought.

The sound around me suddenly came into sharp focus. Telma shrieked, a sundering cry that blessedly few of us had ever heard, but which a primal part of every heart has always known. It was a scream only a mother could produce. Several young children began to sob, and other women picked up the haunting mourner's cry that stopped my heart for the briefest of moments and then sent it racing again.

It was then that I saw one was missing. Kristjan stood behind the sled, while Mikkael engulfed Bastian in a fierce hug. Bastian stood frozen for the briefest of moments, and then he returned the embrace.

"I can take care of the sleigh, Bastian." Kristjan spoke for the first time. His voice was as cold and lifeless as the ice crystals that dropped from his cloak and skittered across the stone.

Bastian turned from his father. "No, let me help I'll take the pelts to the tanner, at least."

Only then did I wonder about the success of their mission. Had they found enough meat to sustain us?

The two boys worked in silent unison while the mourners sang and Telma sobbed in Margeir's arms. I swallowed back my fear and the emotions that wanted to overwhelm me any time I heard the mourning song. Friðfinn and several others took the frozen meat away, but the sleigh was not yet empty; both boys seemed leery of touching what remained under the covering. Finally, with a nod, Kristjan's jaw tightened, and he turned to Margeir and Telma.

"Marko has always been my friend." Kristjan blinked and his throat constricted, but he didn't look away. "But it's my fault he's gone. Do with me as you see fit."

Telma placed a hand to her mouth as tears streamed down her face. She shook her head and embraced my son.

"Kristjan, don't say such a thing. I know you'd never harm him. Don't you dare," her voice broke, "believe that you deserve harm in return. He wouldn't—" A sob crumbled her words. "He wouldn't want that."

Margeir settled his hand on Kristjan's shoulder, his words tight with grief but limned with compassion. "She speaks the truth. Depriving someone else of their son won't bring ours back."

Kristjan nodded, but his shoulders slumped—a posture I recognized, but whose meaning didn't fit here. Had he *wanted* to be punished? What was my son thinking? Had he honestly thought Margeir would require his *death*? That was the punishment for willful *murder*, not an accident. I could recognize malice—I'd witnessed it enough times to know—and what I saw was devastation. Both boys exuded grief from every motion of their bodies, their hands, their stooped postures and downcast faces.

"Please, let me see him." Telma gripped Kristjan's arm.

He nodded and peeled back the fur tarp they'd been supplied for shelter. Stretched out on the sleigh, stiff with either death or the residual cold, lay Marko. Margeir kept an arm around Telma as the two knelt. I couldn't look on. The memories, although eighteen rotations old, were still raw. It was me kneeling beside Sæbjort's still form. I blinked away the images, but they returned. Water lapped around my legs. I could smell the mineral tang of the pools.

Jeeah, help. I took a deep breath and turned from the sight directing myself to take in the rest of the scene.

Mikkael had his arm around Bastian; the other elders, looking on; Friðfinn with his daughter, Tinna. All of them mourned with Telma and Margeir. It wouldn't be right for the chief to leave, but if I stayed, they'd see my tears.

I turned away, scrubbing my cheeks dry, and met the gaze of the one person who wasn't watching the mourners—Josebina. Her gentle expression leant me courage, saying she understood my struggle, but it was also my undoing. I blinked rapidly and headed to my quarters.

I wanted to know what had happened, but now wasn't the time. In private, I'd hold my son and mourn our loss.

* * *

Father... A deep, broad pang pierced Kristjan straight through to his soul, his arms held slightly forward, his body leaning toward his father's retreating form. He'd turned his back on Kristjan. Uncle Mikkael held Bastian, and of course, Margeir was comforting Telma, but there was no one to give a healing balm to Kristjan's heart. He rocked back onto his heels and looked down, finding his best friend's distorted face, grey and pale and cold. No one had understood him like Marko, and now, because of him, Marko was gone.

If only I'd told him to stay. The same thought had plagued Kristjan ever since he'd first seen Marko lying in the pool of his own blood. That sight was stamped on his eyelids, there whenever he blinked, waiting for him to close his eyes. In the three moonsteps it'd taken them to get home, sleep had been fraught and fleeting.

One moonstep waiting beside his body while the storm abated; two pulling him home. Home. What was home without Marko?

Someone touched his hand. He glanced down. A female hand—soft and gentle. Without thinking, he squeezed back. The girl entwined her fingers with his. He turned to see who it was and met liquid brown eyes.

"I'm sorry, Kristjan." Tinna brushed a tear away with her free hand.

His inner voice told him to drop Tinna's hand, but it was the only thing grounding him at the moment. If he let go, he'd flounder back into the morass he'd been in since Marko's death. Even thinking the word brought a chill to his bones.

"It's horrible. I feel so sorry for Telma and the others." Tinna's thumb caressed his hand. "I can't imagine what they're feeling."

Kristjan could—their anger, at least. The injustice. It should have been him roaming the halls of the ancients, not Marko.

Kristjan didn't know how long they stood that way, but his cloak thawed while he stared at nothing, creating a puddle around him.

At last, Margeir helped Telma to her feet. "Thank you, Kristjan, for returning him to us." He blinked rapidly, sending a few stray tears down his cheeks. "I'd like to know what happened, but… I know it's asking a lot of you to tell it twice, and the elders will want—"

"No, Margeir, of course. You deserve to hear it in private."

"Then, please, come with us to our home. We'll let them…" Telma gazed with shattered tenderness at Marko's still form and her face contorted with a grief whose depths Kristjan couldn't fathom. She took a shallow, stuttering breath to finish, "…let them prepare him."

Tinna's aunt stepped forward with an ornate case that held the ceremonial clipping tools. She'd give Marko a final shave and trim his hair. Others would dress him in his best clothes for the final rites. Kristjan had watched the process before, but he'd never expected it to be performed on his best friend.

"Come, Telma, children." Margeir ushered his family through the crowd which opened up to make their way.

Kristjan took a step before he realized Tinna was still holding his hand.

With a final squeeze and a gentle smile, she let go. "If you need someone to talk to, I'm here. Father will give us a quiet place."

"Thank you."

As he passed Uncle Mikkael, Bastian glared at him. *What did I do to deserve that?*

With Bastian he wasn't ever sure. Yet another place Marko would be missed. His friend had helped the two cousins communicate and work through arguments. Now who'd be there for them?

* * *

By the time Kristjan returned to our quarters, I'd finally gotten control of my emotions, but he looked exactly the same—drained, lifeless.

"Welcome home, Kristjan," I offered, clasping him on the shoulder. I wanted to take him in my arms as I'd done when he was younger, but I already knew he wouldn't let me—hadn't for the past five rotations. "I'm… I'm glad you're safe."

"Safe." Kristjan paused, but didn't pull away from my touch.

That was a good sign. I kept the contact, willing warmth into him.

"Yes, I worried about you while you were gone."

"Didn't think I could do it?" For the first time he looked at me. "Well, I guess, I lived up to your expectations for once. I brought home the meat, but not my team."

"Kristjan, that's—"

"I need a bath. I've not been warm since before we left. If you'll excuse me." He brushed past me, then turned at his bedroom door. "You can set up a meeting with the elders so I can answer for what happened."

Elders. I hadn't even thought of that. My concern was for my son—the one who didn't want my touch. The one who walked like a chief, but whose heart had been frozen in the wastes of Toppur. Or maybe it'd happened long before.

Chapter 5

21 Fjorda, 400 AI

Kristjan walked beside his father as one of the many pilgrims that traveled the same path, hardly seeing his feet shuffling across the stone. The passage would soon open into the large stone chamber and its chasm that plunged almost straight down into the depths—into Fivku. Kristjan shuddered at the thought. No one had ever returned from Fivku. Some foolish boys had tried to climb down the chute once, but the heat was too oppressive to survive. One of them had fainted and plummeted to his death; the others had managed to make the ascent and escape but spent several moonsteps recovering from the heat sickness.

According to the Jorvarssons' records, Fivku was the source of Storeheltur's warmth as well as what fed Ferish Pools. When a soul departed for the halls of the ancients, the body was sent to Fivku with the two-fold purpose of keeping beloved ones close and making them part of the warmth and protection they'd enjoyed in life.

Kristjan wanted nothing to do with the Fivku ceremony, but there was no backing out of tradition. Besides Telma and Margeir deserved his presence. So, he traversed the halls with others to pay their respects to a fallen member of the *holdt*.

When they rounded the corner, the way opened into a broad, natural cavern with a high ceiling and no columns to support it. Kristjan always wondered whether it'd one day fall, lacking as it was in the supportive columns that pervaded Storeheltur's occupied caves. *Yoma* of various colors sparkled in the expanse, lending an otherworldly glow to the room. People parted as Kristjan and his father approached, allowing them to pass to the front where Marko's family was already kneeling in a huddle several paces from a polished stone table—the only thing in the cavern fashioned by human hands.

Handi streamed through a *lofti* high above them, shedding its pale light on Marko's body laid out on the slab in his best clothes. Metta had done a wonderful job of shaving him and trimming his hair; he'd have been handsome had his skin not been so waxy and pale.

Father squeezed Kristjan's arm and then stepped to the front, leaving Kristjan beside Margeir. Marko's father didn't even look up. Someone settled in beside him; he glanced over to see that Bastian, Uncle Mikkael, and Aunt Froða were taking their places.

Aunt Froða gave Kristjan a sideways hug. "How are you holding up?"

There wasn't anything to say to that, so Kristjan just shrugged.

"What I thought. And your father?"

"Father?" Kristjan kept his voice low for Marko's family's sake, but he couldn't hide his surprise. "Why would *Father* be affected by this?"

"He still sees her at every passing."

Kristjan knew Father still grieved Mother's death, but that he'd see her in people who bore her no resemblance was startling. Would he see Marko in everyone after this, too?

Father raised his hands and the quiet hum of conversations trailed off. Handi's light waned for a moment, but as Father began to speak it returned. Kristjan reasoned that a cloud must have passed over the moon's face; he was grateful that it hadn't lingered.

"Fellow members of Storeheltur, Bergmundsson family, and elders," Father began in his authoritative voice of compassion—a chief's voice, and one Kristjan wished he possessed. "Any time we send one of ours to Fivku, we mourn together, but this step, even more so, for this step we gather to say farewell to Marko Bergmundsson, who was called to the halls of the ancients in the prime of his youth."

Father regarded the assembly and allowed his gaze to rest first on Kristjan and then on Marko's family. The familiar liquid sounds of the cavern—water traveling, collecting, trailing over and leaving its traces on the living stone—was all that could be heard while he found his words.

"Marko was loved by all, but especially by his younger siblings and parents."

Kristjan tuned out his father's words. He didn't need his father telling him how much he'd miss Marko. Already the hole was beyond explanation. It was as if all Kristjan could feel was pain. There was no way life was going to return to normal after this. *If only…* The words were a litany that ran through his head over and over again, but they never brought peace.

Aunt Froða pinched Kristjan, and he jumped. What had he missed?

"It's time," she hissed at him.

Bastian shook his head and stepped forward. Stilling his racing heart, Kristjan followed. The two of them had been designated to send Marko on the last step of his journey. That way of thinking made it easier to accept the ugly reality of sending his best friend's body into Fivku to be burned up.

"Are you even here? If you were chief, you'd be the one giving the eulogy. Can't see you doing *that*." Bastian's words were intended only for Kristjan's ears. No one else would even have seen his cousin's lips move.

"I'm here, and I'll do my part," Kristjan said through clenched teeth.

"Good. Wouldn't want to have to clean up this as well."

What did Bastian mean? Clean up this as well? What had he had to 'clean up' that had been Kristjan's responsibility? He'd ask later, for now they stood in front of Marko, Handi's light shining on them as well.

"This step, we commend Marko Bergmundsson to Fivku and the keeping of the ancients. May his soul rest in peace." Father intoned the traditional phrase, the signal for Kristjan and Bastian to move Marko from the table to the chute.

Heat hit Kristjan's face in a puff of sweltering air. He blinked to bring moisture back to his eyes. Bastian leaned over and slid his hands under Marko's feet, lifting them onto the lip of the channel. Kristjan grabbed his friend's shoulders. With a nod to his cousin, Kristjan pushed Marko into the small tunnel. Bastian helped guide the body, but once Marko's legs were over the edge, he stepped away. It was up to Kristjan to decide when to give the final farewell.

Why? The question bounced around Kristjan's head. So many *whys*. Why did Marko decide to strike out in the blizzard instead of waiting, just a little longer? Why didn't he see the pit? Why had his pick been drawn out just enough to pierce his thigh? Why must Kristjan be the one to send his friend along the way? Why wouldn't others blame him?

The last was the biggest question. Kristjan was supposed to be the leader—the one who understood the ways of Toppur. The one responsible for the safe return of the team. They hadn't returned safely, and yet, no one blamed him—except himself.

He sighed and blinked back tears. If once they started, he feared they'd never stop, and he couldn't break down, not now—he had to fulfill his last duty to his friend. He owed Marko that much. To the side, Sungvari waited for his nod to begin the chorus that would escort Marko's body to Fivku.

Was Marko's family ready for this? Or was this one of those times in life when what they must do had no regard for what they were ready for?

Kristjan met Sungvari's gaze. Compassion emanated from her presence, giving him the courage to do the thing that shredded what remained of his heart. He wasn't aware of having moved, but Sungvari began to sing. The first note was quiet, almost blending indistinguishable from the hushed sounds of the assembly. The next ones were gentle, almost as if coaxing Kristjan to release his friend. Soon other voices joined Sungvari's.

I'm sorry Marko. It should have been me, not you. I'll miss you; I already do. Bastian's angry with me, and I don't know why—but you would have. I don't know how we'll ever laugh together again without you. Kristjan fought to control the devastation tearing at his threadbare composure—the vision of his many rotations ahead without his closest friend. When he took the chieftain's chair, he'd sit there alone; he'd govern alone; he'd be wandering his own life, lost, until he himself passed into Jeeah's halls and followed Marko down this very fissure.

It was time, and holding onto his friend's body wouldn't change the future; as his father said, a chief often had to do things that pained him. He closed his eyes and with a gentle push sent his friend to Fivku. *As you were in life, may you be in death—at peace.*

Kristjan joined the song, as he peered into Fivku, watching until the dark strands of Marko's hair vanished down the shaft, leaving it bare.

> *The path is smooth now*
> *No danger in sight;*
> *Rest for the weary*
> *A home to enjoy.*
> *Make your way now*
> *Safely to Jeeah.*
> *He'll welcome you to*
> *his enduring peace.*
> *Peace to your soul, friend.*
> *Peace to your family.*
> *Peace to all your friends.*
> *Peace, peace, peace.*

Kristjan turned to face the clan, but only because it was required of him. Margeir met his gaze—and *smiled*! It was touching cheeks traced by tears, but a smile nonetheless How could he? Telma struggled to her feet with Margeir's help. Together they approached Kristjan.

"Thank you, son." Margeir rested his hand on Kristjan's shoulder. "I can't thank you enough for all you've done for Marko."

"I… done for…"

"Kristjan." Telma gripped him in a tight embrace. "You and Marko have been brothers since the step you were born. I'm sorry for your loss."

Kristjan gaped at Telma. What did she mean? *His* loss? What about hers?

She smiled up at him, her grip never wavering. "I'm so proud of the man you've become. Don't blame yourself. Even as wee ones, Marko looked out for you. He could scarcely use a spoon, but he chased you around, trying to feed you from his own bowl while you were busy learning to crawl. When you were learning to walk, he'd hold out his little hands trying to catch you whenever you stumbled. He wouldn't want you to fall into despair. Do you hear me?"

"Yes, ma'am."

Telma patted his back. "That's my boy. Now, you'd better come by and see us still."

"Yes." Margeir squeezed Kristjan's shoulder. "You and your father will join us for the *maltið*."

The *maltið*? That was the meal reserved for the family of the fallen.

"Oh, yes, absolutely." Telma's eyes shone, and for the first time since Kristjan brought Marko home, it wasn't from tears. "You and your father should be there. After all, you were brothers."

This was the second time Telma had used that word—brothers. What did she mean? Of course, Marko was like a brother, but no one had ever said they *were* brothers.

"Then it's settled." Margeir broke into Kristjan's thoughts. "We'll see you and your father at the beginning of the second watch."

With a final hug, Telma and Margeir left. Kristjan remained rooted to his spot, trying to figure out what had transpired.

A gentle touch on his arm startled him.

"I'm sorry, Kristjan." Tinna looked up at him with a somber smile. "I thought you saw me coming."

If he was Bastian, he would have seen her. Why was she constantly at his side?

He mustered a smile. "No problem, Tinna. I was thinking."

"About Marko, yes. He was a wonderful person. It's so sad that he's gone. I can't believe it, and… in such a way." Her voice caught.

Kristjan didn't know what to do. A tear trickled down Tinna's cheek.

"We'll make it, somehow." He patted her on the back. "Marko would want us to continue on."

Tinna wiped her face with a kerchief. "Yes, he would. How are you holding up? I'd think you'd be in tears. I know I couldn't have done what you did today." She shuddered.

"Sometimes you must do what needs to be done."

That was what had gotten him through the moonsteps since the accident. Do what needed to be done. Without thinking of how it looked, he rubbed her back, the motion soothing.

"Well, in my book, you're a hero, Kristjan Jorvarsson. You brought your team back with enough food to feed us for a phase, and stepped up to send your friend on to Fivku." She touched his cheek, her fingers trailing along his beard. "I'll gladly follow you when you're chief."

Chills ran up Kristjan's back and not just from her words. He dropped his hand, but couldn't take his gaze from her brown eyes.

She reached up on tip-toe and whispered into his ear. "Talk to Father."

Then she was gone, leaving a warm spot on his cheek where her hand had been.

* * *

I watched Tinna's tender interaction with Kristjan. Would that thaw him out? Any young man would be distracted by the touch of a beautiful girl—the brush of Sæbjort's gentle fingers on mine still visited me in my dreams, though that blessing had become rarer as the rotations wore on. There, the ghost of a smile on my son's face as Tinna walked away.

"Looks like she may have her way with your son after all." Friðfinn nudged me in the ribs.

"I've been trying to get him to agree, but with everything that's transpired, I've not pushed too hard."

Friðfinn stroked his beard. "Understandable, but when they're under such strain, they need someone to be there for them. You of all people should understand that."

I felt the tension in my jaw tighten and opened my mouth, working the muscles as memories I'd been holding at bay flooded through me. This very hall—but instead of Marko, it'd been Sæbjort who'd lain on the stone until I'd had to push her body into that fathomless pit. I shuddered. Life had been dull and dark for longer than I could track, but I'd come through because I'd had Kristjan to care for. If it hadn't been for the selfless care of Telma and Josebina, I didn't know how either of us would've pulled through.

"Have you spoken to her recently?" Friðfinn crossed his arms, his eyes still on Kristjan, who spoke with people as easily as if it was a birth celebration and not the funeral of his best friend.

I didn't understand how he could do it. I was ready to run from the room, but the chief couldn't do that. Across the way, Josebina rested a hand on Kristjan's shoulder and spoke what were undoubtedly kind words.

"Her?" I didn't want to let on that I understood who or what Friðfinn was speaking about.

"Come now, Geirfinnur. You know as well as I do. The lichen grows closest to the *holdt*, as they say. I see where your son gets his temperament. If you're any indication, my Tinna will be waiting until she's gray before he'll accept the proposal—unless someone else intervenes."

Ignoring what he was implying about me, I focused on my son. "So you're saying we should intervene?"

Friðfinn grinned at me. "That and maybe someone will intervene on your behalf. Or have you not noticed that a certain woman has never taken a husband?"

"There are plenty of women who have chosen to give their energy to the *holdt* rather than to one particular man." I wanted to get this conversation over with as quickly as possible.

"Well, let's take care of your son first, and then we'll focus on you."

If Kristjan was like me, he wouldn't appreciate any interference. I held a sigh in check. Before I could decide what to say, Friðfinn meandered over to Kristjan. I watched as the two conversed. Kristjan was so much my son. He'd learned how to deal with people—even those he didn't want to. The slight tilt of his shoulder was the only indication of his discomfort

In typical Josebina fashion, I didn't hear her until she spoke. "Sæbjort would be proud."

One of the things I loved about Josebina was how she kept my wife's memory alive. Others were more inclined to tell me that it was time to move on.

"Thank you. He's a wonderful son."

"I wasn't speaking of Kristjan, even though she'd be proud of him as well. I was talking about you."

Heat rushed through me. *Would* Sæbjort be proud? Had I kept my promise to her by being there for Kristjan? Jeeah knew I'd tried!

"Quit beating yourself up. You're doing the best you can, and it shows. That's all Sæbjort would have asked of you. Any more is what you place on yourself."

I let out a breath that carried out more tension than I'd felt. "Thank you. Sometimes it's easy to take up the mantle of chief and say I have to be perfect."

"I know." Josebina rested her hand on my arm. "That's why I said something. You've been carrying a heavy load for many rotations. I try to help, but you won't let me."

"How do you see that?" I tried to puzzle through what she'd said.

She smiled, adding to the wrinkles in her face, but they didn't detract from her beauty. "How often have you come to me of your own accord to ask for support? Or help?"

I opened my mouth to reply, then shut it. When *was* the last time? Had I ever?

"I make my point. When the burden becomes too much, I'd love to shoulder some of it."

But I'm chief. It's my responsibility. Yet I'd allowed Sæbjort to be my partner—she was so capable that she could have been chief in my stead. And therein lay the problem. The chilling realization struck that I was afraid. Afraid if I depended that much on a single person again, then I'd fall apart when she was gone, and as this moonstep showed, people passed more quickly than we ever thought or hoped.

I sighed and swiped at a tear. *Sæbjort, would I be unfaithful if I asked Josebina to take your place?*

How could I be thinking this? And now of all times! No, it was best to continue the way things were.

"Geir," Josebina waited until I looked into her deep blue eyes, "I'm not going anywhere. I'd hoped to let you see that over the past eighteen rotations."

"I *have* seen it. You're my best friend, Josebina. I couldn't ask for better."

"But you still cling to Sæbjort's memory." She bit her lip. "Geir, can Marko make his way back up the chute form Fivku?"

I blinked. Where had *that* question come from?

"Walk with me?" Josebina gestured to the side entry which led to the Garður.

I shrugged. My presence wasn't needed here anymore, and if I was being honest with myself, I wanted out of this place of memories. I offered her my arm, and we walked in companionable silence—

another thing I suddenly realized I'd come to depend on for solace.

The archway opened into a wide cavern where a small stream meandered its way past lichen-covered stalagmites to the depths of Storeheltur. The ancients had carved the walls and the various benches and conversation corners along the way, but whether they'd planted the lichen or Jeeah had shed his light upon the area, no one knew. The results were still the same—a vibrant cast of colors magnified by *yoma* of varying shades. A breath of air stirred and a hint of earth, dirt, and something sweet made me feel at home.

How many times had I wandered these paths? Yet, each time, I felt the same peace. It was as if I was close to Jeeah—close to Sæbjort. But this time... I glanced down at the woman at my side. Josebina had been there as well as I'd walked through the Garður. Every time though, she'd been shadowed by her best friend—my dead wife. And that made me think of the image of Marko climbing back up the chute from Fivku. I shuddered as the incongruency of the quiet of the Garður and the terror of the shaft clashed in my mind.

"Why would you ask such a morbid question, Josebina? That's not like you."

Again, she smiled, but the joy didn't quite reach her eyes. "Nor is it like me to allow a friend to wallow in pity."

I was surprised by my own laughter. "That's true." Her expression held steady, though, which sent a chill through me. What had changed? It had to be more than the death of a young man. "What do those two things have to do with one another?"

"Geir, how old is Kristjan?"

"You know as well as I. Eighteen." What had gotten into Sæbjort's best friend?

She nodded. "Eighteen rotations, two hundred and sixteen cycles. That's a long time to stand in front of the passage to Fivku waiting for someone to return."

I choked, then coughed. If I was honest, I could tell her how many moonsteps it'd been, but the fact that *she* knew how long it'd been said more to me than anything else.

Josebina stood there, her hands clasped in front of her and allowed me to process the blow she'd delivered. If Kristjan had been waiting in the cavern of the ancients for even a moonstep waiting for Marko to return, I'd be dragging him from the room to resume his responsibilities, his relationships—his life.

"I'm not—"

Josebina set a finger on my lips, awaking something I had thought long dead. "Think on it."

She turned away, but I reached out for her. "Stay." I surprised myself with the intensity of the request.

"Geir, I can't." Were those tears in her eyes? Had I hurt her somehow?

"Please." I gently drew her to me.

I didn't know what had gotten into me, but I knew that if I let her walk away, I'd lose someone as precious as Sæbjort. She watched me. Those *were* tears she blinked away. I wiped one from her cheek that had escaped, my hand lingering on her cheek.

With trepidation, I did what I hadn't even allowed myself to dream of doing. I leaned into her, drawing her ever closer.

"Geir, it's—"

I interrupted her protest with the softest kiss I could manage, gentle, tentative, but when she returned it, the eighteen rotations of starvation suddenly made themselves felt, and I drank from what she offered, taking it in and letting it wash over me. When we parted, we both were breathless.

"Josebina," I said when my thought had come level again, my hands cupping her face. "I couldn't ask for a better friend." She shook her head and tried to pull away, so I rushed to continue. "But I need more than a friend."

She gasped, and I lifted her face to see her expression.

"What I need is what you've been offering, and I've been too blind—or stupid—to see. You're right; I've been holding onto the myth that Sæbjort wouldn't want me to continue life—all of life." I paused to make sure I had her attention. "Will you become my bride?"

Tears spilled down her cheeks, and she nearly crumpled, clutching at my shoulders like her legs had given out. I pulled her to me. It felt so good to have her in my arms. She was much more delicate than Sæbjort, but her inner strength was just as great. I rested my chin on her head, stroking her hair and rubbing her back while she clutched at my tunic, the sound of broken walls filling her tears with a joy I could hear even in her sobs.

Somehow the Garður seemed different, as if the *yoma* glow that bathed the lichen-coated stone had warmed in our presence. Or perhaps it was only the waking of a heart that had finally returned from the halls of the ancients.

When Josebina's breath had steadied, she looked up at me. I held my breath.

"Geir, I thought you'd never ask. There's one thing, though."

"What?" I wanted to say, "Anything you ask," but held back.

"I'm not Sæbjort."

"No, she'd have kicked me in the backside twelve rotations ago instead of waiting until now." I smiled and leaned closer to her. "So, is that a yes?"

She wrapped her arms around my neck and pulled me to her. The kiss was sweet, comforting, like old friends and new grandeur, utterly alien—something fully alive in itself. Something new.

Chapter 6

21 Fjorda, 400 AI

Kristjan walked into the cavern of the ancients. Handi had passed, leaving only the *yoma* to light the room. It gave the hall a muted and more intimate feel, which was perfect for the *maltið*. He straightened his black tunic and braced himself for the onslaught of emotions.

"Kristjan!" Myr bounced little Glyta on her hip as she came to him. "I'm glad you're here. Marko would have demanded it."

She was right.

"I wouldn't have missed it." He wanted to kick himself for lying to her.

Glyta reached for him, launching herself from Myr's arms. "Mar."

"That's not Marko, Glyta." Myr's voice broke and she swallowed back tears and presented a smile. "That's Kristjan."

"Mar." Glyta held her arms out to him.

How many times had he watched Marko take Glyta, or one of the others, and hold them in his arms? It couldn't be *that* difficult.

Kristjan placed his hands around Glyta's waist and lifted.

"Are you sure?" Myr's eyes were wide, but relief showed in her voice.

"I'm sure." Kristjan adjusted his grip and settled Glyta on his own hip. It wasn't much different than carrying a bag of supplies.

Glyta reached for his hand. Well, a sack of supplies had never squirmed before.

"Hi, Glyta. How are you?"

"Mar." She patted his arm and drooled on his sleeve.

He tried to keep a straight face, but Myr laughed, wiping away tears. "She's getting some new teeth."

Kristjan didn't know how that explained things, but he nodded and hefted Glyta to keep her in place.

"Kristjan, I'm so glad you're here. And you have Glyta." Telma wiped her eyes. "So much like Marko."

He would have given her a hug, but Glyta seemed to be doing her best to fall out of his arms.

"Here, let me take her." Telma reached for the baby. "It seems like only yesterstep you and Marko were this size, vying for me to hold you."

"That's the second time you've talked about Marko and I doing things when we were wee little." He rubbed his shoulder. For a baby, Glyta took a lot of muscle to hold.

Telma smiled and adjusted Glyta. "Of course. The two of you shared so many things from the time you were born."

Kristjan wondered what she was talking about. Telma unwound her hair from Glyta's fingers.

"He never told you?"

Myr glanced between Kristjan and her mother. "Want me to take Glyta so you can talk, *Moði*?"

"Thank you, *kæra*, but I'll manage."

The young girl nodded and left, giving her mother privacy. Kristjan almost would have rather had her stay. He wasn't sure he wanted to know whatever Telma was going to say.

"Who never told me?"

"I never thought it was my place to explain. I'd hoped you had memories of your own, but... No, Glyta." She opened the baby's fist. "You can't pull *Moði's* hair."

Kristjan wanted to be anywhere but here—even a cliff face would be better than the suspense.

"Listen." Telma bounced Glyta on her hip while placing a hand on Kristjan's arm. "Your father was under an enormous strain when you were born. It's a mother's job to care for a newborn, but he took it upon himself to care for you. He wouldn't allow anyone near, other than Froða, and she had her own little one to care for then."

Mother had passed shortly after she gave birth to him. Kristjan had heard the story many times. Father had been deeply hurt, but he fought through the pain and raised a boy Mother could be proud of. What did this have to do with his friendship with Marko, though?

"Marko had seen six cycles when you were born, and I had more than enough milk."

What? Was Telma saying what he thought she was? He blinked as he flushed scarlet, trying to erase the image.

"You needed to be fed. It was the only time your father allowed someone else to take you and care for you. Marko accepted you into his life from the very beginning. The first time Froða handed you to me, I had Marko in one arm. He patted your cheek. Something most infants don't do intentionally, but my Marko did. From that moment on, he'd light up when you entered the room, and when you were old enough to have solid foods, he missed you so much that I finally was able to convince your father to let you come to our house to play." A tear slipped down her cheek. "This is why you belong here this step, at the *maltið*."

From her place in the corner of the room, Sungvari lifted her voice in the *maltið* song.

"I need to get the little ones situated, but Kristjan, know you're as much a part of this family as Marko." Telma gave his arm a squeeze.

He blinked, trying to process what she'd told him. Why hadn't Father said anything? Had Marko known? Most likely. As Sungvari and Telma sang the *maltið* song, Kristjan stood apart. Marko had always been the one to pull Kristjan into the family. Without his friend, he felt like an outsider.

Myr smiled at him as she handed him an unlit candle, then moved on to the next person. By the time Sungvari came to the chorus, everyone had their candle.

Don't mourn without reason.

Don't lose hope.

Light a candle in the darkness.

Remember me.

Remember me.

Telma sang the next section, her voice clear.

I'll be there with Jeeah.

I'll be safe and secure in his arms.

Remember me.

Remember me.

Kristjan couldn't sing. His voice would crack if he tried. Instead, he leaned against the wall with his arms crossed, as if they could shield his heart from the pain. How could this family accept him after what he'd done? It wasn't right.

Margeir was the first to cross to the Fivku chute. A large candle sat where Marko's body had been. The women sang the chorus again; this time Margeir lit his candle and joined his voice to theirs. Each sibling old enough to be able, lit a candle and sang the chorus.

Father stepped up beside Kristjan. "It's our turn, son." His voice was quiet, almost quavering.

With a nod, Kristjan stepped forward. He didn't want to speak with his father now. There were too many questions swirling in his head. Too many memories. He bit his lip fighting the lump in his throat as he stood at the vent.

The words to the chorus resonated through the room, the sound stirring his heart.

Remember me.

Remember me.

I could never forget you, Marko. You've been there for me through fights with Bastian, childhood adventures, first loves, and loss.

The memories swirled around him, as he stood with the candle unlit. If he lit it, he accepted Marko's passing to the halls of the ancients. Marko wasn't ancient. He shouldn't *be* there. Kristjan's fingernails cut into his palm, and he unclenched his fist.

Marko, what will I do without you?

A hand on his shoulder pulled him from his thoughts. Father stood beside him.

"Together?" Father waited for him. "You don't have to do this alone."

And yet, he did. If he was to be a man, he must make it through this.

"Thanks, but I can do it." Somehow.

Taking a deep breath, Kristjan thrust his candle into the flame and joined his voice with the others.

Light a candle in the darkness.

Remember me.

Remember me.

By the second "Remember me," Father was standing beside him, his hands folded in front of him. Had Father deliberately timed it so he didn't have to sing? At least Kristjan didn't have to continue the song. He couldn't have forced the words out.

Margeir stepped forward. "Thank you for coming and singing with us. This step is hard for my family. Losing a child isn't in the order of things, but life often disrupts the natural order. With friends and family, we will survive. Please, join us in remembering our son, Marko. Sit, talk, and share the *maltið* with us."

Telma took Margeir's hand, and the two walked to the head of the table. Their friends from the community brought in dishes and placed them in the center. Marko's siblings took their spots, as did several cousins and other family members.

"Please, Geirfinnur and Kristjan, come." Telma motioned to the empty seats on either side of her and Margeir.

Father nodded his thanks, and they sat down, Kristjan beside Margeir and Father beside Telma.

The food was good, or so Kristjan assumed from the way others ate. He didn't taste it, and mostly pushed it around his plate. He noticed that Margeir didn't eat much either.

Halfway through the meal, one of Marko's brothers laughed.

Kristjan was glad he held his displeasure in check, because Margeir spoke, "What do you find funny, Andri?"

"I'm sorry, Father, but I couldn't help it."

"Go ahead, and tell us. It'll do us good to laugh."

Andri fiddled with his fork then nodded. "I remembered when Marko convinced me to eat the *fletta*. He told me the purple lichen was good for me, that it'd make me grow powerful." Andri smiled. "So, I plucked a huge handful from the cave wall and plopped it in my mouth. You can imagine my surprise when I bit into it! My eyes watered, and I wanted to spit it out. It was so spicy, but I wanted to be powerful and strong like Marko."

Although Kristjan hadn't been there, it reminded him of a similar time when Marko had convinced him to get some younger children to drink the mineral water. Marko could swallow the horrid stuff without nary a flicker of expression. Everyone else gagged, including Kristjan.

"Marko always does… *did* things like that." Myr wiped a tear away. "Except when he was with the little ones. Then he protected them with a passion."

"Oh, but he'd still tease them." Andri jutted his chin toward another brother. "Wouldn't he, Hervin?"

The younger boy laughed. "Marko's the only one who'd tickle me until I cried."

Kristjan squirmed uncomfortably in his chair. This family had always intimidated him, but Marko had drawn him in, making him feel at home.

"What about you, Kristjan?" Margeir's dark eyes held him captive. "What memory is your favorite?"

It was as if the air had been sucked out of the cavern. Kristjan couldn't breathe. It was like that time when… It might not be his *favorite* memory, but it was the first to pop into his mind. Finding his breath restored, he forged ahead.

"Bastian had the crazy idea to go exploring. We were probably not much older than Myr at the time. Marko insisted we take a piece of *yoma* with us. We headed into the unknown with Bastian leading the way." He shuddered as he remembered the cold of that room. "We found an adventure that step. One moment Bastian was in front of us, and the next all of us had tumbled down into darkness—and cold. For some reason that one was cold—almost like being in Toppur. Marko's quick thinking was the only thing that saved us. He used the *yoma* to find hand-holds in the stone. We were able to climb out none the worse for the mishap."

He didn't describe how by the time they'd made it out of the hole, they'd had splitting headaches and fatigue from the lack of oxygen. They'd somehow discovered one of the *bensin*. Father had warned him time and time again to beware of the deadly gas chambers. No one knew why they existed, but they were pockets of death spread throughout Storeheltur. Most had been blocked off. Kristjan wondered what had become of the *bensin* they'd stumbled upon. Had it been barricaded to protect other unexpecting children?

Around him, the conversation had moved on, but his father nodded to him from across the table. There were times when Kristjan wished he could understand the unspoken signs his father used. Was he proud? Sad? Or something entirely different?

* * *

Kristjan did better than I ever had. At Sæbjort's *maltið*, I'd stumbled for words, but mostly remained locked in my own thoughts. Froða had tried to get me to share, but it hadn't felt right. Now, I was glad to see Kristjan smiling and interacting with Marko's family. Perhaps he could avoid shutting out the world as I had done.

At the head of the table, Telma smiled. "I remember how Marko welcomed Kristjan into our family, and then made sure that all of you acknowledged him as a brother as well."

I couldn't help but smile at the memory. Telma had taken Kristjan while I was still numb with shock of Sæbjort's death, but when she'd returned him to my arms, sleeping soundly, she'd told me how the two were made for each other. And they had been. From that moonstep on, they'd been inseparable—but death had no reverence for that bond. I let out a soft sigh.

Jeeah, help Kristjan. May he heal and move forward. Another grim smile spread across my face as I thought of Josebina's words to me and what they'd unlocked inside me. *May he not wait at* Fivku *for Marko to return, but forge new friendships.*

My heart swelled with joy that I'd asked Josebina to be my bride, tempered only by a small mote of apprehension. What would Kristjan say? I'd not had a chance to tell him.

The thought of his displeasure tainted the joy, but the fact that I could have joy at all while sitting at a *maltið* was evidence enough that there was life after death. If only it hadn't taken me eighteen rotations to find it.

Looking across the table at Kristjan, I thought he'd be all right—he'd make it through. He was smiling and laughing with one of Margeir's sons. I never could keep them all straight.

Finally, the meal concluded, and I thought I'd be able to tell Kristjan my news, but when we got back to the house, he excused himself immediately.

"I'm tired, Father. I want to go to Toppur and rest."

"How can you return to the land that destroyed your friend?" The words were out before I could think better of them.

"Destroyed Marko? No, Father, that would be my decision to let him leave our shelter, wouldn't it? It wasn't Toppur that killed him. Now, if you'll excuse me, it's been a long step. You'd know all about those." Kristjan turned and left before I could say any more.

I sank onto the couch and dropped my head into my hands. If Josebina was here, she'd place a hand on my shoulder and comfort me, but she wasn't here. What would it be like to have her here all the time? I'd done my best to keep her out of our home unless Kristjan was around, and even then, I didn't want to feed any unsavory rumors. What good had it done, anyway, if Friðfinn had been ribbing me about her? Who else would rejoice when I finally married Josebina?

The couch was suddenly lumpy and cold. I pushed to my feet and grabbed my cloak. The quarters were too quiet without Kristjan here. I might as well find solitude elsewhere.

I wandered the halls through Storeheltur, my feet making their way back to the Garður where I'd walked with Josebina earlier.

The glow from the *yoma* soothed my spirits. How had life changed so much in mere spans? I closed my eyes and inhaled deeply—the scent of earth, rock, and growing matter blended with the fresh trickle of water.

Jeeah, we can't get through this without you.

There wasn't an audible answer, but it was as if the place itself took a steady breath, as if to say, "Look, at us, Geirfinnur. We've been here for rotations upon rotations, generation upon generation, and have survived."

It had; so too would Storeheltur. And so too would I—with my wife by my side. What a thought! Wife. I let the word swirl in my head like the eddies of water under the bridge where I now paused.

I had to tell Kristjan. If he found out any other way, it'd destroy him. Or more importantly, destroy our relationship. I wasn't blind the boy kept pushing me away. I didn't know whether it was simply his age or whether I'd done something to incite it, but either way, it was time to mend things.

My mind made up, I retraced my steps to our quarters, where I waited until Kristjan returned. It was early in the late watch when I finally heard him. His footsteps were slow and quiet, but I was waiting. He slipped his cloak over the hook and then jumped.

"Sorry, Father. I didn't see you there."

I smiled. "Obviously. I didn't mean to startle you."

"It's late. I'll let you get to bed."

"Kristjan, wait."

He paused with his back to me. His shoulders slumped, but he didn't run away.

"I have something to discuss with you. Maybe it's not the best time, but if I don't say something now, you may hear it elsewhere, and I don't want to do that to you."

I waited for him to turn, but he didn't. Rising, I went to him. How I longed to gather him in my arms as I had done when he was little.

"Elsewhere?" Kristjan faced me, his eyes pained, almost wild. "Like not telling me of my surrogate mother?"

How could he have heard of my conversation with Josebina, and why would he call her a surrogate?

"Yes, Father. When were you going to tell me why Marko always tried to get me to be part of his family?"

"Wait." I gaped at my son as if he'd told me Handi had fallen from the sky. "What are you talking about?"

Kristjan crossed his arms. "When were you going to tell me about the woman who kept me alive after Mother died?"

"Telma?" I tried to keep up with his logic, but it was late, I was tired, and he wasn't making sense.

"Yes, Telma."

"What about her? You saw her every step of your life because you were with Marko." Where was Kristjan going with this?

"Father, didn't you think I'd want to know that she…" Kristjan faltered, looked at the floor, then back at me. His face reddened. "She fed me."

"Yes, she did. I thought she would have told you." Why was this making him so upset?

"She did. Finally. At the *maltið*. She said she'd been waiting for *you* to tell me." Kristjan sighed. "Why didn't you tell me, Father?"

"Kristjan." I reached a hand out but pulled it back when he stepped away from me. "Those steps were… They were chaos. A blur. For me. I was hurting and didn't know where to turn. When Froða said she'd found a mother who was willing to feed you as well, I jumped at the opportunity to keep you alive. When I found out how happy you were there, I knew we'd made the right choice. Does it matter who your wet nurse was? Surely you must have known you had one, since your mother wasn't there to do it?" I hoped the bewilderment showed in my voice, so Kristjan would know I wasn't chastising him for his reaction. "Your relationship with Mark and his family—it started from there, but once you were weaned that phase passed, and your friendship carried on without it. It certainly wasn't the reason you were friends, just the way it started. It seems… I'm sorry, son, but I didn't see the significance; if I had, I would've told you."

At least my son had the humility to look away. Kristjan shook his head. "I guess you're right. It just surprised me when I wasn't needing a shock."

"I'm sorry, son. I never meant to hurt you."

"Of course, you didn't." Kristjan uncrossed his arms and rolled his shoulders toward his room as if about to depart.

For the second time that moonstep, I knew I had to act before someone I loved walked away.

"Don't leave yet—please," I added at the end. "This news would be more shocking than who nursed you."

I tried to smile. Kristjan's scowl curbed my joy, but he stayed, and I forged ahead.

"When your mother passed, I wouldn't have survived if it hadn't been for your aunt, Telma, and Josebina. Between the three of them, I plodded along."

Kristjan tapped a foot. I needed to hurry, and this was something I didn't want to hurry.

"This step, I asked Josebina to be my wife." The words blurted out, not at all what I had wanted them to be.

"You what?" Kristjan eyes widened, and his mouth dropped open.

I couldn't meet his gaze, afraid I'd find hurt, disappointment, or betrayal. Instead, I regarded my soft boots and let my idle thought of resources for new ones wander through my mind and away.

"Josebina has been there for both of us countless times. She's never once tried to take your mother's place, but she—"

"Father," Kristjan said, his sudden grip on my arm a surprise. "If you're happy, it's fine with me, but please don't do anything just because the elders are pressuring you to take another wife."

The strength in his hold surprised me, and the determination in his eye even more so.

"Thank you, Kristjan. I'll admit, Friðfinn did tell me I should, but it only sparked the idea. I'd never take another wife because someone else said I should."

"Good. I'd hate to see you forced into something you wouldn't want. Now, if that's all, it's been an extremely long step. I'd like to get some sleep before the first watch."

"Right. Sleep well, Kristjan."

I watched him leave, so tall and strong. When had my little boy grown up? And why did I feel like he was unhappy with my news?

Chapter 7

22 Fjorda, 400 AI

Kristjan awoke, but for the first time in his life, he had no will to leave his bed. It wasn't that he'd not slept well, or enough; he didn't have any looming tasks waiting for him—this feeling was different. As if there was simply no purpose to rising, or trying to rise, even. He considered rolling over and seeing if he could escape into unconsciousness again, but he heard his father moving about in the kitchen and felt that he ought to make something of the moonstep. It had to be better than the last one, didn't it?

He splashed cold water on his face, hoping it'd help wake him up, but it only made him shiver. He ran his fingers through his hair and pulled on a shirt and pair of trousers, then examined himself in the mirror.

Look at that. The face of a killer

He glanced away, even as a quieter voice answered. *Or the face of a leader.*

"Good step." Father practically glowed as he poured *kaffi*.

Kristjan shoved his irritation down. He *was* grateful that Father was happy. It was a relief, however alien, from the usual somber atmosphere that had worn on Kristjan throughout his childhood. Just because he wanted to sulk this moonstep, didn't mean he had to force Father to do the same.

"Glad to see you happy." He accepted the mug Father handed him. "I take it I wasn't dreaming when I came in last late watch."

Father grinned, and was that red seeping into his cheeks? "No, you weren't dreaming."

"When will your wedding step be?"

His father coughed and splattered *kaffi*. That *definitely* was red in his face.

"Well?" Kristjan couldn't contain a smile at Father's discomfiture.

"I… I guess I hadn't considered that." Father mopped up his mess. "I'll ask… Well, I suppose I'll ask Josebina for some ideas."

"That should work." Kristjan took a bite of a roll.

"You going to join me?"

"What do you mean? I doubt Josebina needs my input on a date."

Father shrugged as he took another sip of his *kaffi* only to find that he'd slopped most of it over the rim. "No, just wondering if you're going to accept Friðfinn's proposal. If so, we'd both be newly married."

It was Kristjan's turn to fight for composure. "Bastian is the one who's interested in Tinna."

"But is Tinna interested in Bastian?" Father refilled his mug, then peered into the cold well. "Looks like we'll need to adjust how we drink *kaffi*. We're out of *geitmjolk*."

The comment brought reality down on them both, and a silence fell. No *geitmjolk*—no money to buy it— because the ore was running out. And that was why Marko was gone.

"I can go look for some of the blue lichen. It'll work as a sweetener." Kristjan offered, trying to break out of the gravity of those thoughts.

"Thank you, Kristjan. You've always been such a considerate son."

Thankfully, Father didn't circle back to the proposal. Maybe, if he was lucky, Kristjan could make it through a moonstep without encountering either Tinna or Friðfinn.

Once the kitchen was clean, Kristjan grabbed his cloak and a basket. Most of the cavern system was warm, but the blue lichen grew in the few places where Toppur's cold seeped down into the caves.

He maneuvered without difficulty between people on their way either to the deeper mines or on their way back. Ahead was where he'd leave the more populated areas of Storeheltur.

"Kristjan," Tinna called to him.

Could he pretend he hadn't heard her?

"Kristjan, wait." The rustle of her skirts accompanied her words.

So much for pretending. He turned to her.

"Thank you." She smiled up at him, her eyes sparkling.

When she looked like that, Kristjan could understand why Bastian would like the girl. She *was* beautiful with her dark hair framing her face.

"What can I do for you?" Kristjan settled his cloak over his shoulders. Maybe it'd give her the hint that he didn't have much time.

"I was wondering if I could walk with you." She glanced down, her lip trembling.

"Is everything all right?"

"I… I'd rather talk in private."

"Of course." He led her to a side cavern and leaned up against the wall. "What is it?"

Tinna broke down, almost immediately devolving into sobs. Kristjan looked at her for a moment, lost, then drew her in under his arm, patting her back. What could be wrong? This wasn't like Tinna. The girl was usually strong and unmovable.

"I…" She wiped her face. "I'm sorry."

"It's fine. What's wrong?"

She took a shaky breath. "I've never had a friend pass to the… I mean, I've had older relatives, but never…" She blew air out.

"I understand."

And Kristjan did. It was very unsettling to have someone who had been full of life and laughter one moment walk with the ancients the next.

"I knew you would, but…" She rubbed her hands together as if trying to clean some spot off them. "I'm sorry. I shouldn't have bothered you. Marko is *your* friend. You were *there*, and I'm dragging it all out and…"

"It's all right; it's… it's awful. I mean… everyone's upset." Did he dare break the surface of his own feelings?

"But it doesn't seem like it! It just seems like everyone's going back to normal now, as if nothing had happened."

He hadn't thought of it in his rush to get away from thinking of yesterstep, but she was right: Everyone was continuing their lives, like there wasn't one life missing.

"Maybe that's their way of coping."

Tinna nodded. "I'm sorry. When I saw you in the hallway, I… I don't know. I guess, I realized it could have been any one of you three…" She wiped at tears her head downcast.

Kristjan rested his hands on her arms. They were so slight compared to his. "Tinna, listen. It was an accident. Bastian and I are back and safe, and you can't live your life constantly thinking of what might have happened."

Those words apply to more than just here.
Lying to the girl. What would Father think?

Before he could really examine those voices, she looked up at him through teary lashes. "Thank you, Kristjan." She threw her arms around him. "Thank you."

For the second time in under a span, he found himself embracing Tinna. This time, though, he was the one drawing comfort from it. He longed for a return to how things had been: him teasing Bastian about trying to woo Tinna, Marko full of life and laughter, and feeling a sense of purpose for his own future, however intimidating it might have been.

When she pulled away, a chill settled into his core.

"I'd better go." Color crept up her cheeks. "See you soon?"

"Sure."

Kristjan didn't know why he agreed. He'd rather allow Bastian to pursue this girl. Besides the more time Kristjan spent around Tinna, the more her father would press his proposal. Yet… she *had* felt nice to hold. No, she was Bastian's.

Tinna smiled through lashes still touched by salt and spun away, her skirts twirling with the movement. Oh, why couldn't she do this for Bastian?

Then a sinking feeling came to him. What if she sought out Bastian as well?

He shook his head. This was getting him nowhere, and especially, not to the lichen he'd promised Father that he'd gather.

* * *

I couldn't remember ever being this nervous to see Josebina, but I stood outside her quarters all but shaking in my boots. It took every ounce of courage I had to call out to her.

"*Goðan.*" My voice barely sounded. I cleared my throat and tried again.

As I spoke, the curtain fluttered, and there she was, smiling up at me. "Good step, Geir. Did you sleep well?"

My mouth opened and closed. All I could think about was kissing her.

"Geir?"

"Sorry." How could I be so juvenile? "Yes… Well, once I got to bed, that is."

As always, she understood me. "Where would you like to go to talk about it?"

"The Garður should work."

"Yes, that would be perfect."

I offered her my arm, acutely aware of her slender fingers on my sleeve.

We passed many people along the way. Most were headed back from having been working in the mines. A few were scurrying to show up for their shift. I wondered about the progress in finding a new lode. We would definitely need it—and soon.

Warm air and the scent of soil and living things welcomed me.

Josebina closed her eyes and breathed in deeply. "I love the Garður. It makes me feel at peace."

She looked it, ease in every nuance of her posture. My heart sped up as I regarded her—this woman who had always been a friend but now had consented to be my wife. Josebina opened her eyes and smiled when they met mine. It was a welcoming smile, yet one that seemed as unsure of our path ahead as I was.

"You wanted to speak with me?" With her eyes on me, she stumbled over a rough patch in the stone.

I looped my arm around her to steady her. She turned into me.

"I..." Suddenly, I didn't know what I'd been saying—or was going to say. All I could think of was her here in my arms. How I longed for this to be permanent—something to look forward to after a long moonstep. She placed a hand over my heart. It was my undoing. I pulled her to me, squeezing her close. She reached up on her tiptoes and cupped my head, bringing it down to her. Our lips met. I knew then I couldn't wait to have the ceremony and call her mine.

I pulled away first, longing for more, but knowing it wouldn't be right to ask. "*Kæra*, when can we have the ceremony?"

If she noticed my use of the term of endearment, she didn't comment. Instead, she placed a hand on my cheek. "How soon can the chief *be* married? If I had my way, it'd be this very step, but I believe there are others who'll demand you go through protocols."

I groaned. She was correct, as always. "I'll find the elders and check with them."

"Was that what you wanted to talk about? Or was it simply that you wished to kiss me again?"

"Mm, that would be wonderful." I agreed, resting my chin on the top of her head and savoring the feel of her body molded to mine. "Mainly, I needed to know when we'd be married. It was Kristjan who reminded me that we needed to decide on a time."

She pulled away slightly but resettled when I tightened my embrace. "How did he take the news?"

"He was more concerned that I hadn't told him Telma had been his nurse," I told her, shaking my head, still baffled by his reaction.

"I could see that. How did he find out about her if you hadn't told him?"

"Telma."

"Then he probably had every right to be upset."

It was my turn to try to create some space between us, but Josebina held me secure. "How do you see that?"

"Think about it, Geir. How would you feel, as a boy barely come of age, if a grown woman explained that she'd *nursed* you from her own breast?"

Suddenly, the Garður was extra warm. "Oh. I see."

"When did she tell him?"

I hung my head. All of Kristjan's awkward anger made sense.

"During the *maltíð*." The words came out in a murmur.

"Oh."

How could one word convey so much understanding for us both?

Footsteps alerted me to someone else's presence. I turned around, but kept Josebina nestled in my arm. If we were to be husband and wife, then the *holdt* would have to find out about it sooner rather than later. Josebina must have agreed, for she tucked her arm around my waist.

"Geirfinnur—" Karva broke off, gaping as he looked between us, then went on, trying to pretend he hadn't thought anything of it. "The elders request your presence."

"Good, because I have something to say to them as well."

Karva didn't respond.

I realized my words had been terse. "Thank you for coming to find me. Are they already gathered?"

"Within the span will be fine."

"Then I'll see you there. Thank you, again."

With a nod, Karva continued on his way.

"Well, that was interesting." Josebina watched the elder's retreating back. "I think we may have surprised him."

I choked. "*May* have? Did you see how his eyes bulged?"

Josebina laughed. "Well, Geir, I suppose you'll need to go prepare for the meeting."

"Not until I escort you wherever you need to go." I looked down at her. "And maybe have another kiss."

She smiled and reached up to me. I couldn't wait to have the chance to grow accustomed to her kisses—and looked forward to never doing so.

Chapter 8

22 Fjorda, 400 AI

Kristjan spent the first watch harvesting lichen. It gave him time to contemplate and replay all that had occurred over the past phase. When he resigned himself to the confusion he felt over Tinna, his mind returned to the thought that had preoccupied him ever since Toppur: everything—anything—that he could have done differently to prevent Marko's death. No matter how he approached it, it all came back to one thing: his permission had been Marko's death sentence. Not even chief yet, and he'd already condemned one of his people—his best friend!—to Fivku. There was no other way to see it.

Everyone else can say what they like. That killer in the mirror will always know the truth.

He gathered the basket and made his way back home. As he neared the more populated areas, the air warmed. It felt good, but soon his fur-lined cloak was too much. He set the basket down and, wiping his brow, pulled the heavy garment off and draped it over his arm.

Bastian rounded the corner; Kristjan gaped at him. His cousin was covered in dirt from head to toe. The only thing not coated was the whites of his eyes.

"Where've you *been*?"

"Well, good step to you as well." Bastian leaned against the wall and rubbed a hand across his face, smudging the dirt even more.

"Sorry. Surprised to see you like this." Kristjan retrieved his basket of lichen.

"What, don't think I work my share?" Bitterness laced Bastian's words. He waved a hand. "Never mind me. Been a long step already."

"I understand. Were you working a new lode?" Kristjan asked hopefully.

Bastian shook his head. "There isn't one, not yet. I was digging looking for one."

Kristjan regarded his cousin. No new vein? That didn't bode well for the community. He remembered the last moonstep before they'd been assigned the hunting expedition.

Before thinking better of it, he mused aloud, "Still think we should keep the dioptase vein to ourselves?"

"There's not enough there to make a difference for Storeheltur." Bastian scrubbed at the dirt on his hand, but Kristjan didn't see it helping the level of filth there.

"I suppose you're right."

"How are you doing?" Bastian pointed to the basket. "Looks like there's enough to feed several families there."

"I'll leave that up to Father. We were low and I offered to gather it. Got carried away."

Bastian chuckled. "Lot on your mind?"

Kristjan kicked a pebble. "Can't quit thinking about it."

"I know what you mean. Every time I close my eyes, I see Marko in the pool of his own blood." Bastian glanced at the floor as if Marko was lying there with them again.

The words brought the scene vividly to Kristjan's mind. If only he could scrub his memory clean of it—that whole nightmarish wait until the blizzard had let them out of that pit. Then again, forgetting wouldn't erase his guilt. He sighed.

"Sorry. Didn't mean for it to come out like that. You're the only person who really understands. You were there. It was your decision that…" Bastian trailed off, looking mortified but at a loss as to how to fix it.

Kristjan kicked another pebble. It bounced down the path, clattering as it went.

"I mean—"

"No, Bastian, you're right. It's my fault. No one else wants to accept it, but it's true."

Bastian crossed his arms. "I suppose you're right. What are you going to do about it?"

That was the problem. No one believed it, other than the only other one who'd been there.

"I'll try to talk to Father again."

"If he still doesn't believe it was your fault, I'll back you up."

Kristjan's shoulders bunched as if he'd been stabbed between them. "Thanks," he mumbled. "I guess I figured you would."

"Well, that's what cousins are for. We may have had our differences, but when it counted, we were always there." Bastian slapped Kristjan on the back. "That's what family's for, right?"

"Thanks. I'll see if I can find Father. You'd best go get cleaned up. You look like something an ice rat dragged to its den."

"Just what I needed to hear." Bastian grinned. "See you around, cuz."

Father wasn't at home when Kristjan got back. He shrugged and began processing the lichen—he might as well make himself useful, but the monotonous movements of cleaning and laying it out to dry again left him with too much time to think.

Do I really just let them sweep this under the rug? What can I do about it?

Marko made his own choice to leave the shelter.

But the decisions of the expedition are the responsibility of the leader; it's his hands in the blood. Any kind of man would own up to that.

When the last bloom was spread out on the counter, Kristjan wiped his hand across his face. If only he could turn off his brain. He was no closer to an answer for how to convince Father that the accident was his fault.

And then what? What is Father meant to do with that? The question rattled around never resting, never resolved.

At last Father came in, his actions slow and dragging as if he'd run all the paths of Storeheltur in under a span.

"What's wrong?" Kristjan hurried to boil water for *kaffi*.

Father ran a hand through his hair and shook his head. With a sigh he collapsed in the chair. "You did all this?" He spread his hands to encompass the now-dry lichen, ready to be crushed and stored.

Kristjan shrugged. "I got carried away."

"It's a blessing, really." Father dropped his hands to his lap. "We *must* find a new lode within two phases, or we'll die."

"Die?"

That seemed an obvious exaggeration, but the pallor of Father's face said otherwise.

"We have enough food for two phases, Kristjan. After that…"

"We'll find more supplies, Father." Kristjan couldn't believe Father was giving up that quickly.

"Maybe, but how do we get the word out that we have ore again? Who'll be the adventurous merchant who'll return to check?"

Kristjan hadn't thought of that, but the answer came to him quickly "We send word to Isholt. They can get word to their next merchant who comes through."

Father smiled, the first since he'd entered the room. "And *this* is why you're perfect for taking my place, son."

Kristjan shook his head. "But, I'm not. Can't you see? I..." He pulled at his beard but pressed ahead. "It was my fault Marko died."

Father strode to Kristjan and placed a gentle hand on his shoulder. "Son, there's something you must learn: You are not responsible for the decisions of others. Marko took the risk when he joined your exhibition. All of you did. He knew the consequences of heading out into the storm. You warned him. He weighed the options and chose what he thought was best. You can't keep blaming yourself."

"But—"

"No, *buts* about it. I won't listen to it."

There was no arguing with Father when he got like this.

"Do you want me to fix a meal?" Kristjan changed the subject.

"Would you mind if Josebina joined us?" His father's eyes twinkled.

It was good to see the slight flush that filled his father's cheeks, but it was also incredibly strange to witness.

"Sure. Go ahead and invite her."

"You're a good man, Kristjan. I'm proud to call you my son."

Kristjan's heart clenched and fell. Father simply wouldn't see it—couldn't believe Jorvar's descendant could be responsible for the death of one of his people. There'd be no justice for Marko.

Chapter 9

23 Fjorda, 400 AI

Kristjan had lain awake for several spans thinking through the conversations they'd had over the meal: when he awoke, the problem was just as debilitating. Storeheltur needed more ore. He knew of one source, but it belonged to Bastian. Was it possible that there was more in the same area?

Swinging his feet over the edge of his bed, he pulled on his trousers and boots. He needed to talk with his cousin. He shrugged into a work shirt and grabbed a bite to eat, then headed to Bastian's house. His aunt answered his greeting at their doorway.

"Kristjan! It's so good to see you." Froða wrapped her arms around him. "How are you doing?"

"I'm fine."

She held him at arm's length and searched his face. Satisfied, she nodded. "Very well, but you let me know if I can do anything for you. Now, what's this I hear about your father finally asking Josebina to marry him?"

"It's true." Kristjan chuckled. "Surprised me, and according to Josebina, she was the only one who'd believed he'd actually ask her. She just wasn't sure whether he'd finally realize he needed to."

Froða laughed. "I'm glad for them both. It's about time your father emerged from his grief."

Grief.

Would Kristjan ever grow accustomed to its whims? He knew that's what he was experiencing, but for now he relegated it to some back corner of his mind. He needed to focus.

"Is Bastian around?"

"He hasn't left yet." Froða stepped away and called into the back rooms. "Bastian, Kristjan's here." With a final pat on the shoulder, she went into the kitchen.

"Hey, Krist—" Bastian paused in the doorway. "Where are you headed?"

"Thought we could explore."

Bastian raised an eyebrow and motioned for Kristjan to join him in his room. "What type of exploration? If I remember correctly, you're deathly afraid of heights. It took both Marko and me to get you back after our last excursion."

Kristjan remembered all too well. "I know, but Storeheltur needs ore."

"I'm not giving up my stash."

"Didn't say you had to," Kristjan soothed. "What if there are more lodes in that area? We could share those."

In the kitchen Aunt Froða hummed while Bastian studied his shelf, already lined with dioptase.

"Fine. If you're willing to brave the cliff, we can go."

"I'll cross that bridge when I get to it."

Sweat broke out over his body just thinking about the climb, but as he'd said, the *holdt* needed ore. Maybe it could make up for—

He cut the thought short. Nothing could make up for what he'd done to Marko.

"Let me grab work clothes and a packet. We might as well mine what we can from my lode while we're there."

In half a span, they were standing before the cliff wall. It looked taller than it had before.

"Are you sure this is the way?" Kristjan studied the intimidating rock.

"Yes, and you climbed it once before. You can do it again." Bastian grasped a handhold and heaved himself up. "See, nothing to it. Just find the right spots to grip."

With a nod, Kristjan steeled himself for the task. One slip of his fingers or boots, and he'd be back on the floor.

Coward.

"Are you coming?" Bastian called down to him. "I thought this was your idea."

"Right. I'm coming."

Kristjan placed one hand on the cold rock. His limbs shook, but he forced himself to continue. The next crevice was just above his hand; he settled his fingers into it and sucked in air with an effort, trying to steady his breathing. His grip felt firm. There was no reason to be afraid. No reason, no reason… But the next hold was a farther reach. Stealing his nerves, he stretched out, managing to graze the rough ledge, but his fingers closed too late and he lost it. Not giving himself time to think, he swiped at it again, locking onto the narrow shelf so hard that his knuckles bent back, and hauled himself upward. Bit by bit he crawled up the cliff face, panting and straining until he made it to the top and heaved himself over the lip to collapse in a heap, sweat-soaked, heart pounding.

"Not bad," Bastian said with a smirk. "Thought I'd have to drag you up here with a rope. Ready to go?"

"Give… me… a moment." Kristjan rolled into a sitting position as far away from the edge as possible.

When he could breathe without shaking, he stood. "Lead the way."

Memories of the last time they'd been here flooded Kristjan's mind. Marko should be with them, but he wasn't.

Because of you.

Oh right. Me.

Murderer.

The light from the *yoma* filled the cavern.

Bastian examined the lines and splotches of greens and blues. "Let's gather some of the best pieces, and then we'll look for more veins."

They worked for maybe a span without a word, the soft *chunk* noises of stones piling into Bastian's gathersack. Every time Kristjan swung his pick, he thought of Marko, and that horrifying moment—discovering the pick protruding from his friend's leg—looped in gory image again in his mind.

At last, Bastian stretched. "You're awfully quiet."

Kristjan shrugged. "Usually, it was you and—"

"Yeah, well, he's not here." Bastian wiped a hand over his face, leaving a streak of dirt along his cheek. "Sorry, that came out wrong."

"I've been thinking of him."

"You and everyone else. Tinna won't even see me because she's 'in mourning,' or at least that's what her father says."

Kristjan wondered about that. Tinna had sought *him* out yesterstep.

"So, did you get a chance to give her the ring?"

Bastian huffed. "Not yet. I was going to yesterstep, but I met Friðfinn instead."

"Oh." Kristjan didn't know what else to say.

"Well, let's see what we can find beyond here." Bastian tapped the side wall, where a vein forked.

Kristjan chose another junction of blue and swung at the wall. Again, the irregular *chink* of picks filled the air.

The quiet was enough to choke Kristjan as much as the dust he raised. He coughed and blew the dust away so he could see.

"Do you have a *yoma* I could use?" He backed away, but it didn't help any. The hole was too dark.

"Think you found something?" Bastian broke a *yoma* off the wall and brought it over.

"Can't tell." Kristjan moved over so Bastian could hold the light forward.

"Take a look for yourself, cuz." Bastian clapped Kristjan on the back.

The dim light of the *yoma* revealed a broad blue streak.

"Let's dig it out more before we take news back to the elders." Kristjan hefted his pick, smiling despite himself and yet trying to quash the hope springing up. Would it be enough?

Bastian joined him, and the two worked steadily, alternating strikes. Where once there'd been a cacophonous reverberation around the cavernous space, now the noise was almost deafening as it rebounded to Kristjan's ears from every direction. When he'd worked up a good sweat, Bastian stepped away. He returned with several *yoma*.

Kristjan gaped. "Is this what I think it is?"

"Well, cuz, looks like you may have what it'll take to make amends." Bastian whistled. "Never thought my little excursion to impress Tinna would lead to such a find."

"What if it only goes for a short run?"

"It's something, Kristjan. There's enough here to load up at least one merchant—and that'll give us enough time to find even more."

"All the same, we'd better widen it, just to be sure."

* * *

Even climbing down the cliff couldn't diminish Kristjan's excitement. Storeheltur would survive, at least until they could mine out another richer lode. They'd traced the vein until their stomachs growled, and now, they were walking the halls together, nearly giddy with relief and delight.

"You'll come get me when you take your father out there, won't you?"

"Of course! It's your find more than it's mine. If it hadn't been for you and Marko, I'd not have gone searching there." Kristjan slung an arm over his cousin's shoulders.

"Well, I just want to see Uncle Geirfinnur's face when he sees it." Bastian grinned. "Think it'll leave him speechless?"

"Who knows."

Sometimes Father could wax loquacious about things, but at others, he'd be utterly unimpressed. Kristjan didn't understand his father, despite everyone else's frequent claims that they were so much alike.

"Oh, come on, cuz. You sound like you've lost..." Bastian glanced away. "Sorry. Wrong expression."

Marko should have been here with them. He would have joked around and celebrated when Kristjan scaled the cliff. Kristjan bit his lip.

"It's fine, Bastian. I'll be sure to tell the elders that you deserve the credit." He smiled and turned down the way to his own quarters.

Why had Bastian had to remind him of Marko?

Why did he have to? Seems a little metal is enough to erase all thought of him for spans at a time.

Kristjan clenched his fists. *What kind of friend forgets after a step?*

The human kind. We can't always be thinking of our losses. Father's remarrying, isn't he?

The pall didn't lift, though, even when he told Father about their find. If anything, it worsened.

"You found *what*?" Father's eyes lit up, and the perpetual gravity in his bearing eased, if ever so slightly.

"I have no idea how far it goes."

Father cut off any further protest. "That doesn't matter. It's the best news the elders will have received since Androw left Storeheltur. As soon as we finish eating, we'll gather the elders and you can show us. Orlaugur will be able to tell how promising of a find it is."

* * *

It was well into the second watch when Kristjan faced the cliff wall for the second time that moonstep. This time, he feared more than his cousin's mocking. All six elders, his father, and Bastian would see his trembling legs. Bastian and four of the elders had already scaled the rock with ease; Friðfinn and Father were waiting for him with Karva not far behind.

Taking an unsteady breath, he placed his hands in the holds.

You've already done this twice. Don't look down, and you'll be fine. But no amount of encouragement steadied his legs.

Closing his eyes didn't help; being blind only made him panic more. He opened them and glanced up. Hafnar waved down to him. If only Marko was here.

Whose fault is that, coward?

Exiling the thought, he forced his arms to move.

By the time he reached the top, his legs were shaking badly enough that he could scarcely stand, and he felt like his lungs were being worked by bellows that were out of sync with his breathing. There was movement beside him, and Friðfinn stood.

"How much further?"

Kristjan nodded toward the find, forcing words through the constriction in his chest. "Just ahead." At least the words came out without a tremor.

He placed his hands flat on the ground and pushed off. His heart slowed back to a normal pace when Karva and his father crested the lip. At least he didn't have to approach the edge to offer them a hand up.

"You fine, son?" Father appraised him with a knowing look.

"Yes, the cavern's up ahead. Bastian's probably already there." Kristjan led the way, focusing on solid ground under his feet to calm his fears.

An exclamation from ahead spurred them along. Kristjan allowed the others to go first. It was only polite, but it also delayed the judgment a little longer. He feared Orlaugur would say that it wasn't worth exploring.

"Where has this been hiding?" Friðfinn gaped up at the ceiling. "The *yoma* alone in here could provide trade for several cycles."

"The *yoma* is nothing in comparison to the dioptase." Orlaugur ran his finger along the vein Bastian had discovered. "Any merchant would brave the ice for this alone."

Bastian beamed and hung his head to hide it.

"This isn't the only lode." Kristjan motioned to where he and Bastian had been working earlier in the step.

With a lingering touch of his finger, Orlaugur crossed the cavern. The other elders gave him space to see.

"You'll want this." Kristjan handed Orlaugur a handful of *yoma*. "It's darker in there."

The elder smiled and accepted the stones. Kristjan's heart beat a rapid staccato that he was sure the others could hear.

Bastian rested a hand on Kristjan's shoulder and whispered into his ear. "Well done. Did you see the look on Karva's face? All of them will be eating out of your hand before we leave here."

His cousin's words did nothing to calm Kristjan's anxiety. Earlier he'd been afraid the find wouldn't meet the standard, but now, he feared the repercussions if it superseded expectations.

Orlaugur stuck his head back out. "Friðfinn, I need your help. Reinar, you can assist him."

The two elders hurried to help. Bastian and Kristjan exchanged glances.

Father smiled encouragement. "You did well, son."

"That you did. Takes a special eye to see the lode behind the gem—to perceive when there's greater value behind the first find." Palmi took a closer look at the original vein tapping his finger in the divot where Bastian had removed the stone for Tinna's ring. "Even moreso to share what he could have kept for himself. Your son is demonstrating initiative, dedication, constructive thinking, a willingness to risk himself for the *holdt*..." His face softened in sorrow. "That trip didn't turn out as we would've wanted, but it did sustain us, nonetheless. He shows care for the *holdt*, care that takes action. I see no reason he shouldn't begin his training now."

Kristjan couldn't believe his ears. Why? He wasn't ready for that. Just because he'd found a strain of ore didn't mean he could handle the affairs of several hundred people.

The chief's seat is a birthright—his son is born to it, and for it. You're born for this.

But not *now*. He wasn't ready.

Or worthy. Murderer, coward…

Orlaugur stepped out of the small alcove, his eyes wide. "The rest of you can take a look. Kristjan, that lode's the most promising I've seen in many rotations, and I've seen plenty of them. You've managed to bring hope back to Storeheltur. You'll make an excellent chief after your father."

Why must they say things like that? Hadn't they seen the fear scaling a simple wall inspired? He wasn't prepared to be leader. Look what had come to pass when they'd put him in charge of just three men for a span of moonsteps! Did they forget so easily?

Chapter 10

23 Fjorda, 400 AI

My son had done it; he'd saved Storeheltur! At last, the elders could clearly see the potential I'd always known he possessed. I wanted to throw my arms around him, but Bastian nudged Kristjan and the two laughed—I would've been an intruder. It struck me with a proud pang that I was looking into his future: leading, laughing, commanding his life—apart from me.

I'd yet to look into the new alcove he'd chiseled out, but I couldn't wait—it must be spectacular to have left Orlaugur speechless. And bewildered as he now was. The elder wandered back to the original band and followed it until it faded into the rock. He fingered the blade at his side, then pulled it from its sheath and chipped at the patch of flaking stone.

"Did you find something more?" Friðfinn joined Orlaugur.

"Maybe. Won't know until we can open this up more. My guess is that this will become our new mine. We'll have to do something about the drop back there, but it looks like this natural cavern is only the beginning."

"That's wonderful news. I'll get to see my daughter married after all." Friðfinn laughed and winked at me.

I mustered a small, perhaps conspiratorial smile, but truly I still worried about how Kristjan would respond to the proposal. We hadn't truly discussed it since he returned from the expedition, but I needed to bring it up again. If I didn't, Friðfinn was sure to, and Kristjan would resent the interference.

Once the elders had scoured every crag and cranny surrounding the new vein, Kristjan led the way back out, but I noticed that Bastian hung back. What was that in his expression? I couldn't tell, but it didn't look like he was as happy as everyone else.

"Come on, Bastian, son." I motioned to my nephew. "You did a good job."

"Thanks, Uncle Geirfinnur." He smiled at me—the same warming look from when he was little.

Together we walked back the way we'd come, but the journey was different with the hope that lightened our steps. There was still a future for Storeheltur.

When we got back home, I clapped Kristjan on the back. "I meant what I said there. I'm proud of you. You've grown even in the last several cycles. You'll make a wonderful chief."

I took a breath. Now was probably the best opportunity I'd get to approach the topic of a wife.

"Have you considered Friðfinn's offer?"

Kristjan rolled his eyes. "Father, I've not had time."

"You've been home for three steps now, and he sent the letter before you left. That means you've had almost three phases to think upon it. What's not to like? Is it the girl? Is she not pleasing?" I had to shake off a surreal sense of detachment; how had I come to discussing the beauty of women with my son? When had he grown up enough for this?

"She's…" Kristjan rubbed the back of his neck. "She's pretty."

"Then what is it?" I pressed, even though I knew I'd hate it if someone had come to me and discussed Josebina this way.

Kristjan huffed out a breath of air. "Bastian's had his eye on her for rotations."

"Why hasn't he spoken up, then? And why would Friðfinn approach you and not him?"

"I don't know. Bastian hoped to give her a ring crafted with the stone he found in that cavern, but whenever he tried, he can't get in to see her," Kristjan said.

"Why?"

"Friðfinn says she's in mourning."

This didn't make sense; she hadn't known Marko well enough that I'd have expected her to be grieving him at any length. Did Friðfinn not *want* Bastian to marry his daughter; was he preventing Bastian from meeting with her on whatever pretense he could muster? Why would he object to my nephew, though? But then I looked more intently at my son and mentally compared the two. Kristjan was more considerate, quieter, less impulsive, and pleasing to a fault. If I was a father of a young woman, I'd choose Kristjan over Bastian any moonstep.

"What does Tinna say?"

Kristjan threw his hands into the air. "Father, why are you pushing this?"

"Because Friðfinn's offered his daughter to you, and it's traditional—not to mention courteous—to give him a reply to such things, especially when it's an elder making the offer."

"Can't I tell him no?" Kristjan flushed and wouldn't meet my gaze.

"Is that honestly what you wish, son?"

A breath of warm air filtered from the vents and swirled around, sending a whiff of earthen damp through the room.

I rested my hand on Kristjan's shoulder. "I know you're hurting, but Friðfinn and Tinna deserve an answer. Go speak with them; ask whatever questions you feel you should. Get a sense for their family, if that concerns you, or even for why Friðfinn made the offer. Then decide. Just remember that a girl will only wait for so long, and her father even less."

"What of Josebina?"

I pulled at my shirt collar. "She's a special case, and she didn't have a father urging her to marry."

"Can I at least wait until first watch? I'm tired. It's been a long step."

That made sense. "Don't you want a meal?"

"I'm not hungry."

I watched my son walk away, his head down. Where was the lilting happiness to his step? How could I revive it?

* * *

When Kristjan finally awoke, it was late in the first watch. He turned over and pulled the blankets around him.

His eyes slid shut, but instead of granting peace, the image of Marko's last breaths sprang up in the dark. He dragged his feet over the edge of the bed, then sat up. Why was Father so insistent on interfering? If he didn't visit Tinna and Friðfinn, Father would only push harder. He sighed and pressed his palms to his eyes. Why must he choose a bride to begin with? What was it that made adults think every eligible man should have a wife, and every eligible woman a husband? His father had lived for eighteen rotations without a woman in their lives. Couldn't he live the same?

He'd told Father he'd at least talk with Tinna and Friðfinn; he might as well get it over with. Paying no attention to the quality, he pulled on trousers and a shirt. He thought he should probably eat something, but nothing sounded appealing. Food was still in short supply, anyhow.

When he pushed past their tapestry and into the main tunnels that ran through Storeheltur, he was taken off-guard by the silence in the passageways, but it made sense. Most people were either working or sleeping off a long shift. Soon enough, they'd have enough ore to return to a less frenetic pace, and trafic would flow through the *holdt* again.

He paused outside Friðfinn's quarters. The brown tapestry depicted the stars and Handi low on the horizon in Toppur. From what he knew, the design had been a part of the Arnorsson family since Storeheltur's founding. The fabric had been replaced multiple times in the last four hundred rotations, but the scene had remained the same.

Realizing there was no use waiting outside a door, he called out. "*Goðan.*" His voice sounded weak in his own ears. He called again, adding a firmness and conviction he didn't feel.

The tapestry moved, and Friðfinn filled the frame. "Kristjan! This is a surprise. Come on in."

"I…" Suddenly, he wanted to run, to back away.

"Have you eaten the mid-meal? We're about ready to have ours."

"Oh, then I can return later." *Or never!*

"Nonsense. There's always room at our table for my future son." Friðfinn slapped an arm around Kristjan's shoulders, which allowed the resulting cough to hide the choking noise that garbled whatever reply he might have made.

Kristjan's heart raced. What should he do? Before he could collect his thoughts, let alone any words, he was walking with Friðfinn into the home, and his stomach took over the thinking, growling at the smell of roasting meat and seasonings.

"When Ebonney heard we'd uncovered a new lode, she decided to celebrate. So, we have the last roast for our mid-meal this step." Friðfinn grinned. "Ebonney, Tinna, what better way to celebrate than with the hero of Storeheltur? Look who decided to join us."

Ebonney set a platter down on the table and brushed her dark hair back. "Welcome, Kristjan. We're glad to have you here." She turned to Tinna. "Fetch another plate and utensils. Frið find a chair, please."

Kristjan glanced about, at a loss as to what to do with himself. Tinna smiled as she returned and set the place for him.

Once everything was ready, Ebonney motioned to the table. "Please, everyone, sit."

Once they were settled, Friðfinn raised his hands. "Jeeah, thank you for providing for our needs. We'll rest on your provision in the cycles to come."

As Friðfinn lowered his hands, Ebonney lifted the platter and served Kristjan, then her daughter. Again,

Kristjan wished to be anywhere but here. Why had Father impelled him to do this?

"Greens?" Tinna smiled at him.

With a nod of thanks, Kristjan added some to his plate. At last, everyone was served. Kristjan lifted his fork to taste the meat, but Ebonney's question interrupted his fork on its way.

"Frið told us of your discovery. How did you think to search out there?"

"It was Bastian, really."

"Your cousin?" Friðfinn's nostrils flared with something resembling disdain. "What did he do?"

Maybe if Kristjan shed Bastian in a good light, Friðfinn would more readily entertain the idea of him courting Tinna. That'd be a perfect way out of at least two messes. "He found the first vein. It wasn't until later that I wondered if there was more to it than what we'd first seen."

"So, it *was* your idea." Tinna's brown eyes sparkled in the candle light.

"Yes." He had to admit that. If not for him, Bastian would have kept the whole thing for himself.

"Then you're the hero father has said you are." Tinna glanced down, but not before she caught his gaze; even that fleeting contact sent his heart racing.

It wasn't until he'd described the mine in detail and Tinna had gotten him to promise to take her to see it that the conversation lulled enough to allow him the first bite. The family talked to one another enough to let him eat in peace at that point, but by then his food had cooled, and the others' plates were empty. When he tried to push his plate away, Ebonney insisted he finish, but it was awkward with everyone else talking and watching him.

At last, Friðfinn stood. "Ebonney, I'll help you with the cleanup. Tinna, why don't you entertain Kristjan in the living room?"

Red filled the girl's cheeks, and again, he couldn't help but notice her beauty. But Bastian had had his eyes on her forever. *What are you thinking?* He hadn't been thinking straight since the moment he'd allowed Marko to leave their shelter.

"Are you all right?" Tinna stared up at him, her hand on his arm. How had he failed to notice her touch?

"Yes, sorry."

"Come." She led him to a couch and sat beside him. "Thank you for coming this step. Father told me about what you did for Storeheltur, but it's not the same as hearing it from you. I'd love to help with the mining."

"That would be up to your father."

"He said you'd be in charge of that."

That was news to Kristjan.

"I... suppose that'd be fine then." Kristjan tried to find a comfortable spot, not because the sofa was lumpy, but rather because the anxiety gurgling like tiny rapids under his skin wouldn't let him stay still.

"How are you doing?" Tinna dropped her hand to his. "Thank you for listening to me the last several times we've met. I've…" She sighed. "I've appreciated it."

"I was glad I could be there."

"Your words helped," she hurriedly continued, as if trying to get the words out before the last ones could land wrong. "I'm doing better, and now that there's something to focus on, it's better than sitting around without anything to do." She turned to him. "But you didn't come to hear me prattle, nor did you come for a meal. What brought you here?"

Now it was Kristjan's turn to look away. How could he ask about Bastian when her hand was resting on his?

"Your father…" He licked his lips. "Well, before we left for the hunting expedition, your father spoke with me."

She squeezed his hand but waited for him to continue.

"He asked me to consider a proposal."

"And?" Her voice was low, tentative. He couldn't tell if she was eager or anxious.

"I don't know if I can make a decision at the moment. Marko…"

"It's a difficult time right now. I can wait."

Kristjan clenched his fist, but Tinna slipped her fingers between his and wedged it gently open.

"Let me help, Kristjan. You were there for me. Let me be there for you."

"Tinna, have you spoken with Bastian?"

"Bastian?" She recoiled, looking… horrified?

"When was the last time you spoke with him?"

She shuddered. "About a cycle ago. He came to me…"

"And?"

What was wrong with her? She should be happy that his cousin wanted her hand in marriage.

"I don't want to talk about it." Tinna turned away, lifting her chin, which was bunched with the effort of holding back something overwhelming. "It doesn't have anything to do with Father's proposal."

"But it does!" Kristjan rose, creating the space he needed from her. "Bastian's had his eye on you for as long as I can remember. It'd be wrong for me…" He trailed off as he saw the tears escape, streaming down her face.

"Tinna?"

She swiped at them with shaky hands.

"Tinna, what's wrong?" Kristjan knelt in front of her.

"Please, Kristjan, don't make me remember."

"But…" What should he do?

Another shudder shook her frame. "Please, promise me that when I go work in the mine, Bastian won't be there."

Kristjan opened his mouth to speak, closed it, and tried again. "Tinna, I don't want to hurt you, but I need to understand. Why are you avoiding him?"

The truth settled like a cloak. It wasn't that Friðfinn didn't want Bastian to see his daughter; it was that the daughter didn't want to see Bastian.

Tinna shook her head. "I suppose if I'm asking you to keep him away, you have to know, and moreso since Father's asked you to—" She blushed, but it wasn't the rosy half-smiling color he'd seen in her before. It was pure shame. "But… Oh, Kristjan, I don't want to cause problems between you and your cousin."

He wanted to ask questions, but waited.

She glanced toward the sounds coming from the kitchen and turned her back to them, folding her hands tightly in her lap and dropping her chin in an almost shameful posture. When she spoke, her voice was a quavering whisper that cracked as it rose and fell—as if she were holding back tears. "About a cycle ago, Bastian came to me. He asked me to walk with him in the Garður. He spoke of his hopes and dreams." Her voice went flat. "Then he took my hand, saying that he wanted me at his side." She licked her lips and clasped her hands in her lap. "I shook my head, telling him no, but he wouldn't listen. I… I tried to resist, but…" The emotion had left her face; she looked like she was far away, barely registering his presence anymore. "I must have given him the wrong impression. That's the only explanation. He grabbed onto me, tried to hold me to him. I shook my way free, but he came after, calling my name."

A dish clinked in the kitchen, but Tinna didn't move.

"He caught up to me; I turned and, as I did, I tripped, or he tripped me. I'm not sure. I just know he was on top of me… there was a rock cutting into my back, but I couldn't get him… his weight… he held me down and—"

"Tinna." Kristjan couldn't hear anymore; Bastian couldn't have—

But he must have. She had no reason to lie.

He set his hand on hers, looking up into her face, flexing his fingers gently against her tight-pressed palms, anything to bring life back to her brown eyes.

"He kissed me, and I felt his hands…" She shrank into herself, wilting, her eyes compressed between lines of anguish. "I struggled, but he must have thought I was… en- enjoying…" She looked sick, pale. "That I wanted—"

"Tinna, it's not your fault."

"But how could he… do that… if I didn't want it? And even if he could, no man would—"

"The word 'no' is hard to misunderstand, Tinna, and no one gets pushed away and thinks he's getting pulled closer." Kristjan struggled to keep his voice soft, gentle.

She met his gaze for the first time, desperation and shame creating something hollow and lonely in her face. "I didn't ask for it, Kristjan. I promise, I didn't, I—"

"I believe you." The rage boiling in his hands, in his chest, was crystallizing into something inevitable, like a boulder already tumbling over a cliff, plummeting toward a fragile scaffold below. His fingers wanted to curl into fists; his voice was a coiled monster, waiting to become a battle cry. If he got his hands on his cousin… "Tinna, I promise he won't be anywhere near you."

The thought of Tinna on the ground beneath Bastian, the violence… He closed his eyes, forcing his breath back to even.

He stood, stretching his legs so that the furious, icy energy coursing through them had somewhere to go. "Have you told your parents?"

"No!" Her face paled.

"Why not?" Kristjan knew that not everyone had so distant a relationship with their parents as he did with his father. Many families shared personal things, and *this* definitely counted as something that should be shared with family.

"Well…" She didn't look up, only examined something on the far wall, her cheeks the only bright spot on her face. "I went with Bastian. I… It was my fault."

"No!"

She flinched, and he softened his tone.

"Tinna, it *wasn't your fault*. It was all Bastian." There was a growl in his voice that he couldn't quite tamp down in time when he said his cousin's name. "You didn't deserve what happened. Tinna look at me." He waited before saying, "No man should do what he did to you. No woman should endure what you endured. Do you understand me?"

"But…"

"No *buts*. It was evil, and it wasn't your fault. So, why won't you tell them? Your mother, at least?"

She scrutinized her hands. "I'm afraid."

Kristjan waited. If she was afraid of Bastian—with good reason—he could understand. He'd personally see to Bastian's punishment.

"My mother'd tell my father, and then…" She bit down on her lip and curled in on herself. "And maybe it's wrong, but I don't want Bastian hurt, and Father… Father'd kill him. I…" She trailed off then looked up at him. "Does that make me a bad person?"

"Oh, Tinna, no!" He strode to her and settled his hands on her slender shoulders. "You're not bad. You're compassionate, kind, and… and beautiful."

"Thank you, Kristjan." She blinked away tears. "May Jeeah bless you."

He didn't feel blessed. He'd lost his best friend, and the hope of an easy answer to the proposal had evaporated, displaced by a horrible knowledge that he'd carry out of the house with him—something no one else knew. He'd planned to punish Bastian, but if it wasn't what she wanted; what did he do? Cover this injustice along with her for the rest of his moonsteps, leave it unanswered? He felt cursed.

He wondered if Tinna felt the same.

Chapter 11

25 Fjorda, 400 AI

Kristjan roused to the sound of Father calling him. He pulled the covers over his head and turned over.

"Kristjan!" Father called again. "The elders have a meeting this step."

Kristjan sighed, but didn't move. "I'm getting up."

"The meeting's in a span."

A span?

"I thought you said it was midway through the first watch."

"And that's in a span. Now get up. I have a meal prepared for you."

Kristjan tossed the blankets aside. There was no going back to sleep now. Sleep had been elusive ever since Marko's death. The whole scene of his death played across the backs of his eyelids whenever he closed them. It wasn't until he eventually drifted off to sleep that he had blessed release—no dreams, only oblivion.

Sitting up, he glanced down at the trousers on the floor. They'd be the easiest to put on, but they were dirty and would raise eyebrows if he walked into the elders' meeting wearing them. But then, why should he care how he looked? What did it matter in comparison to everything else that had transpired in the past three phases? Yet, the elders cared, and as the chief's son, he needed to look the part.

With a sigh, he pulled clean trousers from his stone cubical of shelves and slid into a good shirt. Now for his hair. He ran his fingers through it to comb it down. A glance in the mirror showed that his beard would need to be trimmed soon, but for now it was passable, even though he'd not done anything with it since Marko's service.

The words to the *maltið* song came to mind. Was Marko with Jeeah? If anyone deserved it, it was Marko. Kind, compassionate, faithful. Kristjan shivered as he remembered using some of those same words to describe Tinna. His heart ached for her, and the fury resurfaced. How could Bastian have *done* that? After the elders' meeting, Kristjan would track down his cousin and find out how badly he needed to thrash the man.

"Kristjan!" Father called from the other room.

He took a final look in the mirror, and satisfied he'd pass inspection, went to face the new moonstep.

* * *

I'd watched Kristjan from the moment he'd entered the kitchen until we joined the elders. He was quiet and distracted at home, but here he focused. It was as if the moment we crossed the threshold of the meeting room, he'd shrugged a cloak off. Now, he sat across from me conversing with Orlaugur as if he didn't have a care in the world. I hoped the events of the meeting wouldn't change that.

"Gentlemen, I call this meeting to order. May Jeeah guide our ways and decisions."

Each elder held up their right hand, and then we repeated the pledge together.

"Our lives for the *holdt*. Our decisions guided by Jeeah. Our hopes for Storeheltur."

Eight hands lowered to the table, and I took a deep breath. The pledge was a constant reminder of my position and that I couldn't do this alone.

"Step before last we saw Kristjan's find. This step we need to make a schedule and timeline of action. When can we have a shipment ready? A message must be sent to Isholt, but we know this, and should choose a messenger, but we also have to find out how long we'll need to hold out until another merchant arrives."

Palmi jotted down the questions I posed.

Orlaugur said, "We can start shifts during second watch, and plan them through each watch. That will give us the best outcome. It'll be at least a phase before we have enough to trouble a merchant."

I nodded. "So, we need to make it another phase. How much food do we have left?"

Reinar held out both hands. "I'm not sure. We can send out another hunting party. Have them stay closer to Storeheltur maybe."

"What of hunting here?" Kristjan asked.

"In Storeheltur?" Reinar shook his head. "There's nothing worth hunting here."

"There are ice rats." Kristjan pressed his idea.

"Ice rats?" Friðfinn coughed. "I don't think Ebonney would even allow them in the home let alone prepare and serve them!"

"If worse comes to worse, we'll consider it." I turned us back to safer ground.

Kristjan shrugged, but I could tell there was more going on behind his expression than what he was letting on.

"Who do we send to Isholt?"

Hafnar raised his hand. "I can do that. It's not far, and I've made the trip before."

"You'll want someone to travel with you." I didn't want to take the chance of losing one of our elders. Kristjan moved, as if to volunteer, but I cut him off. "Choose someone you trust, that you've worked with before."

"I'd offer, but I don't think it'd be best for Ebonney for me to leave right now, not with the anxiety she's already feeling about the situation." Friðfinn sat back in his seat.

"That's fine. I'll check with Sigmar. He'll probably be free. We could see about bringing back some supplies from Isholt, as well. They must be in a better position than we are, and if I talk with Nikanor, he'll understand."

Both were good ideas. Out of all the adults in Storeheltur, Hafnar's brother, Sigmar, knew the most about Toppur. He'd taught Kristjan until I intervened and steered my son's education toward what a chief would need to know.

"I'll send a letter with you to Nikanor. From one chief to another, it might give your plea more weight." I glanced around at the men. "Anything else we need to discuss?"

Karva shook his head. "May Jeeah bless us."

We'd need it, but already things were looking up.

* * *

Kristjan had avoided Friðfinn the whole meeting. Every time he looked at the elder, he remembered Tinna's confession. He debated telling Friðfinn, but then he'd break the girl's confidence, something he couldn't inflict on her, not after all she'd already been through. The fact that she'd felt safe enough to confide in him, warmed his heart. He'd deal with his cousin on his own.

A heavy hand fell on Kristjan's shoulder. "Walk with me," Friðfinn demanded.

"Yes, sir." A pall fell over Kristjan.

Somehow, in the conversation with Tinna, he'd failed to talk with her father before leaving their house.

Once they were in the hallway, Friðfinn led them to an alcove with benches lit by *yoma*. Lichen lined the walls, cushioning the sound. The elder motioned to the stone bench carved from the cavern wall.

"First, I want to thank you for coming over yesterstep." Friðfinn leaned against the wall. "It did my heart good to watch Tinna's face lighten. There's been a weight upon her that I don't understand. At first, I thought it was because I gave you the proposal, but the way she interacts with you tells me differently."

What was he to say to that? What did this man see?

"I know you have a lot on your mind, but for my daughter's sake, please give me an answer of your intent by the end of the phase." He drilled Kristjan with his gaze. "Can you do that?"

Kristjan nodded. No words came past the constriction in his throat. He wiped his hands on his trousers and tried to bring moisture to his mouth.

"Tinna asked to see the new mine. May I take her there before they start working?"

Friðfinn's eyes narrowed. "Who all will be with you?"

"Not my cousin, if that's what you're worried about."

The elder's expression eased. "Good. I don't know what it is about that man, but Tinna doesn't wish to see him. As for me, I've never liked him. He's too smooth." Friðfinn fiddled with his ring. "Kristjan, I'm not saying I don't trust you, but I remember what it was like to be a young man. Women have a way of bringing out both the worst and best in us. Take someone else with you. That's a long trek, and there are many places along it where others seldom walk. It'd be easy to feel that no one would know what you do."

Kristjan was glad the *yoma* was the only light in the alcove. He was sure the elder would have seen the heat that rushed to his cheeks at the implication.

"I'll treat your daughter with the utmost respect, sir."

"I know you intend to, but it's best not to tempt our self-control." Friðfinn pushed off the wall with a sigh. "I hope you're able to bring a smile to her face. Take care of her." He settled his hand on Kristjan's shoulder. "If you refuse the proposal, that is one thing, but if a man should hurt my daughter beyond that, he'll find himself at the bottom of a shaft."

"Y… yes, sir."

Tinna was correct to fear her father's anger. Despite the chill in the stone, Kristjan stayed where he was long after the echoes of Friðfinn's footsteps had faded out of earshot.

Who should go along?

And what about the cliff face?

He rubbed his hand across his face. What would they think of him?

What will Tinna think? That she's walking with a coward?

If only Marko was here. How long would that ache remain?

And whose fault is it that he's not here?

As he pondered his predicament, he considered Tinna. Who would *she* want to have along?

See? You can be considerate. The softer voice encouraged.

Only because you're trying to get something you want—selfish.

Kristjan blocked the voices out. If Tinna was avoiding Bastian, would she want any other man with them? Probably not. But he didn't really know any girls. Who could he ask? Again, he thought of Marko, but before the pain could take hold, he thought of his friend's sisters; one of them would be perfect! He hurried off to see if Myr would accompany them to the mine.

* * *

For the third time in two moonsteps, Kristjan stood before the cliff wall. His heart raced, and his hands were slick. He was sure Tinna and Myr would notice the difference in him, but they waited without comment.

He was the one who had to go up first. They'd never been this way before. The weight of their dependency sent his knees to knocking.

Taking a deep breath, he placed his hands in the first hold. "There are crevices that work as stairs. Marko scaled this cliff in no time." He smiled at the memory; however bitter it tasted.

Myr laughed. "He was practically a lizard when it came to climbing."

Something Kristjan had always envied about his friend, especially as he picked his own steps with such care. Each jutting rock held, but not until he reached the top did the tension gripping his lungs finally release.

Tinna appeared behind him, her dark eyes all but hidden in the dim light of the *yoma*. "Are you all right?"

Kristjan nodded, not trusting his voice yet. He gulped in air and stood on wobbly legs. He reached for the wall, but his hand met a soft shoulder instead.

Tinna said, "Hold onto me as long as you need."

"But—"

"I've been in the mines enough to recognize the signs. Is it the height, darkness, or enclosed space?" Her voice was low, so Myr couldn't hear when she crested the ridge.

"Heights." He hated to admit it.

Still keeping up appearances?

He steadied his voice. "Falling more than anything."

"Kristjan, even the best miners have these fears. It's normal." She rested her hand on his. "Thank you for bringing me. Every time I'm with you, I see something great in you. Facing your fears is probably the greatest evidence of it." She sighed. "I suppose I should take my own advice and face Bastian."

"No." The word came out in a growl, and she dropped her hand back to her side. "Sorry. But don't face him, at least not yet and not alone."

"I won't."

"Where's the mine, Kristjan?" Myr stood with her arms on her hips, her blue eyes reflecting the *yoma*.

Kristjan pointed, releasing his hold on Tinna. "Up there. See the bright *yoma*? That's the first cavern."

He led the way, but Tinna stopped him.

"Kristjan, wait." She ran her finger along the wall, lifted her head up, then turned to the opposite side. "Did Orlaugur see this?"

"I don't know." Kristjan hadn't paid close attention earlier. "I think most of the excitement was inside. Why?"

"Looks like there's a good vein of malachite and maybe some copper as well."

"Really?"

She beamed at him. "Yes, really."

"Can you show me what you see?" Myr stood on tip-toe.

"Well, it'd help if we had more light." Tinna glanced around. "There's *yoma* in there?"

Kristjan nodded and jogged for the other room. He returned with several strong pieces that Orluagur had used and kept in the room for developing the mining project.

"Here you are." Her hand brushed his, and his heart did a strange flip-flop. What was that all about?

"Thank you. Myr, see this green line here?" Tinna pointed at the wall. "It goes along here, but then vanishes into the wall."

Kristjan watched her work, his mind more on what her father had said than on her explanation of mining techniques and the ore.

What are you going to do? She's a treasure.

Tinna stretched, running her fingers over the wall to follow some significant striation in the rock.

Oh, a treasure. And Kristjan, coward and killer, is going to be worthy of her?

Of all the women who'd been presented as potential brides, Tinna was the best, but did that mean he should marry her? He wasn't ready to marry anyone at all, but the elders were pushing for it. They might not have said anything to him directly, but Father had made it clear enough that they all looked to him to take a bride—and soon.

"Isn't it wonderful?" Myr bounced on the balls of her feet.

Tinna cocked her head to one side. "Is everything all right, Kristjan?"

He nodded. "Are we ready to move on?"

Myr bounded ahead. "Can I try to find the vein on my own?"

"Go ahead." Tinna smiled at the younger girl, then turned to Kristjan. "What's wrong?"

Kristjan huffed. "Why do you say there's something wrong?"

"Oh, only the fact that Myr asked you several questions, and you just stared into space completely unmindful of her. That's not like you."

He was thankful for the dim light. "I did?"

"And now you're evading my question." She fiddled with her fingernails, picking dirt from underneath them. "Did… did I do something?"

"No, Tinna." He settled a hand on her shoulder. "You're fine. It's me."

Tinna studied him but didn't say a word.

Kristjan sighed. "Your father talked with me after the elder meeting." His hand fit neatly on her shoulder. It felt right. "He gave me a phase to decide on his proposal."

"Oh." The word came out in a puff of air. "I see."

"Tinna! You *have* to see this!" Myr's voice echoed in the cavern.

"Go ahead. I'll be there shortly." Kristjan dropped his hand to his side.

"If it helps any, I…" She faltered and then said in a rush, "I'd like if you accepted." With that she hurried to the mine.

It didn't help. Instead, her father's words came back to him. "*…find himself at the bottom of a shaft.*"

Despite how beautiful she was, he felt woefully unprepared and unsuited to marry, at least not now. Yet, if he rejected the proposal, he'd be hurting Tinna. Much as he might claim Kristjan had a choice, Friðfinn wouldn't take that well, and who knew what form that anger might take?

Chapter 12

25 Fjorda, 400 AI

Kristjan rounded the corner of the passage having left Myr and Tinna at the intersection where they turned off toward their homes and the one heading toward his own. Both of them were eagerly discussing what they'd seen. He smiled at the memory of how Marko's sister had lit up with delight at Tinna's praise. The memory of Tinna's quiet patience and understanding confused him. For so long, he'd considered her Bastian's girl, but after the conversation yesterstep, Kristjan knew that wasn't so — at least as far as Tinna was concerned. He rubbed a hand over his face. What *was* he supposed to do with her? If he asked Father, he'd say to marry the girl. He couldn't ask Bastian, and Marko… He swallowed back the ache.

"Kristjan, there you are." Bastian strode down the passageway. "I've been looking all over for you."

"Looking for me?" Kristjan tried to affect his normal jovial tone, but it fell flat.

"Wanted to talk with you. Do you have a moment?"

"Sure." Now that he was face-to face with his cousin, Tinna's story felt surreal, distant. He almost wondered whether he'd dreamed the whole thing. Shouldn't Bastian look different? Sound different? How could a man force a woman and go about his life completely unchanged by it? "Any place in particular you want to go?"

"Wherever you want." Bastian motioned with an expansive hand.

"What about my thinking spot?" It was quiet and remote, and he had to consider: though the anger he felt had abruptly become stilted and detached from him, it was still there. He didn't know what he'd do with it, but if it came to violence, he'd rather sort it out away from the rest of the Storeheltur.

"The *lofti*?" Bastian huffed out a breath of air. "I'm not dressed for that kind of cold."

"I have an extra cloak you could use. We can grab it on our way."

"Fine." Bastian shrugged. "As long as you have something warm I can wear."

Kristjan led the way into his room where he pulled his cloak from the wardrobe, and tossed a fur to his cousin, then pulled a quilt off his bed. "Here, in case the coat isn't enough."

"That should do. Thanks."

Prepared for the cold, Kristjan grabbed a *yoma* and made his way to the crack in the wall of the corridor that ran between the kitchen and his bedroom. He'd found the small, enclosed space when he was little. At the time, it'd been a world of his own. When Father found him huddled in it, he'd agreed not to block it off so long as Kristjan told him when he'd be there. As Kristjan grew, the stipulation had been dropped, but the haven feeling of solitude in assured privacy had remained. He almost hated to bring Bastian there, now.

The *yoma* threw light into the narrow passage, which slanted gently upward as it wound toward Toppur, but Kristjan could have managed without the stone. The farther they climbed, the cooler it grew.

"How do you enjoy this?" Bastian asked over his shoulder.

"It was far colder than this when we went above to…" But the memory was too fresh dragging Kristjan's spirits down.

"Look where *that* got us."

Their footsteps echoed off the walls. At last, they came to the final turn. Moonlight shaded the walls a purplish-brown, and Kristjan could see his breath billowing like the dragons in the tales of old. The *lofti* opened on a hilltop. Snow drifted into the opening, and Kristjan stepped out into it, smiling.

There, where it'd stood ever since he was a child, was the ice tree, a relic from before the Impact. He often wondered if Jorvar had sat under the sprawling branches gazing up at Handi and Tsiki in their courses above.

Behind him, Bastian coughed. Kristjan turned.

"Sorry, the cold always gets me at first breath." Bastian blew on his fingers. "At least this is out of the wind. I suppose this tree helps. Surprising it's still standing; I'd have thought it'd be eaten away by the elements by now."

"It's always been a reminder to me that there's hope."

Bastian chuckled. "I can see that."

"So, you needed to speak with me?"

"About that." Bastian wrapped the cloak and blanket around his hands and then drew it about himself. "Saw you with Tinna."

A shiver that had nothing to do with the weather ran down Kristjan's spine. He'd wanted to confront Bastian but hadn't thought Bastian would approach him.

"What? No denying it?" Bastian glared at him. "I thought you said you wouldn't steal my girl away from me."

"I didn't steal her."

Bastian cocked his head and chuckled. "Re-ally?" He drew the word out and then snorted. "I've tried to see her to give her my gift and can't even get in the door, but you're wandering Storeheltur with her hand in hand. Explain to me how that's not stealing *my* girl from me."

Kristjan took a deep breath, trying to find the right words. This was, after all, his cousin. But Bastian's indignance had thrown him off-balance; why was he surprised that Tinna didn't want to see him? Why would he expect that she'd ever speak to him again after what he'd done? Was it possible that there *was* some misunderstanding? "Tell me about your time with Tinna in the Garður the last time you saw her."

"What do you mean?"

"What happened between you and her?" Kristjan waited; would Bastian lie to him?

His cousin shrugged. "Not much to tell. We walked and talked. I told her how I longed to have her as my bride."

"How'd she take that?"

"She was very receptive. That's why I can only think that you said or did something to make her change her mind."

"Receptive?" That's not what she'd told Kristjan.

Bastian looked up at Handi. "What do you want me to tell you, Kristjan? There are things that are between a man and his woman."

"Maybe so, but there are certain things that shouldn't be done *unless* you're man and wife." There he'd said it.

Bastian spun around, the blanket dropping to the ground. "What are you insinuating?"

"Nothing. I'm asking what you did with Tinna that step."

"Obviously, you already know something, or you wouldn't be hounding me." Bastian clenched his fists at his sides, his jaw tight. "Fine. I kissed her. She liked it so much she pulled me on top of her. What do you think I was going to do? I gave her what she wanted. When we were done, I left."

"You *violated* her!" Kristjan struggled to keep his voice even.

"Violated? Kristjan, you've not been around women. When they kiss you like that, they're asking for more. Believe me." Bastian shook his head. "I can't believe we're having this conversation." He snatched the blanket from where it'd fallen. "Listen, Tinna's my girl. I don't know what you've done to her—"

"Definitely not what you have, and you don't even realize it. Bastian, she's terrified of you. Wants nothing to do with you."

Bastian's mouth fell open. "Terrified of *me*?" He closed his mouth, opened, then closed it with another shake of his head. "Kristjan, remember when Juli wanted our attention?"

What did this have to do with Tinna? Kristjan smiled at the memory.

"She followed Marko and me around like a pet fox."

"Right, she wanted your attention, but when you and Marko wouldn't give it to her, she came to me." Bastian pulled the cloak tighter about him and stomped his feet to warm them. "Never told you why she quit bothering the two of you. She found what she wanted with me."

Kristjan gaped. "You…" Kristjan shuddered. "You…" He couldn't bring himself to say it.

"Yes." Bastian glared. "I did. We enjoyed each other."

A thought struck Kristjan. He tried to think back to that rotation. It had to be, but… "Is Elias…?" He couldn't finish the question, but Bastian glanced away. "How many, Bastian? How many children do you… have?"

"Only the one."

"But?"

"There might have been one or two more, but they didn't survive."

How… Kristjan felt sick at Bastian's dismissive, almost annoyed tone—as if talking about them was a waste of his time. Living, breathing children, whose tiny lives had been taken straight out of their mothers' arms. His heart ached to think of those women, mourning the loss of their children alone, knowing that Bastian—their father—didn't care.

"Oh, don't give me that horrified look, cuz. I've seen you look at girls, even though you tried to hide it. You've thought of doing what I did, plenty of times, and deep down you'd like to know what it's like, but you're too afraid of what everyone else thinks. We're the same inside, Kristjan; I just have the guts to actually go after what I want. I've watched you over the rotations. You wanted to learn how to mine, but Uncle Geirfinnur and the elders would have had a fit. So you gave it up. Time and again, you buried your own desires because someone else wouldn't like it—the elders would scold you for it, Uncle Geirfinnur would think badly of you, or Marko frowned upon it."

"That's not true."

That's its own lie. The voice was as loud as Bastian's.

Bastian snorted. "Not true? Why aren't you a merchant? Or the expert on Toppur? Why do you still come up here and pine like some lovesick idiot over a world you can't have? Any other person would have fought for what they wanted, but you? No. One cross word, and you give it all up. The irony is that if you'd tried, you'd make a better chief, but when you take that chair, you'll just turn your belly to the elders and be as useless as an eðla lizard in front of a *yoma*."

How had this conversation turned on Kristjan?

"Listen, cuz, you can stay up here mooning over Toppur for as long as you want. I'm going back where it's warm. But…" Bastian waited for Kristjan to look at him. "You think I'm a liar? Or a cheat?" He threw his arms wide. "I'm true to the core. I don't put on a mask to show people what they want to see, and I get what I want. Right now, I want Tinna. Better not get in my way, or we'll have more than words between us."

The steel in his cousin's eyes was more chilling than the frigid winds. Kristjan took an involuntary step back, staring into those eyes that suddenly felt like they belonged to a stranger. Bastian would go to any lengths to get what he wanted, but what would he do with Tinna after he was finished? Would he leave her hurt and used like Juli? If he did, Friðfinn…

"Bastian, her father—"

"Oh, I know Friðfinn. I'll be careful." Bastian glared at him for a moment longer and then turned. "I'll leave your blanket and cloak on your bed," he called over his shoulder.

Kristjan watched his cousin's departing back, his heart racing. Bastian's accusations looped through his mind.

You're a push over. You bend to the will of others.

He pulled his cloak tighter around him, but it couldn't shield him against the barrage of words inside.

He's right. The same inside…

His stomach churned, then another thought struck him. If she was with child, would Bastian abandon her, as he'd done to Juli? Kristjan couldn't imagine him publicly admitting to the tryst, let alone marrying Tinna and caring for them both. Kristjan thought of waiting to find out whether she was pregnant, but if he did, then the birth would be too soon after their wedding—the *holdt* would know that the child had been conceived before their marriage, and even the Jorvarsson name wouldn't protect Tinna from enduring the same quiet ostracizing shame he'd seen inflicted on Juli over the rotations. If he wanted to ensure that she was protected from the stigma, the decision couldn't wait. He'd marry Tinna, and accept the child as his own.

A noble thing to do.

Yet, even with the decision made, it didn't relieve the stress. If anything, his heart felt heavier.

Exactly as Bastian said. Pleasing everyone else. Same as always; good old Kristjan, the worn-smooth stone beneath their feet.

An arranged marriage, though. He'd always thought he'd choose his own bride. But… wasn't that what a chief was supposed to do? Put everyone else's needs before his own?

Bastian's words came back to him. *Time and again, you buried your desires because someone else wouldn't like it.*

It was no use. Kristjan *was* a coward—and he was about to be a promise-breaker, too. Bastian would be livid when he found out what Kristjan was about to do.

Chapter 13

26 Fjorda, 400 AI

I wanted to shout it down a shaft! My son had accepted a proposal to wed Tinna *Arnorsson*. First, I needed to let her father know. With that in mind, I curbed my reaction and made my way down to the newest mine.

Had it been only two moonsteps since I'd traversed this way with Kristjan, leading the elders? The change was so drastic, the place could barely have been recognized. Where before it'd been dimly lit and strewn with rocks, now the way was awash in the multi-colored light of both lamps and *yoma*. Men and women were working to widen the path to allow carts through, and the beginnings of columns, helping support the weight of stone and earth overhead, were already taking form. At the cliff wall, I climbed one of several ladders and stopped at the top, staring.

If I'd thought the change below was great, then this was astronomical! The steady tap of picks was expected, but I had to scurry out of the way of a cart rumbling toward me.

"Clear the way below!" Juli called.

Aldar waited a moment and then dumped the cart into a growing pile of ore below. How had I missed *that* on the way up?

The thunder of rubble tumbling over itself echoed through the confined space.

"That'll do; let's go." Aldar motioned, and the two retreated back the way they'd come.

I watched where they went, and my mouth dropped open. I could have sworn the mine had been straight ahead of where I stood, but a gaping hole glowed off to my left.

Orlaugur's voice boomed through the opening. "Bring the water." His words were followed by steam billowing out of the opening.

Curiosity tugged at me, and I headed to the new mine. I waved the remaining steam aside and watched as people swung pickaxes to enlarge the hole, while others picked up the discarded pieces. Still more sorted the ore into two carts—one to be discarded and one to be refined. I couldn't tell which was which, but hoped with all my might that the fuller of the two was the good ore.

Orlaugur stood with his back to me, shaking his head. "Well done, Mani. You can take a break. Let Erika take your place." He picked up a rock, and I whistled low, the sound escaping me without thought. Even from five paces away, I could tell the beauty of the gem he held.

The elder turned, his face beaming. "Ah, Geirfinnur, take a look at this! Tinna discovered this vein, and the other is just as promising. We've already extracted several wagon-loads of gems, and that's not counting the copper and malachite running along with it. Hafnar and Sigmar had better return soon with a merchant. I wish they wouldn't have left before we'd opened up this wall. We could have sent them with samples of what we have—bet that would've hastened a merchant's steps!"

"That's good news." I took the proffered the crystal, examining it. The cart was three-quarters full of pieces every bit as beautiful as the one Orlaugur had handed me. "Any idea where Friðfinn might be?"

"He's down at the next shaft," Orlaugur said as I returned the gem to him. He tossed it into the cart and went back to directing the workers.

I was glad the elder was distracted. If he hadn't been, he'd have wondered why I was there, and I wasn't sure that I could have kept my excitement in check. As I exited the tunnel, I watched for carts—another was heading to the cliff to dump rejected rocks. I slid along the edge keeping out of the workers' way.

The next shaft was just as impressive with its high ceiling and broad splashes of light spilling into the hallway. The greens of dioptase and malachite wove across the ivory walls studded with the blue of azurite. More workers swarmed through the area. It was much harder to avoid them, but in the center stood Friðfinn. When he caught sight of me, he waved.

I threaded my way past the carts and people until I was in the relative calm around my friend.

"Isn't it wonderful, Geir?" Friðfinn clapped me on the shoulder. "Your son knows what he's looking for. Maybe we should have allowed him to be a miner."

"You know how dangerous the mines are. We can't have our chief caught in a cave-in." I shuddered. When Kristjan had gone through the mining phase, I was glad the elders had cut it short.

"Of course not, but as far as I'm concerned, he should explore more often." Friðfinn laughed. "What brings you down here?"

Glancing around, I realized that if I was to speak with my friend, we'd have to leave. I didn't want to announce the news in front of half of Storeheltur.

"It's a bit loud here. Anywhere quieter?"

Friðfinn cocked his head. "Sure." He motioned me out of the mine, past Orlaugur's and down a ladder.

"Will this do?" he asked once we were around the corner from the tumbling rejects.

"Much better." Now that it was time, I didn't know how best to broach the subject.

My friend didn't make me struggle. Instead, he grinned. "It's good news, isn't't?"

I nodded. "Kristjan agreed."

"Ha! Stars be praised! The boy had me wondering if I'd have to give Tinna over to that lout that keeps pestering…" He seemed to realize who he was speaking to. "No offence intended, but your nephew is nothing like your son."

"Bastian?" I couldn't fathom what he was referring to, but Kristjan had mentioned my nephew, as well.

"The lad won't stop. Tinna's asked me not to listen to him—something I'll gladly do, and now I have an answer for him. Tinna is betrothed to Kristjan. We'll write up the official documents and set a date. Wouldn't want a double wedding, though, would you?"

"I don't think it's fair to Tinna and Kristjan. Josebina and I couldn't care less."

"True. Ebonney will probably want to plan everything out for Tinna. She *is* our only child, after all."

"Well, then, ask the women."

Friðfinn glanced about. "I could probably sneak away. Want to sign the agreement now?"

I smiled. "Are you afraid Kristjan will back out?"

"Well," Friðfinn drew the word out, "not exactly, but with how much work it took to get him to agree, I don't want to take any chances."

"I suppose not." I'd never known Kristjan to renege on his word, but he'd been very reluctant to even consider Tinna.

"Let me explain the situation to Orlaugur. Then I'll be back. We can go sign the document and get Kristjan to sign it as well." Friðfinn scaled the ladder with a grace that belied his bulk.

Soon we were in his study with Kristjan. If I hadn't known better, I'd have said Kristjan wanted to be anywhere but here. He tapped his foot and couldn't seem to keep his attention in any one place.

I settled a hand on his shoulder. "It'll be over soon enough."

That seemed to do the trick.

"Kristjan, this is the contract—the joining of our families. Tinna becoming part of the Jorvarsson household." He looked with a bittersweet fondness toward her. "And your children being of the Jorvarsson line. We'll still need to work out a dwelling for the two of you, as you'll need your own space." He gave a meaningful glance that set Kristjan's cheeks to burning. "But I'd like to let Tinna settle on the one she prefers."

"Of course." There was no hint of Kristjan's feelings in his reply.

"Then we sign it." Friðfinn's signature was confident and bold.

I wrote mine, rotations of practice making it fluid and sure. Kristjan was the last. He paused with the quill raised above the parchment. Then as if he'd made up his mind—yet again—he scribbled his name.

Friðfinn examined the document, then grinned. "Here, a toast to the agreement." He filled three cups with an amber liquid and handed one to each of us before taking his own. "To a new son! Kristjan, I'm proud to have you in the family."

"Thank you. I... I'll do my best to live up to your trust."

"Kristjan, anything you put your mind to, you do well." Friðfinn held the cup high then downed it.

The liquor was bitter and sweet, which felt poignantly apt. My son had finally agreed to take a wife, but that meant he was growing up. Too many emotions swirled inside. If only I could express them to myself, let alone Kristjan.

Friðfinn was the only one who didn't have any trouble with words. "When will the event be, Kristjan?"

"Event?" Kristjan asked with a start. "Wha... what do you mean?"

"What step will we have the ceremony, son?"

"Oh, I... I don't know."

"Well, then let's check with the women. How's that sound?"

Kristjan nodded, but there was no joy in his motions. Nothing like the underlying nervousness and excitement I felt when I thought of Josebina. What was wrong with the boy? Knowing Kristjan, perhaps he was simply afraid of falling short of his new responsibilities. A sliver of doubt wormed its way between my ribs. Had I pushed too much on him?

When we entered the living quarters, Ebonney and Tinna were there waiting for us. Tinna beamed up at Kristjan, and Ebonney glowed as if it was *her* wedding we had been discussing.

Friðfinn rested his hands on his daughter's shoulders. "Tinna, your betrothed has given you the choice of steps. When would you like to be married?"

"Oh!" Tinna looked down at her lap, and Kristjan stared at his feet. "I don't know. How long do we need?"

"At least three cycles." Ebonney rose and stood beside her husband.

"That long?" Tinna glanced up then sputtered. "Oh… I… I mean… It's just… What all must be done?"

Friðfinn laughed, his chuckle filling the space with warmth. "My daughter knows what she wants. She's waited too long already."

"Well, I suppose we could get by with two cycles."

"*Moði*, what all do we absolutely *have* to do? I thought it was a matter of a dress, a ceremony, and a meal."

"True." Ebonney rubbed her chin. "But we don't have much for a meal at the moment."

"Oh." Tinna hung her head.

To my surprise, Kristjan found his voice. "I could make a trip to Toppur and hunt especially for the meal if you wish."

Tinna looked up, her face aglow. "You would?"

Kristjan's cheeks reddened, and he rubbed the back of his neck. "It's the least I can do. How many are we serving?"

Ebonney tossed her arms out as if it should be obvious. "You're the chief's son! All of Storeheltur should attend."

"All?" Kristjan blanched.

"*Moði*, can't it be those who are important to Kristjan and me? Why must everyone come?"

"It's expected." Ebonney's expression was less sure than her words. "Don't you want that, Tinna?"

"I think… I think I'd like a small group—intimate—with family instead of the whole community."

"Well…" Ebonney drew the word out, but then placed an arm around her daughter. "Tinna, this is your special step, and there'll only be one. I know you used to play at holding your wedding ceremony when you were little and you've been longing for it ever since. We need to make it as wonderful as you dreamed it would be."

"*Moði*, I was a little girl." Tinna wrung her hands.

What was wrong with her? I couldn't read her mixed signals.

"Yes, you were, and those dreams are important."

Tinna sighed, then for the first time since Kristjan had offered to hunt, peered into my son's eyes as if seeking assurance.

"I want family and friends. That's who I always thought would be there. I don't like elaborate; the details aren't important. The people are, and Kristjan has agreed to be my husband." She flushed but smiled at him. "The sooner we can do so, the better. Hard as these times are, I'd rather face them with Kristjan." She held a hand out to him.

Kristjan took it gently in his. "I agree. Hunting shouldn't take longer than two steps at the most. How long will it take for your dress to be ready?"

Ebonney sighed. "If you both are determined, we can plan on your wedding step in a phase."

Tinna beamed at her mother. "Thank you!"

"Well, it appears we have a plan." I glanced among the new members of my family. "Tinna, I'm pleased to have you as a daughter."

Her smile was all I needed to know that my son had chosen well. If only he could express his emotions. At the moment he looked like a miner after a cave-in.

* * *

Tinna's hand felt warm in Kristjan's. He couldn't believe he was going through with this, but the way she looked up at him… What else could he do? Besides, better him than Bastian.

Is that how you decide on a spouse?

Kristjan sighed, and Tinna's smile faded.

"It'll be all right." He gazed into her eyes.

"You're sure?"

He rubbed his thumb across the back of her hand. "Very."

She looked down at her feet again and wiped at her cheek. Around them, the adults talked. Ebonney pratted on about details. Friðfinn grinned as if *he* was the one getting married. And Father? He was Father, as enigmatic as always. Tinna stood, keeping her hand in

Kristjan's as if it was a life rope in the dark caverns. All eyes turned to the couple, but Tinna didn't seem to notice.

"Would you go for a walk with me?" she asked.

Kristjan glanced to her parents. They nodded, Friðfinn's grin deepening. Together the two made their way out. As soon as they were beyond the sight of her home, Tinna sagged against Kristjan.

"Is everything all right?" Kristjan steadied her.

She nodded but hid behind her tresses as she often did. "I need to talk with you. Some place quiet, and... private."

Had he done something to offend her? Kristjan raked his mind trying to remember what he may have done or not, but he came away blank.

Tinna squeezed his hand. "I'll be fine. I just need to rest away from prying eyes."

Prying eyes. Kristjan knew the perfect place, but did he dare take her there? She was dressed in a simple gown designed for the warmth of the cavern system, not the cold of Toppur.

"Do you trust me, Tinna?"

"With my life." Her reply stole his breath away.

Marko had trusted him that way.

Look where that got him.

Pushing the thought aside, he led her through the halls to his own quarters.

"You'll need a cloak." He pulled his extra cloak down from the peg, then fastened his own.

There were unspoken questions in her eyes but no fear.

He led her through the narrow slit and up the passageway.

"It's a *lofti*." She kept her voice low as if it could carry all the way back to her own quarters. "Does it go all the way to Toppur?"

"Yes, it's my quiet thinking place."

When they crested the top, their breath came in smoky wreaths. Before them stretched the white snows suffused with the purple light of Tsiki and the paler, purer glow of Handi.

"What is this?" Tinna kept his hand and with her other traced the trunk of the ice tree.

"I like to think that Jorvar himself sat under this tree." Kristjan smiled. "Even here on Toppur, ice trees are rare. The leaves glow in moonlight. When Handi comes out, they turn white as everything else out here, but when it's just Tsiki's light shining on them, they're a beautiful purple color."

"I'd love to see it one step." Her expression told him all he needed to know.

"Then I'll be sure to bring you here."

Tinna turned back to him. "Kristjan…" She looked at their entwined hands. "I… I need to tell you something. I probably should… I know I should… have told you before you agreed to Father's terms. If you wish to back out—"

"Hush," Krisjtan said, squeezing her fingers. "Tinna, I made a choice, a decision. I will follow through with it."

"But—"

"No *buts* I'll let you speak your mind, but I won't change mine."

Her brown eyes filled with tears, and a sob escaped. Kristjan pulled her to his chest and wrapped his cloak around her, shielding her from the cold, but knowing there was more than cold that he couldn't protect her from.

When she quit shaking, she wiped her eyes. He used her cloak to dry them before he allowed her back out into the cold, but she stayed within the circle of his arms, gazing up at him.

"Kristjan, I don't deserve you."

He was the one who didn't deserve her. Such tender beauty. He was sure to shred her if he wasn't careful.

Like the way Marko was?

She inhaled and let out a huff. "I told you of the step in the Garður."

Kristjan nodded, wondering if her confession was what he thought it would be.

I… I guess it must've been the wrong… not that there would be a right… time…" She fiddled with the edge of the cloak. "What I'm trying to say is I don't know how long I'll be able to hide… what happened."

"You're positive?"

"Unfortunately, yes. I denied it for a while, but I've run out of ways to keep lying to myself."

Kristjan bit his lip. He wanted to scream, to thrash Bastian, but any reaction toward his cousin would only frighten Tinna.

"You…" She shivered, huddling in on herself and hiding her face. "You don't have to—"

"Tinna." He waited for her to look him in the eyes. "I gave your father my word. This isn't news to me."

She paled. "How?"

"This isn't the only child Bastian has."

Her lips formed an 'O', but no sound came out.

"When I decided, I figured this may be the case. You shouldn't bear the cost or the shame of his choices. You'll be my wife, and the child you carry, will be mine—ours—and if a son, the next chief after me."

Tinna's eyes widened, and she stifled a gasp, her palm tight against her mouth. Tears worked their way down her cheeks. Kristjan reached out gently to dry them.

"I can't guarantee I'll not hurt you, but I won't leave you."

He pulled her against him, surprised when, instead of melting into his embrace, she pulled his head down to her. Their lips met. When they parted, Tinna's throat was throbbing with her pulse. Kristjan's wasn't much slower. She leaned into his chest, leaving him striving against the craving for another kiss.

Chapter 14

27 Fjorda, 400 AI

Kristjan lay in bed fighting with himself. All his life he'd been told that the chief kept the peace at all costs. The advice had been directed at him from the time he'd seen five rotations and had punched Aldar for belittling Andri. Ever since the scolding he'd received then, Kristjan had held his tongue too many times to count. And yet now, more than at any other time in his life, the drive to beat another person was rapidly devouring the bonds of his self-control. How could Bastian be so thoughtless and base? The memory of Tinna's tears mingled with that of her kiss—and all that it'd awakened in him.

That's a good start for a husband and wife.

And how is that different from Bastian? That's all he wanted, too.

With a sigh, Kristjan rolled over, pulling the covers around his shoulders. He knew he should get up, but he didn't feel like it.

Since when did feelings, or lack thereof, prevent him from doing anything? Yet, he didn't make the effort to drag his feet out of bed. Instead, he closed his eyes, willing his thoughts to be silent. If only it was that easy. When his brain quieted, images replaced the pestering rumination—images he didn't wish to see. Marko—his crumpled body, his blood saturating ground and cloth, his stiff limbs as they handed him to his parents, the sound of his body slipping down the passage to Fivku.

Kristjan shook his head and forced the blankets from him. This was ridiculous. Still, he didn't rise. What was the use? It was like his mind was a piece of ice spun on the floor—out of control and passing the same territory again and again. It didn't matter if he was awake or lying in bed.

A knock on the doorframe finally pulled his attention away from the past.

"Kristjan?" Father called through the curtain. "Bastian wishes to speak with you."

Bastian? The mere mention of his cousin was enough to do what Kristjan couldn't do on his own—get himself on his feet.

"I'll be there shortly."

"Very well." The words were ordinary, but the slight hesitation conveyed so much more.

Putting aside his father's frustration with him, Kristjan pulled on a tunic and a pair of trousers. Within moments, he slipped into the living space. His cousin sat on a couch, fiddling with a loose string on his tunic sleeve.

When he saw Kristjan, he stood. "Need a word with you."

"That's what Father said."

"Where's the best place for a private conversation?"

Kristjan clenched his fists. He longed to feel the crunch of Bastian's nose under them. Private would be best for what he intended. "My quiet place?"

"What is it with you and cold?" Bastian stood. "Guess it's as good as any."

And there'd be no one to hear Bastian scream.

Kristjan didn't know where the thought had come from, and, to his surprise he felt no shame for it—nothing but the rage beneath.

They both grabbed a cloak and wound their way through the *lofti*. The more the temperature dropped, the harder the freeze over Kristjan's heart became, and by the time they reached Toppur, he held no remorse, no anger, nothing. He would deal with his cousin and continue life, no more ghosts to haunt him than when he came.

"So, what did you wish to discuss, Bastian?" Kristjan faced the ice tree, and for the briefest of moments felt the weight of condemnation from Jorvar.

"I thought I made it clear that Tinna was my girl."

"You also made it very clear what you do with your children." Kristjan turned to his cousin. "Want to tell me you intend to marry her and accept the child as your own?"

Bastian's eyes widened for a moment before narrowing in disdain.

"Thought so." Kristjan didn't give his cousin a chance to respond. "Friðfinn was right. You're a lout."

His voice was low, but his actions were swift. He swung an uppercut to Bastian's stomach and followed it with a punch to the cheek that barely rocked his cousin. Bastian, having had more experience with fighting, stayed slightly hunched and allowed the momentum to roll him into a pivot that brought him in closer to Kristjan. He tackled him. The two rolled on the ice, both struggling for the advantage. Soon, Bastian's larger build won out, and he manage to get on top of Kristjan, straddling him while he pinned his hands down in the snow, their faces mere breaths from each other.

Even then, Kristjan felt no fear or dread. He hawked spit in his cousin's face snarling, "You won't have her."

Bastian shrugged, ignoring the spittle on his cheek. "You know, Kristjan, you're pathetic. Can't even put up a proper fight." Bastian snarled. "How am I supposed to respect you, Jorvarsson? You're pathetic. You bow to every word the elders say, and you let your father lead you around on a leash. And then, on top of it all, you go and marry a used-up girl who was mine first. You're no more than an ice rat eating out of my trash."

Kristjan struggled, livid now, but not for himself. Tinna was a better person than Bastian would ever be. She deserved someone to stand up for her, even if it was only him.

"It's not worth arguing about. You can have her, but mark my words, cousin." Bastian glowered down at Kristjan, his breath coming in great steaming gasps. "Storeheltur would be better off without a chief at all than following the likes of you. The *holdt* needs to live and breathe. You'll suffocate it by trying to please everyone else and failing to please anyone in the process"

Bastian held Kristjan down for a beat longer, then rose, wiping the icy globule from his cheek. With a shake of the borrowed cloak, he was gone, leaving Kristjan as cold inside as the snow that melted against his neck. For the longest time, Kristjan lay prone, allowing the chill to creep up his limbs contemplating his cousin's words.

Better off dead. Better without you. The two ideas circled through his mind like the wheel on the ore crusher.

Yet, even though he believed them, he didn't have the strength to follow through. The cold was too painful—it wasn't an end he could endure. He dragged his cloak about him and stood up. He was better off dead. He just needed to find another chance… Another way.

* * *

Kristjan had returned to his room and removed the wet tunic, and now stood bare-chested staring down at his desk. Several papers were sprawled out across its surface. A straightedge and his special rocks held a mechanical diagram in place, and the pencil had skidded across the proposed layout leaving a light trail of graphite. When had he written these up? The memory felt altogether too distant for how quickly he recalled the task, but then he realized: this had been before.

Before the fateful trip to Toppur when life was normal, when he *felt* things. When Marko was alive and keeping the peace between himself and Bastian. But somehow, he doubted that even Marko could've bridged the rift between them now.

He traced the line indicating a tunnel or pipe system from the water reservoir to homes. Maybe he could bring back feeling by completing this project. If nothing else, it may give hope to the colony. Stars knew they needed hope. The mine had granted them some, but now they had to wait for a merchant to come. That would take at least a phase, probably more.

The plans needed some adjustments. But as he settled down to perfect them, he saw his journal and pulled it out instead; maybe he could make sense of what his life had become. He didn't get far.

"Kristjan?" Father stood in the doorway, disapproval written across his face. "I thought you told Friðfinn you were going to go on a hunting expedition."

The breath left Kristjan as if Bastian had tackled him again. How had he forgotten?

Some husband, already forgetting promises to his wife.

"Yes, I'll get ready."

Father cocked his head, lines creasing his face. "Is everything all right?" He came into the room but kept his distance.

"Of course. Why wouldn't it be?" Kristjan shrugged into a tunic.

Had he lied to his father? Why had it been so easy? Nothing was right. Marko walked the halls of the ancients. Tinna carried Bastian's son, and instead of Bastian being called to account, caring for her and the child, Kristjan was marrying her. Where was the justice in all of this?

"Kristjan…" Father took a step with his hand out, but withdrew it and massaged his jaw instead. "Be careful. I'm proud of you. You'll make a wonderful chief—better than I have been."

With that he turned and left. Kristjan staring after him. Wonderful chief? How? Marko was dead, Tinna was pregnant, and Kristjan's marriage was only covering up Bastian's sins. If his father only knew what a 'wonderful' son he had. But if his father couldn't see murder when it was staring him plain in the face,

Kristjan could scarcely expect him to understand what a collapse his son was making of the rest of his life.

Best to set the pondering aside and focus on the hunt. He'd need a sleigh, tent, cooking utensils, stove, fuel, tinder and flint, and bedding. The storehouse would have the first couple of items. He scanned his room. His own bedding would suffice, and a pot or two from their kitchen; if he brought a supply of fuel and his firekit as well, then he could head directly to Toppur after retrieving the sleigh and tent. There was no need to linger here.

After folding his blankets and the dense sleeping pad he'd use to ward against the frozen ground, he wrapped a pot and spoon in the blanket. He secured his knife to his belt and dropped his tinderbox into a pouch. Once all was ready, he pulled his boots on and trudged to the door.

Brushing aside the tapestry, he collided with a petite figure.

"Oh! I'm sorry." Tinna blinked.

Kristjan reached out and steadied her, amazed at how often he had held her hand or arm since returning from his last trip.

"It's not your fault, Tinna. I wasn't paying attention."

"You're on your way?"

Was that a waver in her voice?

"Yes, all that's left is to procure a tent and sleigh."

"Be… be careful." She glanced down. "I… I don't know what…"

He curled a finger under her chin. "Tinna, I'll be here for you."

Her smile was an unexpected reward. "Thank you. I… I don't deserve you. How you can—"

"Hush. You deserve better than the likes of me. You deserve a man who will love you properly."

She shuddered. "I don't think— I don't know what I think any more."

Again, he wanted to slug his cousin, even if it meant another dump in the snow and ice. Somehow, he'd missed what Tinna had said next.

"…back?"

"Sorry, what was that?"

She glanced down but then looked up, her expression earnest. "You'll be back in two steps?"

He nodded. "Maybe sooner if I can find sufficient game."

"Then I'll pray Jeeah will guide your endeavor."

He'd need that, but he wouldn't hold his breath. Look how that had left him the last time.

Tinna glanced over her shoulder, then placed a hand on his cheek. "Thank you, Kristjan." Tears glistened in her eyes, but she blinked them away. "You're a good man. Thank you."

With that she was gone, hurrying down the corridor, leaving Kristjan staring after her. Good man? A good man wouldn't marry a girl without loving her. A good man wouldn't steal the woman his cousin wanted, even if that cousin had— He dismissed those thoughts; they'd do him no good. Best to forget it all and do what he'd set out to do—hunt for his wedding step. Even that idea didn't thrill him, but neither did it set fear in his heart. He sighed and moved along.

* * *

I knew as soon as the curtain fell behind me that Kristjan was gone. It wasn't anything tangible, but the type of knowing a father has. Ever since he'd been a baby, I could tell when he was around. Maybe it was because I'd lie awake listening to his little lungs work and had fallen into the habit of listening for him. No matter how, I knew. He was gone, and the last words he'd heard had been spoken from my heart, but from the way he'd shrugged, I knew they'd not settled in him. If only he'd truly listen.

Our home was too quiet. I fiddled with fixing a meal but wasn't really hungry. I sighed. From past experience, the best thing I could do when I felt like this was to either talk to Josebina or write in my journal. My journal was my way of talking to Jeeah. I never really heard an answer, but once I'd put the words to paper and sought some truth to set against them, it was as if the weight of the problem lifted.

Taking what sufficed as a meal to my writing desk, I sat down. Topmost on my mind was my son. Orlaugur had commended Kristjan again this moonstep. Friðfinn was liable to pop a tunic seam over the match, yet Kristjan didn't see it or acknowledge that he was worthy. It made no sense to me. I just hoped nothing happened to him up on Toppur.

A call interrupted my writing. I placed the quill in its holder and stood.

"Josebina, come in."

By the time I reached the main living quarter, she was there, standing at ease, a smile on her face.

"Geir, how are you doing?" Her blue eyes were sincere.

"Fine now that you're here."

"I thought you might be troubled," she said in the tone of one who wishes they weren't right. "Have you eaten?"

I shrugged. "Enough."

"Then let me rectify that. What do you have in your kitchen?"

Not enough. I'd pushed the extra ration to a family with five little ones. Kristjan and I didn't need the food. Heat filled my cheeks, and I rubbed the back of my neck.

"Ah, well, then come back to my place. I have some of the meat the last hunting party brought back."

Before I could protest, my stomach grumbled.

Josebina shook her head. "When was your last decent meal?"

I could've lied to her, picked a different meaning of "decent" than the one she intended, but I didn't want to. "Probably the *maltið*."

"Geir, that was seven steps ago! That won't do." She reached for my hand and squeezed. "We can't have our chief wasting away." A shy smile crossed her lips. "Nor can I have it said that I allowed my husband to starve."

Husband. Oh, how that thrilled my heart! Eighteen rotations was too long not to hear the word and know it was mine.

"Fine. You've convinced me," I said with a laugh.

Together, we walked hand in hand through the halls. To my surprise, we met no one.

"Where is everyone?"

"The third watch hasn't started yet; those that aren't working at the new shaft are eating their final meal of the step. But probably a third of them are mining—Orlaugur's been keeping them busy."

I knew Orlaugur had prioritized the mining, but not to see *anyone* between my home and hers? That seemed out of character.

"What's troubling you, Geir?" Josebina squeezed my hand.

"Kristjan left on a hunting trip."

She rested her free hand on my arm. "He'll be fine."

"I know that up here." I tapped my temple then my heart. "But here's where I need to believe it. He's been off ever since Marko's death, and I know well what watching a loved one cross to the halls of the ancients can do to a person."

Josebina didn't say a word. She didn't have to. Jeeah knew how she'd watched me struggle through life without Sæbjort.

There were footsteps behind us—hurried. I turned around to see a dust-streaked lad drop his hands to his thighs and suck in air.

"Chief!" He took in a deep breath then rushed ahead. "Come quick! Cave- cave-in."

The final word set my heart to ice and my feet in motion. I dropped Josebina's hand and rushed to the lad, who I now recognized as Margeir and Telma's son, Andri.

"Where?"

"The- new mine."

My mind swirled with the implications as I trotted down the passage, not yet knowing where I was going. We needed that ore more than anything else at the moment, but how many were trapped? Was my first thought of the ore when lives may have been lost? I stilled my racing heart and tried to plan—what would we need?

I turned back to Josebina, only to find her at my side still. I hadn't even been aware of her following me.

"I'll gather a physician, tools, and water, and whatever food we have, by whatever helpers I can recruit. You go assess the situation." Her smile that had been so bright for me earlier, now was gone, replaced by grim determination. "Jeeah help us all."

Chapter 15

27 Fjorda, 400 AI

Andri led me back through the familiar halls, still panting, but even through that his expression was grim.

"Can you tell me anything about it?"

"One moment all was well, the next—" He gasped another breath. "There was a tremor and dust and debris exploded." He rubbed a hand across his face, smudging the grime. "I... I don't know what happened."

I placed a hand on the lad's shoulder. If nothing else, maybe I could ease the shock of what he'd seen.

"We'll do our best to free everyone."

"But..." His lip quivered even as he pulled in more air. "What if they're... what if they're already with Marko?"

The possibility settled like a choking collar around my heart. "Then we trust Jeeah to help us through."

Andri nodded. "I... I did hear voices. They were muffled, but..."

"Then we'll pray that they're all right." *And that Jeeah grants us the wisdom and insight to extract them safely.*

I didn't know what I'd been expecting, but it hadn't prepared me for reality. We came to the sheer rock where the ladders had been set, but one had been knocked aslant, leaning away from the wall, and the other, though still serviceable, had a few bent rungs. Even from the bottom, I could see that the collapse had left no room at the top to stand, but nevertheless, I scaled the battered ladder and rested my fingers on the narrow lip that was all that remained of the ledge—the stonefall occupied the rest. Taking a deep breath, I mustered my knowledge—I did know what to do; I was just afraid of the result. I carefully removed a rock from the pile and tapped on the debris. Would there be a reply?

After waiting for what seemed an eternity, I tapped again. Andri climbed up behind me; looking over my shoulder, I could see his wide eyes in the dim light of the few *yoma* still exposed.

"Where are the torches?" It'd been much lighter the last time I was here.

"They went out in the crash." Andri's voice quavered. "I- it was only my second shift; Father thought I was old enough to work, but I—"

I held a sigh in check. "Good lad. You did exactly as you should have." How could I deal with the enormity of what was before me? "You said you heard voices."

"At first, but there's more rocks here than when I left."

Just what I'd been afraid of—a secondary collapse. How many people were trapped back there? Had any of the initial survivors perished in the subsequent rockfall?

"Who was foreman this shift?" That was one Andri should be able to answer.

"Friðfinn."

My heart sank further yet. An elder. Another horrible thought crossed my mind.

"Was his daughter working?"

Andri looked up at me helplessly and gave an uncertain gesture of his shoulders, his lips parted for words he didn't have.

Someone was hurrying toward us; torches were being lit along the path, the light marching toward us as one after another flickered to life. Orlaugur's grey hair stood on end casting strange shadows as he lit the final torch at the base of the ladder.

"Geirfinnur, how long ago did it happen?" he called up to me.

I turned to Andri, who shrugged again before replying, "Maybe a quarter of a span ago? I came to you as soon as I could."

"You did fine." I hoped he heard in my voice what confidence I could muster, because at the moment I didn't have much.

Jeeah help us! I struggled to take in the magnitude of the barricade in front of me as ice wormed its way deeper into my heart. So much stone… Could we get to them at all, or would we only lose more in the attempt?

"Geirfinnur!" Orlaugur called. The shake of his head said that he, too, was at a loss. "Come down; I need to get up there before I can determine what needs to happen."

Andri was already on the ground. When had he left? In a daze I descended the ladder.

As I touched down, Orlaugur rested a hand on my shoulder. "Geirfinnur, we'll find them." He waited for me to turn around and then repeated his words while holding my gaze with the obsidian will in his eyes. "We *will* find them, but you have to keep steady."

I garnered enough confidence from that to nod and take a deeper breath, whereupon enough tension released in my chest that I became aware of what remained.

Pushing back the despair, I asked, "What do we need to do?"

With a final nod, Orlaugur set his hands on the ladder and said, "Let me go up and assess the collapse. When I come down, we'll know best how to carry on."

If only I could face the situation with as much confidence.

* * *

Kristjan stood outside his tent as the last sliver of Tsiki slid beyond the horizon. He was blind in the utter darkness, not able even to see a hand in front of his face. Still, he waited. Within moments, his eyes began to adjust, and pinpricks of light started emerging all over the sky: the brightest first, a few intrepid sparks in the black, and then, too fast to keep track of them all, dozens, hundreds, a thousand more, in every direction that he could turn, the endless expanse of them... The stars shone in all their glory when they didn't have to compete with the moons.

He could relate so well to the stars. How often he wanted to step out of the light of his father or the elders and just be himself, but everyone looked to him to be the next chief.

You'll do fine. Just like the stars.

Something Marko had once said came to his mind. *Handi and Tsiki might outshine the stars, but the stars are still there.*

Marko. He closed his eyes trying to block out the thoughts, but they only came on the stronger.

How can a man who couldn't protect two strong, capable young men protect an entire holdt? What are they putting their trust in? The fool who killed Marko?

With a shake of his head, he turned to the tent. "Tinna has faith in me," he muttered.

The poor girl Who knows what fate that faith will bring down on her head? The voices were too loud, especially out here in the cold all alone.

Crawling into his blankets, he tried to silence his mind, but it was futile. The interminable litany of condemnation slithered through his heart like wasting worms, chewing holes in his spirit and turning it to rotting pulp. He rolled over, but then Bastian's voice added to the din.

You'll suffocate Storeheltur. We'd be better off without you.

It would be so easy to fall asleep and never wake up. By the time someone found him, it'd be too late. As he lay there, he wondered what it'd be like. No more expectations. No one to push him beyond what he could do. Just blessed peace.

Tinna's brown eyes appeared in his vision. *I don't know what I'd do without you.*

His own reply returned to the echo of her words. *I'll be there for you.*

He sighed and flopped onto his back. What kind of man went back on a promise to a pregnant girl?

* * *

Handi's light woke him. With no one around, he didn't bother running a comb through his hair; he simply packed up and started searching for tracks. Whether it was the weather front that had passed while the moons rested or Jeeah's blessing, Kristjan didn't know, but whatever it was, he was thankful that, within a few paces of his camp, he found what he'd been looking for.

By the footprints, the snow fox was a large one; its paws as large as Kristjan's palm. The meat would be enough to feed both of their families for the wedding feast, and he could even take the pelt and make a cape for Tinna—then she wouldn't have to borrow his to come out to Toppur. He hadn't dreamed much of being married, but once, when he was younger, he'd dreamt of bringing his wife a pelt from the hunt—a trophy of his prowess, his ability to care for and provide for the people who relied on him.

It'd been a much younger boy with that dream. He'd thought such a gift would make him feel worthy. But now he knew it never could, and so the happiness that should have come with that thought was vacant, like a summons unanswered, like a friendship forsaken.

Stretching, he pulled the sleigh and gripped his bow at the ready. At a moment's notice, he could release the sleigh and nock an arrow. His main problem would be sneaking up on the creature. His cloak stood out against the white landscape, while the fox would be camouflaged, but it was all part of the thrill of the hunt—or at least, it had once been. Now, he trudged through the snow with one, onerous purpose; complete the task.

A glimpse of motion in the edge of his vision was his only warning. Instincts took over, and he dropped the rope. As he threw himself aside, he pulled his knife, skidding on the snow. The slippery terrain was all that saved him from the jaws that snapped shut beside his ear when a white mass of fur came down on his ribs, pinning him on his side. His knife arm was trapped under him, and the creature's heavy forepaw had landed on his other hand.

A fierce snarl gave a surge of adrenaline to his muscles, but still Kristjan struggled to roll out from under the massive animal. How heavy *was* this thing? Finally, he managed to eke his shoulder out from under its paw, and its hold slipped, crashing down next to him for a moment before it immediately pounced again, this time facing him down squarely, its slavering jaws dripping on Kristjan's face. Kristjan slammed a fist into the fox's head, but that scarcely fazed it; following it up with a second blow at least knocked it off balance—a fractional moment's advantage, but enough for a deft hunter to use. Throwing his shoulders away from its snapping teeth, he thrust the knife into the chest—or tried to; the first blow hit the sternum and skittered off, leaving a bright line of red that did nothing to relieve the danger. A rapid second strike, though, plunged between its ribs and found its mark—piercing the heart.

Hot, viscous, iron-scented liquid spilled over his hand and onto his face. He closed his eyes and heaved the creature off him, shaking off the blood as he stood, looking over his prize. The enormous beast lay in an expanding pool of its own blood.

Kristjan couldn't look away.

The red soaked into the white snow, staining it crimson, and still, he couldn't break away.

The knife slid from his grasp, landing with a soft *slosh* in the bloody sludge.

Kristjan didn't know how long he stood gaping, but when shivering set into his muscles, it pulled him back to himself. He needed to get warm, and to do that, first the meat needed to be dressed. Shaking the images away, he knelt down and skinned the fox. By the time he'd finished, his hands were stiff, and he couldn't feel his fingers.

Normally, he'd have scolded himself for waiting to clean up, but he couldn't put forth the effort to do so. Instead, he scrubbed his hands in clean snow until the snow had a reddish hue. Then he packed the meat on the sled and spread the pelt over it. Lashing it in place, he set out toward the *lofti* that would take him back belowground. He'd probably be back in time for the final meal of the step. A successful hunt.

Just another task. No dreams trudged back to Storeheltur, either imagined or fulfilled.

* * *

Both moons had fallen beneath the horizon by the time Kristjan pulled the sled into the cavern that served as Storeheltur's antechamber. A solitary torch burned in a sconce, a beacon to those seeking shelter. Its light illuminated the rock cavern, but no people. It wasn't late enough for everyone to be in bed, but the place was deserted. Farther down the tunnels, he could make out a commotion. Had a merchant arrived? That would be the only logical explanation for what he heard, but his was the only sleigh parked outside the *holdt*. Besides, normally, at this time of the moonstep, families were in their own homes settling down for the rest.

It'd be easier to have a helper to move the meat than making several trips of his own or stumbling with a tall stack of the packages. Maybe he could find Andri; Marko's brother had always been helpful.

At least, the thought of Marko's family didn't renew the sting of his friend's death, but that made him feel like scum from the water canals.

What kind of friend stops grieving?

He shook the thoughts aside and went in search of Andri.

Everyone he passed seemed to be in a focused sort of rush. Again, he wondered what was going on but didn't bother stopping anyone. Instead, he made his way down the familiar paths to Marko's home.

"*Goðan!*" he called at the curtain.

Telma tossed the tapestry aside, but when she saw Kristjan, her face fell. "Oh, come in."

"Telma?" This wasn't like the woman at all.

"Sorry. I thought you were your father." She buried her face in her hands.

"I came looking for Andri. Is he available?"

She nodded and wiped tears from her eyes. Keeping her voice low, so she didn't disturb the younger ones who were already in bed, she called to her son. When she turned, she caught a sob.

"What's wrong, Telma?" Kristjan walked toward her, unsure what else to do.

"Don't you know?" Her voice cracked.

"I've been out hunting."

At that moment, Andri appeared, rushing in with a hopeful, expectant look that was dashed as immediately as Telma's had been.

"Oh, Kristjan. I thought you might be the chief."

"That's what your mother said, too." Kristjan looked between them quizzically. "Why were you expecting him?"

"We were hoping for news," Telma supplied.

"About the cave-in," Andri finished.

Kristjan's heart, however detached it may have been, still struck his stomach a muted blow. A cave-in was the worst possible accident in the mines—the very reason he'd been all but forbidden to work in them.

"Father's on the other side," Andri went on, hanging his head and digging one toe into the rug. "I got out, but barely."

"I'm sorry, Andri. I didn't know. I was on Toppur hunting. That's why I came for your help. I have meat to take to Friðfinn." At least the words were sincere.

"Frið—" Andri choked and tried again. "Friðfinn was the foreman on duty."

"Oh." Well, that would change things. "Let's get the meat put away, and I'll see what I can do to help."

Kristjan led the way back to the sled, and between the two of them, they were able to haul it down to Tinna's home. At his call, Tinna opened the tapestry. Her mouth dropped, and then she flung her arms around him.

"You're here! Mother, Kristjan's back!"

Ebonney raced into the room. "Thank the stars!" She took a parcel of meat from Andri. "Tinna, let him go so he can put this away."

Tinna's cheeks turned a bright red. "Here, let me help."

Together, they stowed the meat in a cool space with the household's other perishables.

"Do you need me to replenish your ice supply?" Kristjan appraised the area before closing the door.

"If we were keeping to the plans we'd made, I'd say yes." Ebonney wiped her eyes. "But with Friðfinn…"

Tinna rested a hand on her mother's. "Kristjan's here now. We'll figure something out."

"I don't want you going anywhere near there, Tinna! I can't lose you as well."

"You think we've lost…" Andri's face paled. "We've lost them?"

"No." Tinna shook her head vehemently. "I won't believe that until we've tried everything Elder Orlaugur has suggested. They've been there for less than forty-eight spans."

"Forty-eight?" Kristjan blurted, then caught himself. "It must have happened right after I left."

Tinna nodded. "Everyone's been working ever since."

Kristjan remembered other cave-ins. They were few and far between, thank the stars, but every time, Storeheltur came together to save as many as possible.

"And to what end?" Ebonney sniffed. "My Friðfinn's not back. They've not pulled a single person out of that heap."

"*Moði*, please, let me go with Kristjan. There has to be *something* we can do."

"I won't let any harm come to her." The words were out before Kristjan had a moment to think on them, but they lingered in his throat long enough to sour there. They were the same promise he'd made for Marko.

Ah, more promises all parceled up to be slaughtered. Fate for her faith… He shook the thought away. It wouldn't help anyone.

Nor will you.

Ebonney sighed and shook her head. "I… Oh, fine. I see there's no changing her mind, and she'll just keep pestering me like she has for the past two steps if I say no again."

"Thank you, *Moði*!" Tinna flung her arms around Ebonney and kissed her on the cheek. "I'll be careful. I promise." She turned to Kristjan. "Let me grab a few things first."

Beside Kristjan, Andri yawned.

"Oh, you can take your rest now. Thank you, for your help."

The lad gave a drowsy nod and left.

"Have you eaten?" Ebonney glanced up as if realizing for the first time that she had a guest in her home.

"I'll be fine."

His future mother-in-law placed her hands on her hips. "Let me get you something to take with you."

She went to the kitchen and returned with cups of steaming *kaffi* and flat bread covered with *lauflett*, a greenish spread of lichen. Kristjan took them, but only had time to sip at the *kaffi* before Tinna returned. Although her lips were set in a grim line, her eyes were alight as she nodded to him.

"Take it with you." Ebonney refused the mug Kristjan tried to hand to her.

"Thank you. I'm sure I'll need the energy."

"All I ask is that you do your best to bring my husband home." Her voice broke, and she covered her mouth.

"I will."

It was the least he could do for her. After all, it was his future father-in-law that was trapped in the mine.

His mine.

Chapter 16

28 Fjorda, 400 AI

Nothing could have prepared Kristjan for what he saw when they rounded the corner to the mine. Even his frozen heart skipped a beat. "What?"

Lamps mingled their warm light with the aqueous glow of the *yoma*, illuminating roiling clouds of dry, choking dust that clogged his lungs and sucked the moisture from his tongue. Around them, people filled carts with rubble or ore directed by a foreman, while others pushed them down the passageway to dump them in a shaft or into a separate pile for the good ore which seemed much smaller than the useless rocks. The process was unending. The workers' eyes shone starkly from their dirty faces.

Orlaugur's voice rumbled above the hubbub. "Bring the pipe. Let's see if we can get it in now."

Kristjan searched for the elder, and it took a moment before he recognized him on the ladder. His hair stood on end, and dark lines shadowed his eyes. Reinar, Aldar, and Juli climbed the other ladder each using one hand to balance a tube and the other to keep them secure. Kristjan shuddered at their precarious position.

"They'll be fine, Kristjan," Tinna whispered in his ear.

"No one's had contact with them for two steps?"

The thought was enough to set his heart racing. Every member of the *holdt* was raised with the fear of a collapse—each moonstep in the mines was a brush with death. Storeheltur lived with that knowledge, but it was at moments like these that their fears crawled out of the fissures, screaming to be heard, writing itself on their faces with the reality: *it could have been anyone. It could have been me.*

"Easy, there!" Orlaugur steadied the pipe when it wavered, then gestured the team forward once more and guided the end into the rubble.

The metal slid in handbreadth by handbreadth making its way to those trapped. With still a full quarter of its length exposed, it came to a sudden halt, and Kristjan's heart leapt to his throat.

A groan went up in the cavern.

"Quiet!" Orlaugur demanded. Then he stretched out to the end of the pipe and called. "Can anyone hear me?"

A pebble clattered somewhere, and someone wheezed. Orlaugur waited then called again.

After what seemed like forever, his face eased. "How many of you are there?"

A collective sigh, strewn with exclamations of joy and relief, went up, but was cut short as Orlaugur made a sharp, warning gesture with his chin.

"How many?"

He put his ear to the pipe for a moment then called into it again, "Wounded?" The cavern grew hushed while he listened for a reply; he put his mouth to the opening again and called, clearly enunciating and giving time between each word for the echoes to die down. "Clear… pipe… for… supplies."

He waited again for a response, then, with tension in his face, asked, "Any… dead?"

Utter silence descended at that question. But when Orlaugur turned around, his smile lit his face more than the torchlight. "Everyone is alive."

All around Kristjan the people rejoiced. Some collapsed into tears. Others shouted and leapt, embracing the people around them, while yet others lifted their faces to the ceiling in prayer. Tinna leaned into Kristjan. Without thinking, he wrapped an arm around her and pulled her in closer.

"There's still hope." Her voice was muffled. "There's hope."

Hope. When had he last believed in that?

Chapter 17

28 Fjorda, 400 AI

Kristjan released Tinna, but the smile on her face was some kind of balm, even if it wasn't one that could heal him. She glanced about, then pulled him to the rubble.

She aimed for a particular person, but Kristjan couldn't place the girl, not beneath all the grime on her face, but Tinna called to her by name.

"Juli, how can we help?"

"Tinna, it's good to see you. How's your mother?"

"As well as can be expected. At least, I'll be able to take back good news this time."

"That you can. And Kristjan, your father has done so much to help. Can you give him my thanks when you see him?"

"I can do that. Where can we help?" Kristjan asked, hoping as much as Tinna that there would be something useful to do.

"Right." Juli smiled and said, "This way. We need to get the debris into the carts so it can be cleared away. Only so many can go up the ladders at once, but there's another way up along here."

She led them to a narrow path that wound up a slope that Kristjan didn't remember seeing before. At the top, members of the *holdt* worked in several long lines, removing larger stones by passing them down while others gathered up baskets and buckets of smaller stones and carried them between the files. They worked with such speed that Kristjan could hear a steady rhythm of rocks thunking into the wagon beds, punctuated by the less regular clatter of loose stone and dust being dumped in on top.

"You can join in here. As you remove debris, keep at least one of the larger boulders in place." She pointed out a huge rock at the base of where Arny worked. The ground was bare around its base, and Arny was lugging out a smaller one from behind it. Tinna went around to help, and Kristjan was caught by surprise when someone shoved a bucket against his chest.

"Hey, cuz." Bastian scowled, but it wasn't a wholehearted glower.

"Uh… yeah." Kristjan glanced worriedly toward where Tinna was working.

"What? I'm leaving her alone." Bastian pressed again with the bucket, making Kristjan bring his hands up to take it. "I know when I'm not wanted."

"What are you—"

"I might not be the chief's son," Bastian's tone was derisive, but lacking its usual edge, "but those are my friends back there, too. I'm helping."

Dumbfounded, Kristjan stared after him as Bastian picked his way back along the files and joined other men in hefting the shafts of a full wagon, hauling it down the path so that the next empty one could take its place. Suddenly, he spotted Tinna, holding a large stone and looking very pale, staring in the direction Bastian had gone.

Kristjan let the bucket fall to his side and went to her, reaching out to touch her hand. She didn't look at him, but she clutched at his fingers when they brushed hers

"Are you all right, Tinna?"

What a stupid question. The father of her child used and then left her, and her own father might be dead before we can get to him.

She didn't answer. With a heavy sigh, Kristjan handed his bucket off to someone else and stepped in to head up the line beside hers, keeping close to her in case Bastian came back.

* * *

I couldn't believe Orlaugur's words. Our people were still alive! I couldn't say why it surprised me, but after two moonsteps working non-stop with Orlaugur organizing the shifts, helping Josebina get what food we had to the workers, and calming others' fears, I'd lost track of hoping for relief.

Josebina's smile stretched wide, as tears streamed down her face. She hugged Arny, then another woman that I recognized but whose name I couldn't drudge up at the moment.

"They're alive!" Aldar grinned at me, his face streaked with dirt.

"Yes, they are," I agreed, feeling the contagious joy taking hold of me, yet still watching as an outsider.

In reality, I didn't have a close loved one in there. Of the two people dearest to me, one was in this room, the other on Toppur.

My smile slid. *Keep him safe, Jeeah. Please. I don't know what I'd do if harm came to him.*

"He'll be fine, Geir." Josebina had returned to my side without my being aware of it. She rested a hand on my shoulder. "Kristjan will return."

How could she read me so well? And she was to be my wife… it staggered me to think of it.

"Thank you." I covered her hand with mine and marveled. It was so small, and yet she was so strong, and such a comfort.

Orlaugur made his way to us. "Geirfinnur, come with me," he said. "Josebina, you can come as well, if you like."

"Please." I squeezed her hand.

The crowd thronged around us, eager for news from Orlaugur. They clamored for attention, calling out names.

Orlaugur held up his hands, speaking over those who'd not be silenced. "I could scarcely hear the one I spoke to, so I don't know much; they said there are 'five', and when I asked about wounded, they said 'yes.' We need to give them a chance to clear their end of the pipe so we can hear better. Let this hope sustain you. There *are* survivors."

Some muttered, but most nodded their understanding. With Orlaugur closer, I could see the tension he held in his jaw and how his formerly twinkling eyes were dull. Not all was as he wished.

The organized chaos resumed around us with the *clump* of ore-laden rocks hitting the carts, the heart-stopping rumble as a dislodged stone created a miniature landslide that halted all motion, and the careful but eager return to action. A wheel squeaked behind us, and Orlaugur directed us to the side.

After the cart passed, we followed the trail to a side section where benches had been placed for workers to rest during their shift. Orlaugur motioned for Josebina to take a seat; out of deference, I remained standing, but Orlaugur waved me over to join her.

"Go ahead, Geirfinnur. I won't be able to sit still anyway." He offered a smile and shrugged. "A by-product of the stress."

We waited; true to his word, he paced the length of the alcove twice before he spoke.

"Friðfinn lives." The words were curt, as if he was holding back more important information. "They have a few sack meals that they were able to salvage. I remember seeing *lauflett* in the area, so if they can harvest that, it'll provide what they need for food, but water? That's going to be the first thing we try to send in—if anyone's bleeding, they'll be needing it as soon as possible." He paused and faced me. "If only we had a back way to get into the shaft. There's still tons of debris to remove, even if we can deliver enough supplies to keep them alive until then." He rubbed a hand over his face, streaking the dirt.

"But we've made progress. We know they're alive now." I wanted to encourage him just as he'd done for those in the main hall.

I could tell it'd fallen flat when he grimaced, then resumed his pacing. "Then there's the whole reason we were mining so quickly in the first place. I thought there was enough support, but obviously…" He ran a hand through his hair, adding brown to his greying strands and standing his hair even further on end.

Josebina started to raise her hand to comfort him but restrained herself. Orlaugur wasn't keen on touch, and he had a strong sense of propriety. "Elder, you did the best you could with what you were given. We need time, which we don't have, but you'll do what you can."

Orlaugur smiled; it didn't reach his eyes, but the tension left his shoulders. "Thank you, Josebina. I need to organize the removal. Can you take the news to

Ebonney? She deserves to know that her husband yet lives."

"We can do that." I stood and rested a hand on Orlaugur's shoulder. "Thank you for all you do for Storeheltur."

"Don't thank me until we know whether we'll survive for longer than two phases."

"Very well. Just don't take too much of the burden upon yourself. Allow others to help you."

He nodded and wove his way back into the hall.

"Without him, we wouldn't last two steps let alone two phases," I muttered.

"Let's give Ebonney the hope she needs." Josebina took my hand. "I can't imagine what she's going through right now."

I didn't want to consider it either. I wrapped Josebina into a hug and reached in for a kiss.

"What was that for?" she asked with a smile as she snuggled into my embrace.

"I'm glad I have you beside me."

"Ah. The feeling's mutual. I'm just glad you finally awoke to the fact that you needed me as much as I need you."

I laughed. "You need me?"

"More than you realize, Geir." Her voice was uncharacteristically low, measured, and I turned to meet her gaze, almost startled when I found there a soft, intense expression that immersed me in the words.

Squeezing her fingers, I tucked her hand into my own, and she leaned her shoulder against mine. We walked like that all the way to Friðfinn's quarters.

Chapter 18

28 Fjorda, 400 AI

The chime of a bell echoed through the mine, and all around them people gave weary sighs and wiped at their faces, but everyone moved quickly to clear the way for the next shift.

"Here, let me take that one." Kristjan offered, holding out his arms for the stone Tinna had retrieved.

She gave him a weary smile and did as he suggested. With a final glance about, she nodded. Where before it'd been a wall of stone, now a niche had been carved out within which Tinna could easily sit.

"You did a good job." Kristjan stifled a groan as sore muscles lowered him to the floor. "I don't think I could have done as well."

"Yet you did work steadily. Others noticed."

Noticed? "What do you mean?"

"You're the next chief, Kristjan, and you went to work just like everyone else." Her lip twitched upward as she settled beside him. "Though you're not very recognizable right now with all the dust you're wearing."

Kristjan surveyed the others trudging away. "I suppose I look like the rest of the workers."

"Exactly. That says so much about your character."

He wanted to protest. It didn't say a thing beyond the simple meeting of obligation. It was expected; he complied. If she could only see the truth of him—but then, if she did, she'd probably run, horrified, and hope that he didn't live long enough to become chief and spread his failure to the rest of Storeheltur.

Killer. Betrayer. Hypocrite.

"Tinna?" Orlaugur stopped them. "That *is* you. Will you walk with me?"

"Of course, Elder." Tinna nodded. "Is it alright if my betrothed joins us?"

Orlaugur squinted then grinned. "Well, I'll be! That *is* our young chief under all that dust. I wondered why the lines had increased their output. They had Kristjan Jorvarsson watching them."

Kristjan opened his mouth, but no words came out.

"Yes, come along, and congratulations to both of you. I couldn't think of a better match." Orlaugur led them off to the side while the new workers filed in. I think you should know: your father is alive."

Tinna gasped, and Kristjan put an arm around her, as she gasped out, "Thank you, Elder Orlaugur. Thank you!"

"If you are up to it, I'd like to see if there's been any progress on their end; there should be a few minutes of relative quiet while the workers get set up. Do you wish to come with me?"

"Yes, please." Tinna straightened, her eyes sparkling in the torch light.

What would it do to her if they couldn't get to her father in time? Kristjan didn't want to dwell on that thought. She'd already gone through more than a person should ever have to endure; he couldn't fathom the devastation she would suffer if his mine killed the man who loved and protected her. He'd figure out a way to rescue Friðfinn if it was the last thing he did.

Chapter 19

28 Fjorda, 400 AI

The ladder was the worst for Kristjan, but he kept his legs from shaking—for the most part.

Coward! the inner voice chanted as he climbed each rung. At last, he was standing below Tinna on the ladder.

She leaned out away from the cliff to come even with the end of the pipe It really wasn't that far, but to Kristjan's fear-addled brain, it looked like an uncrossable chasm. Meanwhile, Tinna kept one hand on the rung while the other rested on the tube.

Orlaugur motioned to her, gesturing with dirt-crusted hands. "Call into the tube and then wait."

With a nod, she took a deep breath. *"Goðan!"*

Kristjan felt his heart pounding in his chest. This time it had nothing to do with how high he was off the cavern floor. Would they reply, or had things gone terribly wrong in the time between contacts?

"Tinna?" Friðfinn's voice came through tinny and weak, but recognizable.

"*Pabbi*, it's me."

"Ask him how many are still alive," Orlaugur directed.

She called the question down the metal conduit, but they could all hear how garbled the words became in the pipe.

"I… don't… hear," came the response.

"You'll have to ask one word at a time. As much information as you can in as few words as possible," the elder coaxed.

"How… many… alive?"

"Twenty… eight," came the reply.

Orlaugur's face fell, his whole body stricken. Kristjan gave him a questioning look, and the elder shook his head, whispering so that he didn't impede Tinna's conversation, but Kristjan could see in the set of her shoulders that she heard when he said, "That means they've lost two."

Tinna swiped at tears trailing down her cheek.

"Who… d—" she hiccupped and put one hand over her mouth, unable to continue, but Friðfinn understood.

"Mani. Erika. More… wounded… too."

"How… many?"

Orlaugur overrode her question before Friðfinn could reply. "How… bad?"

"Seven. Bad… two. Need… supplies. Healers."

"We're... working... *Pabbi*," Tinna called, her cheeks tight with keeping the tears out of her voice. "Fast. Fast... as... we... can."

"I... know... *kæra*. But... need... sooner. Try... another... way. Through... Verndandi. Smell... matches—"

Orlaugur suddenly shouldered in close, shouting down the pipe. "Smell?"

"Warm... air... through... hole. Smell... ancients. Verndandi," Friðfinn's metallic voice repeated.

"*Pabbi*... how... big?" Tinna called, and Kristjan knew why she asked. Most *lofti*s were too small for a person, even those that ran all the way to Toppur.

"Don't... know. May... be... blocked... passage. Ground... level."

"Can't... spare... scouts," Orlaugur interrupted. "Everyone... working."

"More... wounded," Friðfinn insisted. "Need... help... soon."

Orlaugur sighed, but said no more.

"Tinna?"

"I... love... you... *Pabbi*."

"I... love... you... *kæra*. I... love... your... mother. Tell... her... please."

"I... will."

Tinna came down a rung. Kristjan moved out of her way before she stepped on his fingers.

Once they were down on the cavern floor, she slumped into his arms. He patted her back, not knowing what else to do. Why was she so often leaning on him for support? It seemed to him this occurred more often than not with Tinna. Would she continue to need comfort so frequently once they were married? Just what he needed; another person relying on him for things he didn't know how to give.

"He's alive." Tinna's voice floated up from his chest. "He's alive!"

"Yes," Orlaugur murmured. "And yet two have passed to the halls of the ancients; meanwhile we're still many spans, if not steps, from clearing the way to them, and two more are in danger of death." He huffed and gripped the edge of the cliff face at the top of the ladder he was standing on.

"So we have to move quickly and find a way to reach them with light and supplies, so they can stabilize the others." Orlaugur glanced down, and his gaze moved from side to side, as if he were drawing maps or running calculations around his feet.

"But what about the other way?" Tinna asked. "*Pabbi* said he could smell warm air coming in."

"And he did find an alcove of some sort behind the mine before the collapse," Kristjan said. "Maybe that's where the survivors have been sheltering. But an alcove doesn't mean there's a way to access it."

Orlaugur shook his head. "Listen, Tinna, I understand you want to reach your father, but he said that it's blocked off, too, so we'd just be facing another mass of debris back there. We've already made progress here; we can't abandon it in hopes of finding something faster, and waste the ground we've already gained here."

Tinna turned to Kristjan. "Please?"

"I'm the last person to know what's right or wrong here. I'm sorry, Tinna. I'll have to go with what Orlaugur says."

With a stiff, tiny nod that didn't come back up, Tinna bit her lip. "I… I understand. At least I can take this news back to *Moði*."

"I'll walk with you." It was the least he could offer. Together they made their way back through the hallways, joining the flow of exhausted workers making way for those who'd rested and were ready to renew the effort. At last, they reached her home.

She cupped her hand against his. "Thank you, Kristjan."

"For?" What had he done? He'd refused to send anyone looking for her father; why would she be grateful.

"For being there for me. I'll see you next step." Tinna reached up and placed a kiss on his cheek and then fled through the tapestry. "*Moði*, I'm back. You won't believe what happened."

Kristjan turned and headed back to his own bed. All the while he felt her kiss and saw her pleading eyes. Was it truly unreasonable to think that there might be a passage that would reach the trapped miners? But it was cut off. Yet, the idea plagued him, worrying at his mind like a mouse at a burlap sack.

He tossed and turned, wishing the thought would quiet, but when he finally silenced it, the voice took its place.

Taking away your wife's hope. Ignoring her pleas. Walking her home and dropping her off like she's a parcel of meat. Not fit to be a husband, a chief, even to exist.

"Be quiet!" Kristjan pulled the pillow over his head, knowing it was futile but unable to bear the hounding words that haunted his mind.

Storeheltur would be better off without you. Tinna would be better off without you.

When he could endure it no longer, he rose. He didn't bother changing clothes, but slipped his belt on along with his knife, then headed into Verndandi to the library. It was said that Jorvar and Bergmund had originally set it up. Some of the tomes predated the Impact. As he pushed the door open, the unique scent of the ancients hit his nose—a blend of arid metal, and dust. As he slid the *yoma* into the glass ball sitting in its niche, he again marveled at the ability of the ancients. Not even Iðna had been able to figure out how to recreate such wonders, and he'd tried many times.

The orb magnified the stone's light, illuminating the room. When set in a holder in the middle of a table, it'd give off enough light to read by, but first, Kristjan needed to find the right book. If there was any mention of the passage Friðfinn had detected, it'd be here in the library.

Kristjan ran his fingers along the edges of the volumes. The first section was all scientific journals, left by Jorvar and the other ancients. Then came the histories. The first few described the Impact, then the resultant founding of Storeheltur. Each chief had added their own volume to the stack.

Yours will sit there one step.

The thought was sobering.

As if anyone would want to read what you have to say.

Kristjan blinked, and moved on.

He needed the book with the maps. At last he found what he was seeking; taking it down, he placed it on the table, then set the globe in the socket. The *yoma* brightened at once, flaring to illuminate the whole surface as if it was bathed in Handi's light. Seeing all the other things the ancients had discovered, they may have figured out how to coax more light from the *yoma* as well.

Opening the book, he scanned the pages. The first were overviews of Storeheltur. Then came the mines, and then Verndandi. That's what he was looking for. He spread it out flat and searched each corner. There were several areas he recognized—the main path, the library, the storage shelter, and the council chambers. Several smaller paths and rooms branched off from the main one.

Withdrawing a piece of paper and a charcoal stub, he recreated the map. When he was certain that he could follow the trails back to the main passage, he replaced the volume, withdrew the *yoma* globe and closed the door, leaving the library as he'd found it.

Kristjan oriented himself with his map, and then set out for the first trail. He hadn't gone far before finding a wall of rubble where the path should have been. Was this Friðfinn's blocked passage?

He glanced at the map, working out how close he might be to the mine, but it was far too great a distance to think that they were the same closed tunnel. If, somehow, they were connected, Orlaugur was right that the faster way would be from the front—the amount of debris to fill a passage all the way from the mine to where he stood would be astronomically more to move.

He turned back and made for the next option—a passage that led him down for about three hundred paces and then ended abruptly in a *lofti* that dropped further away below him. At one time there may have been a bridge, but there wasn't so much as a hint of one now. He raised his *yoma* high and gave his eyes time to further adjust to the darkness, but try as he might, he couldn't see anything that hinted at a trail continuing on the other side; the passageway marked on the map must refer to the *lofti*, burrowing down, far further than he could see. If there was a way through to the mine, it'd have to involve dozens of fathoms' worth of rope to make the descent, not to mention the difficulty of getting back up to the level where the miners were trapped.

He retraced his steps. One more to explore before he returned with the news that at least he'd tried. He wasn't perfect, after all. *Just ask Marko*. He sighed. Best to dismiss those thoughts for now. They weren't helping.

The way was dim and lonely. Normally when he traversed Verndandi there were others with him, but now, the paths were deserted. He checked his map. Somewhere up ahead should be the turnoff.

A dark corner loomed in the path, matching up with the branching lines in his sketch. Something skittered away from him—probably an ice rat. They liked the quieter sections of Storeheltur. He'd have to mention this area to the young hunters. As long as people didn't *know* they were eating rat, they would be fine, wouldn't they?

He followed the creature into the dark. When he couldn't see anymore, he pulled out a *yoma* and used it to guide him down the passage, though he quickly lost track of the ice rat. A *lofti* admitted a beam of Tsiki's purple light onto the walls. He left the light behind him and pressed on.

After another hundred paces, the path turned downward. He shivered as a cool breeze tickled his neck, and he wished he'd brought his cloak. If it stayed this chill, or the temperature continued to drop, he'd have to go back for it, but for now, he ducked his chin closer to his body and hunched his shoulders.

For having fallen into disuse, the path was unusually clear. He wondered who would have been last to walk it; would Jorvar have traveled this way? He pictured the father of Storeheltur with a severe countenance and a stern way about him. If Jorvar could see the mess Kristjan had made of his life, he'd scowl and shake his head.

See? What good is it for you to continue to afflict people with your presence? The voice returned. Kristjan almost thought he heard it echo through the tunnel.

Bastian's words joined in. *Storeheltur would be better off without you.*

He shivered. Any time he contemplated finding a way to die, he came away blank—yet another failure.

Kristjan snorted. "I can't even figure out how to kill myself."

The breeze ruffled his hair, and he stopped in his tracks. Something about this temperature sent his skin prickling. There it was: the briefest hint of a sour smell as if food had gone bad. A *bensin* was near. The question was: was it crossable? Would there be a path around, let alone one that could bring him to Friðfinn? But even if it did, what good would it be to bring wounded and weak miners back through the toxic gases?

He sighed and turned back. This too was a dead end. Dead, like Marko, like the pair of miners wounded in the collapse, like Kristjan himself should be. He peered over his shoulder into the darkness. Could he just…

walk into it, never to return? The idea played over and over in his mind. He wasn't sure how long he stood staring into the void before he blinked and took a step away from the sour smell.

The paper rattled in his fingers, and he settled his left hand over his right to still the tremor. His second step was less steady, and he looked back once more.

Storeheltur would be better off. No more desperate, loveless betrothals. No more fatally foolish leadership. No more disappointing the Jorvarssons' legacy.

But what would it be like? He remembered how his lungs had ached when he, Bastian and Marko had stumbled upon another *bensin* so many rotations ago. But could it be that it'd hurt because they'd fought the vapor? What if he just breathed deep, let it fill his lungs, refused to cough it out? He could close his eyes and let it steal his air, let himself drift into sleep with nothing more than a headache before it was all over.

Somewhere, far off, a chittering noise pulled him back into himself, his feet wavering, his weight on his toes, as if ready to move ahead. It'd be so easy.

He shook his head and turned back, a sick feeling abruptly bursting in his stomach. Maybe the library would have more maps that could help.

Kristjan thought he'd set the morbid thoughts aside, but by the time he pulled open the steel door of the library, they were circling him again.

Coward. You have a way of helping the holdt, *and you reject it. Are you so selfish that you can't even do the decent thing and let Storeheltur find itself a better leader?*

"Be *quiet!*" The words echoed around the room.

Kristjan rested both hands flat on the table and took a jagged breath. He had to gain control of his thoughts and his life. Ever since that fateful trip to Toppur, everything had been spinning out of control, from Marko's death, to Bastian's crimes, to his own betrothal. On top of all that, Storeheltur could last only another phase without imports, and he had no idea whether their neighbors had managed to recruit any. Steadying his shaking hands, he found the book that held the map of Verndandi, and set it back on the table.

At least you can face Tinna knowing you've done your best.

But had he?

What if you can't find a way to save her father? What then?

He pushed the thought aside and focused on the lines—lines with clear, objective meanings and no question about their purpose. They were a shelter of certainty in a world where failure and doubt were all he could feel, a place where he could hide from the fickle feeling and vicious voices that dogged him—at least for a little while.

After that… there was always the *bensin.*

Chapter 20

29 Fjorda, 400 AI

"**G**oðan!" Josebina woke me from my slumber. I darted out of bed.

"Easy, Geir; all's well. I brought you something to break your fast." Josebina bustled about the kitchen.

I stood in the doorway to my room, hair probably a tousled mess, and watched her. This was what I'd missed for too many rotations—watching the one I loved caring for me.

She unwrapped a pan, then pulled down three plates. "Go ahead and wake up Kristjan. There's enough for all of us."

"Right." I croaked, cleared my throat, and tried again. "Let me get dressed."

Only then, when she turned and red flooded her cheeks, did I realize that I was standing there in my undertunic and nothing else. Fleeing to my room, I pulled on trousers and boots. What had I been thinking? How could I face her?

"Geir." Her voice, right outside my door, trembled. "Food's getting cold."

This was Josebina. The woman who'd cared for me while I grieved; the one who was to be my wife. Soon we'd share more than meals together. The thought sent heat rippling through my body. How I longed to hold her close!

"I'll be out." I ran fingers through my hair and then came into the main room.

She chuckled and flattened a stray strand down onto my head. "Have I told you I've always wanted to do that?" Her hand rested on my cheek.

My heart raced. "Do you mean to tell me that I've gone off with my hair sticking up for the past eighteen synods?"

Her smile lit up her eyes. "Maybe, but I wouldn't have let you go to an elder meeting in disarray."

"That's comforting to know."

"Well, now, you have me to help you. The people of Storeheltur won't recognize their chief." Again, she chuckled.

I pulled her to me and kissed her. For the briefest of moments she resisted, still turned toward her preparations, and then she melted into my arms, her lips seeking mine. When I pulled away, I could barely breathe.

"Let me check on Kristjan. I don't think he'd appreciate walking in on us kissing."

Josebina ran a hand through her hair. I didn't think I'd messed it up, but then again, I wasn't thinking of appearances when I'd kissed her. I wanted a repeat, but she'd asked me to do something. What was it? Oh, yes. Kristjan.

Right. I'd best wake up my son. How things had changed! He used to wake *me* up with the smell of *kaffi* every moonstep, but recently, I was fortunate if he made it out of bed before the second watch. I took a deep breath to fortify myself and slid the tapestry aside. I blinked.

"Kristjan?" When there wasn't an answer, I went to his bed. "Kristjan."

Nothing. Where was he? The covers had been thrown aside, his pillow tossed against the wall. His cloak still hung on the hook by the door. I shook my head. What now?

As I turned to go, I saw his quill discarded on the desk—normally, the place was as tidy as the ancients' laboratories. Papers lay strewn across it, with pencils on top, and a journal was open. The light illuminated the page and the neat script that was so characteristic of my son.

WHY DID MARKO HAVE TO GO THE WAY OF THE ANCIENTS? IT WOULD'VE BEEN BETTER IF IT'D BEEN ME. I WAS THE ONE IN CHARGE OF THE EXPEDITION, NOT MARKO.

WHY CAN'T THEY SEE THE TRUTH?
A USELESS EXCUSE OF A MAN.

The words were like a slap to the face. I blinked. Useless? Kristjan? He was the most useful person I knew. The elders were eager to set him as chief. If I hadn't been so proud of him, I might almost have been insulted by how ready they were to accept him.

BASTIAN WAS RIGHT.
STOREHELTUR WOULD BE BETTER
OFF WITHOUT ME.

"No!" Oh, Jeeah, please! No!

I scanned the page, seeking more information, context, anything to tell me that my son didn't truly believe the final words in his journal. The thought was enough to send chills and sickness through my body. I'd guarded him so carefully, loved him so deeply, and now… Never again did I wish to watch a loved one die.

"Geir?" Josebina rapped at the door frame. "Is everything all right?"

I tried to speak but only managed a strangled noise that brought her hesitantly into the room. When she saw that Kristjan wasn't there, she came to my side, and seeing where my hand was clenched on the page, scanned the words. She sucked in a breath. "Oh, no…"

"What do I do?"

Josebina set a hand on my upper arm, squeezing—not comfort, but camaraderie. She was with me, strengthening me, even though I couldn't yet feel strong. "First things first, do you think he left with this on his mind?"

"I... I don't know." Who would have thought my son even considered these things?

"Has he been acting any differently lately?"

I thought of the long first watches of waiting for him to wake, of the growing distance between us these past synods. It must have shown in my face.

"Then we need to find out where he is. Would Tinna know?"

Tinna! Of course. Kristjan couldn't seriously be contemplating taking his own life when he was to be wed. But then... if Bastian had been poisoning his mind... and the betrothal hadn't lifted the malaise that'd been hanging over my son, either.

A knot settled in my stomach. "Josebina, can you check with her? I'm going to find my nephew."

"Go take care of Kristjan. I'll be here when you return."

With a nod, I left. The familiar passages led me to my sister's.

"*Goðan*, Froða."

"Geirfinnur!" She gathered the tapestry aside in one hand to greet me. "What brings you here? Gossip has it that you finally decided to take Josebina as a wife." My sister gave me a hug. "Sæbjort would be proud of you."

"You really think so?"

Froða wiped at her eyes as she stepped away. "Of course I do."

"I… appreciate that. You, ah… I suppose you would know."

Her face sobered. "But you didn't come here for my congratulations. What can I do for you?"

"I came to see Bastian. Is he here?"

"In the kitchen; he was just getting something to eat before bed. He had a late watch in the mine recovery."

"Good. I'll ask him how it went." As she headed into the back recesses of their house, I called out, "Is there a place we can speak in private?"

She turned back to me, her head cocked to one side, but as always, she trusted me. With a quick nod, she said, "You can have the place to yourself. I'm about to go on shift—Orlaugur has at least one healer waiting in case we're able to get to them—or even learn anything about their condition."

With that she led me back toward the kitchen where Bastian was just pushing back his cushion from the low table.

"Uncle Geir's here to see you; I'll see you later, Bastian. I should be home before Father, but if I'm not, please tell him where I am."

"Yes, Mother." His tone was only nominally respectful, and his eyes were hard as he regarded me. He waited until she had left before asking, "Uncle, what can I do for you? Have a seat."

I took the seat generally reserved for Mikkael, while Bastian sat back and stared me down. Now that I had my nephew face-to-face, I wasn't sure how to broach the subject. How many times had Bastian and Kristjan sat in front of me for mediation of some infraction or argument. But I'd never seen this stony set to my nephew's chin, or the flint-grey edge to his gaze.

"Uncle Geirfinnur?" Bastian prompted.

I set my chin likewise and met flint with ice.

"I found some of Kristjan's writings in his room."

Bastian tapped an inconsistent rhythm with a finger. "I don't mean to be rude, Uncle, but I've had a long step of hard work and no rest yet. I'd like to go to bed."

"Of course." I straightened and forged ahead. "Why would you have told Kristjan Storeheltur was better off without him?"

Of all the possible reactions, I hadn't expected Bastian to *laugh*. He threw his head back and guffawed. "Do you hear yourself?" He chuckled and shook his head. "This is *Kristjan* we're talking about. The ever-conscientious people-pleaser."

"I know. That's why I want to know why you'd say something like that."

"Look, Uncle. I've said many things to Kristjan. Mostly trying to get him out of his rut, or out of frustration because we're very different people. I don't remember telling him Storeheltur would be better off without him. I *do* know that not everyone's as enamored of him as you are."

I leaned back, trying to find a more comfortable spot on the cushion. "What do you mean?"

"Think about it. What does Kristjan do best?" He paused just long enough for me to process the question, then answered it himself. "Please everyone. But that brings its own list of problems. He'll be able to please one person, but to please another, he'll have to go back on what brought the favor of the first. It's not exactly the stability we look for in a leader."

Bastian stood. "I know you're well-intentioned, Uncle, but really, trying to ask me about something I said to Kristjan who-knows-when?"

"Did you happen to see Kristjan on your shift?"

He snorted. "What's *really* going on? Did the two of you have a spat, and that's why he's gone now and you're here looking for him?"

I recoiled. A spat? "No." The word was weak. "No," I repeated with more force.

"Well, it's nice to know that you're finally seeing what everyone else has known for a long time: the 'perfect' heir has a fault in his stone." Bastian sneered; his farce of a smile downright derisive. "I wish you a good step. Stars know we could use one."

Was this my nephew? I'd always known him to be less diplomatic than Kristjan, but outright rude?

"Bastian," I called out before thinking. He turned as I asked, "What's *really* wrong between the two of you? You've always been friends."

"Friends?" His eyes narrowed. "Is that what you call someone who goes behind your back to steal the girl you wanted?"

"Tinna?" Kristjan had tried to tell me, but I'd never seen any interest between Tinna and Bastian.

"No, Myr." Bastian's sarcasm was thick. "I don't see your son walking around holding anyone else's hand."

"But it was Friðfinn who made the arrangement. I'm sure Tinna is able to stand up to her own father."

"What girl can say no to that man? He's rough and has a hard hand."

I blinked. Was Bastian describing my friend? I'd never seen those traits in Friðfrinn.

"Oh, he might not show them in a council meeting, Uncle, but the elder has a firm grip on his family. And don't get me started about his temper. Why do you think I didn't speak with him about Tinna?" Bastian clenched his fists. "But Kristjan knew how I felt. He promised to leave her alone, and what do I find? He's *betrothed* to her! *My* girl. The one I've had my eyes set on since we were children."

Kristjan had said something about that in those first moonsteps since Friðfinn's proposal, but not again since. What was going on? Was it simply the jealous rivalry for a woman's hand? For some reason, I didn't think so.

"There's more isn't there?"

Bastian bowed his head, pursing his lips uncertainly. "I don't relish speaking badly about someone—especially to their father—but..." He twirled his thumbs.

"But what?"

"I found them together—alone."

Again, I blinked. What was Bastian implying?

"Oh, don't look so innocent, Uncle. You know what I'm saying. I confronted Kristjan, and that's when he told me he didn't care about what I thought. He had Friðfinn's blessing, and I didn't. So don't be surprised if you have a grandchild on your hands sooner than you expect. Now, if you'll excuse me, I need sleep."

He strode from the room, leaving me staring at his back, trying to comprehend the idea of Kristjan—my son—violating Jeeah's law. Had I really so misjudged him? Of course, I wasn't blind to the ways of young people in love; was that why they'd pushed for a ceremony sooner than Ebonney had wanted? It would explain Kristjan's sudden change of mind. He would want what was best for the child, after all.

My heart plummeted to my knees. This wasn't the reason to marry someone, and it was bound to lead to pain at best, resentment and bitterness at worst. If only, I could spare my son the consequences of his own decisions.

Chapter 21

29 Fjorda, 400 AI

Kristjan pushed the map away. If there was an answer, he wasn't finding it here. Another failure to add to his growing list. He sighed. Why couldn't things just *work* right? He'd wanted to take hope back to Tinna, but here, seven spans later, he was just as useless to the rescue efforts as he'd been when he'd begun

With heavy feet, he made his way toward the mine, thinking that perhaps some progress had been made that he could tell her about. When he rounded the corner from Verndandi into the more recently constructed trails, he almost bumped into someone.

"Oh, excuse me. I didn't…" He trailed off.

Bastian's glower creased his face like a glacial crevice. "Of course you didn't see me. You're always focused on yourself."

Kristjan stepped back as if struck. Where had this new degree of hatred come from?

"Bastian?"

"As if you didn't know why I'm angry with you? You have some nerve. What? Did you go crying to *Pabbi* when I said you weren't fit to be chief?"

"Wh- what do you mean?" Kristjan couldn't believe his ears. "I've never repeated anything like that to Father."

"No?" Bastian's scowl deepened. "Then why'd he come to my quarters when I should've been sleeping, demanding an explanation for me wounding his precious son's sensitive little feelings?"

Where could Father have gotten that information? And why would he have confronted Bastian with it? At the moment, Kristjan really didn't even care, but Bastian did. And Bastian was blocking his way.

"I don't know what happened. I was in the library trying to find a way to help the miners—"

"Naturally. Trying to please Tinna and rescue Friðfinn. You disgust me, Kristjan. Despite your failures, you keep going—keep trying. You know washing the outside of a cup does you no good if the inside's filled with grime. That's all you are. You clean up on the outside so people think you're so wonderful, but inside?" Bastian waved a hand as if to ward away a nasty smell. "Inside, you're pathetic, worthless, and selfish."

"How dare you!" Kristjan finally found his tongue. "I'm pathetic? Look at you. How many children do you have running around Storeheltur without a father? Everyone thinks Bastian is an upright citizen—"

"Upright?" Bastian laughed. "Oh, no, cousin. No one thinks that. They know who I am, because I don't go around covering it up. I do what I want and take what I need."

"Without regard for how it hurts anyone else." It was invigorating, experiencing some kind of *feeling* again, even if it was this burning anger. How long had his heart been ice? Kristjan stepped forward into Bastian's space, raising his chin defiantly as he stared his cousin down. "What do you care for the benefit of the *holdt*? You're just looking out for yourself."

Bastian swung, his fist connecting with Kristjan's jaw, sending Kristjan reeling. "Stay away from me with your self-righteous prattle. I don't want to see you again. You take one hit and retreat; you won't even fight back. You're weak. You're no kind of leader. We would *all* be better off without you."

The words hit far harder than the punch. Kristjan leaned against the wall, breathing heavily, as Bastian stomped off. His cousin's footsteps echoed through the corridor as condemning as his words. "

Jorvar would be ashamed. Even he'd think like Bastian does. He'd have the best interests of the holdt *at heart.*

Kristjan hung his head. He found no answers in the grey rock trod by countless feet over the rotations. With a sigh, he tossed his head back.

What use was it? He was worthless. Couldn't even *feel*. No excitement about being betrothed, no dread that his future father-in-law was trapped under tons of rock, no shame for his failures—not even love for his betrothed.

He banged his fist against the rock wall, setting the ridge of his hand to stinging. It *felt* like something. Sensation, crystal clear, ringing through his skin and bone; a bolt of lightning in the grey haze. He punched the stone again, feeling the rip of skin being left behind and the aching shock that ran through his bones like sharp-edged static. He cradled his wrist to his chest, watching with fascination as blood welled from the scrapes, dribbling down his wrist. It made him fearful, somehow, but far greater was the thrill of *feeling*; the experience of being alive was suddenly thrown into stark relief by the pain still rippling through his hand and arm.

A slow smile, two parts relief and one part awakening, spread across his face, pulling at muscles that hadn't been used in too long. He rubbed at the wound and winced, but the renewed pain sent that same flood of vitality through him. It was proof that he was still alive, that he wasn't completely asleep inside.

Kristjan blinked. What was he *thinking*? What kind of person had to resort to hurting himself just to know he was alive? He must be damaged, broken beyond repair.

But we already knew that.

Whatever the other voice might have said was lost in the whorl of the thoughts that followed.

He *was* broken, and people were following him straight into that broken state. He couldn't stop it, but maybe he *deserved* to have every other avenue of feeling anything be cut off, leaving pain as his only option. That seemed right. He'd exist by suffering, and it'd be a just punishment for Marko's death, for betraying his cousin, for failing Tinna and the miners—the retribution that no one else would mete out. The pain was a way to punish his own sins.

That idea was an indescribable relief, at the same time that it sowed a feeling of despair. It wasn't what he wanted; he wished deeply that things could go back to normal, to how they'd been before Marko died and everything fell apart, when he could laugh and explore and hunt and think and pray. But that life was lost now, and rightfully so. This was all that was left to him.

He wiped the blood off on his tunic and went back to his room.

* * *

I was at my wits end when I finally stumbled upon Josebina back at my quarters. In all my wanderings, I'd not seen Kristjan, nor had anyone I'd spoken with. The somber look on my betrothed's face spoke of the same results.

"Where could he be?" I couldn't help pacing. My son was missing; from the last thoughts in his journal, he might already be dead!

"Geir," Josebina said, pulling me into her embrace and running her hand through my hair. "He'll return, and all will be well."

I hoped desperately that she was right. The only other time I'd felt this helpless was when Sæbjort had died in my arms. I wouldn't survive losing Kristjan.

Several steadying breaths later, I could think straight. "Where could he be?"

"Where does he like to go?"

"Of course!" I flung my hands in the air as I spun toward the hook where my cloak hung. "Toppur."

Josebina's smooth brow furrowed. "Toppur?"

"He found a *lofti* when he was young. He uses it to think." I snatched up the thick cape and paused. Kristjan's cloak, which he should have taken with him if he'd gone to Toppur, was hanging beneath mine. Either he wasn't on Toppur, or he hadn't brought it with him. And the only reason, I could think of for him to leave it behind cast a harrowing cloud into my thoughts.

No. I'd find Kristjan whole and well, wrapped in a blanket. He hadn't wanted to disturb my sleep when he went up or didn't plan on being up there long enough to need his cloak. I took it down and gave it to Josebina, who looked at me with somber understand before putting it on.

With Josebina enveloped in Kristjan's fur-lined cloak, I led the way up. I hadn't realized how long the *lofti* was nor how steep. By the time we emerged into Handi's bright light, I was puffing, my air breath billowing like clouds from the buildings of the ancients.

It took me a while to determine that we were alone. Josebina gaped, her eyes bright with wonder.

"Is this the first you've seen Toppur?"

She nodded, her mouth open in a circle.

Despite the grim situation, I smiled. She looked younger and somehow even more beautiful. The lines etched from rotations of worrying over and waiting for me smoothed out.

"It's… It's beautiful, Geir. I see why Kristjan would want to come here to think." She trailed a hand over the bark of the ice tree. "Is this the one Jorvar spoke of?"

"Maybe? Never really thought of it."

"'Despite the weather, it blooms with ice and lichen, providing shelter and comfort for the soul.' At least—" She pulled her hands back to the warmth of Kristjan's cloak. "At least, that's what I've read."

Comfort for the soul. I could use that. Maybe that's why Kristjan enjoyed this place. But there was no comfort to be found beneath its branches, not this moonstep, because he wasn't here now.

"Let's go back. He's not here." My words were harsher than I'd intended, and the lines returned to Josebina's face. "I'm sorry."

"No, you're right. Maybe Kristjan will allow me another opportunity to visit later."

If we could find him. I was more than halfway back, hastening through the passage, before I caught the sounds coming from the other end. Footsteps? Quickening my pace, I followed them the rest of the way down the *lofti* and on to Kristjan's room. Had he returned?

"Kristjan, are you here?" I cried out as I wheeled around the corner and shoved the tapestry aside. "Kristjan!"

He stood, his face pallid, his hand clenching his leather-bound journal.

"I'm here, Father."

I didn't care whether he wanted a hug or not; I enveloped him in my arms, but he didn't return my affection. In my embrace, he was as stiff and motionless as the statue of Jorvar in Verndandi.

"Are you all right?"

His eyes were devoid of their usual life—their attentiveness, their keen observation and clever curiosity.

"I'm fine."

Even his voice didn't sound right.

"Are you sure?" I held him out at arm's length and searched his face.

"I said, I was fine. What more do you want?" He pushed me away. "Were you meddling with my things?"

"Meddling?" I repeated. What was he talking about?

He held up the journal. "Did you snoop through the whole thing? If so, you know all about my failures.

Maybe now you'll believe me and tell the council I'm not ready to be chief." He turned and flopped down on his bed.

"Kristjan..." It was all I could think to say. Where had this come from?

"That's my name."

"What's wrong?" My heart felt like it was being ripped out of my chest like mined ore.

My son stared up at the ceiling, his body limp on his bed. When he spoke, his voice was back to the dead sound he'd been using since Marko's death.

"You ask, but do you really care to hear? I tell you, but you don't listen. I'm tired. Let me sleep."

Tired? "It's not even the second watch!"

"And I was up through the late watch looking for some other way to get to Friðfinn. Like everything else I do, it was a failure." He closed his eyes, effectively cutting me out of his life and ending the discussion.

At least he was home—and alive. If he'd...

I cut off the thought and made my way back to Josebina's comforting arms, feeling like my soul was suddenly threadbare and ready to rip in two, but I knew I wouldn't give up. I couldn't, I couldn't conceive of a world in which I'd let this separation, this wounding of his soul, stand. He was my *son*, and if the sheer depth and ferocity of one person's love could save another, then somehow, I—we—would figure out how to help Kristjan.

* * *

Kristjan waited until his father's footsteps faded. At least, Father hadn't lied and denied prying into his life. What all had he read? And why would he have told Bastian? That was the real question, but again, his heart had frozen over as surely as the ice tree outside the *lofti*.

Maybe that was the way to escape his life. He could go up to his special spot and think. He could be free of the condemning voices forever and find rest in the place where he felt most at peace.

Contented by the formulation of a plan, he smiled but didn't move. His limbs felt as heavy as an ore cart filled to the brim. Maybe after a nap, he'd have the energy to climb the *lofti*. Father wouldn't think anything of him leaving; he'd take his cloak so that there'd be no questions, then shed it when he was ready.

At last, the elders will recognize the disappointment you are. He could see Bastian's grin and almost spoke out loud to silence the voice, but there was nothing to argue. It was right

"I'm a disappointment," he whispered.

Yes, you are, the familiar voice persisted, its words somehow both condemning and seductive. *Always have been—second to Marko all along. Then you killed him. The better of the two of you. What makes you think you deserve any peace?*

"I don't." He rolled over.

Maybe he should go now while he still had the gumption to do so, but turning over had taken what little energy he'd had left.

Storeheltur needs a strong chief, a man like Bastian or Marko, not a wimp who can't even get out of bed. Who do you think you are? You condemn those who take action and get what they want and kill the one who would have made a better chief than you.

The image of Marko's still body and the stark contrast of blood on snow returned to his vision. This time, though, Kristjan remembered something new—the pick—the one that had killed his best friend—had been a birth-step gift from Kristjan.

See, you did *kill him. Not only did you take him on the journey, it was your gift that did the deed. It might as well have been your hand.*

Horror fell over him like a shroud. He was surprised to find that, deep within, he'd held onto some hope that everyone else was right, that it was nothing more than an accident, but this revelation rooted out that hope and threw it into a fire.

And yet, through all these thoughts, nothing brought him above the surface of the morass that held him under; nothing broke through; he couldn't feel remorse or anything beside the growing weight of understanding—knowing what thorough harm he'd done to everyone he'd ever tried to help. What sort of friend was he? What type of agony had Marko felt as he died? Something dug into Kristjan's ribs, and he reached over to tug it out from under himself—his knife. He'd put it on out of habit when he'd gotten up. He worked the sheath off his belt and then pulled the blade from the leather.

It'd been a gift from Father when he'd seen his twelfth rotation.

You're a man now, son, Father had said. *You're old enough to carry a man's tool. This was passed on to me from my father, and from his father to him all the way back to Jorvar himself. Care for it well and you can hand it on to your son.*

Over the rotations, it'd stayed as polished and sharp as the step his father had handed it to him. A simple rasp of the stone had brought the edge back to life when it'd dulled, but that was never as often as other knives in Storeheltur. Whatever magic the ancients had used to create it, it was an exceptional blade.

Now as Kristjan examined his reflection in the blade, he remembered the feeling in the hall after meeting Bastian. His body still reacted to pain. He turned the knife around and fiddled with the edge. Always so fine. His finger slid along it, leaving a red line. He hissed at the keen, burning pain, his heart racing, but a moment later the sense of alertness and vitality started coursing through him once more, and he took what felt like his first deep breath in spans.

He used the edge of his tunic to sop up the drop of blood that landed on his blanket. He'd be able to explain away a nick on his finger, but not if it was any more noticeable than that. There had to be a way to achieve

the euphoric rush without leaving marks for the world to see—he'd have to hide them. He rolled up his sleeve and ran the blade across his forearm—savoring the sensation that flowed with his blood. One line, another, another—he breathed deeply, gritting his teeth for another.

When he tried to make the next cut, he found that his thumb was slick with blood, and he was abruptly aware of the sheet of crimson spreading over his arm. So much! How badly had he hurt himself? Was it dangerous? Did he need a healer? Suddenly frantic, he swiped away the red, but it welled up too quickly to make out how deep the cut might be. Snatching up the first piece of fabric he could find—a discarded pair of trousers—he pressed hard against the wounds, trying to staunch the bleeding. His heart raced, quickening the flow. He panted, his eyes tearing in fear while silent sobs worked their way in and out of his open mouth— they had to be silent, or Josebina and his father might hear, and he couldn't let them know. They wouldn't understand; they'd be terrified. They'd treat him like a child; he'd have to see the pity and horror in their eyes. His father would treat him like a fragile cup, and his life would become even more restricted than it already was.

What does that matter? You're living for the next round of pain; who wants to protect that kind of existence? Do you really think you deserve to live when your best friend *is dead by your hand? Your whole life is in blackness. It's not worth carrying on. This proves it—you have nothing to live for. You're a hazard to the ones you love; spare them any further suffering, and end your own. Everyone wins.*

Within a few moments, the bleeding had slowed, and he was able to lie back, tucking the bloody trousers under his arm to catch what still oozed out. Closing his eyes, Kristjan waited for his body to calm, intensely aware of the hammering of his heart, the tightness in his chest. Tears he didn't understand squeezed out from beneath his eyelids. He didn't want to die.

I don't want to die.

Neither did Marko, and you killed him, but you won't take your own life?

I don't want to… I don't want to…

But you don't want to live, either. If you ever manage to kill yourself, it'll be by accident. That's how pathetic you are.

Kristjan rolled over and huddled into his pillow, letting the voice say what it would. He couldn't fight it anymore.

Chapter 22

30 Fjorda, 400 AI

Kristjan stood when he heard voices.

"He's in his room. I'll go get him. Have a seat and wait here."

Who was Father talking to, and why was there such tension in his voice? But then, why wouldn't there be? The *holdt* was surviving on a thread, and miners' lives were at stake. Kristjan bowed his head with the weight of it all.

Kristjan frantically searched his room for any stray smears of blood; he found none, but just to be safe, he threw his covers over the pillow and pulled his sleeve down to conceal his wounded arm.

Father poked around his bedroom curtain. "Oh, good, you're still up. You have a visitor."

"Who?" Kristjan kept his voice low. Best not to appear rude.

"Your betrothed."

Tinna? What did she want?

Kristjan nodded, and slipped past Father. Tinna sat on the edge of the chair, her face pale. She rubbed her hands together, then smoothed down her tunic over her trousers. The dust that puffed from her clothes at the touch led him to conclude that she'd been at the mine. When she saw him, she bounded to her feet and ran to him, clutching at his wrist. He tried not to grimace at the waves of pain it sent through the fresh cuts.

"There's been a second collapse."

Father strode toward the door, and when neither Kristjan nor Tinna moved, he turned. "You're coming with me."

"No, Geirfinnur. I want to look into something my father suggested. He said there was another way."

Kristjan's heart sank. He'd already searched for that way without luck.

"I want Kristjan to help me." She looked up at him, her eyes pleading as much as her words.

"Fine." Father's words said one thing, but his eyes narrowed. What was that all about? "Remember that you're not yet wed. Honor Jeeah with your ways."

Tinna's cheeks flamed to life, and Kristjan dropped her hand, his stomach performing a small flip.

"Father—"

He held up his hand. "Kristjan, I was a young man once as well. I understand what it's like."

Tinna trembled beside him.

"You know nothing about us, Father, if you think—
"

"Not now, Kristjan. I'll discuss things with you in private when we both return home. For now, I have another emergency to care for. All I ask is that you remember Jeeah in your actions."

As if he wouldn't! Kristjan wasn't Bastian. Bastian would take advantage of the situation, as he'd done in the Garður.

"Geirfinnur." Tinna's voice was steady, almost commanding.

Father turned back to her.

"I trust Kristjan with all of my heart. Not once has he done anything that he should be ashamed of. And you, of all people, ought to have known that." Kristjan was shocked at the reprimand in her voice. He'd never dare to speak so sharply to his father! And from his father's expression, he was just as surprised by the scolding tone as Kristjan, but he answered with good grace, though his words were characteristically firm.

"My apologies, Tinna, but sometimes, when you're betrothed or even before, you dismiss propriety and take early what should be waited for."

"And as I said, that is *not* Kristjan."

With a final glance at the two of them, Father nodded and left. Where had that come from?

Tinna squeezed his wrist. "Will you help me find the back way into the mine?"

"You honestly think it exists?"

"It has to. It's the only way. Otherwise…" She covered her mouth with her hand. "Otherwise, Father's lost along with the rest of them."

Kristjan pulled her to him. "We won't let that happen."

She rested her head against his chest for a moment. "I knew I could count on you."

Poor little wretch, putting such confidence in someone who's already thinking about leaving her behind along with the rest of the world! Her faith in you will break her heart when you finally take the coward's path out.

With her here in his arms, it was easier to push the condemning voice with its alluring idea aside, but he knew it'd return in force when she was gone.

Together, they walked hand in hand through the hallways toward Verndandi. He didn't have the heart to tell her that he'd already searched to no avail, but the library was the best place for answers. Maybe she'd discern something he'd missed.

When they came to the library, Tinna paused. "It always fills me with awe when I go in here. It's like the ancients are looking down on me. Will I be found wanting?"

"You?" Kristjan pushed a stray strand of hair behind her ear. "You're perfect, just the way you are."

She bit her lip. "Not if men touch me the way Bastian did." She shivered. "Even your father thought you were going to do the same."

"Tinna, he's wrong. I'll not hurt you."

"I know, but…" Tears filled her eyes and she brushed them away. "Is it wrong to *want* someone to hold me?"

"No. Father holds Josebina. I've seen them together when they don't realize I'm watching. He's even kissed her." He didn't know why he told her this, but it seemed right.

"Yet, you've…" She glanced away.

"I've what?" Kristjan tipped her head back up.

"You've never kissed me of your own accord." Red again filled her cheeks, which only heightened her beauty.

"We've kissed, Tinna."

She bit her lip. "Yes, but that was me. Do you not want me?"

That kiss had proven how base he could be. He wanted her, but he'd not use her to sate that craving.

Tinna slid closer to him until he could feel her heartbeat and see the pulse of it in her exposed neck. How could he tell her no?

With slow movements, he leaned down and kissed her. At the contact she immediately caved into him, her arms circling his neck, her fingers running through his hair. He forgot all else, but the feel of her and his desire, until he pushed her back to the library door and pressed against her body. Her squeak of surprise jarred him back to himself like the sting of an *edla* lizard. He jolted, dropping his hands, breaking the kiss, staggering apart from her.

Tinna reached for his hands, but he shook his head. What had he been thinking?

You weren't. The voices were back. *You were just taking what you wanted—who are you to condemn Bastian when you do the same thing, given half a chance? You two are family, all right—two wheels on the same cart.*

He hung his head and turned away. "I..." He tried to gain his breath, his voice. "I'm..."

"Don't!" Tinna cried. Tears spilled down her cheeks. "You..." she sobbed. "Is it because Bastian already had me? Is that it?"

"Tinna, *no.*" How could she think this was *her* fault? "It's me. I..." He faltered, but she deserved the truth, after all she'd been through and the obvious anguish he was causing her now. "I want you, but in the wrong way. It has nothing to do with your soft spirit, your love of your family, or the way you help those around you. It's..." His eyes trailed to her lips and started down her body before he closed them for a breath and forced his gaze back to her face. "You're beautiful. I want you for that. But that's no better than what Bastian did." Kristjan clenched his fists at his side. "I won't be like him."

She turned away from him and opened the door he'd thrust her against, her features a mixture of rage, fear, and grief. "And you're so terrified of being like him that you won't even touch me? You can't possibly see how this might be *different*?"

"I just—"

"Let's just find Father."

"Tinna." He reached for her, but she pulled away.

"Find my father, Kristjan."

Ah, she finally saw your cowardice, and now she's angry. Angry at the man she's now bound to. Once you're married, she'll feel just as abandoned as Bastian left her, but she'll have no alternative anymore. Unless of course—

"Shut *up!*" he growled under his breath as he entered the library.

Tinna had already lit the *yoma* lamp and stood gazing up at the bookshelf. Her shoulders shook, and he wondered if she could even read the titles of the volumes through her tears. He wanted to assure her, somehow, but he didn't want to lie, either—he'd been selfish, and he knew it.

Ignoring all else, he hefted the tome he'd used earlier that moonstep from its place on the shelf and opened it on the table. He flipped to the section that mapped Verndandi and slid his own map from his pocket where he'd stored it.

"What's this?" Tinna was right behind him, her voice low, no more evidence of tears in the carefully even tone.

"I couldn't sleep and came here. These are the passages, I've explored. Those are deadends. This one led to a *bensin*."

She shivered. "A *bensin*? How far in did you go?"

"I'm fine." He didn't confess that he'd considered wandering in and not coming back out.

"Was it deep?" Her question brought him up short.

"I don't know. Why?"

"Maybe there's a way around it. Will you show me?"

"Tinna," he said, "you can't do something that will harm you—or the little one."

"No?" She cocked her head. "Who says? Bastian doesn't want this child. What makes you think I do?"

He sucked in a breath. "But… you can't kill him."

She traced the way on the map. "I suppose not."

Kristjan took a chance and reached out for her. His hand settled around hers. "Tinna, I gave you my word that I'd protect you and your—our—child. Don't you believe me?"

Hard to protect them from Fivku, but you were already considering that.

He shut the voice out.

"But why? He's not yours. Won't you despise him as much as I despise what happened to me?"

"It's not his fault. None of this is. It's not yours either, for that matter." He allowed his hand to travel up her arm and cup her chin. "You're strong, caring, and attentive—everything a child needs in a mother. If there's someone in this scenario who's out of place, it's me. I'm not—"

She shook her head decisively, and the command in her tone surprised him. "Don't. I've heard you tear yourself down all my life. You say you're never good enough, but that's not true. Who brought back food for us to survive when hope was dying? Who found the mine that will sustain us for rotations to come? Who was kind enough to betroth a used-up girl?"

He kissed her fingers. "Not used-up. A girl with backbone and grit like I've never seen before. A girl the ancients would be proud of."

"Well, if that's the case, then show me this passageway. It *has* to lead to Father."

With a nod, he led the way. For some reason, it didn't seem so far from the library with Tinna beside him. Their footsteps echoed down the passage, a testament to the barrenness of the place. Far sooner than he'd expected, they stood at a chasm, shivering in a chill breeze wafting across.

"This is it." She squinted into the darkness. "How far across?"

"I don't know."

She lifted a *yoma*. "I can see the other side."

Tinna knelt at the edge of the cliff. Kristjan put a hand on her shoulder.

"It's not deep, and the odor isn't very strong—the *bensin* mustn't be very close by. My guess is the gasses have settled here beneath us, but they didn't originate here. That means it'll be fine as long as we don't linger here."

But it was a sheer drop. His knees shook with the thought of scaling it in the dark.

"Kristjan, you can stay here."

Oh yes, leave your betrothed to venture into danger while you sit here mewling over a little crack in the ground.

"No, I'll go along."

The *yoma* added sparkles to Tinna's eyes, as she said, "You know, you're wonderful. I couldn't have asked for a better husband."

He clenched his teeth shut and knelt beside her. "Where do we descend?"

"There." She pointed.

A narrow path wound down and across. If it hadn't been so close to the edge, Kristjan wouldn't have been nervous, but it was barely broad enough for a single person.

Tinna took his hand and led the way. He kept his eyes on her shoulders, and somehow his limbs obeyed him, despite shaking. As they shuffled across, the odor became stronger, especially at the lowest point of the path, but nothing that was too unbearable or dangerous.

Once on the other side, Tinna kept his hand. "Where now?"

Kristjan took a steadying breath and surveyed the forking path before them. One way led up and the other off to the left.

"I think we'll have to explore them both." He tightened his grip on her hand as she pulled away. "Together. You know as well as I the dangers of exploring alone, and besides, if you're right, we might encounter a *bensin* somewhere above."

She nodded and bit her lip. "You're right. Which direction?"

"You choose." It was the least he could do for her.

"As far as I can tell, the mine is off in that direction." She pointed to the right. "That means, we take the upward path first."

The *yoma* cast enough light to walk, but no more, and as they left the better-lit passages behind, the deep, cave-black darkness fell around their small illuminated circle. It would've been easy to think they were the only ones in Storeheltur. Had anyone traversed these paths since Jorvar?

They traveled upward until Kristjan wondered if they'd come out in Toppur. The air cooled, confirming his suspicions, and the darkness began to thin until he spotted a ray of Handi's light streaming in through a *lofti*; when they were closer, they could feel the icy air spilling in from above. The light, though, shone on a metal door, its make strongly reminiscent of the one at the library in Verndandi—something left over from the ancients. It was rimed with frost, and Kristjan doubted whether the handle would have the freedom to move even if he wanted to chance it.

"Where does it go?" Tinna shivered.

"My guess is it's an exit to Toppur. I'm not willing to open it without cloaks, though; that ice on the door is only a hint of what's on the other side."

Tinna's teeth chattered, though Kristjan managed to keep his jaw still.

"Let's get you out of here." He turned her around. "We'll explore the other way."

She nodded, but her eyes didn't shine like they had before.

When they came to the fork, Kristjan led the way down and to the left—away from the mine. Tinna kept looking over her shoulder.

"We'll figure something out."

"Will we?" She tightened her grip on his arm.

Kristjan stopped and turned to her. In the light of the *yoma*, her face was painted with stark shadows, but he could still read the anguish there.

"Tinna, I promise, I'll do my best to find a way to your father."

A single tear slid down her cheek. He caught it on his thumb.

"Thank you." She sobbed, and he drew her into an embrace. "I don't know what I'd do without *Pabbi*."

"You're the strongest girl I know. You'd pull through, but you won't have to. We'll free him and the others. I promise."

She shuddered, then slowly calmed. As she wiped her tears, she looked up at him. "Thank you. Thank you for understanding."

"Of course; you can't hold it together indefinitely."

"But I can't be like *Moði* either."

"I see."

And Kristjan did. How often had he seen Ebboney's outbursts; they'd always seemed extreme. The more time he spent with his betrothed, the better he came to understand her. What would he learn about her in a lifetime together?

A lifetime? You'd tie her down to your miserable self for that long?

Kristjan wanted to tell the voice to be quiet, but he couldn't deny the truth—she was better off without him. But what would be the gentlest way to set her free?

You know, but you're too cowardly to follow through.

Chapter 23

30 Fjroda, 400 AI

Kristjan focused away from the girl in his arms and the annoying voice in his head. He squinted. Was that another split in the path ahead of them?

"Tinna, let me see that *yoma*."

She dropped it into his hand. He held it aloft and moved forward, but stumbled. Holding the light lower, he found that the ground was littered with rocks, but the path *did* fork. The right-hand passage turned back on itself—back toward the trapped miners.

"That..." Tinna caught her breath, but already her eyes shone anew in the light of the *yoma*. "That's the right direction."

"Let's mark the way back, and then we'll try this passage." He might want to rid Storeheltur of himself, but he didn't want to take Tinna with him.

After fashioning a clear arrow from the loose stones to point them home, he led the way down the path. The other passages had been clear though unused. This was fraught with debris as if the stones had been shaken from their rightful places, though Kristjan didn't see the fracturing or shifting layers that would've warned of instability.

After a hundred paces or so, the rubble cleared up, leaving the path easier to follow, and Tinna immediately sped up, tugging at his arm. "Come on, Kristjan!" she urged, and he hurried to keep up with her. Just as suddenly as she'd begun, she stopped, so abruptly that he had to put a hand out against the wall to avoid crashing into her.

"What's wrong?"

The path went on ahead, but Tinna was looking at a steel door similar to the one that let out onto Toppur, but this one had no handle.

"Is… is this it?" she whispered.

"The only way to find out is to call out or knock."

Tinna looked so small and fragile in the light of the *yoma*. Without thinking, Kristjan wrapped his arms around her waist from behind and settled his chin on her head.

"You're not alone. Whatever comes our way."

She sagged into him, and he planted a kiss on the top of her head. Tinna gazed up at him, her eyes brimming. Kristjan longed to ease the pain. He kissed her forehead, and she closed her eyes, letting him continue down over her lashes. When he pulled away and moistened his lips, he tasted salt there.

"I'll be here."

More promises to break! Are you trying to set a record before you abandon her?

Kristjan wanted to shut the voice out, but it was irrefutable and persistent; in a moment of rebellion against that despair, he chose what he wanted. He nudged Tinna around to face him and looked into her liquid brown eyes.

"Tinna, no matter what we find here, this remains." He leaned down and kissed her.

All of his confusion and passion mixed together, and he pulled her as close as he could. She melted against his body. When his breath ran out, he pulled away but ran his hands through her hair. Then he knocked on the door behind her.

The sound was a dull thud that barely carried down the passage; he doubted anyone on the other side could have heard it. He pounded against the metal with bruising force, sending stinging pain through his hand, but the sound was more muted than he wanted or expected. However, this time there was a faint echo. Tinna scrambled forward, but he held her back.

"Easy, that was only my knock. It wasn't a reply."

She slumped against him. "I can't take this."

"Yes, you can. You're stronger than you think."

A third set of blows yielded no more answer than the first two.

Tinna covered her face with her hands.

"We're not even sure this is the right place." Kristjan gathered her again in his arms, watching the door, waiting.

She nodded, and her hair tickled his nose. "You're right, but I can't get away from the feeling that this is it. Orlaugur said the mine side had rocks piled in front of it. Maybe *Pabbi* and the others cleared it away and found the door."

He didn't have the heart to ask her why they didn't reply if that was the case. Instead, he motioned further down the path.

"Let's see what we can find that way."

With a lingering look, Tinna nodded. "I... I suppose."

The trail wound up and then down again. Several more doors lined the way, some opening into storage rooms, while others wouldn't budge. Those they called through and knocked on, but to no avail. At last, they came to a solid wall—the end of the path.

"Come." Kristjan took her hand, not missing the defeat in her shoulders and the yearning in her eyes as she stared at the dead end. "It's time to head back. We'll need food, and your mother will be worrying about you by now."

He didn't add what his father must be thinking.

Tinna nodded but stilled him with her free hand on his chest. "Promise me we'll stop at each one on the way back."

"Of course."

Her eyes lit up. "We need to call through the bottom!"

What was she thinking?

"*Pabbi* said the air coming through the bottom of the passage smelled of the ancients. That means there's a crack we can communicate through."

It was worth a try.

At the first door, Tinna crouched down and yelled in. "*Goðan*! Anyone there?"

They waited for what felt like an eternity, but there was no reply.

"It's the first. There are many more." Kristjan rested a hand on Tinna's back. "Besides, the open doors here are all storage rooms."

She nodded and stood. "Let's go to the next."

As Tinna stood, Kristjan paused. Had that been a sound? Probably an ice rat. Yet, there it was again—a dull clank.

"Tinna," he whispered her name, straining to hear where the noise had come from.

She turned toward him, but her wrinkled brow smoothed as her eyebrows shot up. They stood immobile in the middle of the passage, straining to hear.

Another metallic thud was followed by a weak, "Is… there?"

Tinna rushed to a door they'd missed. It was partially hidden under dust and grime.

She dropped to the ground and cupped her hands around her mouth, yelling through the crack at the bottom. "We're here!"

"Help! We're trapped."

"Yes." Tinna choked, then controlled her emotions. "You were in the mine with Friðfinn. This is his daughter, and Kristjan Jorvarsson is with me. We'll get you out."

"Praise the stars!" The man coughed. "Friðfinn said this would work. Can you open the way?"

"Ingvi, is that you?" Tinna asked.

There was another cough. "Yes. Can you get this open?"

Kristjan searched for a handle but found nothing. The metal was smooth and featureless under all the dust, so he asked, "Do you see a latch on your side?"

"No." Ingvi's voice was strained. "We thought it was on the other side."

"We'll figure it out." Tinna paused, and when she spoke again, her voice was quieter. "Please tell my *pabbi* we'll find a way."

"I… I will."

Tinna sat on the floor with no sign of rising, her fingertips against the metal, as if she could will the door open by sheer force of resolve. Kristjan couldn't leave her there, and if they stayed much longer, his father would send a search party for them.

He knelt down. "Come, Tinna. We need to go."

She nodded but didn't move, other than the shaking of her shoulders. Kristjan wrapped his arms around her.

"Shh. As you said, we'll figure it out."

"B… but…" She swallowed back a sob. "But *Pabbi*…"

"I know. We'll get him out."

Tinna gripped his shirt and sobbed.

He stroked her back and hair until she calmed. Then he lifted her tear-stained face and said, "Listen to me. I don't know how, but we'll find a way. I promise."

"You're sure?"

"Well, we are to be wed, and that can't happen without your father, right?"

That brought a wavering smile to her face. "Thank you, Kristjan." She pulled his head down to her and kissed him until he lost his balance and pulled away.

He offered her a hand up and wiped her tears with the other. Her smile was a reward that almost made him feel again. Almost let him smile back

* * *

Tinna pulled Kristjan through the corridors, eager to return to share the news. He didn't have the heart to remind her that this route was just as blocked as the other. She smiled and waved at people as they hurried on, until they all but ran into his father.

"Chief Geirfinnur!" Tinna bounced on the balls of her feet. "We've found them!"

"*There* you are." Father's expression was as cold as the stones on Toppur.

Tinna instantly stilled and just as abruptly deflated, cringing down next to Kristjan.

"We've been looking all over for you, Kristjan. I want a word with you. Tinna, you may go home."

She bit her lip but shook her head. "I… I need to be there with him, Chief."

Father's expression didn't ease; if anything, it grew harder. "Very well."

He led the way to their quarters. Tinna clung to Kristjan's arm. Was she trembling?

"It'll be fine." he whispered to her, but she still shivered.

Father thrust the tapestry aside and gestured them curtly to the couch. Tinna kept Kristjan's hand in hers, and he sat next to her.

"Where have you *been*?" Father didn't wait for a reply. "Do you know how long it's been? People will talk. You're a betrothed couple wandering into unknown depths of Storeheltur alone." His scowl deepened, and he leaned forward. "Kristjan, you should know better. I've *raised* you better."

"Father, we went to the library and then explored the back entrance to the mine."

His father threw up his hands, shaking his head. "It doesn't matter what you *say* you did. It's the appearance that matters."

"Yes, that sounds just like you. I've heard it my whole life: 'You're a Jorvarsson; you'll be chief next. Make sure everyone knows how perfect you are.'" Kristjan rose, his fists at his side. "Well, I've done it. I've impressed everyone, Father—everyone but *you*!"

Tinna pulled on Kristjan's hand, but he paid no heed. It felt good to finally make Father hear what he'd been burying for rotations upon rotations.

"I was the one who led the first expedition to bring food back when it was running short. *I* was the one who discovered the new mine, and *I* was the one who took Tinna beyond where anyone has ever traveled in Verndandi and discovered the back entrance that brought us straight to the trapped miners. All that's not good enough for a Jorvarsson. No, I need to do it all while keeping up appearances that all's right with the world when nothing's right. I've put the mask on long enough, Father. I'm done with it. No more 'appearances.' Let people think what they will. They already do."

Father paled and took a barely-noticeable step back. "Kristjan?"

"Yes, Father. I've had enough. If I can't please everyone, I might as well not be here. Storeheltur would be better off without me."

Tinna's hand slipped, but she tightened her grip, her nails biting into the raw flesh on Kristjan's wrist, bringing a fresh wave of pain and vitality that he desperately needed.

"Kristjan, *never* say that again." Father pressed forward, his finger pointing at Kristjan. "You are loved and *needed*. You'll be the perfect chief after me. In fact, other than this incident, I've never feared you'd do any wrong—never suspected you of it. That's why I'm concerned. You disappeared on me earlier this step, and now you take your betrothed into the darkest areas of Storeheltur—alone."

"Enough, Father. Out with it. What do you think I did to her?"

Tinna stood, coming to Kristjan's side, and steadied her voice. "You should address me, too, not discuss me as if I couldn't hear you."

"Of course, Tinna, but," Father lowered his voice. "It's just that when two people are betrothed, they often…" He rubbed the back of his neck. "They can want things—good things. But things that should wait…" He licked his lips. "Things that should be… had… only after they're wed. When they're alone, the inhibitions that normally keep the… that keep such desires at bay… well…"

Kristjan watched his father struggle and felt a grin stretching out his mouth. If Father was going to accuse them of indecency, he could at least enjoy watching him flounder trying to verbalize it.

"Well, let's just say, it can become more than a person can bear, and they do things they wouldn't normally do." Father pushed the words out in a rush.

Tinna forged ahead, having found courage from some place Kristjan couldn't fathom. "And you think we gave in to those… desires?"

Father brushed his foot across the carpet, watching the pattern it made. "I'm not saying… I mean."

"Yes, you were." Kristjan joined Tinna's defense. "You all but said I would take her when we left."

Red crept up Father's neck. "I… well… I…"

"What, Father?"

He turned to Kristjan. "Son, you were against the betrothal, wanted nothing to do with it, then suddenly changed your mind. That makes people speculate. What happened?"

Tinna sucked in a breath, and Kristjan squeezed her hand.

"I saw reason is all, Father. You and Friðfinn were more than happy to jump at my change of heart. An arranged marriage is traditional if one or both parties have no particular prospects in mind."

Father squinted at Kristjan. "There's more, though, isn't there?" He paused, then as if making up his mind, he squared his shoulders. "Tinna, I would've asked this out of your hearing, but you stayed, and I must know. Kristjan, is Tinna pregnant."

A cry escaped Tinna, and Kristjan wrapped his arm around her. How *dare* Father bring this upon her!

"Is that why you wished the ceremony as soon as possible?"

"You have no business meddling, Father."

"Don't I? I still have the option to void your marriage agreement."

"You wouldn't!" Tinna covered her mouth.

"I wouldn't want to, no, but I also deserve to know what my son has done."

"He's done—"

Kristjan cut her off. "Yes, Father, Tinna is pregnant."

Beside him, Tinna gasped, looking frantic. Kristjan kept a firm grip on her. "And, yes, that is why I agreed to marry her." He took a deep breath. At least in this, he could keep his promise—follow through, and protect her as he'd sworn to do. "The child is mine. I went through with the betrothal in order to provide for the little one, and give him the father he needs."

Father seemed to wilt. "Oh, Kristjan."

"Kristjan?" Tinna whispered.

He patted her arm. "It'll be fine." How often had he assured someone this step without any real conviction?

Liar, liar, liar...

He shook the thought aside.

Father rubbed his hand across his face. "When?"

When? What did Father mean?

Tinna kept her head lowered, her tone resigned. "From what I understand, the child should be born in the middle of Endanleg."

Father ticked back through the cycles on his fingers. "It's been that long since… No, I don't want to know." He let out a long breath. "Why, Kristjan?"

"Why?" Kristjan repeated, incredulous. "You mean: why did I agree to marry her and give the little one a father?"

"No." Father shook his head. "Not that."

"You said it yourself, Father." Kristjan's gut twisted. Up until now, his words had been technically true; he hoped to keep it that way. "A man and a woman have desires, and they can run away with them."

It hadn't been *his* desires that had run away, but either way, the implication was clear.

You wanted *to.* The voice was loud. *You crave the same things; you're the same kind.*

"I see." Father hunched his shoulders with another sigh. "I suppose we won't have to explain anything to the elders."

"Preferably not." Kristjan squeezed Tinna's hand. "For Tinna's sake—she doesn't need the added stress. Not only is she pregnant, but she's trying her best to rescue her father—what we *were* doing when you accosted us."

"How, exactly, do you claim you were doing that? There's nothing back in Verndandi that would help."

"You're wrong there." Kristjan smiled. He had proof that there was more; the problem was figuring out how to open that door. "We made contact. Ingvi was going to take the news to Friðfinn."

"You…" Father shook his head. "You *spoke* with Ingvi? Where? When? Did you tell Orlaugur?"

"We didn't have the opportunity. You dragged us here to stand trial before we could find him."

"Well, let's find Orlaugur and tell him about it!"

"We still don't have a way in." Kristjan hated to be the bearer of bad news, but he couldn't let his father run off with false hope to give Orlaugur. "The door has no handle, and I don't see a way to open it. Ingvi said it's the same on the other side. So there must be some secret that the ancients left behind Can you help us?"

Father stood still, his fingers framing on his chin. "If it's a device of the ancients, you might find what you need in the library. Either way, Orlaugur needs to hear about this."

Kristjan glanced between his father's set expression and Tinna's hopeful one. Orlaugur wasn't likely to have the answers; he'd thought that finding an alternate route was hopeless to start with.

What good can you do? You failed Marko, and you'll fail Tinna.

The only way he'd fail was if he didn't try.

Then what? The longer you draw the hope out, the harder her fall. The jaws are opening to crush her; how long until they close?

Chapter 24

30 Fjorda, 400 AI

I strode through the halls oblivious to my surroundings but for Tinna trailing behind me. I couldn't believe it. Kristjan had found another way to the trapped men! The exultation was quickly replaced with despair as I remembered that my son had also let the fire leave the lantern, and now he was forever connected to Tinna, whether or not they married. I'd hoped for better for Kristjan. Was he marrying Tinna out of obligation? It was noble, but I'd wanted him to find a girl he loved.

My musings were cut short by the girl herself. "Chief Geirfinnur." Her voice was soft, almost timid as if afraid, and I could hardly blame her after the way I'd confronted her and Kristjan.

"Just Geirfinnur, or if you feel comfortable with it, Father." I slowed my steps so she could catch up.

Tinna nodded, but she was clearly preoccupied with whatever she wanted say. "Don't be angry at Kristjan. He…" She watched her feet for several steps before looking up and stopping, wrapping her arms around herself. "He promised to claim the child as his own, but it's not his. Bastian—"

I shook my head to clear the confusion. "What does Bastian have to do with any of this? He said he found the two of you…" I'd been so bold in the center of my own home, but here… I glanced about; no one was near, but I lowered my voice nonetheless. "Bastian said he found the two of you together alone."

She laughed a mirthless laugh. "Bastian found 'us?' *He* said…? I should have known." She wiped burgeoning tears from both eyes, her voice thick when she said, "Bastian's jealous. He's the father, and not because I wanted it."

My breath left my chest, leaving a sucking crevasse in its place. Bastian… I couldn't finish the thought. And he had the *gall* to accuse my son? My nails bit into my palms, and I opened my fist.

"Thank you," I managed to choke out. "Thank you for telling me. And… Tinna," I made eye contact with her. "I'm sorry for what my nephew did. It was wrong."

"D… don't tell Kristjan, please. He… He wants this child to be his, and not let me suffer like…"

"Like what?" But as soon as I asked, I could see that it was the wrong question. "Like who?" I didn't want to press at her pain, but I needed to know—Mikkael needed to know what his son had been doing.

Tinna shook her head.

"But there was someone else?"

She nodded, enough for what I needed.

"Thank you. I'll get to the bottom of it."

* * *

The closer we came to the cave-in, the more people we passed, and the clamor around us grew to the point that even if Tinna had been in a talkative mood, I wouldn't have been able to hear her.

As we rounded the corner, Orlaugur's voice boomed above the commotion, "Watch out!"

Workers scrambled out of the way as one of the potential passageways collapsed. Dust billowed as the rocks tumbled down.

"Back to work," Orlaugur called out as the air cleared. "Make sure to keep the supports steady."

Immediately, teams ran to carry out his orders. He turned toward us, the haggard lines clear for all the *holdt* to see, but his face lit up when I caught his eye.

"Geirfinnur, what brings you this way?"

"Tinna has good news." I beckoned the girl forward to share what she and Kristjan had discovered.

At first the lines eased across Orlaugur's face, but then he shook his head. "Tinna, I told you before; it won't work."

"But…" At a nod from me, she persisted. "Kristjan and I spoke with one of the men. He said he'd relay my message to Father."

"You *spoke* with someone? Who?"

"Ingvi."

A brief flicker of hope crossed Orlaugur's face, but just as quickly evaporated. "Why isn't he here now?'

Tinna glanced at the rock floor. "There was no knob on the door."

"Exactly!" Orlaugur threw his hands in the air, but when Tinna flinched, lowered both them and his voice. "Tinna, you know how the ancients were. Their ideas were far beyond ours. The *yoma* light in the library is only one example. We have no way of knowing how it works. There are all kinds of locked doors scattered throughout Verndandi—all with no way to access what's behind them. Don't think we've not tried—the stone in Verndandi defies even the best of our tools, and those doors are something else entirely. There's either a power mechanism that we don't have access to, or some magic that the ancients used to carve out Storeheltur and work that metal. I'll not waste my time—or that of my workers—trying to chip through the granite down there." He paused, pity replacing the exasperation on his face. "I'm sorry, Tinna. I truly am. Your father's my friend. I'm doing all within my power to rescue him and the others."

"I…" She licked her lips. "I understand. Thank you."

With that, Tinna turned and left. I watched her go for a brief moment before returning my attention to Orlaugur.

"That bad?" I asked.

"You of all people should know, Geirfinnur."

He was right. I'd tried deciphering some of the plans the ancients had left but to no avail.

"What can I do to help?"

"Pray." Orlaugur surprised me with his answer. "That's all any of us can really do. Pray for a quick death." He shuddered. "For all of us."

"All… all of us?" I sputtered.

What could he mean?

"At this rate, I can't even retrieve the ore we mined, let alone open up a new shaft that will provide for Storeheltur's needs."

All of Kristjan's hard work had been wasted? There was no hope for the *holdt*? I blinked, welling up with rage that had nowhere to go, no one to blame, nothing to do. All was lost. Hundreds of rotations of Jorvarssons, keeping this *holdt* alive, and now it'd come to an end because of an unlucky collapse? Where was Jeeeah's plan in all of this? My devastation was balled up in my fists, and I could feel the tension of helpless fear coiled in my chest.

But it wasn't Orlaugur's fault. So instead of saying words I would regret, I nodded.

Pray. Stars knew how often I'd been on my knees talking with Jeeah over the past rotations. Recently, I'd found other things to occupy my time. Now—now it'd be best to take my distress to him again, but this time, I'd not be alone. Josebina would be beside me.

"Thank you, Orlaugur. I'll be praying. May Jeeah shine his light on us."

* * *

Kristjan waited until the curtain fell before coming to his feet again. What was he going to do? The miners didn't have many moonsteps left. They'd be starving and needed water. But what could he do?

Nothing. You're worthless. Useless.

He punched the wall, briefly comforted by the rock biting into his skin and the jarring impact in his fingers.

"I can do *something*," He muttered.

Hurt yourself doesn't count.

How long had that voice been with him? It felt like rotations, but it'd gotten so much louder since Marko's death, and it was so hard not to believe it. It was always with him—tearing him down.

Telling you the truth.

Truth. The one thing he'd prided himself on, and now he'd live a lie for the sake of a girl and her honor.

He shook his head to clear it of the unwanted thoughts. What good was this doing him or the trapped miners for that matter? He needed to *think*!

The library was the only place that might have a chance of helping them. So, for the third time in less than a moonstep, he found himself back on the paths to Verndandi.

Kristjan paused in front of the library door, feeling a sick tide of guilt spill over him at the memory of how he'd held Tinna, how he'd kissed her, taken—*what you always wanted anyway. It's just how Jeeah made men—hungry for a woman. There's no escaping it, not unless you take yourself out of this world. All it'd take is a walk down that path.*

He peered off toward the *bensin*. He could follow the way down, right now—it might not be the source of the gasses, but if he stayed down long enough, it'd work anyway, and no one would think to look for him there before his lungs had stopped, letting his heart follow suit. It wouldn't be painful—or if it was, he'd die feeling more alive than he did now, and any suffering would be just punishment for Marko's death.

The image of his friend sprawled in the snow returned full force, followed by the cold-clay feel of Marko's body as Kristjan and Bastian pushed him over the ledge into Fivku. But Kristjan wouldn't rest there. The death of a criminal was exile to Toppur—a death sentence with no retrieval. The *bensin* would do just as well.

His foot caught on uneven ground, and Kristjan caught himself clumsily against the wall. When had he left the library? He glanced over his shoulder and saw that it was almost out of eyeshot. His gaze lingered on it.

One specific page, in one specific book, on one specific shelf—if it's there at all. Yes, the cowardly hypocrite about to give up on life itself is going to go on what even Orlaugur thinks is a fruitless search and emerge victorious? Be a hero? Storeheltur doesn't need more of your 'heroics.' Take yourself out of the picture; it's the only honorable thing you can do now.

A sigh escaped him. He'd told Tinna he'd make a way.

Another oath you can't fulfill. She'll disown you when you can't give her what she wants—you saw her reaction. You can neither rescue her father nor love her as a husband. What would she want with you once she realizes that?

Kristjan turned back toward the abandoned path. He couldn't do good for anyone by living. And was it even *worth* living if the only things he could still feel were pain and—his stomach turned—lust. The craving he felt with Tinna was just proof of his hypocrisy and lies, and the pain didn't last long enough. The sting was gone from the scrapes on his knuckles, and even probing at the cuts on his forearm only produced a dull ache.

And yet, for once the voices were silent. He lifted his foot. It felt so heavy. Then another step. The second was easier. Soon, he was staring down into the *bensin*. The narrow path still set his knees knocking. Maybe the gasses *wouldn't* be his end. It'd be as he'd always feared: falling.

A footfall echoed down the path. Was someone there? He spun around, his heart racing, but saw no one. Yet it came again, a scuffle, a pebble skittering off rock, an inhale of air. These weren't the sounds of an ice rat.

"Who…" He cleared his throat. "Who's there?"

"Kristjan?" Tinna's voice floated to him, followed by the tap of her feet.

He calmed his heart and went to meet her.

"You're here!" She embraced him. "I knew you wouldn't give up. Did you find the answer in the library?"

He shook his head, too numb to respond, but Tinna didn't seem to notice. She took his hand.

"Come on. Let's go look."

She pulled him back to the library—toward life. But what kind of life?

They paused before the door. Tinna traced the knob.

"This is so simple. Just turn and it works. Why can't *their* door be like that?"

He didn't have the heart to lie to her and say again that they'd figure it out. Best if he tried to distance himself from her; that way it wouldn't hurt so much when he was gone.

"Where do we look?" Tinna crossed to the middle of the room. Kristjan didn't know when she'd opened the door, let alone lit the *yoma* lamp. "Do you have any idea?" She turned to him with an earnest expression that faded when she studied his face. "Kristjan? Is everything all right?"

"Yes." He shook himself and tried to focus—really look at her. "You've been crying. Why?" he asked, closing the distance between them.

She glanced down, her hair veiling her face, then brushed it away. "Orlaugur has condemned them."

He blinked. "Who?" The elder wouldn't pass judgment on anyone.

"*Pabbi* and the rest. He says there's no way in from Verndandi, but while we were up there another escape route collapsed. They weren't even halfway through."

Kristjan couldn't bear the sorrow in her eyes. He slid his hand along her cheek, wiping away a tear she'd missed.

"We'll figure something out."

Not even enough backbone to keep your lying mouth shut.

Tinna leaned into his hand, then wrapped an arm around him, pressing into his body.

"I knew I could trust you. Where do we look?"

Where indeed? Shelves lined every wall; each shelf held hundreds of volumes. If only he knew the system the ancients had used to organize the library. There was one, but Kristjan couldn't easily recall it, and he'd only ever really perused the histories himself.

"Our best chance is for each of us to start at one end of a shelf and make our way to the middle."

Tinna glanced about the room and sighed, then she nodded. "Let's start with this one."

It was as good a place as any. He went to the far end and picked up the first book: *Plants and Animals of Ardatz*. That wasn't what he was looking for. The next one was similar, as were the next three. All described various forms of life on Toppur before the Impact. There were numerous pictures; one in particular stood out—what looked like a snow fox but with a red snout and tail, tipped with white that stood out against the green around it. This had been Toppur before the Impact? He shook his head and put it back. *Snow Creatures of Toppur* was more of what Kristjan was accustomed to. White animals in snow and frozen environs filled the pages.

"Looks like this is all animals and plants," he said as he ran his hands along the shelf, skimming the titles.

"And here, too." Tinna didn't pause in her perusal. "Who knew there were this many animals in Storeheltur?"

"Not just the settlement, but up on Toppur as well." Kristjan met her in the middle. "Next shelf?"

They continued finding histories, geography, sciences—beyond anything Kristjan could comprehend, and even what looked like plans for creating some mechanism to assist in the mines. None of it made any sense to Kristjan. One by one he slid each one back to its spot until he once more met Tinna in the middle.

"This is hopeless!"

"No, it's not. We've only covered two shelves out of…" Kristjan paused and glanced about. "Fine, two of five hundred!"

It was an exaggeration, but it did the job. Tinna smiled.

"You're too good for me." She reached up and kissed him.

The contact drew him in as steadily as a *yoma* in a dark tunnel. He needed her. How could he have listened to the voices? She could keep him steady.

When she pulled away, she quirked an eyebrow at his expression. "Maybe I'll get you to love me, yet."

Love. Was that what this was? Kristjan didn't think so, but then, he didn't know what it *did* feel like. He'd watched Mikkael and Froða, always working together, like they were orbiting around each other as they raised their children, solved problems, and washed their dishes, but he still felt that he'd know more about "love" if he'd been able to see how his own mother and father had been together. Would his mother have understood him better? Would she have had some kind of wisdom to offer? He'd never so much wanted to know the answer as he did now.

With an extra kiss on his cheek, Tinna said, "Only four hundred ninety-eight shelves to go."

Chapter 25

30 Fjorda, 400 AI

I allowed my feet to lead me where they would. My mind was a jumble of loose, unsorted rocks.

Jeeah, if ever you've been present, now's when we need you. I… I can't do this on my own.

Too much rested on my shoulders. The whole *holdt*? My breath caught in my chest, and I stumbled, catching myself against the firm rock wall of the hallway. What was I to do? Think!

That was the problem. My thoughts whirled around, a chaotic mess as shifting and uncertain as the stone that kept collapsing on the rescue endeavors. With an effort of will, I wrested one answer from the torrent.

Food. We needed food first.

The next came more easily: we needed a way to keep ourselves supplied with tools and other necessities that we couldn't create here. Isolated at the northern tip of Eelarga, we'd die without support from the outside. No matter how the ancients survived, this was now, not then. What could we trade merchants if not the ore?

"Geir?" Josebina's voice broke into my ponderings. "Geir, are you all right?"

I shook my head, and she came to me, as she always had.

"Here, come in. Why would you wait outside my door without calling?"

Why indeed? My feet knew where I'd find the help I needed, even if my brain couldn't think clearly.

"Let me get you a cup of *kaffi*. I have a few leaves left, and Kristjan gave me some of the blue lichen to help sweeten it. Have a seat." She pointed me to the couch, while she bustled about her kitchen heating water and brewing the *kaffi*.

Why, indeed? I'd thought I'd been following my own feet, but an earnest gratitude stretched my heart as I realized that Jeeah had brought me to the help I needed. *Thank you for providing me with a woman like Josebina.*

Only Jeeah could have fit the two of us together and led me to her door in the midst of my anguish. I rested my face in my hands, my elbows on my knees. In the comfort of Josebina's home, the swirling mass of looming catastrophes didn't seem quite so overwhelming. I could view each one as it was, not as a *shkatað* ready to devour a snow fox or anything that happened into its path.

"Here, it's still hot, but it'll help." Josebina handed me a mug. The outside all but burnt my hands, I wouldn't dream of putting it to my lips at the moment.

"Thank you." I set it aside, but at her frown, picked it back up—by the handle this time.

"Now, what's bothering you?" She sipped her *kaffi* with a little slurp; I wasn't sure how she could do that without scalding her tongue.

Where to start? Josebina would say 'the beginning.' But where was the beginning? With the collapse? The food shortage? The depleted mines that had brought on both of the others?

"Tinna's pregnant," I blurted out.

Josebina sputtered, a dribble of *kaffi* trailing down her chin. I was surprised by it, too—didn't I have weightier things to consider?—but it must've been what was heaviest on my heart.

"Sorry." I wiped a hand over my face. "They went searching for a secondary entrance to the trapped miners, and I confronted Kristjan about something Bastian had said. Kristjan claimed the little one, but later, Tinna told me the truth. Kristjan wants to protect her. As far as Storeheltur is concerned her child is his."

"Who…" Josebina wiped the *kaffi* from her chin. "Who all knows?"

"My guess is, Bastian, Kristjan, and Tinna. If Friðfinn knew, Bastian wouldn't be alive."

"Those are strong words, Geir."

I closed my eyes. "But they're true. Friðfinn sees family as the most important thing in his life; even his position as an elder takes a distant second. No one harms his family and gets away with it."

"I see. This isn't what you needed on top of the rest of the issues in Storeheltur. Why would you have pushed for the information?"

She knew me too well. "Bastian said…" I realized I was alone in her home and that what Bastian had reported to me could have just as easily been said of Josebina and me. "Bastian said he found them together—alone."

"Hm. And did he say what they were doing?"

I shook my head. "He strongly implied it. He told me not to play innocent, that I understood what he was saying. How could I have believed him? Why would I so readily think that of my own son?"

Josebina set her mug down and reached for my hands. "Geir, you have a lot you're responsible for. You're too close to Kristjan to see things objectively. He's pushed you away as he's tried to mature. It's natural. You also love him so much, that you'd do anything for him. It's one of the reasons I love you. I've watched the two of you as he's grown up. Give him space. Treat him as you would any of your elders."

"Thank you, *kæra*." The endearment slipped from my lips.

She smiled at me.

"There's more." When she didn't back away, I forged ahead, explaining about the cave-in, the lack of ore, the need for food, and the *holdt's* imminent collapse. "Whatever happens, though, I want to spend these last steps with you as my wife. If Friðfinn can't, and Orlaugur's too busy, then one of the other elders can perform the ceremony. Is that all right with you?"

Josebina wiped a tear and nodded. "You know I'm ready to be your wife, Geir. I'd make it final this step if I could, but I want Kristjan and Tinna to be there with us."

"Then we'll find them and go first to Karva, and if he won't, we'll make our way through the other elders."

"Yes, *kæra*. That sounds perfect. Then we'll deal with the other issues as husband and wife." She lifted her face to mine—my wife, soon—for however long we had left.

I managed not to spill my hot *kaffi* all over her as I kissed her, but it was a near thing.

* * *

Neither Kristjan nor Tinna were at home; my house was empty, and Ebonney hadn't seen Tinna in a few spans. Where else would they have gone?

"Oh, of course! They're probably at the library." Kristjan was tenacious; Orlaugur's deterrence wouldn't have convinced him to give up, and Tinna would certainly have joined him. I turned, pulling Josebina along. "Let's go."

"Geirfinnur! Geirfinnur!" The voice of a young boy chased us down as we went.

"Andri?"

Why was Marko's brother running down the hall waving at me? Had there been another catastrophe?

"Geirfinnur, come quickly! They're back."

"Slow down, boy, and explain."

Andri sucked in air for the surge of words. "Elder Hafnar and his brother have returned from Isholt with visitors and supplies and they're waiting for you so they can unload them! They brought meat and flour, and even some dried fruit! Come!" He turned and sprinted back the way he'd come, then skidded to a halt as he realized I hadn't followed. "Are you coming?"

Josebina's gentle touch stirred me from my trance. "Go. We'll find Kristjan and Tinna afterward. Besides, maybe Hafnar will want to marry us."

Her last words warmed my insides more than the *kaffi* had.

"Yes, I'm coming. It's not appropriate for the chief to run through the passages of Storeheltur. You can take the news back that I'm on my way."

I couldn't help but chuckle at how he barely even nodded before he dashed down the hall as if a snow fox was after him.

"Let's make our way a bit more sedately." Josebina laughed. "But I don't blame him if there's dried fruit!"

Andri had already snatched a bag of fruit by the time we arrived.

"Take that to Arny, and ask Reinar to return with you," Hafnar called after the lad's departing back. "Geirfinnur!"

Hafnar enveloped me in a wet embrace—his furs dripped with melting ice.

"Glad you made it back." I wiped at the larger patches of water that were already soaking into my tunic. "How was your journey?"

"Look!" He waved a hand at ten sleighs covered with furs. "Your letter to Nikanor worked. He sent eight of his men with us to bring what we need."

I wanted to be anywhere else but here. We had no ore to return with the men, and what were ten sleds full of food if we had no way to sustain ourselves? It would only prolong our starvation. Yet, I couldn't spurn his work or bring myself to quench the joy that exuded from him and spilled over into the people who'd gathered to help divide it up and store what was left— if any. I focused instead on the snow-covered furs.

"Did you encounter a storm?"

Hafnar shrugged. "Thank the stars, Sigmar led us through without a problem! Now, come let me introduce you to our visitors."

I was surprised to see how many had come. The journey in good weather would take four moonsteps. In the middle of Fjorda, the winds blew and made the weather unpredictable.

"Nyvarð," Hafnar called over the commotion, "I'd like you to meet the chief of Storeheltur."

A tall, broad-shouldered man strode toward us unclasping his furs. His voice boomed and echoed off the cavern walls. "Hafnar's told me so much about you, it's as if I already know you."

I glanced at Hafnar and he shrugged with a grin.

"Don't believe half of what he told you, then." I held out my hand.

Nyvarð gripped it, crushing it in his mighty paw. "Now, that doesn't sound like any chief I've ever known. They want their fame to be spread far and wide. Don't worry, I'll be sure to share with Nikanor all the great tales Hafnar told me."

"I… I appreciate it, though perhaps I'd like to hear them first." I glanced at Hafnar and cocked my head. Rubbing my hand, I tried to bring circulation back. "What all did you bring us? Andri mentioned dried fruit."

"Aye, that we have. It's the best of last season. A merchant brought an overstock and we've not made it through all of it. Nikanor thought you'd want it."

"Thank you. Anything is welcome at this moment."

"Well, we have to stick together out here in the wastes of Eelarga. If Storeheltur falls, we'll be the furthest north, and we don't have as many rich mines as you."

I hadn't thought of it that way, but it made sense. Many merchants traveled through Isholt only because they were on their way to trade with us for the plentiful ore we sold.

"Well, once more, I thank you." I offered my hand, trying not to wince as Nyvarð gripped it again. "I'll have a place prepared for you and your party."

"I can see to that." Josebina smiled at my side.

"Oh, how could I be so rude?" Heat flared up my neck. "Nyvarð, this is Joesbina, my betrothed."

"Betrothed? Well, I'll be!" Nyvarð's grin spread out under his craggy nose. "That's something Hafnar didn't tell me. Congratulations! Here." He bowed then shuffled over to a sled and rummaged through the contents. Before long he returned with a package wrapped in skins. "This is my gift for you, Josebina. May it bring blessings on your ceremony."

"You don't h—"

"Shush! I wanted to. It's not every step a chief gets married. It deserves a celebration."

"Then thank you." Josebina accepted the gift and pulled one side of the fur back to reveal several different items wrapped in thin paper to protect them. All were frozen.

"They'll need some thawing, but you'll find a roast, several potatoes, and dried apples."

My mouth fell open. "*Apples*?"

Nyvarð laughed, the sound filling the chamber, and several people stopped what they were doing to glance at us. He waved his hand at them, gesturing for them to continue. "They're my favorite as well. Enjoy, Chief Geirfinnur."

"Thank you." What a pleasant surprise on an otherwise gloomy moonstep.

"Chief Geirfinnur!" Although Andri used the same exuberance from when he'd come to get me earlier, it sounded muted compared to Nyvarð. "Chief Geirfinnur, I brought elder Reinar."

The elder gawked at the sight before him. Then he closed his mouth and settled a hand on the lad's shoulder. "You want work, Andri? I've got plenty for you. First, we divide everything up by category—meat here, vegetables there, staples over there, and fruit in the far corner."

"Looks like Reinar has everything under control." I nodded to the elder. "It was good to meet you, Nyvarð, but I was going to find my son when I was called."

"Oh, of course, by all means. I wouldn't want to come between you and family." Nyvarð nodded. "Thank you for your time."

"My pleasure." I motioned for Hafnar to join me.

"What is it?" He unbuttoned his coat, revealing a layer of heavy skins.

"What would you say to performing a ceremony during the third watch?" I couldn't keep the grin from my face.

"Ceremony?" He cocked his head then he smiled. "You two?"

I nodded.

"I'd be honored." Hafnar turned to Josebina. "I thought you might have gone ahead while we were gone."

"There were other things to consider, but now—"

"I'd be glad to! Who all will be there?"

"Just family." The severity of our circumstances weighed down on my shoulders again. "Kristjan and his betrothed, Tinna."

Hafnar's jovial expression fell. "No one else?"

I sighed. He needed to know the affairs of the *holdt*. Keeping my voice low, I explained our situation—the discovery of the secondary mine, the rich lodes within, and the collapses that kept our men trapped inside. "That's what we have. Nothing to satisfy a merchant and only enough food as what you brought back."

"That…" Hafnar shook his head. "I…"

He spoke what I felt—words could not suffice to mourn the death of a *holdt*. My *holdt*.

Chapter 26

30 Fjorda, 400 AI

Despite the grim news that we didn't have the ore for the merchant that was coming in a cycle, I couldn't help but feel a ray of hope. I was getting married. If Jeeah could resurrect my heart to love a woman again, then surely, he could provide a way for us to survive.

One look at Kristjan's face was all it took to tell that he didn't have the same faith I did. I longed to cheer him up but didn't know how. Before I'd settled on anything to say, we'd arrived at Hafnar's quarters.

I gathered my courage about me and wiped my palms on my trousers. My voice trembled as I called the greeting. We didn't have to wait long before Sungvari opened the tapestry for us to enter.

"Welcome, Geirfinnur." She gave Josebina a hug. "I'm so excited for you."

Hafnar straightened out his tunic as he entered the room. "Come on in. Geirfinnur and Josebina you can stand here." He motioned to a spot in front of the couch. "Kristjan, you'll be beside your father, and Tinna, you can stand beside Josebina." His eyes twinkled. "Unless, you wish to be wed as well…"

"No, thank you."

"Yes, please!"

Kristjan and Tinna answered at the same time. Tinna's cheeks flamed red.

"I thought you wished to wait for your father," Kristjan said, reaching for Tinna's hand.

She wiped a tear from spilling down her cheek. "I'd like to, but…"

"We'll give it another step to rescue him." Kristjan lifted her chin. "Will that work?"

A brief nod was her only reply.

Hafnar cleared his throat. "I should have considered your family, Tinna. Forgive me."

"There's nothing to forgive. Now, let's give Josebina the step she's been waiting for."

I couldn't help but admire my future daughter-in-law. She had taken the teasing and the allusion to her father's demise with grace, despite being under her own stressors—the pregnancy, the *holdt's* looming knowledge of it, must be taking a toll.

Josebina took my hand, a quizzical look on her face, as Hafnar laughed, saying, "Geirfinnur, come now; you're the one who requested the ceremony. Are you ready?"

"Of course." I ran a hand through my hair and looked to Jesebina, realizing I'd missed something. I tried to focus—to be present for this moment—for my wife. I took her other hand in mine and looked at her beautiful face, and it set my feet on solid stone. My heart was full.

Whatever I'd missed must not have been too important, for Hafnar began the ceremony with the traditional words. "This step, we come together to join two people into one. Just as Handi and Tsiki light Toppur, separate yet in step with each other, so too is a man with his wife. Each unique in their own way, yet, lending light to the other. As you walk the paths of Storeheltur, may you both shed light like the moons."

The words brought back memories, but I let them pass over me. Sæbjort would want me to rejoice in this moonstep—this ceremony.

"Do you have a symbol of your promise to each other?"

I nodded. Despite the hurried ceremony and the upheaval in the *holdt*, I'd commissioned a ring from Iðna.

"I have a ring," Josebina said with a quiet, yet firm voice.

It shouldn't have surprised me, but it did. We hadn't discussed this part.

"Geirfinnur?" Hafnar turned to me.

"As do I." I pulled it out of the pouch at my side.

Iðna had outdone himself in designing the piece.

"Good, then Josebina, would you place the ring on your betrothed's finger?"

I held out my left hand for her. She settled it in her palm and slid a solid silver band onto my finger. Silver, not copper. She had to have saved and traded with a merchant for it. I marveled at it, then her, speechless.

"I've been hoping for many rotations, Geir." Her smile was small, but proud, and her happiness limned her face like the glow of a lantern. How had I been blessed with such a woman?

Josebina went on. "Handi and Tsiki guide our steps, so as a token of my pledge to you, I have chosen a silver ring in the shape of Handi. Silver to reflect its light. As the moons are ever in sync, may I ever be in step with you. My life for yours as long as Jeeah wills."

May it be for the rest of my life. I squeezed her hand.

"It's your turn, Geirfinnur." Hafnar grinned. He seemed to be enjoying my bewilderment.

With Josebina's hand settled in mine, I slid her ring into place. The light reflected from the dioptase, gleaming more green than blue.

Suddenly, my mouth was dry. I worked moisture to my lips. "This ring is evidence of my devotion to you, Josebina." Why was this so hard to express? "As long as I live, you will be as valued as the gem on your hand. You're the only one who will hold my heart. I… I love you."

Her smile was far greater than my words could have evoked, but it said that she understood what I couldn't say—as she always had. She squeezed my fingers as we both looked to Hafnar.

"As elder of Storeheltur, and with Jeeah's blessing, I pronounce you man and wife. You may kiss your bride."

All else melted away as I reached for Josebina, only to find her meeting me and pulling me to her. Our lips met in a sweet embrace.

"Congratulations!" Hafnar was the first to intrude on our triumphant kiss. He held out his hand. "I'm glad you finally had the gumption to ask her." He glanced over at Josebina. "Keep him in line."

Her smile didn't dim in the slightest. "I plan to," she said, winking at me.

Tinna stepped forward, and Josebina hugged her. "Soon, it'll be your turn, sweet girl, and your father will be there."

"I hope so."

Kristjan stood awkwardly. On impulse, I reached out for him and drew him to my side.

"Thank you, son. I appreciate it."

"I'm happy for you." Although his words were right, his tone was off. I released him, and he stepped back.

"We have a meal waiting at home. The first real one since you left," I said with a nod to Hafnar. "Froða prepared it for us. Thank you again for your contribution."

"Glad to see you finally married. I won't keep you from your meal. Enjoy the rest of your step." Hafnar winked at me.

The back of my neck heated up. It'd been a long time since a man had alluded to such things regarding me, and I was suddenly as bashful as a young man.

Hafnar clapped Kristjan on the shoulder. "If you want me to perform your ceremony, all you have to do is ask. Then you'll join the rest of us in wedded bliss."

"Thank you. I'll let you know. We haven't discussed anything yet."

"Well, get to it then. Your girl seems eager to have you."

It was Kristjan's turn to be flustered. He muttered something incoherent.

Hafnar laughed. "Go on, then. I've not seen my own wife in too many steps."

Sungvari shook her head, her dark locks shifting at her shoulders. "Don't listen to him." But she reached up and kissed him.

Josebina took my hand and led me from the room. As we reached the hall, she reached up and whispered, "As much as I like seeing you blush, it makes one wonder: do you think you can bear what's coming later?"

I couldn't speak, even when she winked at me to assure me that she was teasing. This moonstep, when we went to bed for the rest period, it'd be together. The thought set my heart racing. At least we hadn't planned a reception with the whole *holdt*; we wouldn't be required to drift among guests and greet every well-wisher, only savor the time with family and the meal my sister had so generously prepared before we retired to my—no, *our*—room, I blushed again, but I also squeezed Josebina's hand and took another kiss.

Chapter 27

30 Fjorda, 400 AI

unt Froða had outdone herself. As soon as Father shouldered the tapestry aside to carry Josebina across the threshold, the scent of roasted *shkatað* overwhelmed Kristjan. His stomach grumbled. The last he'd eaten a good meat had been when he'd had the meal with Tinna and her family.

"Are you hungry?" Tinna smiled at him.

"Aren't you?"

She shook her head. "For the past couple of phases, food hasn't gotten along with me. From the few discrete conversations I've had, that's normal."

Normal not to be able to eat? But she was carrying a baby. She needed her strength, but what did he know of pregnancy? He wasn't like Marko who had many siblings.

What should've been a pang of longing crawled through his heart. His friend would have been overjoyed to see Father married. If only… If only, it was as easy as wishing. Then Marko *would* be here, as would… Bastian. Kristjan's face heated, and he clenched his fists. If only, he could bring his cousin to justice, but in so doing, he'd cast Tinna in a bad light, make her the subject of scrutiny and suspicion, and Bastian had already shown himself capable of outright lies to divert such things from himself. Kristjan couldn't put her through that.

A light touch on his arm brought him back to his surroundings. "Is everything all right?" Tinna studied him.

Kristjan nodded. It wasn't, but there was no need to add to her worries. If she could smile while her father's fate hung in the balance, he wouldn't mar that.

How self-centered of you. Standing around with a stupid look on your face while your pregnant betrothed stands waiting on you, worrying for you. You should end her worry and let her have her life back.

He offered his arm to Tinna. She took it, and together they sat down at the table. Father had already seated Josebina and was giving her another even longer, lingering kiss when Aunt Froða came in.

"Geirfinnur, you're making your son blush," she chided him as she juggled a large platter in one hand and a basket in the other. "And you'd better not rush through this meal! I've spent the last several spans preparing this. You'll enjoy it and allow Josebina to savor every bite."

"I'll savor it." Josebina didn't take her eyes from Father.

Kristjan found his fork and traced intricate swirls in the gravy and mashed vegetables. It was far better than watching the newlyweds.

Beside him, Tinna chuckled. "Will we be like that?"

Her words had been intended for his ears alone, but Aunt Froða had chosen that moment to reach across the table and set down the basket. "Of course you will. By the time you're wed, he'll be yearning to show you exactly how happy he is to have you in his life." She winked and turned to Kristjan, who'd intensified his tracing of the pattern with his fork. "And if you're as devoted to her as my older boys are to their wives, she'll be eager to let you."

Kristjan all but choked. Why had all the adults in his life started speaking so openly, commenting on the… intimacies… of married life?

Froða rested a hand on Kristjan's shoulder. "And don't let this young man fool you. Give him a kiss or two, and he'll have you before an elder in no time."

A kiss or two? Tinna *had* kissed him, but all it'd done was ignite his desire, not make him want to marry her.

Just like your cousin. He felt the heat crawl up his neck.

Froða laughed at the color in his cheeks. "See? He's already thinking about you."

Kristjan would've given anything to leave the table, but this was, after all, his father's wedding meal. It was unheard of for the family to desert the guests of honor. He forced his thoughts to the food, but even the tantalizing scents no longer held his interest.

"Now, Froða," Josebina rescued him, "leave them be. Tinna's had a long step or two. Give her time, and you'll be helping me prepare her wedding meal."

"Thank you." A timid smile lit up Tinna's face.

Was she actually looking forward to being married? Kristjan thought she only wanted a way to have her child without disgrace. Then he remembered the kiss at the library. She wanted more. No, he corrected himself, she *needed* more.

And you can provide that for her. You've felt the same as she does—is what she wants wrong?

Kristjan clutched his fork, trying to push the voice aside, wishing he could stab it. He couldn't give in to such cravings; he'd make her feel the same way Bastian had.

Tinna reached under the table and squeezed his knee. "Don't mind them, Kristjan," she whispered.

His heart raced at her touch. He knew he should probably move her hand, but he didn't.

See, your lust rules you.

"Thank you, Tinna." He glanced about and saw her empty plate. "Would you care for bread?"

He lifted the cloth from the basket, and steam escaped. He slid a warm slice of bread onto her plate and passed her the butter—actual *butter*! It'd been almost a full cycle since they'd had any in Storeheltur. He quickly slathered some on his own slice and bit into it. The creamy, oily blend had melted into the bread. He closed his eyes. At least he could enjoy this. When he looked up, Tinna hadn't eaten a thing. In fact, she looked pale.

Suffering, and you sit beside her.

Kristjan ignored the voice. "Do you need to go?"

Tinna shook her head but bit her lip at the same time.

"Are you sure?"

"Shh." She glanced over to Father and Josebina. "I don't want to ruin it for them."

Ruin it for them? Kristjan looked at his father. He took in the set of his shoulders, the lift of his lips, and the way he glowed. Never in his life had he seen his father so at peace and contented. He'd never considered it, but Father had always had a gloom about him. Now, it was gone.

"All right, but let me know when you're ready. I'll walk you back home."

"Kristjan, you're tired. There's no need."

There might not be a need in her eyes, but no other man would allow their betrothed to wander alone after the final meal of the step.

Still keeping up appearances. How hypocritical.

He shoved the thought aside with a bite of roast. What more could he do? He *was* betrothed to Tinna whether he liked it or not. He might as well act the part.

They ate in silence—or at least Kristjan did. Tinna moved her food around her plate without eating, while Father and Josebina talked quietly, their heads tilted toward one another, their eyes warm and liquid, their smiles bright and shining, heedless of anyone else at the table.

At last, the meal was finished. Father stood, taking Josebina's hand. "Thank you, Froða, for this wonderful meal. You've blessed us."

"It's my pleasure, Geirfinnur. Don't even think of helping clean up; I know you have places to be." She winked at them.

Red crept up Father's neck. At least he had the decency to blush at the implications.

"I'll walk Tinna home," Kristjan said. He could give them privacy.

Josebina hugged Tinna. "Thank you, both, for being here."

Kristjan didn't know how they had helped besides standing with them at Hafnar's, but if it made Josebina happy, he was content.

Tinna took his offered arm, and they left.

"You'd think there was no one else in the room but the two of them." Kristjan shook his head.

"It's so sweet. Do you think..." Tinna studied the path in front of them.

"Do I think what?"

"Never mind."

Now what? Had he said something? Done something?

"Kristjan, you don't have to walk me home."

"No? Don't you want me to?"

"Only if you want to."

He let out a deep breath and stopped in the middle of the passageway. "Tinna, you're my betrothed."

She still didn't look at him. He turned her to him and bent to look her in the eye. "What has you concerned?" Were those tears?

"I… Never mind."

"Never mind? You're about to cry."

"It's just…"

He waited for her to go on, but she didn't. "Just… what?"

"I'd always dreamed of my husband looking at me the way your father looks at Josebina."

Another failure to add to the list. He tried to keep his voice even, but an edge crept in nonetheless.

"I'm not my father."

"Of course not."

They stood that way for several moments. Down the hall, a gust of warm air belched from a vent. When Kristjan could stand it no longer, he took her hand.

"Tinna, I'm your betrothed. I thought that was what you wanted."

"It is, but…"

"But what? I can't change something if you don't talk to me."

"It's no good if you change just because I want you to. I want it to come from you. From here." She placed her free hand on his heart. "I don't want to make you *act* like you love me, Kristjan. I want you to love me because you *want* to, because you *do*!"

Didn't taking her even though she was bearing his cousin's child count for something? Wasn't that love?

"Just take me home. It's been a long step, and we still haven't figured out how to get Father and the others out."

"As you wish." Frustrated, defeated, he offered her his arm again, but her hand where it touched him was stiff and vacant of any warmth.

Love can grow. It can begin in small things.

He almost reached over to cover her cold fingers with his other hand, offer her some reassurance, but the other voice preempted him.

You really believe you're doing her a favor, don't you? But she wants someone who loves her for herself—not as a responsibility. You'll suffocate her.

For once he didn't tell the voice to be quiet. It was right. He would suffocate everything around him. He'd killed Marko. If he couldn't find a way to unlock the door, he'd kill Friðfinn and the other miners. If he remained on this path, he'd condemn Tinna and her child to a cold, loveless existence, and he knew what that did to a person. Best to end his life before he killed anyone else.

Chapter 28

30 Fjorda, 400 AI

After leaving Tinna, Kristjan didn't want to return to his own home, despite how tired he felt. The dejection in Tinna's eyes still haunted him.

End it. You'll spare yourself and everyone else any further misery.

The question was how. The voices had enough answers, but none of them appealed to Kristjan. Or at least he wouldn't admit, even to himself, that they did. His feet betrayed him. Before long, he found himself standing outside the library.

All you have to do is go to sleep. The gas from the bensin *will do the rest.*

Yet he couldn't without trying one more time to find the answer to the door without a knob. More out of habit than anything, he dropped the *yoma* into the globe and set it in the middle of the table. The light flared to life while Kristjan walked around the edges of the room examining the different spines. One particular section had always baffled him. It held maps of a sort, but they weren't of Storeheltur. It was as if someone had mapped out smaller items like he'd done with the water system and not gotten around to finishing.

You never finish what you start, or if you do, it ends in disaster. This whole mining accident was your fault. If you hadn't shared the ore find with the elders, there wouldn't have been a collapse.

He pulled out a book. As he puzzled over the precise lines and geometric shapes, he realized it *wasn't* a map; it was some sort of design. But of what?

"Generator." He read the word.

What was that? What did it produce? He turned the page. *Vault.* His face scrunched in concentration as he tried to puzzle out the layout. It looked familiar. On the opposite side, it said *Lightbulb.* It showed a circle with arrows. He read.

> *Place the minerals in the bulb. When connected to the magnets, the resulting energy will power the minerals for several hours if not days.*

Kristjan scratched his head. The word days referred to moonsteps, but before the Impact. What were "hours?" The minerals looked like the *yoma.* Could this be explaining the *yoma* light? Either way, this book held the most hope he'd found so far for a way to unlock the door.

He turned page after page, each design as foreign as the ancients.

You're wasting your time.

With a sigh, he closed the cover, but his finger caught in the back. As he pulled it out, the page fell open to yet another picture, but it was the words at the top of the page that gave him pause. In a different hand than the earlier entries, this one seemed to be added later.

> *KEYPAD.*
> *THE CURRENT DESIGNS ARE FAILING. WE CAN'T KEEP POWER TO THEM. DOORS ARE SLOWLY CLOSING TO NEVER OPEN AGAIN. A FEW OF THEM CAN STILL BE POWERED WITH THE SAME MECHANISM AS THE MINERALS AND MAGNETS. WITH THAT IN MIND, I'VE SET ASIDE A KEY OF SORTS IN THE VAULT ALONG WITH THE BOOKS TO EXPLAIN HOW TO USE IT. PLACE THE MINERALS IN THE SMALL GLOBE, ALONG WITH THE MAGNETS. TOGETHER, THEY CREATE A CHARGE, ENOUGH TO POWER THE KEYPAD IF PLACED IN THE SOCKET ABOVE IT. THE CURRENT CODE IS 20–21–07–09–32.*

Kristjan scrutinized the words, trying to comprehend them. Keypad. He knew what a key was, but how was a key also a pad? Could this be the answer he'd been looking for? But where was the power mechanism? He glanced about. At the end of the shelf, the books gave way to miscellaneous items, all of which had been deemed trivial knick-kancks, relics from the ancients.

What could it hurt? He picked up each item—a block of wood, a hunk of metal, and a deteriorated piece of cloth. Behind them all lay a glass ball with black stones inside. There was a clasp on the side. With a shrug, he snapped it open. The ball hinged open. The black stones weren't necessarily heavy, but what good would they do? He resealed it and went back to the book, placing the ball on the table in the light of the *yoma* lamp.

After re-reading the passage, he still was no closer to understanding what needed to be done, but he was confident that this orb was the key. If only he could figure out if the black stones were the minerals or magnets. He picked up the ball and peered into it, but no revelations came from the examination. With a sigh, he set it back down, but his finger slipped, sending it rolling across the table.

He grabbed for it but only managed to knock it back toward the middle, where it bumped up against the *yoma* lamp. The stones flared brightly at the contact, then dimmed again as the sphere rolled past. Kristjan gaped, and in his shock, he almost let the glass ball run off the opposite edge of the table before he could snatch it up.

Taking a deep breath, he opened the globe and placed a single *yoma* inside. It gave off a soft hum and the *yoma* glowed more brighter than it had on its own.

"Stars be praised!" Kristjan removed the *yoma*, and it returned to its natural brightness. "Only one way to find out."

He slid the *yoma* into a pouch and glanced around for a safe way of transporting the ball. Even apart from its fragility, the thought of accidentally dropping it into the *bensin* on the way across was catastrophic.

He paused at the thought of the poison pit. Was he really going to go through with his idea?

Are you so fickle you can't make up your mind? You're worthless—worse than an ice rat, no good to anyone. Why do others need to die because of you?

"I'll get Friðfinn free, and then I can leave."

Putting pretty words on it now? You can't even be honest with yourself *about what you're going to do?*

With a sigh, he tucked the hem of his tunic into his belt and knotted it there, leaving a small gap at the top; he dropped the ball into the makeshift pouch and walked a circuit around the room, then jumped a few times and ran a few steps to make sure it was secure. Once he was satisfied that nothing would slip, he took a final glance around the room then removed the *yoma* lamp from its socket and closed the door.

The way seemed brighter for some reason, and soon he came to the *bensin*. As he made his way across the path with shaking legs, he wondered how he'd get to the bottom. There wasn't enough of the deadly gas along the sloping trail.

He'd work that out later. Now he had a door to unlock.

Before he knew it, he was standing in front of the blocked entrance. What was he even *looking* for? He pulled the *yoma* from the pouch so he could see better. The door was made from the same metal as the library door—smooth and heavy. The only seams were the large gap at the base and the pair of thinner ones that framed its edges. He doubted he could've slid a piece of paper through the side cracks.

Pad. He pursed his lips, chewing on the bottom one, and ran his hands along the door but without result. Could it be something *beside* the door? It couldn't hurt to look. His fingers caught on every bump and crevice in the rock on the left side of the door. He reached as high as he could on the right side, and slid his fingers down. A jagged edge poked his middle finger. He pulled it away, but not before his pinky trailed along a smooth surface—as smooth as the door.

With the *yoma* in one hand, he examined the area. A square piece of metal stared back at him at about shoulder height. He cleared the dust from it, and found an indent.

His hand trembled as he pulled the glass ball out of his tunic. He opened it and set the *yoma* inside, taking care to seal it tight. The light from the *yoma* illuminated the pad. It was an unadorned metal square with a spot for the globe.

Please, let it work.

Kristjan touched the ball to the indent. The black stones jumped to the wall leaving the *yoma* suspended in the middle of the sphere. There was a faint hum above the pounding of his heart, and the metal… awakened? Came alive? The glowing forms of numbers appeared on its surface.

"Now it makes sense!" Kristjan shook his head and removed the orb.

It released with a *chk*, and the black stones fell back to the bottom along with the *yoma*. Not bothering to remove the *yoma*, Kristjan stuffed the ball into his pouch and darted back down the hall. He slowed at the *bensin* and sped back up after he'd crossed it.

Once at the library, he recorded the numbers on a piece of paper that he stuffed in beside the sphere. Then he retraced his steps at a run.

This time, his movements were sure as he placed the orb in its spot and touched the numbers: two, zero, two, one, zero, seven, zero, nine, three, two. At first there was no change, but a heartbeat later there was a faint click, and then a low, building rumble. Kristjan jumped back, forgetting the orb in an ingrained reflex to dodge falling rock. The sphere stuck to its socket, and the sound of stones skidding and crashing against each other came from behind the door.

Someone shouted. Kristjan scrambled back to the door which was now cracked open.

"Are you there?"

"Help! Please!"

"Friðfinn!" a woman called; Kristjan thought it might be Mari. "Friðfinn, we're saved!"

A grey face appeared in the crack; the whites of the eyes bright as Handi. "Is it true?" Ingvi asked. "Can we get out this way?"

Kristjan nodded. "I can lead you out. Does anyone need help walking?"

Ingvi hung his head. "Those who can't walk; won't be coming out."

"How…" Kristjan didn't want to ask, but he had to. "How many?"

"Too many."

Mari's voice turned frantic. "Friðfinn! Friðfinn! No!" It ended in a wail.

"He wasn't doing well." Ingvi didn't look back into the cave. "He gave his portion of water to others. Then… Well, then he was trying to figure out a way to get the door open. He'd given up and turned his back to it when it opened and the rocks…"

You killed him! You killed your betrothed's father!

There had to be another explanation. Friðfinn wasn't dead. He couldn't be. Not like this. Not now after Kristjan had found a way to free them all. It *had* to be a mistake.

"Stand over there." Kristjan pointed, then thought better of it. "If the door shuts, touch these numbers on the pad." He handed Ingvi the slip of paper.

It'd serve you right to die trapped.

Kristjan shook the thoughts aside, and strode into the cavern. The faint glow of *yoma* lit the area, but it was too big of a space to fully illuminate with what few there were. Several thanked him, clasping his hand as they passed to freedom, but none of them were Tinna's father. He almost didn't recognize Margeir. Marko's father had shriveled in the last three moonsteps. Then again, what would it do to a person to be locked away without food or water, and only a few *yoma* to see each other by?

The last to stand was Mari. She shook her head as she turned toward him, her shoulders shaking.

When she reached him, she sobbed. "Thank you. I know we can't bring him out right now, but it doesn't feel right to leave him."

"I'll see to him."

Even in death, the elder was imposing. Blood streaked his face from where Kristjan assumed a rock had struck him. His clothes were dusty, and his hair was sticky and matted around the fatal wound. But his face had been smudged mostly free of the grime and blood. Mari must have tried to do that much for him.

Kristjan looked around for something he could use to move Friðfinn and happened upon an empty ore cart. With a heavy heart, Kristjan retrieved it and started to maneuver the weight of his father-in-law's body into the bed of it.

"What are you doing, son?" Margeir called.

"I can't leave an elder here."

"Well, let me help then."

Kristjan doubted Marko's father had enough strength left to do any good, but Margeir took Friðfinn's feet and helped Kristjan hoist the elder onto the cart. When they pushed it out, they saw that someone had propped the door open with several rocks.

"Didn't want you trapped in there." Ingvi grinned.

"I appreciate it. Now, let's go; I don't think the cart will fit down the path, so we'll have to leave—" A swallow of bile burned Kristjan's mouth. "—leave Friðfinn behind."

Several nodded, and Margeir smiled encouragement. "He's not trapped anymore; we'll send others to return for him. Lead the way, son."

As they began to make their way back, Ingvi and Margeir walked beside him, their exclamations of delight grating against the heavy sickness simmering in Kristjan's spirit. Behind, the other miners talked among themselves, some sharing dark-humored or strident, brazing jokes, others crying in relief, but all hurrying along the path as best they could in their weakened state.

When at last they arrived at the place where the path descended into the crevasse, Ingvi sniffed and threw up a hand. "Hold! This is dangerous. You expect us to walk through a *bensin*?"

"It's not bad." Kristjan glanced about, but most were already backing away. He raised what he hoped was a soothing voice, calling out, "The gas doesn't originate

here; it only seeps into the pit, and the path doesn't go all the way down, either. I've come and gone several times, and in any case, it's the only way out."

Margeir stepped forward. "Son, you've already saved us once. I've no reason to doubt you." With that, he started across, followed by Ingvi, and the rest quickly fell into file, picking their way cautiously, but not fearfully along the bridge.

Finally, Kristjan crossed over after them and led the rest of the way home. As they left Verndandi and came into the well-traveled halls of Storeheltur, they began to be recognized. They shouted out to friends as they spotted them, and the jubilant cries roused those who'd been sleeping. Kristjan began to hang back as, within moments, the paths were flooded with exhilarated people; the laughter, tears, and embraces were overwhelming, and he felt somehow fearful of being swept up in it. He felt he ought to go to Orlaugur—otherwise it could be that no one would think to tell the mine workers that they could, at last, give up the rescue effort.

Because it's too late for Friðfinn. You saw to that. Coward. Liar. Murder.

He ignored the voice and kept walking, his footsteps echoing the accusations. When he finally came to the mine, he was thankful for the noise. It drowned out the litany of condemnation.

Orlaugur called out. "Clear the way! When was the last time anyone had contact with them?"

Someone replied, but Kristjan couldn't hear.

"Friðfinn!" Orlaugur put his mouth right up to the pipe and shouted. "Friðfinn! Can you hear me?"

It was like a pick driven into Kristjan's heart. Friðfinn would never hear anyone again. He walked the halls of the ancients—with Marko.

Instead of yelling across to Orlaugur, he made his way through the rubble. Rocks littered the floor— evidence of another collapse or two. Before he was ready, he'd made it to the bottom of the ladder.

"Orlaugur," he called up.

"Kristjan, what brings you here?" The elder's face was ragged as he descended the ladder, and even among the grime, Kristjan could see the dark circles.

Kristjan waited until Orlaugur was on firm ground before replying. "I have news."

The elder sighed and shook his head. "No, son, Tinna already tried to convince me to try the other way. It's impossible."

"I hate to disagree, Orlaugur, but I opened it."

Orlaugur gaped at him for a moment, then slowly cocked his head and ran a finger through his ear. "I must have dirt and dust clogging my hearing. What was that?"

"Margeir is with Telma and the rest of his family. Most of the others are safely in their homes. I found the key. The door's open so anyone can enter through the back way." He held out the map he'd drawn in the first place. "You'll go through this area here, where it smells like a *bensin,* but it's not. The gasses leak into the chasm, but the path leads you across without injury."

Orlaugur was still dumbfounded, gaping at him. "What…? Well… how many made it out? What about Friðfinn?"

Kristjan hung his head but couldn't bring himself to say what he should have. *I killed him.* "He… he didn't make it. Someone said he gave his rations to others in need, so he was too weak to…" *Survive what I did to him.*

Orlaugur sagged against the ladder. "Gone?" He covered his face. "No. It can't be."

"Margeir helped me get his body onto a cart. It's resting in the passageway. I…" He took a deep breath. "I need to tell Tinna and Ebonney."

"Go. I have plenty of workers here to help bring him back."

Seeing the dismissal, Kristjan turned.

"Kristjan." Orlaugur waited until Kristjan glanced back over his shoulder and said, "thank you. Well done."

Well done? Well done killing off Friðfinn? Good job, you killed Marko. Who else should you kill? How about yourself, before you harm anyone else you love?

But first he'd tell Tinna, and maybe…

Who was he fooling? She'd never forgive him for her father's death. Best put that hope aside and be done with it.

Chapter 29

30 Fjorda, 400 AI

A sound woke me. Was that Kristjan? Where had he been? I turned and found Josebina beside me. Warmth filled all the formerly lonely places of my heart. Taking care not to disturb my wife—wife; the term felt so foreign and yet so right—I crawled out of bed and pulled on a pair of trousers.

Out in the living room, I didn't see anyone. I padded to Kristjan's room and softly called his name. No sense in waking him if he hadn't been what I'd heard. There was no answer. Some inner sense said to check.

His room was empty. I could have sworn he'd been exhausted. He hadn't slept last moonstep either. An unease settled in the pit of my stomach. Maybe some warm *kaffi* would help. I didn't need the energy it'd bring, but if I brewed it at half-strength, it might help.

I set the pot to boil and pulled out the ingredients. There was even some *geitmjolk* if I wished, but I decided to save it for Josebina instead. Restless, I paced the kitchen. Once my *kaffi* was ready, I took it to the living room and sat in my favorite chair. I set my mug on the table beside the chair and paused. What was this? That was Kristjan's hand writing.

FATHER,

I'M SURE YOU'LL HEAR THE NEWS WHEN YOU WAKE, BUT I WANTED TO GIVE IT TO YOU STRAIGHT. THE PASSAGE THROUGH VERNDANDI DID LEAD TO THE TRAPPED MINERS. THERE'S A BOOK IN THE LIBRARY THAT EXPLAINED HOW TO UNLOCK IT.

I gasped. Kristjan had found a way to rescue Friðfinn and the others?

THE DEVICE WORKED, BUT IN THE PROCESS, OF OPENING THE DOOR, I DISLODGED ROCKS. ONE OF THEM HIT FRIðFINN IN THE BACK OF THE HEAD. BETWEEN THAT WOUND AND HIS WEAKNESS FROM BRAVELY SACRIFICING FOOD AND WATER FOR THE OTHERS, HE HAS GONE TO THE ANCIENTS. IT WAS MY FAULT. I KILLED HIM.

Killed him? How? That was an accident. Why was Kristjan writing this, rather than telling me in person? My gut clenched, and my stomach roiled, threatening to disgorge my wedding dinner.

TO SAVE YOU THE DISGRACE OF LIVING WITH A MURDERER FOR A SON, I HAVE TAKEN THE PUNISHMENT IN MY OWN HANDS. I'M SORRY, FATHER, BUT STOREHELTUR IS BETTER OFF WITHOUT ME.

LOVE,

Kristjan Jorvarsson

I stopped breathing; my chest collapsed; there was no sound left to me. What had he done? Where *was* he?

A strangled gasp worked its way into a shout. "Kristjan!"

"Geir?" Josebina ran to my—our—bedroom door, wrapped in a blanket. "Geir, what's wrong?"

Her voice propelled me to action. "*Kristjan!* Where are you?"

"Has he left again?"

I thrust the note into her hand and searched for his cloak. It was where it belonged, hanging next to mine. The thought crossed my mind, that Josebina would soon hang hers there as well, and I felt guilty for wasting thoughts on such things. Where would he have gone? Was there anyone else he'd tell first? I must've just missed him; I must've woken because I heard him leaving.

"Tinna! She'll know where he is."

"Go. I'll meet you there once I'm dressed. Unless he's up on Toppur?"

"No, his cloak is…" I choked on my words. If he'd gone to the icy wastes with such darkness in his spirit, then the cloak hanging on its peg might mean nothing. He could be up there right now, freezing.

My feet dashed for the *lofti*, propelling me at reckless speeds up the rocky passage until I emerged under the ice tree. I broke into a sweat that turned to shivers as I surveyed the empty landscape with its pristine coating of snow. He wasn't there.

I raced back to our living quarters to find Josebina dressed and ready. I grabbed her hand and pulled her along. We ran down the passageways. To my surprise, by the sounds filtering through the tapestries, many families were awake.

When we reached Friðfinn's home, I hesitated to call out, but a cry from inside moved me to action.

"*Goðan!*"

Tinna opened the curtain, her eyes red and her cheeks streaked with tears. "Oh, Geirfinnur, I thought you were Kristjan again."

"Where is he?" I didn't waste time. "Where's Kristjan?"

Her pale face, turned lighter yet. "What do you mean? He was heading back to get some sleep after rescuing the miners. I sent him home. There was nothing more he could do here."

I shook my head. "No, he's not at home. He left me a note, said…" How could I repeat it?

"We're afraid he's going to harm himself." Josebina rested a hand on my arm. "Would you know where or how he might do that?"

"H- harm himself?"

I nodded. "He thinks… he thinks Storeheltur would be better off without him."

Tinna gasp was close kin to a devastating cry. "No! I… I need him!"

"I know you do. Where do you think he may have gone? He didn't go to Toppur."

"The library?"

What could harm him there? Despite the uncertainty, I turned to go, but Tinna stopped me.

"The *bensin*!" She turned back inside. "*Moði*, I'm going with Geirfinnur to find Kristjan. I'll be back later. Will you be all right with Aunt Metta?" She must have received a reply, but she didn't wait for long. "Let's go. I'll lead the way."

The path to the library was familiar ground for me. To my surprise, Tinna didn't pause there but hurried on. The scent of rotten food mingled with cooler temperatures was my warning.

I stopped, but Tinna hurried ahead, calling over her shoulder, "It's fine. It's not a true *bensin*, but if he fell in…"

Or jumped in? I didn't know what to expect, but it wasn't what I saw.

* * *

The passages were clearing by the time Kristjan left Tinna's. Even though Tinna had insisted he return home to sleep, the voices condemned him for abandoning her. What kind of man left his betrothed to grieve alone?

Who do you think you are? You worthless lump of dung. Murderer. Liar. Do everyone a favor and be gone before the first watch—you don't want to see how they look at you once they wake to the news. They'll want you dead, anyway. Spare them the trouble. It's the least you can do.

Tinna's haunted eyes flashed before him as he walked unseeing toward his home. They'd been alight with hope when he'd first arrived, but he'd dashed it to bits and left her in tears—tears even his embrace couldn't dry up.

You're useless to her.

"Go away!" The words exploded with such force that several people turned to see who had said them. Heat rushed to his cheeks, and he mumbled an apology.

Great, now I'm looking like a lunatic!

Still concerned with appearances, murderer? Murderer, murderer, murderer…

The accusations rang with each footfall. He couldn't get away from them. By the time he reached his home, the litany had worn a track in his mind, something he could feel even when he didn't hear the words.

What's the penalty for murder? Death. The penalty for murder is death. The penalty for murder…

The implication hung in the air as he pushed aside the tapestry and entered his house. Soft snoring carried from his father's room. Father. What would he say when he found out? The news would kill him! His beloved son, a disgraced killer.

Save him the shame, or are you too cowardly for that? You'd rather drag the Jorvarsson name through the ice with your deeds?

But he couldn't do that. He yanked his cloak from its place and hurried up the *lofti*. Maybe he could find solace on Toppur. But when he came to the mouth of the tunnel, out of breath and with the voices swirling in his head, he found no moonlight waiting to receive him. The shadow of Jorvar's ice tree seemed darker for the lack of light, blocking out even the stars.

Even Jovar condemns you.

The weight of the last several phases fell upon Kristjan's shoulders. He couldn't take it anymore. He'd killed his best friend, accepted a betrothal to a girl he didn't love—a girl who carried his cousin's child—instigated a mining accident, and murdered his future father-in-law. As if that wasn't enough, the rest of Storeheltur would soon follow, starving to death; his rescue of the miners had been merely a stay of execution. He'd failed in every way.

He peered up at the ice tree. "What would you have me do? I can't live up to your expectations, Jorvar. I'm not the great man you were. I couldn't even save my best friend—let alone all of Storeheltur! What do I do?"

Silence met his demand. Not even an ice rat scurried in the tunnel behind him. No wind blew. Nothing.

Kristjan buried his head in his hands. "Why?"

The voices returned, soft and soothing. *Because you know the answer. You know what you should do, but you don't have the honor to do it. Go, climb into the* bensin *and save Storeheltur from the curse you carry. No wonder your mother died birthing you… everyone should've known then.*

That though should've knifed into his heart and made him cry out, scream, sob, rage—something—but it didn't. It just felt right. Like the last step in a pattern, or dark-vision developing into its full clarity—the final piece finding its place.

He turned around, never touching the white crust of ice or the tree that stood, black and angry, against him.

His steps dragged at first, but by the time he'd hung his cloak beside Father's he was able to think clearly.

Father had Josebina now. He'd be fine. Tinna wouldn't want to see him ever again anyway, not after he'd killed her father. Everyone would be better off without him. He could do this.

He strode to the door, only to pause at his father's chair. Father deserved an explanation at least. It didn't take long to write a note and leave it on the table beside the chair. Once that was done, he wondered about Tinna. Sighing, he returned to his room and wrote a hasty message. Satisfied that Father would find it and give it to her, he left it on his desk and walked out into the living room.

The place held many memories, some with Marko, but mostly with his father. Was he willing to give this up?

What? You'd back out now? You know what to do. Be worthy for once in your life and do the right thing.

Kristjan hung his head and crept from the room. He found his way to the *bensin*. His skin stippled from the cold. Where were Orlaugur's workers? Had they already come by with Friðfinn? Or would they round the corner ahead and wonder what he was doing? Maybe they could dissuade him.

Hoping for someone to rescue you? Like Friðfinn hoped you'd rescue him? Coward. Be a Jorvarsson — this is the only way to live up to your name: Do what must be done.

He stood at the dip in the path. The chill was more pronounced here, and the stench of decay filled his senses. Staying here, though, wouldn't do the job.

His knees shook as he walked closer to the edge. How far down was it? Would the fall alone be enough?

Trying to find a way down, he noticed in the shadows of the dip that the path widened ever so slightly, and he forced himself to explore the edge. To his surprise, he discovered hand-holds and remembered the times Marko had encouraged him to climb. With a deep breath, he descended into the cold and dark. Each step sent a chill down his spine until he was shivering. On a ragged breath of rancid air, he gagged, and his hand slipped. His stomach leapt into his throat, as he fell. There was no way to gauge how far. As his body slammed into the ground, shards of agony erupted from his ribs and one knee, stealing his breath, and his head bounced off the stone immediately after. He struggled, trying to gasp and finding that he couldn't, his lungs spasming as they sat empty. When finally he did manage to draw in air, it was the fetid gas that flowed in, burning, clogging his throat, as if an ice rat had gotten lodged there, and was trying to scratch its way out.

His heart raced as the realization hit. He was in a *bensin* with no way out. Was this really what he'd wanted? To die like this?

You deserve no less.

He knew that; he *knew* it, but suddenly he wished he'd found some other way, waited, tried… something. Anything. He tried to turn over to see how far up the lip of the chasm might be, but the agony in his body prevented it. He choked on the gas, and his eyes watered; an inevitable sense of *ending* took over his thoughts. He was past hope. He was dying.

Marko, is this what you felt? The image of the blood-stained snow and Marko's pale, staring eyes returned to him—his only company in his final moments.

That felt just as right as it was inescapable.

Another cough wracked his body. He didn't remember coughing when he'd stumbled into the *bensin* with Marko and Bastian so many rotations ago. Was this different? He shivered and his breathing shifted to shortened, shallow gasps. Was that *yoma* ahead? Was someone coming? He blinked and the dots faded away, only to return elsewhere. His head felt heavy, as if it was pressing more firmly into the rock on which it rested.

Give up. Breathe it in.

Kristjan hadn't thought he was capable of feeling anything, but a tear trailed down his cheek to the dirt, followed by another and another. *Marko, I'm sorry. Friðfinn, I didn't mean to kill you. Forgive me. Father, forgive me.*

With one solitary sob, he closed his eyes.

Justice had been served.

Chapter 30

30 Fjorda, 400 AI

In the light of the *yoma*, the path leveled out, but nothing was there. Where was my son? Tinna cast about, her face creased with worry.

"He *has* to be here." She held the *yoma* over the gaping pit to the side of the way. "There! I think I see someone!"

She crouched down, but Josebina stopped her. "You're pregnant. This gas wouldn't be good for the child."

"I…" She looked at her feet. "I don't care."

"But does Kristjan?" Josebina's hand was firm, her voice soft.

Tinna bit her lip.

"I'll go. He's my son. Tinna, if you want to do something, you can go get more help." I wasn't sure what I'd find at the bottom, but there was no way I'd be able to bring Kristjan back to the surface on my own. "I could use more *yoma*."

She nodded. "I'll get the lamp from the library."

With that she was gone. Josebina reached for me. "Be careful, Geir." Her eyes shone in the dim light, but her voice held no quaver. "I know what he means to you, but you need to come back as well."

I wiped a tear from her cheek. "I'll be careful. Jeeah knows how much I love my son, but I love you, too. We have many things to look forward to in the rotations ahead."

She smiled, and I kissed her. "When Tinna brings back the lamp, I'll need it to see. Can you figure out a way to get it down to me without breaking it?"

"I can do that. You'll also need these." She ripped the bottom of her tunic and handed me the strip.

"What—"

Josebina waved her hand to silence me and tore another strip. This one she tied around my nose and mouth. "It's not much, but it has to be better than breathing in the fumes directly."

"Thank you."

We shared a wide-eyed moment of fear, and then I began the descent into the pit. I felt around for a foothold, then found purchase for my hand on a rock that jutted out. Another foothold, another rock. Step by careful step I moved.

Before I was even half-way down, light flared around me. The *yoma* lamp had arrived. I chanced a glance up to see it suspended in a basket. In its glow, I sought my son. He lay on his side, his face pale, but that could have been the *yoma's* light.

Jeeah, don't let me be too late!

I couldn't hurry this, or I'd slip. My heart raced, and my hands turned clammy. What would I find at the bottom? How long had he been here? I'd been too agitated to ask Tinna when he'd left her place.

At last, my foot found solid purchase. The chill was much worse here.

Kneeling, I felt his skin—cool to the touch, but that could have been from the air temperature. His lips were tinged with blue. Not a good sign. Was he breathing?

Please, Jeeah.

I wetted my finger and held it beneath his nose. The barest breath of air chilled my skin.

Thank you!

But already, I could feel the light-headedness beginning. I wrapped the extra cloth around Kristjan's nose and checked for other injuries. He seemed to be all right, but I worried about fractured bones or, worse, internal injuries that'd escape my quick inspection. The way he was lying, suggested that he'd fallen, unable to move from how he'd landed—that alone told me he was more injured than he appeared. I tried to get him onto my shoulders, but the exertion made me draw too deep a breath, and I was wracked by an immediate coughing fit that doubled me over.

What could I *do*? Maybe I could at least sit him up. The higher up, the less toxic the gas.

I draped his arm across my shoulders and used it to pull his body across them, but by the time I'd let another round of coughing pass, I was growing dizzy. I knew I couldn't manage to stand up under his weight—I'd accomplished nothing.

Please, Jeeah, we need help! I… I can't do this on my own.

And then I waited.

Long moments, congealing into what felt like an eternity, and every time I checked Kristjan's breathing, I feared there'd be nothing to find. Was the weak little stream of air I felt waning still further, or was I imagining it? I wanted to scream, to shout for help, for anyone to hear me and come, but I knew I couldn't. I had to keep my breathing shallow, take in as little of the toxin as possible. I had to be conscious when help came; I had to be able to take my son out of this pit of death. I desperately wanted to wrap my arms around Kristjan and shield his face from the vapors, but I feared obstructing what little healthy air was still mingled with the gas at this depth. My son, the pride of my life and the steady beat of my heart, lying in a chasm, trying to throw away his own life.

How had I *missed it*? How had I not seen how he was suffering until it was too late? My grief wracked my body while I sat in that pit with him, helpless, his limp form draped over my shoulders, deluged by my own failures, failures I'd hoped he'd forget or overcome, but which had plainly added up to something more fearful

than I could ever have conceived. How many times had I wanted to go to him and held back? How many times had I failed to listen to him? How many times had I simply put off responding to what I did hear, then let it be lost in the mundane tasks and responsibilities of daily living? Those little catches in his voice; the times when his tone hadn't quite matched his words, how he'd turn away from me as if in pain… Why hadn't I just opened my mouth and *spoken*? My son had been falling down a mine shaft, and I'd been standing at the top wondering why he wasn't talking to me. How many chances had I had to break and bridge that silence?

Would I ever get another one?

While my thoughts roiled, the headache set in; the slight cough I'd had since alighting here intensified until it was hard to breathe in between. We were both running out of time. When I felt for his breath, it was hardly more than a whisper, and it was too long before another one came.

"Kristjan," I wheezed, shaking him. "Kristjan!" And of course, the cough redoubled, sending my lungs into spasm. I felt him slipping from my shoulders and clutched at him, leaning into the wall, gripping his limbs with all my remaining strength while my body fought the poison. *Jeeah, please… not my son. Not my son. Please, I need another chance.*

* * *

Some place, something rumbled. Tinna hadn't had enough time to go get help, so what was it? Not another cave-in; the thought sent a shock of terror through me, but the sound didn't abate as a collapse should have. Instead, it came closer, and then I heard Josebina's voice. I couldn't distinguish the words, but the urgency was unmistakable.

"Geirfinnur?" Orlaugur called down to me.

"Help!" My throat ached, and I doubted that he could've heard me.

"I'll be there shortly. Hold on."

Hold on. I'd hold my son to the last.

Thank you. The miracle of help; it'd been sent. Jeeah had answered.

Soon, Orlaugur stood before me a rope in his hands and his freshly-washed hair dampening the edges of his tunic that he'd wrapped around the lower half of his face.

I struggled to do as he commanded—every miner knew how to tie a safe harness for exploration—but trying to situate Kristjan so that I could do that work was too much for me; I'd grown too weak.

"Get up there." Orlaugur motioned toward the wall. "You'll be no good if you pass out."

"Not... without... my... son." Each word was painful, but he needed to understand.

Orlaugur shook his head, but quickly helped me knot a harness around Kristjan's hips and shoulders.

"You'll go up with him. I'll be behind you both." Orlaugur called up to Josebina, "Now!"

Kristjan's Rise

The rumble came again, but with it, Kristjan moved. The weight left my shoulders. Then his arm lifted from my neck. If I was to stay with my son, I needed to climb. Each step, brought me out of the gas, but still Kristjan hung limply from the lifeline. Below me, Orlaugur began to cough, but I couldn't spare the focus to check on him; my fingers were scarcely holding to the wall as it was.

After what felt like a span, I came up to eye level with a pair of boots. Josebina's boots.

Tinna gasped. "Kristjan!"

I collapsed to my knees on the path, and Orlaugur was close behind me. Air wheezed through my lungs, and I stripped the mask off. The rumbling stopped. I didn't have the energy to investigate its origin.

Josebina rubbed my hands in hers. "He's safe."

It was a reassurance. I wanted to see with my own eyes, but when I tried to move my head, a wave of nausea ran through my body. Gulping back bile, I waited for my stomach to settle.

"Andri, go get Froða. Tell her it's *bensin* gas poisoning." Margeir knelt down beside me and smiled. "Be thankful we were here to bring Friðfinn back to his family. Otherwise, you'd still be down there."

I nodded, and at least my head didn't swim with the motion.

"Kristjan, wake up." Tinna sobbed. "Wake up!"

Margeir's countenance fell. "I'll see what I can do for him."

"Th- thank you." I managed to get the words out while Josebina helped me sit up.

"He needs good air." Margeir rested a hand on Tinna's shoulder. "Will you let me try?"

"Please."

Was there nothing I could do? I tried to stand, but Josebina put a heavy hand on my shoulder.

"Easy, Geir. You'll be dizzy if you stand right now."

"Kris… tjan."

"Hush." Josebina smoothed my hair back. "Jeeah has him."

I bit my lip. There was nothing left for me to do. My son lay sprawled beside me, his betrothed crying next to him. Meanwhile, I could barely breathe, let alone walk.

Margeir bent over Kristjan and tilted his head back, pinching his nose, then sealed his mouth to my son's so he could force his own clean air into Kristjan's lungs; a moment later he took both hands and pressed sharply down on Kristjan's stomach, vacating the stale air before he bent to breathe for Kristjan once more. I knew the procedure, but never had it seemed so agonizingly slow, so ineffective. I watched with void in my stomach and a knife in my chest, coughing and wishing Kristjan would do the same. Waiting.

A fourth cycle.

Waiting.

A fifth.

Jeeah, please. Don't save me just to take him. Take me, take me; I'll go to the ancients! Spare my son!

Then suddenly, I saw a tiny movement, barely a flutter, but I cried out when I saw it. Kristjan's chest, rising. Falling. Margeir gave a sound of relief and strafed his knuckles against Kristjan's breastbone. The flutter became a true inhale, a weak gasp, followed by a cough and then a moan.

A sob erupted from my throat, and I fell forward onto my hands and knees to be nearer to him, and this time Josebina didn't hold me back. I cupped my hand against his face, felt the pulse of blood in his neck.

"Alive!" I cried, heedless of how my throat scraped itself raw to make the sound. The pain was nothing to the dreadful fear now relieved. "Jeeah, he's alive. Kristjan." I stroked his hair back from his face. "Kristjan, I love you, son. I *love you*."

* * *

The first thing Kristjan knew was excruciating pain and his father's voice somewhere nearby, saying things he couldn't yet decipher. His leg throbbed, his lungs burned, and his chest ached. It felt like someone had dropped a boulder on it. He couldn't bring himself to open his eyes, but the voices around him told him all he needed to know. He was alive.

It should have sent his heart plummeting in despair, but instead a strange warmth stole over him. He'd failed, but he was *glad*. There in the last moments as he felt his lungs clog and his breathing fail, he'd realized that he didn't want to die. His problems hadn't been resolved. He'd live with the *holdt's* disdain for the two lives he'd taken. But he was alive.

"Kristjan, oh, Kristjan."

Tinna? She was here? How?

"Give him room," Margeir instructed, and Kristjan felt a hand leave his face. "He's breathing on his own. When Froða gets here, we'll take him to Ferish Pools. The waters will help heal his lungs."

How did Marko's father know so much about healing? Would he have been able to save Marko? The image flashed through Kristjan's mind. No, too much blood. No one was able to staunch that type of wound.

Kristjan's heart ached as if pierced by a knife—a pain that had nothing to do with the *bensin* gas and everything to do with the death of his friend. Was there a way to fix a broken heart? He desperately hoped so. It was good to feel again, but it hurt. Before he could stop it, a tear trickled down the side of his face. Tinna wiped it away.

"Hush, we're here," she whispered into his ear. "Your father found your note. I brought him here. If..." She trailed off. "I won't dwell on that. I'll be grateful we made it in time."

As would he. Part of him cringed at the idea of causing such a frantic scramble on his behalf, but the other part was glad that they'd found him.

Selfish. Failure. A man who can't even find honor in death—a burden on them all.

He ignored the voice. It didn't matter. He was alive, and while he lived, he had a second chance.

Chapter 31

1 Fimmti, 400 AI

Kristjan closed his eyes and allowed the others to work around him. Tinna was clutching his hand as if she'd never let go. He didn't blame her, but he still couldn't understand how she could forgive him. Maybe when she saw her father's body that would change. He let it go; she was here. That was all that mattered at the moment.

At least Father… Tinna had mentioned him. Kristjan forced his eyes open to see her face hovering over his. "Hush, all will be well. Margeir's here, and he sent for your aunt. She'll know what to do."

She would.

"Kristjan." Father's voice came from his other side.

Despite the weight of his head and the pounding inside his skull, Kristjan forced it to move. He dreaded the condemnation he'd see, but putting it off would accomplish nothing.

"Oh, Kristjan." His father's words were soft, barely an exhale of breath. And his eyes—they were full of love.

Kristjan blinked, wondering if the gas had addled his brain. Father would be scolding him—for trying to run away from his responsibilities, for refusing to face the consequences of his actions, for…

"My son, I'm…" Father swallowed back either a cough or a sob, Kristjan wasn't sure which. "I'm sorry."

Sorry? Father? For what? Kristjan tried to form the words, but they wouldn't come out past the pain in his throat or the burning in his lungs. Nevertheless, his father understood.

Father rested a shaky hand on Kristjan's shoulder. "I… I pushed you away. I didn't mean to, but I did. For that I'm sorry. Will you forgive me?"

None of this made sense. Tinna and Father had found him, Father wanted forgiveness, and instead of lying in the halls of the ancients, he was lying in the dip in the path—as if he'd never fallen.

"Geirfinnur." Margeir leaned over from above Kristjan's head. "It's best if he doesn't try to speak. Depending on how long he was down there, he could damage his voice if he tries too much before we get him to the pools."

Father nodded and reached for Kristjan's face. With hands as tender as Telma with Glyta, he wiped away the last of Kristjan's tears. The motion brought more.

Why hadn't he done this sooner? Maybe if he had, I wouldn't have listened to the voices.

"Shh, my son." Father coughed, but left his hand on Kristjan's face. "There's something you must know."

Margeir handed Father a water skin. "If you insist on speaking, drink first."

Father nodded and took a long draught. When Margeir was satisfied, Father said, "Never again believe the lie. Storeheltur is *not* better off without you. Do you hear me?"

Kristjan managed a nod.

Tinna squeezed his hand. "*I* need you, Kristjan."

"As do we." Josebina leaned over Father's shoulder. "That's three people. Can you promise me you'll stay here? For us, if nothing else?"

Again, Kristjan nodded. He couldn't understand it; why were these people saying they needed him? Josebina had Father, and Father had her and all of Storeheltur. Tinna… She couldn't mean it. Not after what he'd done.

"Andri, you didn't say I had three patients." Aunt Froða stood with arms crossed looking down at him.

"Three?" Kristjan ignored the warning and spoke anyway. Was Father hurt? And who would the third be?

Tinna saw him glancing around and nodded toward another prone form. "Orlaugur helped your father get you up here."

"And why did he need two grown men to help get him back up here in the first place?" Froða glared at him.

"He fell."

"Fell? Kristjan?" Despite her questions, Froða was already bending down by his feet, and as she surveyed him, she bumped up against his foot, evoking a guttural yell. "What?" Froða shook her head. "No one told me I had other injuries to care for."

She examined first one foot, then the other. Kristjan whimpered.

"I'm going as easy as I can. Andri, run back to my place. Tell Mikkael I need my splint bag. He's got a broken leg." Froða dug into a bag at her side. "Each of you need these." She held out a type of lichen with a dense leafing pattern. "Place it over your noses and breathe through it and drink as much water as you can. How long were you down there?"

"Only long enough to get the rope around Kristjan." Orlaugur coughed.

"And you, Geirfinnur?"

Father shrugged. "Until help came."

"I see. Josebina, will you keep him from speaking now? I can tell from the rawness of his voice that it was too long. Once I can care for Kristjan's leg, you're all moving away from here. Orlaugur, if you're able to, you should leave."

"Won't you need me to get Kristjan home?"

"I think others can do that."

Orlaugur glanced about. "I only see Tinna, Josebina, and Andri as anywhere near healthy enough. Sorry, Margeir, but I'm not sure you could lift him."

"I see your point." Froða waved one hand in accession. "Then for now, those who are healthy, should make their way further up the path. We'll call you when ready. I don't need more patients to manage."

Kristjan held onto Tinna's hand. He knew he should let her go, but something about her presence was a balm to his soul.

"P- plea…" He coughed, and Froða scolded him.

"Hush. You'll only make things worse." She glanced to Tinna. "Did you not hear me?"

"He needs me." Tinna's normally timid personality had taken on an edge as if contesting Froða's authority.

Froða shook her head. "Fine, then at least cover your nose and mouth." She handed a scarf to Tinna and wrapped one around her own face as she bent over Kristjan.

Kristjan was afraid Aunt Froða would question or scold him, but she only bustled around him muttering under her breath. For as long as Kristjan could remember, Aunt Froða had been the one who was there when anyone got hurt. It comforted him to know he was under her care. He shut his eyes and took a shuddering breath. All would be well.

You've proven you're a coward, murderer, liar, and failure. What's going to be 'well' when Storeheltur is saddled with that for their chief?

Maybe the words were true, but he didn't have to listen to them.

You're learning. Sometimes, it takes falling to regain your feet.

For once the other voice didn't drown out the softer one. What a change—refreshing. Life-giving. Could it be that through this, he'd learned something valuable?

Not you, the louder voice condemned.

Kristjan shut it out and mulled over the implications. How could he more often hear the gentler voice in his mind? How did he keep finding the truth that let him live?

Aunt Froða's voice brought him back to the present. "Thank you, Andri. Kristjan, this will probably hurt. I'm going to have to realign the bone."

He thought he was prepared, but the agony was beyond anything he could've imagined. Kristjan yelled, squeezing Tinna's hand.

"Shh." She smoothed his hair from his forehead.

Another raw howl echoed in the enclosed space as Aunt Froða gave another sharp motion of her hands and his leg shot through with shards of fire.

"That's the worst of it." Aunt Froða steadied his leg and wrapped it firmly.

The pain eased to a rhythmic throb, and Kristjan breathed a sigh of relief that shuddered in his chest, ice and magma stuttering through his ribs

"I..." Father wiped at his eyes. Were those tears? Why? "I'm sorry, son."

"Now, Geirfinnur, will you be satisfied?" Froða placed her hands on her hips. "He's as bandaged as I can get him. Now all of you need to get to Ferish Pools. Andri, I can use your help now."

Father stood but wobbled, and Josebina supported him. Froða shook her head but didn't comment.

Andri and Orlaugur bent down beside Kristjan. Each placed one of his arms over a shoulder, then slid their free arms under his legs forming a chair of sorts.

"One, two, three." Orlaugur grunted as he lifted.

Together, they carried him up the path to a waiting ore cart. Was this one they'd brought to take Friðfinn home? Kristjan didn't have the willpower to inquire. All that mattered was that he was alone in it. Tinna took his hand again and walked alongside.

"Geirfinnur, you should join him." Froða's voice carried down the way.

"I'm able to walk." Father coughed, and Josebina pursed her lips, then hauled him toward the cart by a gentle but inexorable grip on one hand.

"Go as gently as you can, but get them to the pools." Froða shook her head. "I'll be along as soon as I gather my things. I'll bring some tea as well."

Kristjan didn't hear any more. The cart hit a bump and he groaned. As it picked up speed, it jostled and clanked its way down the passage. Each jolt sent another wave of agony up Kristjan's leg and through his ribs. Part of him longed to pass out and not feel the pain, but the other part of him was grateful he was alive.

* * *

Soon the warmth of the pools seeped into the passage and replaced the metallic dryness of Verndandi. The humidity and the pungent odor brought back the memories from eighteen rotations ago—another hurried trip to Ferish Pools. I took a steadying breath. My son would be all right; he *had* to be.

Kristjan coughed and groaned, clutching his side.

"We'll make it through this, son."

"Th—" Another cough wracked his body. "Thank you. But…" He sighed. "I don't deserve it."

"Set those thoughts aside. They're what led you to that *bensin*."

Kristjan nodded, then gripped his leg as we hit a particularly large bump.

"Sorry," Andri called up. "We're ready to get you down from there. Geirfinnur, I think you can come down on your own. Kristjan, do you want someone up there helping you?"

With a grimace, Kristjan shook his head, but I waited to see what he'd do. He might not be capable of as much as he hoped. He slid first one leg and then the other over the edge.

"Jeeah help me," Kristjan muttered as he slid down into Andri and Orlaugur's waiting arms.

He already has.

Josebina was there when my feet met the ground, appearing as she so often did, a stolid presence that was close enough to lean on without demanding that I do so. "How are you?"

"Better than Kristjan."

She shook her head and kissed me. "I didn't ask about your son. I needed to know how my husband is."

I smiled. How I needed her! "I'm well. The air is already soothing my throat."

"Now." My sister set her burdens down on a bench carved into the wall and surveyed the room. "Any woman who's shy needs to leave. These men are going to get into the pool, and I doubt they want to do that fully clothed."

Tinna blushed but didn't relinquish her hold on Kristjan's hand. Josebina must have noticed for she squeezed my hand and slipped over to the girl, whispered something in her ear, and the pair made their way out.

"Kristjan, you need to be completely immersed in the water. The rest of you didn't have as much contact with the fumes, so you won't have to submerge, but the more of you is in the water, the faster you'll heal."

Andri and Orlaugur set Kristjan on the ledge—the place where Sæbjort had labored in water, murky with red, her weight on my legs… My vision betrayed the present and went to the past, and suddenly I could scarcely think of where I stood, what I needed to do. My only instinct was to look for Josebina, but she'd gone, and it wasn't until I heard Kristjan's voice again that I could return to what lived.

"I can't… My leg won't let me—" Red ran up Kristjan's neck.

"Don't worry, son." Margeir patted Kristjan's shoulder. "We'll help."

While Kristjan slipped out of his tunic, we helped him out of his trousers and down to his underlayer.

"Go ahead and lower him to me." I held out my arms for my son.

The memories fought for control, but I didn't let them. This was now. I had Josebina and Kristjan to care for. I couldn't be swallowed by old sorrow. Sæbjort was gone, but I knew that by caring for her son, I honored her memory.

With care, I maneuvered Kristjan to one of the submerged benches. Then I sat beside him.

"Thank you… Father."

"Hush, no talking. Just let the water and minerals do their job."

Froða laughed. "The same goes for you, Geirfinnur. Andri, you might as well see about getting fresh clothes for these two, and Orlaugur."

"I'll be fine." Orlaugur squatted beside the pool. "I wasn't in there very long."

"Thank you, Orlaugur." I looked up to the elder and caught his eye. "I…" I didn't want to think of it, but it needed to be expressed. "I couldn't have done it without you."

"You're welcome."

He was ready to say more, but my sister slapped the back of his shoulder. "Enough! No more talking."

I tried to smirk at her and settled onto the bench, allowing the water to buoy up my legs and soothe away the pains I carried.

Chapter 32

1 Fimmti, 400 AI

Kristjan opened his eyes. When had he been returned to his own bed? Had it all been a dream? The murmur of feminine voices outside his room drew him out of bed—or would have, if the pain hadn't immediately shot up his leg, piercing him with the wash of memory—all that had happened. His inhalation of breath sent his lungs into a coughing spasm which ended in a groan—he must've cracked at least one rib in the fall. Nothing to be done about that, though—his aunt had told him that much. They'd heal in their own time.

Tinna and Josebina rushed into the room.

"Easy, Kristjan." Josebina pushed him back down into the pillow. "We don't want you taxing either your lungs or your leg. Froða has it splinted up but says you need to stay off of it for at least two cycles."

Two *cycles*? "But…"

"It'll be fine." Tinna brushed his hair back from his face. "Rest."

But he couldn't. The *holdt*. The mine. Would they survive two cycles? Despite his frantic thoughts, his body categorized fighting either of them as a waste of resources. He rubbed his eyes.

"How… how is…"

"Shh, Kristjan." Josebina pulled the blanket up.

"Please, I need to know." He knew he sounded desperate, but he didn't care. How could what others thought affect him after almost dying?

"Is that my son?" Father pushed the curtain away, his eyes somber.

"Stubborn like you." Josebina shook her head. "Just be sure he gets the rest he needs."

Father hugged Josebina before she could slip past him. "I'll be sure to take care of him, but if he's my son, he won't rest until he knows all's in order."

With a shrug, Josebina left. Tinna stood close, as unmoving as granite, as if she'd never belong anywhere else, and was afraid of losing that place. He didn't blame her. She'd lost too many people in too short of a time, and the best he could do to reassure her was take her hand, so he did. She squeezed in response, the motion somehow grateful.

He almost thought he heard a condemning voice, telling him how inadequate it was. But Tinna's face said something different, and he chose to believe her instead.

"I'll try to answer your most pressing questions—at least, as best as I can guess them." Father sat down

beside him, drawing his attention away from Tinna. "First off, the miners made it out safely. The door you found is still open which provided us with access to the ore. Nyvarð will return with his fellow explorers to Isholt, but not empty-handed. They'll have samples of the ore to share."

It was as if a weight lifted from Kristjan's chest. Merchants would return to them; they'd have what they needed. Storeheltur would survive. At least… he hated to think it, given the grief he'd caused his betrothed in the doing, but… at least it all hadn't been for naught.

As if you did anything to help.

Kristjan longed to silence the voice, but instead, the quieter one replied. *You brought food when there was none; you faced your fears to search for the new mine.*

Which led to trapping men and women and killing your betrothed's father. Yet the voice didn't hold the power it had before.

And you rescued the miners, opening the mine to send ore back. You've helped your people.

He had. It felt strange to not heed the negative voice. "…proud of you."

Somehow, he'd missed what Father was saying; it didn't seem that Father had noticed, though, because he went on without pausing.

"You've done much of valor. From providing us with food, to marrying a girl to protect her honor."

Kristjan blinked. "What?" The word was hoarse and screeched.

Father glanced at Tinna and then made eye contact with Kristjan. "She told me what you'd done. Your secret is safe with me, but know that I am proud of you. I think, though, that we're going to have to bring Hafnar and Ebonney here soon."

Things were moving so quickly. Father smiled, and with a final squeeze of Kristjan's hand, he left the two of them alone.

"Ti—"

She quieted him with a tap to his cheek. "He's correct. We can't wait much longer. Father would've wanted us to get married. Unless, we figure out a way for you to walk without using your leg, you'll not be able to attend the *fivku*. As soon as it's over, maybe even before the *maltið* I want to become your wife…" She faltered and hung her head. "That's… that's if you still want me."

Look what— Kristjan shut down the voice.

"Tinna, I'd be honored to have you as my wife. But there's one thing you must know." He waited for her to look at him, and then patted the bed beside him. Once she had settled, he said, "I still hear the same voices— the ones that told me that…" Kristjan shrugged and winced as even that motion somehow connected with his leg. "I've always felt the pressure of being Jorvar's successor. Somewhere in that, I started hearing things in my head, like someone was speaking to me. Telling me what to do—or reminding me of how I'd failed."

"And it told you you were worthless? That there isn't a future left for you?" Her hands shook as she placed them in her lap—but there was a solemn hush to her voice that spoke of familiarity. He nodded slowly, trying to make out the expression on her averted face. Did she understand?

"Yes. And it felt true, after hearing it for so long. After I killed—I mean, after Marko died, it got worse and worse, until I..."

Just speak the words. They'll free you.
Coward.

"I tried to kill myself."

There it was spoken, and the irony wasn't lost on him. The voice that had condemned him had been the final push to let the shame be set free, cast into the light that could devour it.

"I'm not proud of it—"

Tinna reached over and wrapped her arms around him—that hurt, too, but he didn't care. Her tears dripped onto his shoulder. He blinked and patted her shoulder, not willing to let her know that even that pressure was painful. He was sure he'd cause her enough pain in all their rotations together—he could bear this without complaint.

When her sobs had eased, she didn't draw back. "I... I was so frightened. Without you..." She sniffled, burying her face tightly against his neck and clutching at the back of his tunic. "I'd be lost without you. You mean the world to me. Please… stay here."

Storeheltur needs you. Your betrothed needs you. What will you do?

For once the harsher voice had nothing to add. It was as if it held its breath waiting for Kristjan's answer.

"I'll stay for you, Tinna." He took a shallow breath. "And for our child."

She raised up to see him. "Our?"

He nodded. "Our. That gives me two reasons to stay."

"Thank you, Kristjan." A shaky smile spread across her face. "But…" Her smile dimmed. "We make a good match. You hear voices, and I have dreams."

Kristjan waited for her to go on, but she hid her face in his chest.

"Dreams, *kæra*?"

"Of… of Bastian, and what—"

Kristjan held her close. "Hush. From now on, I'll be beside you when you have them. You can curl up in my arms and know you're safe."

"Really?" She looked up at him with such trust and love.

At one time, he'd have believed the voice that said he could never live up to that trust. But for now, at least, he felt that simply being there for her might be enough to begin with—and to keep that promise, they needed their own ceremony.

"Now, I suppose you need to go speak to your mother. I would, but…" He grinned at her. "I'm sorry that the ceremony may be held in my bedroom." Heat rushed up the back of his neck, and he found everything else in the room to look at.

Tinna giggled, summoning his attention despite himself. "Some would say that's the best place to have a wedding ceremony." Her cheeks were red, but she held his gaze. "I won't complain."

"Then go work out the details. I can't wait to make you my wife."

To his surprise, he meant every word of it. He wanted to care for her, to have her beside him, holding him steady against the storms to come.

* * *

I couldn't help but notice the smile on Tinna's face, as well as the red in her cheeks, when she finally came out of Kristjan's room.

"Is everything all right?" I couldn't help but grin at her.

The flush colored her face even more brightly as she nodded. "I... Chief Geirfinnur..."

"Take a deep breath, daughter."

Tinna complied, then plunged ahead. "Could you ask Hafnar to wed us? I'd like to do so as soon as possible—maybe even before the *fivku.*"

"Thought that might be the case. What will your mother say?"

"I... I don't know. I hope I can convince her it'd please *Pabbi*."

"Then you go talk with her and bring her back here by the third watch if she'll be swayed."

With a nod, she was gone. Couldn't blame her. If I was in her shoes, I'd want to be married as soon as possible.

With a thought, I sought out my wife—it still felt strange to think of her that way; even moreso was the term of endearment that so easily fell from my lips.

"*Kæra*, could I ask you to prepare something special for Kristjan and Tinna?"

Josebina glanced up from chopping up dried fruit. "Already working on a pie."

My heart swelled with gratitude. *Jeeah, how did I ever deserve her?*

"Thank you."

As Josebina dropped the fruit into the pan and sprinkled some spices over them, she asked, "What are we going to do about housing?"

I hadn't even thought of that! "I'm sure they'll want their own place eventually, but for now, he needs his own bed. We have time; I'll discuss it with Kristjan later."

"I can just imagine how that will go." Josebina grinned at me. "The pair of you, stammering at each other, you with that wonderful blush in your cheeks."

I started to wave a hand in an anxious bid to skip over the topic, but caught on her last words. "You think it's wonderful?"

Her grin widened as she nodded and poured water into the pan and stirred. "The pie will be ready when its needed. Are you off, then?"

I nodded. "Hafnar."

"Then you'd best get." Her words were softened by her smile.

As I was on my way to Hafnar's house, Orlaugur found me; his solemn face reminding me that there was both joy and grief among my people.

"Do you have a moment, Geirfinnur?"

I nodded, wondering what this was about. "Any place in particular you'd like to speak?"

Orlaugur shrugged. "Private would be best."

Realizing we were close to the Garður, I led the way. When we came upon a bench, Orlaugur sat and invited me to join him.

"What can I help you with?" My curiosity finally got the better of me.

The elder didn't reply right away. That was never a good sign.

"Geirfinnur, have the elders placed too much pressure on Kristjan?"

I blinked. Where had this come from?

"Before you answer, think carefully. Even though Kristjan tries to hide it, the elders saw his fear of heights when he introduced us to the mine. Yet, he was at the bottom of that *bensin*. Why?"

Yes, why. Despite having read Kristjan's letter, I still couldn't believe it.

"He'd already brought the miners safely past. Why was he back there?" Orlaugur asked.

I wiped a hand across my face. How much should I tell him? Or should I make Kristjan tell? Although it was my son's place to do so, it felt wrong to put him in that position; I could at least share what I understood—which wasn't much.

"Orlaugur, you must promise me you won't speak of this to Kristjan." I waited for his nod before continuing. "According to the note he left me, Kristjan believes he was responsible for Friðfinn's death."

"What? What can he have been *thinking*? He *rescued* those people."

"Yet when he opened the door, it dislodged the stone that killed Friðfinn. He felt—feels—responsible."

"So… what was he doing going back there? Going back to try to work out how to find it could've been avoided?"

I sighed. "No. He… someone told him that Storeheltur would be better off without him."

Orlaugur sucked in air, then rested a gentle hand on my shoulder. "Oh, Geirfinnur. And he believed this lie?"

"Yes. Enough so that he purposely tried to take his own life."

Orlaugur gaped, his mouth opening and closing wordlessly. I weathered his confusion, which mirrored my own, hoping in some way that he'd find reason in it where I couldn't. How could Kristjan be so blind?

At last, Orlaugur turned to me. "I... I don't know what to say, Geirfinnur. How are you holding up?"

I shrugged. "I really don't know," I said with a tremble in my voice. Orlaugur's grip on my shoulder tightened, and I swallowed, blinking rapidly. "I haven't had a lot of time to process what I missed. How I could've let him..." I buried my face in my hands, holding the sobs at bay, but they leaked between my fingers anyway. "I let this happen to him. Sæbjort wouldn't have let... if she were alive, he wouldn't..."

My shoulder rocked with the force of Geirfinnur's tug on it. "But Jeeah gave *you* to him, and you were doing your best. The boy hid his pain wel—I've wondered sometimes at how... active, and capable, he seemed after Marko's death. I think we all believed he was just incredibly resilient, that he'd withstand whatever came. Even a chief can only act on what he knows, Geir, and even then, you can never walk another's path for them. You can only change so much—and you didn't know."

I nodded, sucking my grief back down into my chest in stuttering gasps that I silenced one by one, focusing on the pressure of my friend's fingers and the tight clasp of my own over my mouth. "I can't let it happen again," I whispered.

"I know," Orlaugur replied softly.

I swallowed, letting my feelings settle slowly, while Orlaugur released his hold on me and simply sat, waiting while I calmed.

At last, I managed to wrest my mind back to the present and then to the near future. I gave my friend a weak but grateful smile.

"I'm here for you, if you ever want to talk through things," he offered.

I nodded once more. Thank you. But this step…" I pushed to my feet and drew an expansive breath, looking ahead, toward Hafnar's house. "I'll be celebrating. My son's becoming a husband." The thought washed over me, as alien as it was invigorating, and I was utterly suffused with the gratitude that accompanied it—so filled with it that it stirred me to say, "I can't wait to tell him how proud I am of him."

"You think he sees more clearly now, then?"

"I don't know, but I think so. And Tinna… I think she'll be good for him."

"I couldn't agree more. Congratulations, Geir."

As Orlaugur walked off, I contemplated his words. What a mess Bastian had made of things. Maybe it was time for a longer talk with my nephew, but first I had to see Hafnar.

Chapter 33

1 Fimmti, 400 AI

Froða answered my call at her door. "Geir! Welcome. Come in. Come in."

"Thank you. How are you doing?"

"Fine. I should be inquiring about that son of yours. Is he staying off that leg?"

"I believe so, but you may want to pay him a visit. Is Bastian home?"

My sister eyed me with a cocked head as she nodded slowly before calling. "Bastian, Uncle Geirfinnur's here to see you." She turned to me. "I'll check on Kristjan."

Bastian entered from his room, glancing between me and his mother's departing form. "Uncle."

I motioned to the chairs in the sitting room and took one of them. Bastian settled warily in another. I studied my nephew; he glared back at me.

"Is there something you need, uncle? If you're just going to stare at me, I have other things I could be doing."

"Bastian." I leaned forward, trying to quell the roiling disgust in my gut. How could this be my nephew—the one who had tagged along to elder meetings and anything else he could when he was younger? "We have some things to discuss."

"Like what? How your son isn't fit to be chief?"

I blinked.

"Oh, I know. I heard Andri talk. Said Kristjan fell down a *bensin*. That's one thing Kristjan would *never* do. He'd never go near a cliff face unless he had a death wish—so, he must have been heeding my advice. So, will you believe me now that he's unfit?"

My mouth worked, but my brain was stuck. "Unfit? *Unfit*? How do you see that, Bastian? Who else would take my place?"

At least my nephew had the grace to glance away, but it was only momentarily, and when he looked back, his eyes were hard. "Me. Didn't I do just as much as your precious son to help rescue the miners? I've been working all watches." He held up his hands which sported broken nails, scratches, and dirt deep into the creases of his knuckles.

"*I* listened to my supervisor and worked in the dirt, not running off for watches on end through the deserted halls of Verndandi with my betrothed. No, *my* girl was taken from me and given to my cousin. The cousin who everyone thinks is so good."

Bastian stood, gesticulating, angrily. "For rotation after rotation, I followed you around, listening to what it means to be chief, befriending Kristjan to see how he would do, and watching as he failed time and again. I vowed early on to be his opposite. You can't please everyone, but there's one person I can please." He puffed out his chest and jabbed his finger against it. "Me. So I did. And you, Uncle, you believed him; just like everyone else. You believed the façade he put up— 'Ooh, Kristjan, he's so confident; he's so capable. But you weren't there." His voice softened, and he blew a breath out. "He let Marko go out into that whiteout. Because he had to please *everyone*, he didn't stand up for what he *knew* was right. It's Kristjan's fault."

I worked my jaw to release the tension in it. Kristjan had tried to tell me it was his fault, but I'd not listened— but I'd also believed Bastian once before, and that'd been an incalculable mistake.

Bastian stopped in front of me, but he lifted his face toward the rocky ceiling as if to see through to Toppur above. "We should have waited out the storm—at least another step—but Marko found that *yoma* and convinced Kristjan we needed a better shelter." He sank his face into his hands. "Kristjan should have *stopped* Marko! It should have been Kristjan not Marko who died. Kristjan was the leader; he should've been the one out in the storm. That's a leader's place."

It was the first inkling I'd had of the raw pain my nephew felt at the death of his friend, and it staggered me. He'd never said a word; hadn't shed a tear, either at the Fivku or since. I stood and reached out a hand to place on his shoulder, but he flinched away, rubbing at his eyes and smudging them with dirt.

"Well, Uncle? What do you say to that? You taught me that a leader takes the responsibility. Do you call allowing your best friend to run off in the middle of a storm on Toppur and then 'falling' down a *bensin* being responsible?"

I let out a deep breath, praying for help. "Bastian, son, a leader is more than responsible for those around him. He's responsible for his *own* actions as well. If a leader did as you say and lived to please himself, we'd not have unity in Storeheltur; we'd not survive here, hiding from the frozen wastes on the farthest reaches of an icy continent. We live only because we think of one another and care for each other. The leader must think of everyone else and make sacrifices to allow the larger community to thrive."

Bastian shook his head, but I forged on.

"Son, what you've done in looking out for yourself has left others hurting and has created a burden that you left them to bear alone. That's not what a chief does."

"How?" Bastian jerked his head up.

"How have you hurt others?" I repeated incredulous. I waited, but he only shrugged. Picking up my jaw, I started listing things off on my fingers, advancing on him a little further with each one. "Anna miscarried your child, and she was forced to grieve alone, but she never named you, so her family kept her disgrace as quiet as they could and mourned in isolation. Margret suffered still more; you took a woman with no family, no husband to care or comfort her when she bore a child, and that healthy child died suddenly less than a phase later, leaving us with questions that she wouldn't answer. Then there's Juli who's endured the lasting scorn of the *holdt* for having a child without a husband."

I paused gauging the effect my words might have on him. But the only expression he showed was in his eyes—shock that I knew. No remorse. No pain. No shame—no decency.

"Then there's Tinna. The one that you openly say is 'your' girl. She's pregnant, and based on when she believes the child will arrive, Kristjan had nothing to do with it. *You* did."

Bastian waved a hand as if swatting at a bug. "You have no proof. You name names, but Uncle, none of those girls have said a word as to who the father was. As for Tinna, she wanted me. We'd been talking about being betrothed. What else is a man supposed to do when she kisses like that?"

My heart seized within me at the callous lies. What he described didn't remotely resemble with the girl that would shortly be my daughter—nor did it explain the utter shame and choking grief she'd displayed when she told me what my nephew had done.

"Well, Uncle. I'm tired."

That was the last straw. I summoned the weight of all my authority, drawing my shoulders back and straightening. "Bastian Helgisson *stop*."

His eyes widened, and he even cowered a bit.

"You say you wish to be chief of Storeheltur, but you have yet to prove that you would care for its people. In fact, you've shown outright disinterest in those who are closest to you over the past three or four rotations. Your actions of obeying Orlaugur and working in the cave-in are only what a normal citizen would do—and has done. But a chief would have taken responsibility for his *children*. Bastian, you had one who died prematurely, another who died under mysterious circumstances, another who yet lives not knowing he's yours, and a fourth who will be born and raised as a Jovarsson. You have done nothing to help provide for the needs of the first three, and from the looks of it, you had no interest in claiming the fourth."

My ire was aroused, thinking of those poor young girls. I knew what it was like to raise a child alone, but I'd at least had the sanctity of a marriage—and I knew that Kristjan's mother had loved him just as much as I did. It was no one's choice that took her from us, but Juli—and her son—lived, knowing that they'd been discarded.

"As if that wasn't enough to make you unqualified to be chief, you go around whispering lies into the ears of my heir so that he thinks the *holdt* is better without him here. No chief—from Jovar on down to me—would *ever* tell a member of his community that Storeheltur is better without them. Even when we have a recalcitrant miscreant." I gave him a withering look. "We don't ostracize them with such words. Instead, we work with them to bring them around."

"And if they don't? What then, Uncle?" Bastian had also straightened, his arms stiff at his sides, his hands balled into fists. "You send them off to Toppur to die."

I shook my head. "Not until all other options have been sought, and even then, only if they've killed one of us." I regarded him. "Bastian Helgisson, you are guilty of that. One child and the near death of Kristjan. Are you going to deny that if I brought this to the council, they wouldn't condemn *you*?"

His mouth dropped open, but he slammed it shut, his throat working. "You wouldn't." His words were barely audible. "You wouldn't," he repeated only marginally louder.

"As chief, I must look out for the good of *all* members of Storeheltur. Who else are you going to use and then throw under the rockfall, Bastian? Who else must *die* for you to see the error of your selfish ways?"

"No! You wouldn't. Not to your sister. You wouldn't."

I closed my eyes briefly. "Bastian, I'm prepared to do this, but I don't *want* to. Please, do you not honestly see how inconsiderate, selfish, and terrible your actions have been?"

"Inconsiderate? All of those girls liked what I offered. Tinna's the only one who didn't come back for more. How was that 'inconsiderate and selfish'? As for Margret, we were both young. She shouldn't have done what she did. I guess…" He let out a puff of air and shook his head. "We were both scared kids. What would you have had me do? Bring disgrace down upon the family? *Moði* and *Pabbi* were caught up in Johann's wedding at the time. And Juli…" He folded his hands in front of him and picked at the dirt under the nails. "She didn't want anything to do with me afterward. It may have had something to do with my attitude, but she's avoided me ever since."

I softened my tone, offering a plea to Jeeah that he'd listen. "And do you blame her?"

Someone passed in the hallway, their footsteps the only sound as I waited for my nephew's reply.

"No. I suppose not; put in that light. Pft." He threw up his hands. "What would you have me do? That was two, almost three, rotations ago, Uncle. I'm not Kristjan, to go groveling for someone's approval when I know I'm not going to get it."

I sealed a spiteful retort behind my lips and measured my response, consciously unclenching my teeth to reply. "And I don't want you to be him. The differences between us all are critical to our survival, our well-being. We need the insight of those who see things differently." I drew in a deep breath. "But you need to make things right with Juli. At least offer to provide for her and your son."

Bastian shook his head. "It's been too long. She won't want to talk to me."

My heart sank. "You won't even try?"

He shrugged. "There's no use."

I'd hoped to spare my sister and her family the pain, but I couldn't simply let him persist this way. Bastian's actions had already led to the murder of an innocent child. What if the next young woman decided to end her own life after what he did to her?

"Bastian, if you'll not hold yourself to account for your actions, then I must do it instead. I cannot—I will not—sit idly by while you destroy the lives of *our* people."

"What are you going to do?"

I felt my mouth tighten over words that I hadn't yet chosen, then let out the few that seemed right—the only ones that might leave the door open for mercy.

"What I must."

Then I left. Bastian yelled after me, frantic, but I didn't look back. My spirit was more burdened than if I'd shouldered all the fathoms of rock overhead.

Chapter 34

1 Fimmti, 400 AI

By the beginning of the third watch, we were all back in Kristjan's room. Ebonney appeared abashed, but Hafnar was grinning as if *he* was the one to be wed. Kristjan struggled to sit up. I helped him.

"Thanks." He mumbled. "I can at least be upright when I get married."

Hafnar chuckled. "Why bother? Stay there, and you'll have that much easier of a time once we've left you two alone."

"Hafnar!" Ebonney blurted. "You're an elder!"

"And a man." But he did bring his face back to a more solemn demeanor.

Tinna took her place beside Kristjan, who reached for her hand. "We're ready."

"Jeeah set Handi and Tsiki in the courses above."

The traditional words flowed over me. Josebina slid her hand into mine. Together we watched as my son pledged his life to Tinna. Even Ebonney smiled and wiped tears from her eyes as the young couple kissed.

May Jeeah bless you, Kristjan.

* * *

The reality of being wed was so foreign that it felt surreal, and yet, Tinna's hand in his felt right.

You'll fail at this just as you have at everything else you've done.

The words struck him as if they'd been a physical blow. He tried to push the thoughts away, but they persisted like an ice rat over a bit of garbage.

"For the newlyweds." Josebina stepped forward with a plate and two forks. "It's not much, but I thought it would be a way to celebrate."

Ebonney gasped. "You didn't?"

Josebina smiled. "They needed something."

"Thank you." Ebonney glanced away, then looked back up blinking away tears. "Friðfinn's mother made us a pie when we were wed. I'm... I'm glad my daughter can have the tradition as well."

"And here you are." Josebina handed a fork first to Tinna and then to Kristjan. "Cut a piece off and feed it to your spouse."

"Or..." Hafnar grinned. "You could be mean and make a mess."

Tinna shook her head minutely.

She just told you how you can care for her. All these small ways, you'll know, and you can show her—starting with this one.

With a shaky hand, Kristjan lifted a small bite to Tinna's lips. Why did they look so lovely? He wanted to reach up and pull her in for another kiss, but he fought the impulse. Tinna, however, leaned closer, and followed the bite she offered him. Sweet dried fruit and flaky crust melted in Kristjan's mouth, and then even sweeter was Tinna's lips on his. There was a moment of happy exclamation, laughter—family celebrating them coming together—and then Kristjan forgot all else and pulled her to him.

His ears were ringing, when he pulled away.

"Careful," Hafnar teased. "With those injuries, you can't go getting rowdy too quickly."

"Thank you, Hafnar." Despite how the elder's allusion made him blush, Kristjan had the clarity of mind to hold out his hand in gratitude.

"My pleasure, son. Take care of that woman of yours."

"Yes, sir. I will."

And Kristjan meant it. He'd care for Tinna with all his might.

Ebonney pulled Tinna into an embrace. "I'm so happy for you."

"Thank you, *Moði.*"

"You're welcome. At least there's one spot of bright light on this step." She moved away. "I should go help Metta. The sending will be at first watch."

"I'll be there, *Moði*."

Ebonney nodded and left.

Josebina caught Tinna up in a hug, while Father went to Kristjan's side.

"Well done, son." Father fiddled with his wedding band.

"Come, Geir." Josebina pulled his hand into hers. "We have some things to take care of as well."

Father smiled at her. The look was so different from his accustomed expression—it still shocked Kristjan. How could one person cause such a difference in another? Would that be what he was like with Tinna?

Before he realized it, the only one left in his room was Tinna—his wife. She folded her hands, her hair hiding her face. Kristjan wanted to go to her, but he was stuck in his bed. His eyes drooped, but he forced them open. What would she think of him if he dozed off?

Perfect husband.

Kristjan chuckled. He was far from perfect.

"What?" Tinna asked.

"Look at me. Most husbands are eager to get their wife to bed, and I'm stuck unable to do anything at all."

Red filled her cheeks, but she came to him and sat on the edge of the mattress. "Thank you."

"For?"

"For even thinking of it." She fiddled with the ties of her belt. "Remember when I asked if you wanted me?"

He remembered. Remembered how he'd scared her.

"I guess, what I was really asking was if you loved me. Bastian said he did, but what he did felt wrong. Made me feel vulnerable, dirty… consumed." She shivered. "I… I want to believe that it can be different."

Kristjan reached for her hand, stilling its restless fiddling. "Tinna, if anything, I don't deserve you. Yes, I want you. I was afraid I'd be like Bastian."

"No!" Her whole body spoke the vehemence of the word, and then she caught his eyes, her gaze earnest, and set her palm against his cheek. "Never. There's no way you could be like him. Your touch has never made me feel…" She paused, but hurried on. "You've always made me feel like a lady."

A silence fell between them, drawing out too long, and Tinna looked down, again fiddling with the ties of her belt. Kristjan longed to ease her discomfort, but he felt a similar shyness. How did old married couples become so relaxed about this? Hafnar made it a joke, but Kristjan wasn't even sure how to invite Tinna to bed this moonstep, when it was certain that nothing was going to happen.

"I… I suppose I should go get…" Tinna stood, but Kristjan reached for her hand.

She froze, then looked down at him, gazing into his eyes. Oh, how he longed to do more than look at her. He moved her hand closer to him, and she yielded. Their lips met in a tender embrace, sparking hope of more, but not this moonstep.

He patted the place beside him and slid the blankets back. Red flushed her cheeks, but she took the offered spot. With his eyes half closed, Kristjan pulled the blanket up around her, and put an arm around her, pulling her to his side. She snuggled in with a contented sigh.

"I can't offer much more than this, but sweet dreams, Tinna."

She rested her head against his chest, her hand at his heart. "And you, *kæra*."

The term of endearment floated through Kristjan's mind over and over. *Kæra*. Beloved.

You don't deserve that.

Maybe he didn't, but it felt wonderful knowing she loved him. Would he be able to one moonstep reciprocate?

What type of husband would you be if you didn't?

True, but beloved. Yes, he could get used to this. His head rested on hers, and he fell asleep to the scent of Tinna's soap. It was refreshing and made him feel at home.

* * *

Some point in the middle of the rest period, Kristjan awoke with a yelp; something had knocked into his leg, and he rolled away, trying to protect it from whatever—

It was Tinna. She was thrashing in bed, making pleading sounds garbled by sleep, and when he reached out to touch her shoulder, she fairly leapt away from him, coming awake with eyes wide and unseeing, panting like she'd been running from a snow cat, clutching the blanket around her and whimpering.

"Tinna?"

A muted cry was his only answer, and she wilted, shuddering, softly sobbing. "I'm sorry. I—"

"It's all right; it'll be fine."

She shook her head. "I'm sorry. Go back to sleep."

"*Kæra*." He was surprised by the ease with which he called her his beloved, but it must've been right, for she sniffled and looked toward him in the scant light of the *yoma* lamp.

"It's fine," she whispered. "I'm sorry. I can go sleep somewhere else—"

"It was a dream, wasn't it?" Even though he phrased it as a question, he didn't wait for her nod but continued, "Remember what I said. You're not alone. He's not here; I am, and I'll never take anything from you. You're as safe as I can make you. Come." He held open his arms.

After a moment, she scooted closer, and he wrapped an arm around her.

Tinna caught a sob, then collapsed into his embrace, her body shaking. He held her, kissed her hair and her tears, rubbed her back, and comforted her the best he could.

"I… I'm sorry." She wiped at her eyes.

"Shh. You have nothing to be sorry for."

"But… it's… our wedding."

Kristjan chuckled. "And I broke my own leg, like an idiot, which is the only reason we're not both too exhausted for dreams right now," he told her teasingly. "If anyone should be apologizing, it's me."

She smiled as another tear dripped down her cheek. He caught it with his thumb and leaned in to kiss it away. Instead of finding her cheek, though, his lips met hers. As gently as possible, he kissed her, until she melted against him and his heart raced. Her hands trailed up his back to his hair, and without thinking, he pressed more strongly. When he broke away, his breath was coming in jagged gasps.

"It's… me, *kæra*. All I'll ever do is care for you."

"All?" She played with his hair. "You don't think you'll want more when your leg is healed?" She brushed her lips against at his ear, sending his concentration flying apart.

"What?"

"You said you're only going to care for me, but I thought you might want more."

"Oh, I want more, all right. Between two people who mutually want and who are married…" He rubbed at his neck, only to find her hand there. How could he say this? "Tinna—"

She cut him off with another kiss which ended in a fierce hug. "You want me. You *want* me!"

"I do." Now he was confused. "Tinna, what's wrong?"

"Everything, and nothing." She sighed. "Remember back at the library? I asked if you wanted me, but you said no. Said you were no better than Bastian. It made me feel just as dirty."

"Oh, *kæra*, I'm so sorry."

She shook her head. "I… I've dreamed of a man loving me like *Pabbi* loves—loved—*Moði*, all my life. And then Bastian came along. He gave me attention, then…" She dropped her eyes, her hand stilled in his hair. "I didn't like it. I thought… I thought it was me. When I pushed away from him, he mocked me. He…"

"Shh." Kristjan pulled her to him. "Bastian's a brute. He knows nothing of caring for anyone. Of treasuring them."

"But, then you didn't want me."

"I was wrong. I didn't know what I wanted. *Kæra*, I was listening to lies. Lies that said I was no better than Bastian if I loved you. You had a loving mother and father to watch all your life. I've had nothing. Father always said to watch appearances. This feeling was new and exciting, but frightening. I didn't know what to do, so I ran. Look where that got me? Down a *bensin* with a broken leg—not wanting to die, but without the help of my father I would have."

"I'm glad you didn't."

He grinned. "Me, too. Now, maybe we should start over." He pushed himself to a better position and gave Tinna some space, grimacing with the effort. "If I had the ability, I'd get down on one knee as it's said Jorvar did. Tinna, will you be my wife? I'll care for you, love you, and provide for you as Jorvar did for Iunn. When I can, I'll get you a token of my love to show to the world."

Tinna sucked in a breath. "You… you'd do that for me?"

"You're my beloved. Took me long enough to figure it out—to know it's okay to love someone. Tinna, will you love me?"

She nodded, her hand at her mouth, tears shining in her eyes. "Thank you, Kristjan. Thank you."

His heart melted within him. How could he have been so blind to the treasure she was?

Tinna laid down beside him, careful of his leg. Soon her breathing evened out. Kristjan ran his fingers through her hair.

See, you do know what is precious. Care for her, my son.

Chapter 35

2 Fimmti, 400 AI

Tinna had tried to dissuade him from making the trip to the ancients' hall, but Kristjan wouldn't hear of it. His wife was grieving; he wasn't about to leave her to face this alone, however much his leg might ache. For once, he felt certain that he was doing the right thing. He only wished that Marko could've been with him through that journey, keeping him smiling through the pain, offering the teasing support that only a brother could. His friend would've been more than willing.

Indeed. He loved you just as much as you loved him.

The thought brought tears to Kristjan's eyes. Had he really loved Marko so well that it could've matched the visible devotion Marko had for him? Maybe, maybe he had really been a better friend than he'd thought after Marko's death. Maybe it actually had been a tragic mistake, even if it'd been his decision. His doing, but perhaps not his fault.

When Hafnar carried him in, the chamber was filled to overflowing. It seemed that every member of Storeheltur had come out to pay their final respect to all who'd perished in the collapse, including the elder.

Father-in-law. Kristjan corrected his thoughts. *Friðfinn would've been my father-in-law.*

Beside him, Tinna sat with her back straight, her hand gripping his—the only sign of the emotions running through her. Ebonney, on the other hand, was sobbing inconsolably. Her sister-in-law wrapped an arm around her, to no discernable effect—if anything, she wept harder.

Kristjan's gaze wandered to the others in the room. Mani's wife was sitting quietly, holding her son close. Behind her sat Aunt Froða, Uncle Mikkael, and Bastian. Kristjan averted his gaze from his cousin and squeezed Tinna's hand. She gave him a soft smile.

Father strode to the front, standing beside his friend's body.

Taking a deep breath, he raised his hands. "People of Storeheltur, this step we honor those who've gone before us—they were precious to us, friends, fathers, a mother, and an elder. Mani leaves behind his wife and two young sons—a family that knows well how devoted he was to them, and how hard he worked to give them the best he possibly could—both of himself, and of the comforts he could provide.

"Erika was a miner by trade but a jeweler by passion—she took delight in every facet of the gems we produced, a delight that she both deeply felt and eagerly shared. Her sisters and father will miss the brightness of her in their lives.

"Friðfinn Arnorsson dedicated most of his adult life to our *holdt*. He worked the mines, led our people, and gave of himself. Those who were on shift with him know full well the sacrifices he made to give others the best chance at survival."

Kristjan couldn't help but feel the pang of guilt. If it wasn't for him… He shook his head, and Tinna glanced at him.

"Are you all right?"

He nodded.

Murderer.

You rescued many others.

Why did the truth feel so double-edged? How could he live with both in mind? Kristjan forced his thoughts to what Father was saying.

"Every person is destined to walk the halls of the ancients at some point in time. Jeeah holds each man's steps in his palm. Friðfinn, Mani, and Erika were called to the halls of the ancients and to Jeeah's side. It's hard for us to understand why, but Jeeah knows best. Of all people, I understand this. I fought with grief for rotation upon rotation, but only recently found the peace in

Jeeah that'd been waiting there for me all along. May you all find his peace."

Father waited with bowed head while Mani's family slid their brother down the chute. Kristjan remembered all too well the sensations but ground himself with Tinna's presence. Next Erika's sons guided her body into Fivku. Finally, Father stepped to Friðfinn's side. Orlaugur joined him. They stood erect while Karva, Hafnar, Reinar, and Iðna each placed a hand on Friðfinn's shoulder and whispered a few words that no one else could hear. When the other four stepped away, Father and Orlaugur picked up the body and carried it to the mouth of the passageway, releasing their friend — Tinna's *pabbi*—to the halls of the ancients. Beside Kristjan, Tinna shuddered, and her shoulders trembled, but she never looked away. He had to marvel at her strength.

Standing over Fivku's empty entrance, he saw his father, his face an alloy of sorrow and contentment as he found Josebina's eyes and smiled gently. Kristjan had always watched Storeheltur's chief carry himself with an aloof stoicism during these ceremonies, but now he could see that shield for what it'd been—protecting a wound. Now, that wound had been healed, and it seemed that a healed man could experience both grief and joy in the same moment. Would Kristjan himself ever be able to do that?

Sungvari raised her voice once more, just as she had for Marko, but this time, listening to the hymn, Kristjan found that its meaning didn't feel quite so mysterious,

so distant and removed. At last, he felt that the words
held a glimmer of something he could grasp:

> *The path is smooth now*
> *No danger in sight;*
> *Rest for the weary*
> *A home to enjoy.*
> *Make your way now*
> *Safely to Jeeah.*
> *He'll welcome you to*
> *his enduring peace.*
> *Peace to your soul, friend.*
> *Peace to your family.*
> *Peace to all your friends.*
> *Peace, peace, peace.*

Epilogue

27 Endanleg, 400 AI

Kristjan couldn't take his eyes off his child, cradled in Tinna's arms. Wondering eyes stared unblinking at their mother. His wife was exhausted, but she smiled as little Friomar wrapped his tiny fist around her fingertip.

"I'm so glad for you," she whispered to the baby. Then she shifted from Kristjan's shoulder, tucking her chin up to look at his face. "And you."

"Likewise, *kæra*. You were incredible."

"So were you, Kristjan. I couldn't have done it without you."

Men are worse than useless in birth. She's just being kind.

You did everything she asked, and more. You were close by; you stayed awake with her through the long spans; you supported her and held her hand when the pain was overwhelming. You did everything a man can.

Kristjan leaned into that second voice—it'd grown stronger in the past seven cycles—and closed his eyes in a practice that'd seemed to help make it easier to hear. *Thank you, Jeeah, for the chance to hold my son; thank you for his life, and hers; thank you for the honor of being with Tinna while she brought him into this world, and for what little I was able to do for her. Thank you that I'm still here.*

Careful, lest he somehow mar those delicate fingers, he stroked Friomar's soft little knuckles. His son. It still felt beyond him—like it must be a mistake.

It is a mistake, letting a cursed man play father to a child. Ignorant, cowardly, useless—

Friomar has a father, and it's because you chose to give him that. Imperfect, but loving—and that's the perfect way for a father to begin.

It still hurt, thinking of all the ways he might fail this helpless little person. But he pressed into the truth that gave life—that promised things could always change. He hadn't known how to love Tinna, either, when they first began, but he'd learned, and would continue learning.

"I'm going to fix you that tea Aunt Froða left," he told her with a gentle kiss on top of her head. "Some fruit, too?"

Her smile was bright and grateful. "Yes, thank you, *kæra.*"

He slid out of bed and went to the kitchen to retrieve the treat he'd set aside a cycle ago. The merchants had been coming in droves of late; once the mine had been opened back up, news of the spectacular quality—and quantity—of ore and gems available in Storeheltur had spread quickly. By the time Kristjan's leg had healed enough to bear his weight, Storeheltur was practically flooded with all the luxuries it could ever want—spices, fruits, new tools and carts, wool and cotton, tea leaves, medicines, and *kaffi* and *geitmjolk* enough to fill every coldbox in the *holdt*. Kristjan had tried not to take too much advantage of his new position as an elder on the council, but he had nudged a few people to let him trade first for the apples, so that he'd have them as a gift for Tinna when Friomar was born. *Thank you for apples,* he prayed with a smile. *Thank you for ways to care for my beloved.*

While the water boiled, he thought of Aunt Froða, and all the ways she'd helped Tinna through the birth. *Thank you for her knowledge; Jeeah, thank you for her care.* But as always, thinking of Aunt Froða was followed by thoughts of her son. It'd been six cycles since he'd been sent into exile—shipped out with a merchant who'd agreed to establish him in an apprenticeship or some other position far from Storeheltur—and it'd be eighteen more before he'd be allowed to step foot in the *holdt* again. Privately, Kristjan wasn't sure that he'd ever return; Bastian might very well revel in the liberty that the wider world could provide and live out his remaining moonsteps in empty indulgence. For his parents' sake, at least, Kristjan hoped he'd miss the *holdt* enough to reflect on his selfishness and come home contrite. But if Tinna never had to see his cousin's face again, he'd have been hard-pressed to be grieved. But Marko… How Kristjan wished his friend could've lived to see his son. Marko would've helped him care for Friomar, taught him just the right way to bounce the baby when he cried, laughed at the spit-up that'd no doubt soon be staining Kristjan's clothes, made jokes and mischief—he'd have been the perfect uncle. He'd have loved Friomar as if he was his own—just as he'd loved Kristjan as his own brother. A pang of grief that could only come from lost futures pierced Kristjan's heart. But Marko, he knew, wasn't grieving; if his friend could watch from the halls of the ancients, he'd be smiling. The words to the *maltið* song returned to Kristjan, a balm that'd often comforted and strengthened him in the cycles since his own encounter with death.

> *Don't mourn without reason.*
> *Don't lose hope.*
> *Light a candle in the darkness.*
> *Remember me.*
> *Remember me.*

Safe with Jeeah. Kristjan smiled through his tears.

Tinna gave a cry of tender delight when she saw the apples Kristjan brought her, and he felt her happiness echo back to him.

He kissed her, then their son, and settled back in beside her. *Thank you that, for this step, I can feel happy.*

It wasn't always so; some moonsteps were dark and hollow, and simply moving out of his bed felt like more than he could manage. But some weren't—and that was something he'd once thought impossible. He'd given up too soon; he knew that now.

Thank you, Jeeah, that I lived to learn it.

Hope

Good books, like good movies, move us. They draw us into a world, introduce us to characters we love, and sometimes, hit closer to home than we'd like.

Can you relate to Kristjan or even Tinna? They were hurting and, alone, incredibly vulnerable to their circumstances. As Kristjan learned, crying out for help isn't a weakness; it's strength because it requires courage to admit you can't do it on your own.

If you've thought of death by suicide, and especially if you have a plan for it, *please* reach out to the suicide hotline in your country. That's 988 in the United States. They will talk with you either via text, chat, or phone and give you what you need to listen to the right voice. Remember: suicide is a permanent solution to a temporary problem and leaves others with pain, questions, and sorrow.

Kristjan also went through thinking that feeling pain was better than not feeling at all. Are you there? Are you using self-harm as a coping mechanism? Then I ask you to text CONNECT to 741741 in the US; if you're international, you can connect with help via www.helpguide.org. Self-harm can become an addiction; don't let it get ahold of you.

Or are you like Tinna, trying to ignore abuse that happened, trying to cope on your own? Sexual assault is never easy to deal with, and it often leaves life-long scars, but it doesn't have to leave eternally open wounds. RAINN is an organization that is ready to help you, and you can get in touch with them at www.rainn.org.

Whether you're struggling like Kristjan with hearing the condemning voices, self-harm, thinking of suicide, or like Tinna having endured abuse, the scars don't have to define you. They can be transformed into beauty. But how?

It's a day-in and day-out struggle, and sometimes you may wonder if it's worth trudging through the hours until bed. Or you may lay in bed counting down until the next day. This is where you have control over your life. Changing your perspective *is* possible, but it's not easy. Even though I can list the steps, it takes a daily choice to listen to the father of life rather than the enemy of our souls. Both are very real and active in our lives today.

How do you go about changing your perspective? Here are some actions you can take *now*. As I said, easy to write them but much harder to do them. If you're physically unable to do them yet, you may also be a person who benefits from medication—not that it fixes everything, but sometimes, it makes it possible for *you* to begin to fix things.

1. **Care for your physical self.**

While we're not exclusively physical beings, how we care for our physical body has an effect on our emotional and mental wellness, and vice versa. If you care for one aspect of your being, the others benefit; if you neglect one, the others suffer.

Rest is essential to our mental wellbeing. Sometimes, we just need to sleep, and we'll feel better. With this, also check your diet. Are you eating properly? Are you missing or choosing to skip meals? Nourishment and adequate sleep often do wonders for your energy and your emotional state; asking a friend to share a healthy meal with you can also give you not only energy, but connection.

Getting outside, even for a few minutes a day, can also help. The sun's UV rays are a necessary ingredient for your body in producing vitamin D, which helps lift your mood and gives you energy. Fresh air also creates a feeling of "difference" that can help jostle your emotions and thoughts into a better place.

Physical contact with a safe person creates a chemical reaction that helps your body discharge negative emotions and make room for positive ones. If you can get a hug from a friend, take it; if you have a friend who'll hug you for 30 seconds or longer, it has immense benefits to all aspects of your being. You might also consider getting an animal that you can pet and snuggle with and care for. Their affection can be a balm to the soul.

2. On hard days, make one small change.

This kind of darkness thrives on and repeats the idea that nothing can or will ever change, and you can defy that in small ways that are low-cost on your hard days. Pick one thing you can muster the will to do, something easily achievable. Wash one dish or fold one piece of laundry; answer one text; eat one healthy snack; do one push-up; write one line in your journal; walk outside for one minute. Then recognize what you've just accomplished: it's something, done on a day when the 'voice' told you nothing was possible. Plus, by acting in defiance of it, you've proven that it can lie to you—and that's a powerful truth to perceive. Even leaving your bed, getting in the shower, or retrieving a snack from your kitchen can count. It's okay to do what you can and leave the rest—though, often, if you write one line or do one push-up, you'll end up doing more and feeling better than you thought was possible that day.

3. Start a thankfulness journal.

A merry heart does good like medicine. That's what the wise king penned almost three millennia ago, and it's still true today—now, though, scientists have confirmed it. So grab a composition notebook, a note app on your phone, or a document on your computer and start recording the things you're grateful for. At first it might be hard, but look around you and see the world with eyes for the miracles—however small. It may surprise you how your perspective changes.

4. Get your focus off yourself.

Ouch! That sounds harsh, but it's said with love. When we're in a state of depression, we're really focused on *our* problems, on what went wrong to *us*, and how terrible everything is for *us*.

Sound familiar? There's a simple (but perhaps still difficult) way out: focus on someone else. Volunteer someplace. Libraries, rotary clubs, schools, food banks, shelters, and more are all looking for people to do the work. At first you might be doing this with the sentiment of "might as well try something," or out of a sense of obligation, but then it may surprise you how much changes and you find yourself eagerly anticipating your next shift, or you discover that your problems don't seem as insurmountable as they did before.

If volunteering regularly feels like signing up for a marathon right now, choose something smaller to begin with. Text a friend who's also suffering and let them know you're there if they want to talk; write a "just because" card to someone with a memory that'll make them smile; pull a few weeds out of your neighbor's flower bed, or offer to pick up a few groceries for them while you get your own. It doesn't have to be big to make an impact—on them or you.

5. **Adopt uncertainty.**

Believing that things *might* change is a powerful force against the darkness, which would like to convince us that our future is set in stone. Practice telling yourself that the day *might* not get better, but then again it *might*; that your friend *might* be happy to hear from you; that this *might* be the day that the incessant rain stops; that you *might* find a purpose for your pain; that you *might* learn a new truth that makes living easier. We don't know the future (whatever that 'voice' may say), and a year from now life *might* look incredibly different from how it does right now. Believing that it could change means you'll be open to the change when it presents itself; you'll live with your eyes open and be able to recognize the opportunities that brush up against you.

6. Remember.

What does that mean? Remember what? Ah, this is another kind of journal. It's one of your life. Remember how you've come through hard times. How just at the moment you didn't think you could take another step, strength was provided. Walk through life with eyes that focus ahead, look back on where you've been, and give thanks through it all.

7. Know the One in charge.

In Kristjan's story, he began to see hope when he cried out to Jeeah. The same is true for us. Learning who Jeeah is is the first step, but realizing that he has control of our lives is second.

Just like Geirfinnur governs the *holdt*, loving the people and caring for them, so also Jeeah is watching over us. He loves *you* and wants the best for you. You may scoff at that because of followers of his that you've know; there are many out there who claim to know him, but the way they live doesn't at all resemble Jeeah's character—like Bastian. He wanted to be chief, even claimed to know what needed to be done, but in reality, he was fundamentally unwilling to fulfill the purpose of the role—to work in the best interest of others. We can't completely rely, then, on others to get to know

Jeeah. He would have to tell you about himself—and he has.

To learn about Jeeah in our world, you can contact Harvest to receive a Bible for free (https://harvest.org/request-material/). Kristjan had to wait for Geirfinnur's expression of love and affection before he knew how much his life meant to his father, but you don't have to wait. It's been written down for you—the words of life. Harvest can also connect you with someone who knows Jeeah themselves and walks with him daily.

I pray that your journey will be one that brings you to Jeeah, rather than distancing you from him. I've seen both paths taken, because it's our choice to make, and sometimes we choose based on a lie that's been given to us—or at least a twisted truth. But I know from experience that true, lasting hope that can never fail, no matter the circumstance, is found only in him, and to be in his presence is to know true peace—a peace that deepens in proportion to your suffering, as you continue to encounter just how good and loving he is. Maybe that's the first miracle for your journal.

If only one person finds Jeeah and his hope because of this book; or if you choose to live because you've read Kristjan's story, then it's accomplished its purpose. I want you to live, but more than that, I want you to experience the joy of living, of looking back and cherishing the times of darkness for the light that you found within them—light you'd never have gone looking for otherwise. If you know Jeeah and his works, you know that every pain in your life can be redeemed. Some way, somehow, someday, we'll understand. Until then, we hope in Jeeah.

5945 AI

He had his staff, knife, water skin, and cloak. What more could a man need?

Birds twittered in the trees along the river, and from time to time he heard the splash of leaping fish. Graen beat down, and Paskal pulled his hood up to protect against the harsh rays. He'd been traveling since the first watch, and from Handi's position in the sky, it must be coming up on the second. The moon had slid far to the north, barely visible with Graen's rays against it. He took a sip of his water, feeling satisfied with himself. Two more moonsteps along the River Ree, and then he'd turn back. By then, having survived on his own for six moonsteps without any help from the clan, his father would have to acknowledge that he was no longer a child. All the condescension and disrespectful dictatorship he suffered under his father would come to an end, and he'd finally receive the respect a member of the clan deserved.

As he walked, he spied a tall boulder that cast a long patch of shade, and the river was close by wafting its cooler air up along the bank—the perfect place to rest and take a meal.

The bread was stale, but that was expected—Graen's heat sucked the moisture from everything. The jerky revived him, though, and the dried fruit was a nice sweetness at the end. He thought about trying his hand at fishing, but a nap sounded better—he could always string up a line when he was rested. He leaned back with his arms cushioning his head and pulled the generous hood over his face to block out Graen's perpetual rays before closing his eyes. It was so nice to relax without anyone telling him what to do. He could practically see Uncle Theodor scolding Elias for not getting fine enough sand for the glass maker. At least this moonstep it was Elias, and not Paskal, who had to scoop the sand that had been laying in Graen's hot rays. A smile worked its way across his face. This was much better than glass-making under Uncle Theodor's judging eye, or living with Father's perpetual disgruntlement.

He wasn't sure how much time slid by, but when he awoke, it was with a start. What was different? He couldn't tell. The water was still rushing by; he still lay in the shade… Disoriented, he turned over—or tried to. Something held him in place.

"Easy, no need to ruin a perfectly good cloak." The deep voice startled Paskal.

He tried to move the hood out of his face, but his arms were bound to his sides.

"Who are you?"

"Doesn't matter who I am, it's a matter of you being so stupid as to go to sleep along my path." The male voice held a chuckle but ended with cold, hard as steel. The man leaned closer. "If I help you up, are you going to add to your stupidity and try to fight?"

Fight. Paskal had a knife somewhere, but what good would that do if he couldn't move? He needed the help this man would provide.

"I'll not fight you."

"Good, you might learn quickly."

Without warning, strong arms sat him up. "Not going to pass out on me, are you?"

Paskal wasn't sure. He was lightheaded, but it soon dissipated.

"Let's get you with the rest of them."

The man flicked Paskal's hood back, making him blink as he adjusted to the brighter light. White teeth glared from a dark face. One of the front teeth was crooked. The man spat on the ground, leaving a brown spot. The scent of tabak juice accosted Paskal's nose.

With a flick of his wrist, the man unhooked Paskal's cloak clasp; for a moment, Paskal felt whatever was binding his arms to his sides release, but it just as quickly reasserted itself as the man flipped the cloak over his own shoulder, leaving Paskal exposed to Graen's light.

"Now, get moving, boy."

"I'm not a boy!" Paskal turned, only to be slapped across the face.

The man's ring scraped across Paskal's cheek, leaving a burning sensation behind the sting. The man wiped the ring on his trousers, glancing down at it as if to check for damage. It glowed a deep red.

"Ready to defy Olechario again? I'll let you see my true power." The man's forehead pulsed with ruddy light.

Paskal blinked. Was he seeing things? No, the man's temple and wrists glowed! He'd heard of the *jiddee'adar*, those who could manipulate the elements, but he'd never met one. Why *now* of all times?

"I see you recognize this." Olechario pushed his wrist into Paskal's face, washing it in intense heat. "Now, move, boy." Olechario stared him down, defying Paskal to say a word against the belittling title.

Paskal swallowed. He'd let it slide this time. What else *could* he do? He moved his feet; at least he could walk. Olechario gripped Paskal's arm with as much force as the glass vice, and with almost as much heat, too.

They rounded the boulder, and Paskal stared. A pair of horses hitched to a small wagon. It was what was inside it that caused Paskal to shudder. Young men and women sat crammed into the back of the wagon, their heads down. Olechario pushed Paskal toward the wagon bed. Paskal blanched. He'd heard of slavers, but the clan had never had contact with them—never had the need for slaves, even if Paskal and his friends had complained that their parents used them as such.

"Up you go, boy." Olechario hefted Paskal into the air.

Paskal blinked at the heat that swelled around his feet as they left the ground. The slaver gave him a push, and Paskal fell onto a patch of bare boards in the wagon.

Whether the others had moved or Olechario had forced a space open, Paskal didn't know, but he struggled to sitting as best he could with his arms strapped to his sides. No one met his gaze. With deft movements, Olechario trussed Paskal's ankles together.

"Put your head down and relax. You'll be working hard soon enough."

Olechario climbed onto the bench in front and dropped Paskal's pack and knife onto the floor. The slaver picked up the reins, and the horses started off.

For the first time since waking up, Paskal thought about his predicament. Would his father be able to search for him? He'd explained his intent to go on this journey, despite Father's disapproval, but he'd made Elias promise not to tell anyone else where he planned to go or how long he was going to be gone. There was no hope. Uncle Theodor and his father had been proven right. He was still a boy—a slave boy now.

About the Author

Kandi J Wyatt lives with dragons, most in human form--and some even blow fire! She spends her days providing space for teens to be themselves, inspiring them to be more than meets the eye, and spilling hope into their world. When she's not hanging out with fictional characters, Kandi's chilling with family watching anime or playing games. Her toddler granddaughter keeps her running--often in circles--and full of joy.

If you enjoyed this book, sign up for her newsletters to be the first to know about publishing news, receive book recommendations, occasional free gifts, and continue the discussion of hope. You can find out more at www.kandijwyatt.com.

Dare to Hope

Do you feel like Kristjan? Are you seeking courage to face another day, hope to survive, or would you rather just escape your real life?

I hear you. That's why the Dragon Rider Society exists. Each Tuesday, you receive an email to help you get through the week. Whether it's book news, books for you to nab, hobby hints, insights into your favorite characters, or topics that help you delve deeper and give you hope that despite your circumstances you, too, can live without fear.

Is once a week not enough for you? Then come over to my Discord channel where you can join the Dragon Den and have daily encouragement and interact with others who, like you, long for a found family where the number one rule is respect. No judgment found here.

I hope to see you there. Go to www.kandijwyatt.com to find the links.

More by Kandi J Wyatt

Dragon Courage series

Dragon's Future

Dragon's Heir

Dragon's Revenge

Dragon's Cure

Dragon's Posterity

Dragon's Heritage

Dragon's Winter

Myth Coast Adventures Trilogy

An Unexpected Adventure

An Unexpected Escapade

An Unexpected Exploit

Available in Paperback and Hardback Omnibus

with additional short story

Myth Coast Adventures

Four Stars over Ardatz

Sovereigns:

Uprooted

Blessed

Exalted

Determined

Resolved

Divided

Appointed

Ascended

Available in complete boxed set with matching spines
Companion Hardback with all the Dragon King's journals and songs
Dragon Journal

Journeys:
Kristjan's Rise
Paskal's Hope

Standalones
Journey from Skioria
To Save a Race
The One Who Sees Me

Novella
The Apprentice of Amadan Dubh

Children's Picture Book
Tea for Dragons

Short Works
"A Ride Home" published on Havok
"Worlds Collide" (a Four Stars Over Ardatz short) published on Havok
"An Unexpected Weapon" (a Myth Coast Adventures short) published in *Mythical Girls* anthology
"Running from Memories" published in *Fantastic Creatures* anthology

"Creator vs Created" published in *Finding God in Anime* devotional anthology

"Daddy's Girl" published in *Finding God in Anime vol 2* a devotional anthology

"A Reason for Pain" published in *Finding God in Anime vol 2* a devotional anthology

"Time—It's Only a Perspective" published in *Finding God in Anime vol 3* a devotional anthology

"Rest of Our Lives" published in *Finding God in Anime vol 3* a devotional anthology

www.ingramcontent.com/pod-product-compliance
Lightning Source LLC
Chambersburg PA
CBHW021331310726
48971CB00001B/75